THE CHINESE CLASSICS

颂 大雅 詩經

THE SHE KING
GREATER ODES OF THE KINGDOM
ODES OF THE TEMPLE ALTAR

［英］理雅各　译释

JAMES LEGGE

上海三联书店

图书在版编目（CIP）数据

《诗经·大雅颂》译释：汉英对照/（英）理雅各（Legge，J.）译释.
——上海：上海三联书店，2014.1
（中国汉籍经典英译名著）

ISBN　978 - 7 - 5426 - 4457 - 2

Ⅰ．①诗…Ⅱ．①理…Ⅲ．①汉语—英语—对照读物
②古体诗—诗集—中国—春秋时代Ⅳ．①H319.4：I

中国版本图书馆 CIP 数据核字（2013）第 268298 号

诗经 · 大雅 颂

译　　　释／理雅各
责任编辑／陈启甸 王倩怡
封面设计／清风
策　　　划／赵炬
执　　　行／取映文化
加工整理／嘎拉 江岩 牵牛 莉娜
监　　　制／吴昊
责任校对／笑然
出版发行／上海三联书店
　　　　　（201199）中国上海市闵行区都市路 4855 号 2 座 10 楼
网　　　址／http：//www. sjpc1932. com
邮购电话／021 - 24175971
印刷装订／常熟市人民印刷厂

版　　　次／2014 年 1 月第 1 版
印　　　次／2014 年 1 月第 1 次印刷
开　　　本／650×900 1/16
字　　　数／450 千字
印　　　张／14. 5
书　　　号／ISBN 978 - 7 - 5426 - 4457 - 2/I · 791
定　　　价／58. 00 元

中国汉籍经典英译名著
出版人的话

出版这样一套书与当今中国文化走出去的需要分不开。

其实,仅仅就中国传统文化走出去而言,近代以来已经有浓重的笔墨,只是那时的走出去大都是由西方的传教士实现的。那时的好多传教士在向中国人传播教义及西方科技的同时,自己更是为中国文化所吸引并且深入其中,竟然成就了不少有名的汉学家。在这些人中,英国传教士理雅各是非常典型的一位。

理雅各(James Legge,1815—1897 年)是近代英国著名汉学家,伦敦布道会传教士,曾任香港英华书院校长。他是第一个系统研究、翻译中国古代汉籍经典的人。

理雅各在传教和教学的过程中,认识到了学习中国文化的重要性:"只有透彻地掌握中国的经典书籍,亲自考察中国圣贤所建立的道德、社会和政治生活,才能对得起自己的职业和地位。"理雅各系统地研究和翻译中国古代的经典著作。在中国学者王韬等人的辅助下,从 1861 年到 1886 年的 25 年间,陆续翻译了《论语》《大学》《中庸》《孟子》《春秋》《礼记》《书经》《孝经》《易经》《诗经》《道德经》《庄子》《离骚》等中国的经典著作,共计 28 卷。当他离开中国时,已是著作等身。

理雅各之前的西方来华传教士虽也对中国的经典著作做过翻译,但都是片段性的翻译,而且由于中文不精,译文辞句粗劣,歧义百出。理雅各在翻译的过程中治学严谨,博采众长,他把前人用拉丁、英、法、意等语种译出的有关文字悉数找来,认真参考,反复斟酌。除此之外,他还与中国学者反复讨论,最后才落笔翻译。理雅各翻译的中国经典著作质量绝佳,体系完整,直到今天还是西方世界公认的标准译本,他本人也因此成为蜚声世界的汉学家。理雅各的译作是当之无愧的英译名著。

从英译的水准来看,或许是现今不易超越的。主要是译者当时所处的语言环境是中国文言文作为书面语言的原因。精晓文言文的直接英译,与现实白话理解后的英译相比,前者肯定会与原意更为贴近,况且理雅各又是得到了当时精通中国经典著作的中国学者王韬等人的辅助。当然,今天的人们有理由去挑战一百多年前的译作,但作为历经一个多世纪仍为西方世界普遍认可的英译经典,依然还会继续发挥其曾有的版本作用。

理雅各译作的重要代表《中国经典》(*THE CHINESE CLASSICS*),首版于1861至1872年的香港。此次以"中国汉籍经典英译名著"名义出版的各书,是依据牛津大学1893至1895年出版的理雅各《中国经典》的修订版。

"中国汉籍经典英译名著",是从理雅各的《中国经典》中选出对中国典籍原著的译释,舍去了各卷含有的绪论、前言及所附的参考文献,这样也就更为突出了典籍原著。

原《中国经典》实行的是汉英对照加英文注释的方式,汉语部分使用的是当时的书面语言繁体竖排。为了适于现实的阅读,此次出版均将汉语的繁体竖排,改为简体横排,并将英文注释中的汉字繁体改为简体。

在原《中国经典》中,理雅各对中国经典著作汉字的多音字和需要特别注明的字,都在字的四角画圈以示在注释中说明。这次出版将其改为在字的正上方标注着重号(黑点)。

原《中国经典》对汉语原文的断句标点,采用的是当时的方式,与今天现代汉语式的断句标点存有很大差别。为了保持理雅各译释的面貌,仍然用原断句标点。

另外,为了改变原书过于厚重的形态,这次出版还将原书的大开本改为小开本;将原《中国经典》的1—4卷拆分为七种书,即《论语·大学·中庸》《孟子》《尚书·唐书-夏书-商书》《尚书·周书》《诗经·国风》《诗经·小雅》《诗经·大雅-颂》。每书300页左右,便于选择使用。

理雅各的译作至今还是西方世界公认的标准译本,说明它适应着西方世界的语言和理解。这种影响了西方世界一百多年的情形,从接受心理的角度看,是很难被取代的。

随着中国在世界的影响力不断提升,中国学者的对外学术交流也更加活跃,交流中对中国文化的讲解和诠释,需要有相应的英译本作为参考,理雅各的译作无疑是适当的选择。

同时,理雅各的经典译作,还是翻译学、语言学、比较文学、历史和经典诠释的重要文献,是研究和实践汉译英的重要参考和借鉴。

相信,借用昔日西方学者译释中国文化经典并传播到西方的成果,延续和助推当今中国文化在世界的影响力,一定可以取得事半功倍的收效。

2014年1月1日

目　录

THE SHE KING.

PART III.

GREATER ODES OF THE KINGDOM.

BOOK I. DECADE OF KING WAN.

ODE I. *Wăn wang.*

诗经

大雅三

文王之什三之一

文王

一章
文王在上。于昭于天。周虽旧邦。其命维新。有周不显。帝命不时。文王陟降。在帝左右。

1　King Wăn is on high;
Oh! bright is he in heaven.
Although Chow was an old country,
The [favouring] appointment lighted on it recently.
Illustrious was the House of Chow,
And the appointment of God came at the proper season.

TITLE OF THE PART.—大雅三, 'Part III. Greater Odes of the Kingdom.' Little can be added here to what I have said on the title of Part II. The rendering of 大雅 is not according to the literal meaning of 雅; but it is more descriptive of the odes, and more intelligible, than a literal translation would be. The term 'greater' is given to the pieces because of their comparatively greater length, and the themes of several of them, which are of a more exalted kind than those of Part II., being occupied with the history and the virtues of the ancestors of the House of Chow, and founders of the dynasty. The first eighteen pieces are 'the Correct Ya (正雅),' and are attributed to the duke of Chow.

TITLE OF THE BOOK.—文王之什, 三之一, 'The Decade of king Wăn; Book I. of Part III.' As in the last Part, the odes should be arranged in tens; and each Decade takes its name from that of the first ode in it. Luh Tih-ming observes that in this Book king Wăn is the subject of the first eight odes, and king Woo, of the last two.

Ode 1. Narrative. CELEBRATING KING WAN, DEAD AND ALIVE, AS THE FOUNDER OF THE DYNASTY OF CHOW, SHOWING HOW HIS VIRTUES DREW TO HIM THE FAVOURING REGARD OF HEAVEN, AND MADE HIM A BRIGHT PATTERN TO HIS DESCENDANTS AND THEIR MINISTERS;—ATTRIBUTED TO THE DUKE OF CHOW, FOR THE BENEFIT OF THE YOUNG KING CHING.

二章

亹亹文王。令闻不已。陈锡哉周。侯文王孙子。文王
孙子。本支百世。凡周之士。不显亦世。

> King Wăn ascends and descends,
> On the left and the right of God.

2   Full of earnest activity was king Wăn,
> And his fame is without end.
> The gifts [of God] to Chow
> Extend to the descendants of king Wăn;—
> To the descendants of king Wăn,

St. 1. Acc. to Choo, the first two and the last two lines are to be taken of the soul or spirit of king Wăn in heaven; and to explain them otherwise is, simply, to explain them away. Maou makes 在上 in l. 1 = 在民上, 'was over the people;' and l. 2 = 'Oh! his virtue was displayed to Heaven.' Then in l. 7 陟降 = 'he ascended and descended;' *i. e.*, he did what was right in the sight of Heaven above, and what was good in the sight of men below. On l. 8 Maou says nothing; but Ch'ing took 在 in the sense of 察, 'to examine,' and interprets all the line—'King Wăn was able to see and know the mind of Heaven, obeyed it, and acted according to it.' Yen Ts'an, dissatisfied with these explanations, says, 'King Wăn's virtue was in accordance with Heaven. He ascended and descended, advanced and retired, as if he were always on the left and right of God, so that not a single movement of his was other than the action of Heaven.' The inadequacy of all these explanations of the text is sufficiently evident. Këang Ping-chang admits it in reference to ll. 7, 8, and adopts Choo's view, that the language can only be taken of Wăn's spirit (以神言).

But we must adopt it also in ll. 1, 2. 在上 is simply—'is on high.' The writer is not thinking of Wăn as 'over the people,' but in reference to the wonderful attributes of character which made him the object of the divine favour. He is called 'king Wăn,' as having been *kinged* by the duke of Chow, after the subjugation of the Shang dynasty, when Woo in his old age received the appointment to the throne (Doctrine of the Mean, XVIII. 3);—not that he ever assumed the title of *king* himself. It was an error in the scholars of the Han dynasty to suppose that he did so, originating with Sze-ma Ts'ëen. The appointment of Heaven lighted on Wăn, but it took effect only when his son Fah became the sovereign of China as king.

Ll. 8—6. Ch'ing is literally correct in saying that the history of Chow dates from the removal of Wăn's grandfather, king T'ae, to the territory so called, as I have related on the title of I.i.I; but Yen Ts'an is correct, as regards the spirit of the ode, in saying that it is the House of Chow (周家), after and before its settlement in Chow, that the poet has in view. 其命 in l. 4 is the 'appointment of Heaven' that the sovereignty of the kingdom should be in the Chow family. The statement that the appointment was 'new,' or 'recent,' shows that we should not translate 命 by decree. On the use of 有 in l. 5, see on II. v. VI. 6. Maou observes that 不显 and 不时 are to be taken as affirmative of 显 and 时. We may do this, or take the lines interrogatively. The 时 = 当其时, 'at the proper time.' I translate both 帝 and 上帝 by 'God.' The single term has that meaning, and the 上, 'High,' is equivalent to the definite article. The one is the *Elohim* in Hebrew; the other is the *Ha-elohim*.

St. 2 tells us how the blessing of Heaven rested not only on the person of Wăn, but extended also to his descendants and his ministers. In l. 1, 亹亹 = 强勉之貌 'the app. of strong exertion,' In 2, 令闻 = 善誉, 'good praise,' = fame. In 3, 陈 is explained by 敷, 'to diffuse,' 'to give.' The line is quoted, once and again, in the Tso-chuen and the Kwoh-yu, and always with 载 instead of 哉. Maou explains 哉 by 载, which it is much better to take in its frequent usage as an expletive particle, than to attempt, with K'ang-shing to give it the meaning of 始, 'to begin,' which it also has. It appears also more in harmony with the ode to understand God as the subject of 陈锡, than king Wăn, as Ying-tah does;—so that the

三章
世之不显。厥犹翼翼。思皇多士。生此王国。王国克
生。维周之桢。济济多士。文王以宁。

四章
穆穆文王。于缉熙敬止。假哉天命。有商孙子。商之

In the direct line and the collateral branches for a hundred
    generations.
All the officers of Chow
Shall [also] be illustrious from age to age.

3   They shall be illustrious from age to age,
    Zealously and reverently pursuing their plans.
    Admirable are the many officers
    Born in this royal kingdom.
    The royal kingdom is able to produce them,—
    The supporters of [the House of] Chow.
    Numerous is the array of officers,
    And by them king Wăn enjoys his repose.

4   Profound was king Wăn;
    Oh! continuous and bright was his feeling of reverence.
    Great is the appointment of Heaven!

line=上帝敷锡于周. In l. 4. 侯=维,—as often. 孙子, has no more meaning than 子孙, 'sons and grandsons,'=descendants. The usual order of the terms is changed here for the sake of the rhyme. That no peculiar meaning is to be sought in the form of the expression appears from its recurrence in st. 4. This line is under the govt of 敷锡, or may be taken as in apposition with 周. L. 6. 'The root and the the branches' denote the eldest sons by the recognized queen, succeeding to the throne, and the other sons by the queen and by concubines. The former should be the kings, and the latter the nobles of the kingdom, through a hundred generations. The former would grow up directly from the root, and the latter would constitute the branches of the great Chow tree. Ll.7,8. And not only the descendants of Wăn, but all the officers of the House of Chow should share in the favour of Heaven through him. 士, 'officers,' should have its most extensive application. 不显,—as in st. 1. 亦 may here have its force of 'also.'

St. 3 continues the subject of the officers of Chow, for the duke of Chow knew that only through their loyal attachment would the throne be secure. In l. 2, 犹=谋, 'counsels.' 翼翼=勉敬, 'zealous and reverent.' L. 3. 思 is here an initial particle,—as in II.vii.IV. 皇=美, 'admirable.' Ll. 4, 5. 'The royal kingdom' is the kingdom of Chow,—both the original Chow, and the general dominions which the House had obtained through Wăn and Woo. L. 6. 桢=桢干, one part for the whole of the wooden frame by which adobie walls are raised, so that the term has the idea of erection as well as of support. Ll. 7, 8. Choo finds in 济济 here only the idea of 'numerous;' Maou adds to that the idea of good deportment,—as in II. vi.V. 2. I prefer to take l. 8 of king Wăn in heaven, in his spiritual condition (文王之神; Foo Kwang).

St. 4 returns to king Wan and sets forth his great virtue of 'reverent attention' to his duties,

孙子。其丽不亿。上帝既命。侯于周服。

五章
侯服于周。天命靡常。殷士肤敏。裸将于京。厥作裸

将。常服黼冔。王之荩臣。无念尔祖。

There were the descendants of [the sovereigns] of Shang;—
The descendants of the sovereigns of Shang,
Were in number more than hundreds of thousands;
But when God gave the command,
They became subject to Chow.

5   They became subject to Chow.
The appointment of Heaven is not constant.
The officers of Yin, admirable and alert,
Assist at the libations in [our] capital;—
They assist at those libations,
Always wearing the hatchets on their lower garment and their
    peculiar cap.
O ye loyal ministers of the king,
Ever think of your ancestor!

through which it was that the dominion of the kingdom passed to this House from that of Shang. Ll. 1, 2 are quoted in 'The Great Learning,' Comm. III. 3, and then expounded. See the remarks on them there. L. 3. 假 = 大, 'great.' Choo makes the line = 'The great appointment of Heaven rested on him;' but that term seems rather to be descriptive of the appointment of Heaven, and 哉 to have its usual force of admiration. L. 7. 丽 = 数, 'numbers.' In ll. 7, 8, the meaning seems to be more vivid if we take 命 as I have done. 侯 = 维, as in st. 2. Wang Taou says that both here and there it = 乃, a force which 维 sometimes has. 于周服 = 服于周.

St. 5, carries on the subject of the descendants of Shang, and concludes with an admonition, drawn from their case, to the officers of Chow. There is in the st. an element of proud feeling in the triumph of the author's dynasty. Ll. 3, 4. By 殷 (the previous dynasty was called indifferently that of Shang or Yin) 士, I think,

we must understand both the descendants of Shang and their ministers. They are described as 肤 (= 美) and 敏 (= 疾), 'admirable and active.' When they appeared at the court of Chow, they assisted at the sacrifices of the king in his ancestral temple, which began with a libation of fragrant spirits to bring down the Spirits of the departed. The libation was poured out by the representative of the dead, and the cup with the spirits for that purpose was handed to him by some of those who assisted at the service;—here it is represented as done by the officers of Yin. 裸 = 灌, 'to pour out as a libation.' Choo defines 将 by 行, and Ying-tah, by 送;—we must take the two characters together, with the meaning which I have given them. L. 6. 黼 is the lower garment with the hatchets embroidered on it, though, as Ying-tah says, we are not to suppose that the blazonry was confined to that one figure. 冔 was the name of the cap, as worn, during the Yin dynasty, at sacrifices. The Hëa had used the 收, and the Chow used the 弁. The officers of Yin

六章
无念尔祖。聿修厥德。永言配命。自求多福。殷之未

丧师。克配上帝。宜鉴于殷。骏命不易。

七章
命之不易。无遏尔躬。宣昭义问。有虞殷自天。上天

之载。无声无臭。仪刑文王。万邦作孚。

6   Ever think of your ancestor,
Cultivating your virtue,
Always striving to accord with the will [of Heaven].
So shall you be seeking for much happiness.
Before Yin lost the multitudes,
[Its kings] were the assessors of God.
Look to Yin as a beacon;
The great appointment is not easily [preserved].

7   The appointment is not easily [preserved]
Do not cause your own extinction.
Display and make bright your righteousness and name,
And look at [the fate of] Yin in the light of Heaven.
The doings of High Heaven,
Have neither sound nor smell.
Take your pattern from king Wăn,
And the myriad regions will repose confidence in you.

used their peculiar cap;—by way of honour, and also by way of warning. In ll. 7, 8, the writer turns to the officers of king Ching, and admonishes and stimulates them. 荩＝进, 'to advance,' i.e., never to cease in the maintenance of their loyalty. Their 'ancestor,' of course is king Wăn.

St. 6. Ll. 2—4. 聿 is merely the initial particle. 厥德 is not to be understood of the virtue of king Wăn, but of that of the officers who are addressed; and 厥 = 'your.' 言 is the particle; 配 = 合, 'to match,' 'to accord with;' 命 = 'the will of Heaven,'—Choo says, 天理, 'heavenly principle.' 自 = 'as a matter of course,' 'this is the natural way.' As Choo expands ll. 3, 4:—而又常自

省察,使其所行,无不合于天理,则盛大之福,自我致之,有不外求而得矣.—In ll. 5—8 we have the case of Yin again produced. See the 'Great Learning,' Comm. X. 5. See also the Shoo, V. xvi, 8, on the phrase 配天, equivalent to l. 6 here.

St. 7 continues the admonition in st. 6, converging, in the conclusion, from the officers of Chow to the person of king Ching himself. In l. 2, 遏,＝绝, 'to extinguish,' = to ruin. In l. 3, 宣＝布, 'to spread abroad;' 昭＝明, 'to make bright;' 问＝闻, in st. 2. In l. 4, 有＝又, 'moreover;' 虞＝度, 'to calculate,' 'to estimate.' 自天,—'from Heav-

II. *Ta ming.*

大明

一章

明明在下。赫赫在上。天难忱斯。不易维王。天位殷

適。使不挟四方。

1　The illustration of illustrious [virtue] is required below,
　And the dread majesty is on high.
　Heaven is not readily to be relied on;
　It is not easy to be king.
　Yin's rightful heir to the heavenly seat
　Was not permitted to possess the kingdom.

en,' *i, e.,* from the point of view of Heaven;—seeing how Yin's fall was brought about by Heaven, in consequence of the disobedience of its kings, and their neglect of their duties. See ll.5,6, in the 'Doctrine of the Mean,' XXIII. 6. If the doings of Heaven be thus, how can they be studied and known? The answer is in ll.7,8. King Wăn might be considered as an embodiment of the virtue of Heaven, and he could be studied and imitated. 仪＝象, to resemble;' 刑＝法, 'a pattern.' 仪刑文王＝取法于文王,—as in the translation. 孚＝信, 'to believe.' 作孚,—' will arise and repose confidence in you.

The rhymes are—in st. 1, 天, 新, cat. 12, t. 1; 时, 右 *, cat. 1, t. 2: in 2, 巳, 子, *ib.;* 世, 世, cat. 15, t. 3: in 3, 翼, 国, cat. 3, t. 3; 生, 桢, 宁, cat. 11: in 4, 止, 子, cat. 1, t. 2; 亿, 服 *, *ib.,* t. 3: in 5, 常, 京 *, cat. 10; 寻, 祖, cat. 5, t. 2: in 6, 德 *, 福 *, cat. 1, t. 3; 帝 *, 易, cat. 16, t. 3: in 7, 躬 (prop. cat. 9), 天, cat. 12, t. 1; 臭, 孚 *, cat. 3, t. 1.

Ode 2. Narrative. HOW THE APPOINTMENT OF HEAVEN RESTED ON KING WAN, AND DESCENDED TO HIS SON, KING WOO, WHO OVERTHREW THE DYNASTY OF SHANG;—CELEBRATING ALSO THE MOTHER AND THE WIFE OF KING WAN. See on the title of II.v. I.

St.1. Ll.1,2 are certainly enigmatical, Choo says that 明明 is 德之明, 'the brilliance of virtue,' and 赫赫 is 命之显, 'the manifestation of the will of Heaven.' To

the same effect in a measure is the view of Yen Ts'an. He says, 'The first two lines contain a general sentiment (泛言), expressing the principle that governs the relation between Heaven and men. Acc. to l. 1, the good or evil of a ruler cannot be concealed; acc. to l. 2, Heaven, in giving its favour or taking it away, acts with strict decision. When below there is the illustrious illustration *of virtue*, that reaches up on high. When above there is the awful majesty, that exercises a survey below. The relation between Heaven and men ought to excite our awe.' I believe that Yen-she has appreciated the sentiment of the lines; but it is difficult to bring it out in the brevity of a translation. Maou refers the lines, erroneously, to the virtue of king Wăn, which was displayed among men below, and gloriously seen by Heaven. In ll.3—6 we have the same sentiment of the changing of Heaven's favour, and the same illustration of it, that run through the Part.

Ode 1. 忱＝信, 'to be trusted.' 斯 is the final particle. L.4='He who has not an easy position is the king.' The idea is not that of gaining the throne, but of retaining it. 'The heavenly seat' is the throne, the seat given by Heaven to him who is called 'its son.' 殷適 ＝殷之適嗣, 'the legitimate heir of Yin;'—referring to Show, the last sovereign of that dynasty. 挟＝有, 'to possess.' 四方, ＝ the middle State and all the feudal States of the four quarters,＝the kingdom. We must bring down 天 from l. 3 as the subject of 使.

二章
挚仲氏任。自彼殷商。来嫁于周。曰嫔于京。乃及王

季。维德之行。大任有身。生此文王。

三章
维此文王。小心翼翼。昭事上帝。聿怀多福。厥德不

回。以受方国。

2   Jin, the second of the princesses of Che,
From [the domain of] Yin-shang,
Came to be married to the prince of Chow,
And became his wife in his capital.
Both she and king Ke
Were entirely virtuous.
[Then] T'ae-jin became pregnant,
And gave birth to our king Wăn.

3   This king Wăn,
Watchfully and reverently,
With entire intelligence served God,
And so secured the great blessing.
His virtue was without deflection;
And in consequence he received [the allegiance of] the States
    from all quarters.

St. 2 refers to the father, and especially the mother of king Wăn. She was a Jin, the second daughter of the prince of Che. As Maou gives the first line,—挚 国, 任 姓 之 中 女. The 氏 belongs to 任, and precedes it by the inexorable law of the rhyme. Where Che was has not been ascertained; but we may presume from l.2 that it was within the royal domain of Yin. The critics, at least, say that this is intended by the combination of Yin-shang, the two names of the Yin or Shang dynasty (挚, 商 畿 内 国 也). 周 is best taken as in the translation. 曰 is the particle. 嫔 = 妇, 'to become wife to;'—as in the Shoo, I. 12. 京 is the 'capital' of Chow; so denominated from the fortunes of the family when the ode was written. The 乃 及 in l.5 shows that the mother of king Wăn is still the main subject of the stanza. 王 季 is the title conferred by the duke of Chow on his great-grandfather;—see the 'Doctrine of the Mean,' XVIII. 3. The best way of dealing with the

之 in l. 4 is to take it as = 其, 'only virtuous was their conduct.' It makes the 行 descriptive of the 德. Ta'e-jin is the honorary name of the lady. 身 = 怀 孕, 'pregnancy.' Chinese writers celebrate Ta'e-jin in the highest terms. 'When she was pregnant with king Wăn,' says Lëw Hëang, 'her eyes looked on no improper sight, her ears listened to no licentious sound, and her lips uttered no word of pride. When the king was born, he was intelligent and sage, so that when his mother taught him one thing, he learned a hundred things; and in the end he became the founder of the Chow dynasty. The superior man will say that T'ae-jin could commence the instruction of her child while he was yet in the womb.'
St. 3 is all occupied with the virtue of king Wăn, which made him the object of God's favour. Choo explains l. 2 as 恭 慎 之 貌, 'the app. of reverence and carefulness,'—the same as the 敬 in ode I. 4. 昭 is defined by 明, 'brightly;'—the meaning appears to be what I have given. 聿 is the particle. 怀

四章

天監在下。有命既集。文王初載。天作之合。在洽之

陽。在渭之涘。文王嘉止。大邦有子。

五章

大邦有子。俔天之妹。文定厥祥。親迎于渭。造舟為

4　Heaven surveyed this lower world;
　　And its appointment lighted [on king Wăn].
　　In his early years,
　　It made for him a mate;—
　　On the north of the Hëah;
　　On the banks of the Wei.
　　When king Wăn would wive,
　　There was the lady in a large State.

5　In a large State was the lady,
　　Like a fair denizen of Heaven.
　　The ceremonies determined the auspiciousness [of the union],
　　And in person he met her on the Wei.

is defined by 來, 'to make to come.' 回＝邪, 'crooked,' 'perverse.' 受方國＝受四方侯國之旧,—as in the translation.
St. 4 introduces the queen of king Wăn, as specially provided for him by Heaven. Ll. 1, 2 refer to Wăn, as singled out by Heaven to occupy the throne. It was hardly necessary to put 'on king Wăn,' in brackets, as they are merely brought up from l. 3. 集＝就, 'to come to,' 'to settle or light on.' 載＝年; 初載＝'in his early years.' Thus his bride would be about the same age as himself. 合＝配,—'a mate.' Hëah is the name of a river, on the north of which lay the capital of the State held by the father of T'ae-sze. The Shwoh-wăn quotes the line with 郃; and Maou originally had 合 alone. The 水 was added in the Han dynasty. The river is supposed to have been in the pres. dis. of Hoh-yang (郃阳), in T'ung Chow (同州), Shen-se. 涘,—as in I. vi. VII. 2, et al. In l. 7, Choo defines 嘉 by 婚礼, 'the marriage ceremony;'—certainly marriage is one of what are denominated the 嘉 or 吉 ceremonies: and we may adopt Choo's view, so that the meaning of the

line is as I have given it. Even Yen Ts'an here follows Choo in preference to the old explanation of the term as meaning 'admired.' The great State is Sin (莘), to which the young lady belonged.
In st. 5 we have the marriage of Wăn and this lady. It would be hard to say what specific idea the writer had in his mind in the 2d line, descriptive of the grace and other attributes of the lady. 俔＝譬, 'to be compared to.' Han Ying read 磬, which has the same meaning. 妹,—'a younger sister;' but here simply ＝少女, 'a young lady.' L. 3 is descriptive of the preliminary formalities; 文 is defined by 礼, 'ceremonies;' and 祥 by 吉, 'lucky,' 'fortunate.' Yen Ts'an says, 'The tortoise-shell was consulted, and gave a favourable response. Then they determined by the ceremonial observances that the thing was fortunate, and presented the bridal gifts (卜 而 得 吉, 則 以 礼 文 定 其 吉 祥, 而 納 币 焉). All things being ready, the young prince went in person to meet the bride, and made a bridge of boats for her to cross the Wei by. The boats were moored across the stream, and then planks were laid upon them, so that the lady might walk over. Morrison, under the char. 俔, gives the stanza thus:—

梁。不显其光。

六章
有命自天。命此文王。于周于京。缵女维莘。长子维

行。笃生武王。保右命尔。燮伐大商。

七章
殷商之旅。其会如林。矢于牧野。维予侯兴。上帝临

> Over it he made a bridge of boats;—
> The glory [of the occasion] was illustrious.

6　The favouring appointment was from Heaven,
　　Giving the throne to our king Wăn,
　　In the capital of Chow.
　　The lady-successor was from Sin,
　　Its eldest daughter, who came to marry him.
　　She was blessed to give birth to king Woo,
　　Who was preserved, and helped, and received also the appointment,
　　And in accordance with it smote the great Shang.

7　The troops of Yin-shang
　　Were collected like a forest,
　　And marshalled in the wilderness of Muh.

'Of a great nation there is a daughter,
Comparable to the angelic sisters of heaven.
The elegant presents have determined his bliss;
In person he meets her, on the banks of the Wei.
Build the boats; make a bridge;
Spare nought to illustrate his glory.'

Translating at random as Morrison did, for the purposes of his dictionary, it was not to be expected that he would give the verses correctly, according to the tenses they must have in their connection with others. It became a statute of Chow that a royal bride should be brought across a stream on a bridge of boats, king Wăn having thus set the example. 不显,—as in I. 1.

St. 6 carries on the narrative to the birth of king Woo, Wăn's son, who was to wrest the sovereignty from Yin. L. 3. 于周于京, 'in Chow, in the capital,'=in his Chow capital (于周之京). Ll. 4, 5 must be taken closely together, in order to make any construction of them. 缵 = 继, 'to continue.' T'ae-sze is called 'the continuing lady,' as the successor to T'ae-jin, whose praises were declared in st. 2. 维莘 plainly means—'was from Sin.' Choo takes 行 = 嫁, as in the translation. Maou would connect it with the 行, in st. 2. Yen Ts'an agrees with Choo, referring to the use of the term, in I. iii. XIV. 2. It is difficult to give or to understand the force of 笃, 'real,' 'sincere,' 'to give importance to,' in l. 6. Choo takes it as I have done,—天 又 笃 厚 之. The 天, thus understood, must be brought on as the subject of the verbs in l. 7. 右 = 助, 'to assist.' The 尔 cannot be taken as the pronoun of the 2d person;—we must regard it as a final particle, or as = 之. 燮 = 和, 'harmoniously;'—we must suppose here 'in harmony with the will of Heaven.' Choo says, 顺 天 命.

女。无贰尔心。

八章

牧野洋洋。檀车煌煌。驷𫘝彭彭。维师尚父。时维鹰

扬。凉彼武王。肆伐大商。会朝清明。

We rose [to the crisis];—
'God is with you,' [said Shang-foo to the king],
'Have no doubts in your heart.'

8   The wilderness of Muh spread out extensive;
     Bright shone the chariots of sandal;
     The teams of bays, black-maned and white-bellied, galloped
          along;
     The grand-master Shang-foo
     Was like an eagle on the wing,
     Assisting king Woo,
     Who at one onset smote the great Shang.
     That morning's encounter was followed by a clear bright [day].

Stt. 7, 8 are occupied with the decisive battle, which issued in the overthrow of the dyn. of Shang, and gave the throne to king Woo. In st. 7, l. 1, 殷商,—as in st. 2; 旅=师, 'multitudes.' L. 2. Comp. the Shoo, V. iii. 9. L. 3. 矢=陈, 'to be displayed' 'to be marshalled.' 牧野,—see on the Shoo, V. ii. 1. In l. 3, Choo takes 侯 as the particle 维, so that the meaning is, as I have given it (我 之 师 为 有 兴 起 之 势). Ch'ing refers the 侯 to Woo, here called marquis from Shang's point of view;—which is very unlikely. Këang Ping-chang and many others take the line as saying, 'We of Chow and the princes on our side arose (予 周 以 诸 侯 兴 起 而 陈 于 牧 野 之 地). Ll. 5, 6 are well taken by Këang as spoken to king Woo by Shang-foo, who commanded on the side of Chow. 临 女,—'has come to you;'=is with you. 贰=疑, 'to doubt.'

In st. 8, 洋 洋=广 大 之 貌, 'the app. of being wide and large.' 檀 车,—see on I.

ix. VI. 煌 煌,—see I. xii. V. 1. 𫘝,—is defined as 'a bay-horse, black-maned, with a white belly (骊 马 白 腹). 彭 彭,—as in II. vi. I. 3. 尚 父,—seen on the title of I. viii. 师=大 师, 'grand-master. 时=是, 'he was.' 凉—'to assist;' as if it were 亮, with which the line is quoted in the Books of Han (王 莽 传). Maou explains 肆 by 疾, 'rapidly;' Choo, by 纵 兵, 'let go his weapons.' 会 朝,—'the morning of the meeting,' i. e., of the battle. 清 明=而 天 下 清 明, 'and all under heaven was clear and bright.'

The rhymes are—in st. 1, 上, 王, 方, cat. 10: in 2, 商, 京 *, 行 *, 王, ib.: in 3, 翼, 福 *, 国, cat. 1, t. 3: in 4, 集, 合 *, cat. 7, t. 3; 涘, 止, 子, cat. 1, t. 2: in 5, 妹, 渭, cat. 15, t. 3; 梁, 光, cat. 10: in 6, 天, 莘, cat. 12, t. 1; 王, 京 *, 行 *, 王, 商, cat. 10: in 7, 林, 兴 (prop. cat. 6), 心, cat. 7, t. 1; 旅, 野 *, 女, cat. 5, t. 2: in 8, 洋, 煌, 彭 *, 扬, 王, 商, 明 *, cat. 10.

III. *Mëen.*

绵

一章

绵绵瓜瓞。民之初生。自土沮漆。古公亶父。陶复陶

穴。未有家室。

1　In long trains ever increasing grow the gourds.
　　When [our] people first sprang,
　　From the country about the Ts'eu and the Ts'eih,
　　The ancient duke T'an-foo,
　　Made for them kiln-like huts and caves,
　　Ere they had yet any houses.

Ode 3. Metaphorical and narrative. THE SMALL BEGINNINGS AND SUBSEQUENT GROWTH OF THE HOUSE OF CHOW. ITS REMOVAL FROM PIN UNDER T'AN-FOO, AND SETTLEMENT IN CHOW, DOWN TO THE TIME OF KING WAN. The gradual rise of the House of Chow has been adverted to in the notes on the title of Part I. T'an-foo, it is there stated, removed with his tribe from Pin to the plain of Chow, in B.C. 1,325; and we have here an eloquent account of his labours in founding the new settlement. Duke Lëw, to whom is ascribed the previous settlement of the tribe in Pin, in B. C. 1,796, is celebrated in the second Book of this Part; but what we read of T'an-foo, in the 1st stanza of the ode before us, is hardly reconcileable with the accounts of his distant predecessor, nor with the sketch of life in Pin, which forms the theme of I.xv.I. It is not history which we have of the early days of the tribe in Pin, but legends, and legends dressed up by the writer or the writers of the odes, carrying back into antiquity the state of things which was existing around them in their own day.

St. 1. L. 1 is metaphorical, designed, evidently, to give us the idea of the growth of Chow from a very small beginning. Choo says that large gourds are called *kwa*, and small ones *tëeh*, from which Williams explains the two characters together as 'large and small melons, *met.* posterity.' But 瓞 (*i. q.* 瓜, with 勺 on the right) is the gourd near its root, where it begins, very small as compared with the 瓜, when it has grown and extended, with a vast developement of its tendrils and leaves. So had the House of Chow grown and increased, small at first, and ever becoming larger. Këang Ping-chang says, 绵 绵 之 瓜，本 方 初 生 之 瓞, making it clear that he did not understand *kwa* and *tëeh* as two different plants, but as one, in the early and developed stage of its growth. 绵 绵，—as in I. vi. VII. The line is metaphorical really, though Maou makes it allusive, as introductory to the whole of the stanzas. It is so introductory; but it is itself metaphorical.

Ll. 2—6 certainly give us the idea of the tribe of Chow coming first into notice in the time of T'an-foo, in the country about the two rivers mentioned, and living there in habitations of the most primitive description. This is irreconcileable with the accounts which we have of it under duke Lëw nearly five centuries earlier; nor will the student think that the difficulty is lightened by Wang Gan-shih, who says, 'The State of Chow [this can only be understood of the tribe, which afterwards settled in Chow] had nearly become extinct. Subsequently it occupied the country about the Ts'eu and the Ts'eih, and began to revive, so that the people are here spoken of as first originating there.' The Ts'eu and the Ts'eih were two rivers in the territory of Pin, and are not to be confounded with those of the same name in the Shoo, III. i. Pt. i. 75. We need not enter into the various discussions about them. 自 土 沮 漆 = 自 居 于 沮 漆 之 旁, 'from the time of their dwelling on the banks of the Ts'eu and Ts'eih.' 古 公，=先 公, 'the ancient duke;' 亶 父 is to be taken as the name. The personage was the grandfather of king Wăn, and appears as 'king T'ae' in the list of the kings of the Chow family. He is here called 'duke,' as the ordinary designation of the prince of a State after his death. 陶 is 'a kiln for making pottery;' used here for 'to make in the shape of a kiln.' 复 is explained in the dict. by 累 土 于 地 上, 'raising up earth above the surface of the ground,' and is said to be, in this sense, interchangeable with 覆, 'that which covers or overshadows.' These kiln-like huts and caves were the dwellings in which the tribe of Chow lived in the 13th century before our era. They were left open, it is said, at the top, for the purpose of light. 家 室 together = regularly constructed houses.

二章
古公亶父。来朝走马。率西水浒。至于岐下。爰及姜
女。聿来胥宇。

三章
周原膴膴。堇荼如饴。爰始爰谋。爰契我龟。曰止曰
时。筑室于兹。

四章
乃慰乃止。乃左乃右。乃疆乃理。乃宣乃亩。自西徂

2   The ancient duke T'an-foo
     Came in the morning, galloping his horses,
     Along the banks of the western rivers,
     To the foot of [mount] K'e;
     And there, he and the lady Këang
     Came, and together looked out for a site on which to settle.

3   The plain of Chow looked beautiful and rich,
     With its violets and sowthistles [sweet] as dumplings.
     There he began with consulting [his followers];
     There he singed the tortoise-shell, [and divined].
     The responses were—there to stay, and then;
     And they proceeded there to build their houses.

4   He encouraged the people and settled them;
     Here on the left, there on the right.

St. 2 commemorates the removal of T'an-foo from Pin to the plain of Chow. Of the circumstances in which the removal took place Mencius has given us a graphic account, very much to the honour of the ancient duke;—see Men. I. Pt. ii. XV. 1. 来,—'came;' *i. e.*, came from Pin. 率 = 循, 'along,' 'following the course of.' 浒 = 水厓, 'banks.' The 'western waters' are probably the Ts'eu and Ts'eih. Mount K'e, called also 'Pillar of the sky,' is 10 *le* north east from K'e-shan dis. city, dep. Fungts'ëang. The prince's wife was a Këang; she is commonly spoken of as T'ae-këang (大姜). 爰,—as commonly, = 'there.' 聿 is merely the particle. 胥 = 相, 'together.' The term indicates that T'ae-këang was capable of advising her husband,—a worthy predecessor of T'ae-jin and T'ae-sze. 宇 = 宅, 'the site for a settlement;' the term here has a pregnant meaning here,—'to look out for such a site.'

St. 3. The plain of Chow lay south from mount K'e. 膴膴 = 肥美貌, 'the app.

of being rich and beautiful.' 饴 denotes sweet cakes made of rice. The soil in the plain of Chow was so rich, that vegetables, elsewhere very inferior, grew in it so as to be like those cakes. The 荼 we have met with repeatedly as the sowthistle. About the 堇 I am not sure. Choo calls it the 乌头, or 'crow's-head;' but more modern critics all will have it to be the violet; and as such it is figured in the Japanese plates. The roots of this yield an emetical substance; but I have never read of their being eaten. Attracted by the appearance of the plain, T'an-foo proceeded to consult and divine about making his settlement here. According to Mencius, his people had followed him in crowds from Pin. 契 is used here for an instrument which was employed in scorching or firing the tortoise shell;—'to scorch.' I cannot tell why 我 is used before 龟; but it is better to neglect it in translating. The 曰 .in l. 5 is understood by Choo of T'an-foo thus reporting the result of his consultations and divinations. I have taken it rather differently.

东。周爰执事。

五章
乃召司空。乃召司徒。俾立室家。其绳则直。缩版以

载。作庙翼翼。

He divided the ground into larger tracts and smaller portions;
He dug the ditches; he defined the acres;
From the west to the east,
There was nothing which he did not take in hand.

5   He called his superintendent of works;
He called his minister of instruction;
And charged them with the building of the houses.
With the line they made everything straight;
They bound the frame-boards tight, so that they should rise
     regularly.
Uprose the ancestral temple in its solemn grandeur.

St. 4 speaks of the general arrangements made by T'an-foo for the occupancy of the plain of Chow. We cannot translate the 乃 which occurs so frequently. 'Accordingly' would convey its force more nearly than any other term I can think of. Choo defines 止 by 居,—'to assign the place or quarter of residence.' The left and the right,' i.e., the east and the west, would be determined with reference to the site which had been fixed on for the town, that was to be the capital or residence of the chief himself. L. 3,—see on II. vi. VI. i. 宣 has been taken variously. K'ung Ying-tah adopted Ch'ing's view, that the word = 时 耕, 'to assign the times of ploughing and other agricultural operations;' Choo takes it as = 布 散 而 居, 'dispersed the people all over the country.' Neither of these interpretations commends itself. Much better is another which Choo mentions, and which I have followed;— 宣 导 其 沟 洫, 'dug the ditches, large and small,' i.e., made all the arrangements for the irrigation of the fields, which the peculiar system of husbandry and the division of the land required. 亩 is to be taken verbally,— as I have done. L. 5 seems to come in awkwardly; but we must take it as an account of the whole of the newly occupied territory, from the west, where it was nearest to the old site of the tribe in Pin, on to the furthest point towards the east to which it extended. Then

l. 6 has still T'an-foo for its subject. 周 = 遍, 'universally.' 'all round.' 爰 cannot be translated. Choo expresses the whole line very well as = 靡 事 不 为.

Stt. 5, 6, and 7 all describe the processes and progress in erecting the buildings of the new settlement, and especially with reference to the residence or palace of T'an-foo himself. These processes took place under the direction of a superintendent of works and a minister of instruction; but I do not not believe that T'an-foo had at this time two officers at all corresponding to those who bore these names subsequently, when the Chow dynasty was consolidated, and whose functions are described in the Shoo and the Chow Le. The string or plummet was used so that the walls were made perpendicular and square. The building frames were firmly bound together (缩 = 束), and raised as the space enclosed by them was completed, the lower board in the frame being removed and placed above. The same process was continued, tier exactly above tier, till the walls were carried to the required elevation. This is the meaning assigned to 以 载 (上 下 相 承 也, 言 以 索 束 板, 投 土 筑 讫, 则 升 下 而 上, 以 相 承 载), though it is getting more out of the 载, which simply signifies 'to contain' the earth, than the term can well convey. The intimation in the 4th line is interesting. The first building taken

六章
捄之陾陾。度之薨薨。筑之登登。削屢馮馮。百堵皆
興。鼛鼓弗勝。

七章
乃立皋門。皋門有伉。乃立應門。應門將將。乃立冢
土。戎丑攸行。

6　Crowds brought the earth in baskets;
　　They threw it with shouts into the frames;
　　They beat it with responsive blows;
　　They pared the walls repeatedly, and they sounded strong.
　　Five thousand cubits of them arose together,
　　So that the roll of the great drum did not overpower [the noise of the builders].

7　They set up the gate of the *enceinte;*
　　And the gate of the *enceinte* stood high.
　　They set up the court gate;
　　And the court gate stood grand.
　　They reared the great altar [to the Spirits of the land],
　　From which all great movements should proceed.

in hand and completed was the ancestral temple. The chief would make a home for the Spirits of his fathers before he made one for himself. However imperfectly directed it was, religious feeling asserted the supremacy which it ought to possess. In st. 6 we have the bustle and noise of the building graphically set forth. 捄 denotes the constant 'carrying of earth to the frames in baskets (盛土于器);' 陾陾 ＝众, 'all,' 'multitudes;' 度 is 'the throwing the earth into the frames (投土于板);' 薨薨, 'the noise of the people (众声),' their chattering and shouting; 筑 is 'the pounding of the earth;' and 登登, the blows of one long pestle answering to another. When the wall was thus reared, they pared or scraped it, till it was clear of all protuberances and made smooth (削屢), and then it gave a sound, when tapped, represented by 馮馮. L. 5. See II.iii.VII.2. 皆 should, probably, be 偕,＝俱, 'all together. L. 6. see on II. vi. IV. 3. The drum was beaten to stimulate the workers; but so many were they, and so cheerful and active, that the sound of it was almost drowned in the noise which they themselves made. St. 7 relates to the building of the palace and grand altar; but they are described, unfortunately,

with reference to the palaces of T'an-foo's descendants when they had become sovereigns of the kingdom. The residence now reared was but a small structure apparently, consisting only of two buildings, an outer and an inner, leading to which were two gates. Subsequently the royal palace consisted of seven buildings, two more than those which constituted the palaces of the princes of the States. Belonging to it were two gates called the 皋門 and the 應門, which the princes could not boast of, and these names are here given to the gates of T'an-foo's residence. 皋門＝王之郭門, and 應門＝王之正門 or 朝門;—as in the translation. 有伉＝高貌, 'high-looking;' 將將＝严正, 'severe and exact.' 冢土＝大社, 'the grand altar to the Spirits of the land.' See the note on the Shoo, III. i. Pt. i. 35. 戎丑＝大众, 'great and universal,' meaning all great undertakings, and such as required the cooperation of all the people. These were preceded by a solemn sacrifice at the grand altar. As Choo says, 起大事,动大众,必有事乎社,而后出谓之宜. T'an-foo would raise an altar, appropriate to his own circumstances; but it is here thus grandly described with reference to the royal position of his descendants.

八章
肆不殄厥愠。亦不陨厥问。柞棫拔矣。行道兑矣。混
夷駾矣。维其喙矣。

九章
虞芮质厥成。文王蹶厥生。予曰有疏附。予曰有先
后。予曰有奔奏。予曰有御侮。

8　Thus though he could not prevent the rage [of his foes],
He did not let fall his own fame.
The oaks and the *yih* were [gradually] thinned,
And roads for travelling were opened.
The hordes of the Keun disappeared,
Startled and panting.

9　[The chiefs of] Joo and Juy were brought to an agreement,
By king Wăn's stimulating their natural virtue.
Then, I may say, some came to him, previously not knowing him;
And some, drawn the last by the first;
And some, drawn by his rapid successes;
And some, by his defence [of the weak] from insult.

St. 8. Ll. 1, 2 are taken of T'an-foo in his relations to the wild hordes, which, as described by Mencius, obliged him to withdraw with his tribe, from Pin. He could not prevent them from showing their barbarous dispositions, but amid all his trouble from them, and subsequently, he showed his own great qualities. 肆 is defined in the Urh-ya by 故, 'therefore;' and by 故 今, which I do not know what to make of. Choo explains it by 遂, adding that 'it carries on the discourse from what precedes.' Here it= 'thus although.' 殄=绝,—'to disarm.' 愠 =怒, 'anger.' 问 we have met with before, —in the sense of 闻, 'fame.'

Ll. 3—6 describe the gradual clearing of the country, and bring us down to the times of T'an-foo's son and grandson,—the kings Ke and Wăn. 柞 has occurred already,—an oak and thorny. The *yih* is by some said to be the same tree; but it appears to be different, and is called, in the Urh-ya, the white *juy* (白樱), 'a thorny, shrubby tree, growing to the height of 5 or 6 feet, and bearing a red fruit, like an ear-pendant, and eatable.' The country had been all over-grown with these, affording shelter to the wild tribes; but gradually the trees were 'thinned'—

so we must take 拔 —and roads were 'opened' (兑=通, 'to be made passable'). On this the barbarians, here called 'the Keun hordes,' could no longer keep their ground. 駾 is defined in the Shwoh-wăn as 'the app. of a horse hurrying on rapidly;' and here = 'fled away rapidly.' L. 6 represents the barbarians flying with open mouth (喙=口). Choo defines the term by 息, 'to pant.'

St. 9 brings us to king Wăn, and the States, one after another, coming to him to hail him as their leader. Joo and Juy were two States on the east of the Ho; but their positions cannot be sufficiently defined. 质 is explained by 成, and 成 by 平; 质 厥 成 = 'decided their strife and made peace.' The story of their case, as related by Sze-ma Ts'ëen, Lëw Hëang, and others, is this:—Their chiefs had a quarrel about certain fields, or a strip of territory, to which each of them laid claim. Unable to come to an agreement, they went to lay the matter before the lord of Chow; and as soon as they entered his territory, they saw the ploughers readily yielding the furrow, and travellers yielding the path to one another, while men and women

IV. *Yih p'oh.*

棫樸

一章
芃芃棫樸。薪之槱之。济济辟王。左右趣之。

1   Abundant is the growth of the *yih* and the *p'oh*,
Supplying firewood; yea, stores of it.
Elegant and dignified was our prince and king;
On the right and the left they hastened to him.

avoided one another on the road, and none of the old people had burdens to carry. When they got to the court, they beheld the officers of each inferior grade readily giving place to those above them. All this made them ashamed of their own quarrel. They acknowledged the error and folly of it, agreed to let the disputed ground be an open territory, and withdrew, without presuming to appear before the prince of Chow. When this affair was noised abroad, it is said that more than forty States tendered their submission to Chow. Choo says that he does not understand l. 2. I have followed Yen Ts'an's view of it. He takes 生 as meaning 'the natural conscience (本 然 之 良 心),' as inseparable from man as his 'life,' and 蹶＝动, 'to move;' thus connecting the line closely with the preceding. By the 予 曰 in ll. 1—6, we are probably to understand the writer of the ode, delivering his own opinion as to the causes which gave king Wǎn his great and ever increasing influence. The last three characters in every line are applicable to himself,—his attributes or the effects of his attributes. This is not the view of Maou or Choo; but Këang P'ing-chang gives it, and I can see no other reasonable mode of construction. Këang's words are, 文 王 之 兴，自 予 言 之，则 曰 以 其 有 疏 附 耳，能 宣 布 德 泽 使 民 归 也，以 其 有 先 后 耳，能 前 后 相 导，使 无 过 举 也，以 其 有 奔 奏 耳，能 使 四 方 喻 德 奏 功 也，以 其 有 御 侮 耳，能 奋 扬 武 卫，折 冲 威 敌 也．

The rhymes are—in st. 1, 槱 生 (prop. cat. 11), 穴 室, cat. 12, t. 3: in 2, 父 马 *, 浒, 下 *, 女 宇, cat. 5, t. 2: in 3, 胝 (prop. cat.

5), 饴 谋 *, 龟 *, 时, 兹, cat. 1, t. 1: in 4, 止, 右 *, 理, 亩 *, 事, *ib.*, t. 2: in 5, 徒, 家 *, cat. 5, t. 1; 直, 载, 翼, cat. 1, t. 3: in 6, 陕 (prop. cat. 1), 薨, 登, 冯, 兴, 胜, cat. 6: in 7, 门, 门, cat. 13: in 8, 忼, 将, 行 *, cat. 10: in 8, 恺, 问, cat. 13; 拔, 兑, 驳, 喙, cat. 15, t. 3: in 9, 成, 生, cat. 11; 附 *, 后, 奏, 侮 *, cat. 4, t. 2.

Ode 4. Allusive and narrative. IN PRAISE OF KING WĂN, CELEBRATING HIS ACTIVITY, INFLUENCE, AND CAPACITY TO RULE. Such is the account, substantially, given of this piece in the Preface, and accepted by Choo. I do not wish to call it in question, but we have not the same amount of internal evidence as to its subject, as in the three preceding odes; nor is it without its difficulties,—as will appear in the notes.

St. 1. The *yih*,—see on last ode. The *p'oh* has not been determined. The Japanese plates do not give a figure of it. It is described as a dense and shrubby tree. 芃芃 has been met with several times. The meaning which I have given of 槱 (Choo says, ＝ 积) is determined by the previous 薪. Këang says, 'L. 2 is introductory to all the rest of the piece. 薪 之 indicates the gathering of the wood for to-day's use, and serves, allusively, to introduce ll. 3, 4 and st. 2. 槱 之 indicates the storing up of the wood for future use, and serves to introduce stt. 3—5.' 济 济 is here defined by 容 貌 之 美,—as in the translation. 辟 ＝ 君, 'ruler;' 辟 王 is understood to be king Wǎn. 趣 is defined in the dict. by 疾 and 遽, expressive of 'rapid movement.' L. 4 indicates the States everywhere—on the right and on the left—hurrying to acknowledge the claims of the lord of Chow.

二章
济济辟王。左右奉璋。奉璋峨峨。髦士攸宜。
三章
淠波泾舟。烝徒楫之。周王于迈。六师及之。
四章
倬彼云汉。为章于天。周王寿考。遐不作人。

2   Elegant and dignified was our prince and king;
On his left and his right they bore their half-mace [libation-
     cups];—
They bore their instruments with solemn gravity,
As beseemed such eminent officers.

3   They rush along,—those boats on the King,
All the rowers labouring at their oars.
The king of Chow marched on,
Followed by his six hosts.

4   Vast is that Milky Way,
Making a brilliant figure in the sky.
Long years did the king of Chow enjoy;—
Did he not exert an influence upon men?

In st. 2. we have the lord of Chow,—again called 'prince and king,'—in his ancestral temple, assisted by his ministers or great officers in pouring out the libations to the Spirits of the departed. The *chang* was a semi-mace (半 圭 曰 璋); *i. e.*, the obelisk-like symbol of jade, called a *kwei*, was cut into two parts, each one forming a *chang;* but we are not to understand here the *chang* simply, but a libation-cup, of which it formed the handle, and called 璋 瓚. The handle of the king's cup was formed by a complete *kwei;* of a minister's, by a *chang*. Choo says, that as his officers stood on the chief's left and right, the *chang* would always be turned towards him, as they performed the libation, so that l. 2 has the same significance as l. 4 in last st.;—I do not see the value or point of the remark. 峨 峨 = 盛 壮, denoting the grave formality with which the officers went through their business. 髦 = 俊, 'eminent.' Kĕang expands l. 4:— 髦 士 奉 璋, 威 仪 节 度, 皆 得 其 宜.

St. 3. 淠 = 舟 行 貌, 'the app. of a boat in motion.' 烝 = 众, 'all.' 楫 'an oar;' here, = 櫂, 'to row,' 'to use the oars.' These rowers, all working willingly, are allusive of the alacrity with which the people followed the chief of Chow. Choo defines 于 by 往; but it is better to take it, as we have hitherto done in similar cases, as the particle. 六 师 = 六 军, 'six armies.' But only the king led '*six armies*' into the field; and hence l. 4 could not be appropriate to the Head of the house of Chow, till king Wăn's son, Woo, actually acquired the sovereignty of the kingdom. Kĕang here brings in the allusive force of the 櫂 之 in st. 1, so that the six armies correspond to the stores of wood laid up for future use. They had been prepared by Wăn, but were used only subsequently, by Woo.

St. 4. 云 汉 is another name for the 天 汉 of II. v. IX. 5, the 'Han of the Clouds,' the Milky Way. 倬 = 大, 'great,' 'vast;' or 'brilliant.' 章 = 文 章, 'elegant figures.' 'King

五章

追琢其章。金玉其相。勉勉我王。纲纪四方。

5   Engraved and chiselled are the ornaments;
     Of metal and of jade is their substance.
     Ever active was our king,
     Giving law and rules to the four quarters [of the kingdom].

V.   *Han luh.*

旱麓

一章

瞻彼旱麓。榛楛济济。岂弟君子。干禄岂弟。

1   Look at the foot of the Han,
     How abundantly grow the hazel and the arrow-thorn!
     Easy and self-possessed was our prince,
     In his pursuit of dignity [still] easy and self-possessed!

Wăn,' says Choo, 'died at the age of 97; hence the terms 寿考.' 遐=何, as in II.ii.VII.4,5, *et al.* 作人 =='stimulate men;' as Choo says, 变化鼓舞之. The stanza, acc. to Këang, found its fulfilment when king Woo arranged the orders of nobility, &c., as related in the Shoo, V.iii.10, making the earth glorious as the Milky Way does the sky; but he was only completing the work of his father.

St. 5. Ll. 1,2 seem to be allusive of the state of the kingdom, made goodly and great by Wăn and Woo, like the most precious substances, gold and jade, wrought on by skilful workmen. 追 (read *tuy*) == 雕, 'to engrave,' 'to make figures on;'—with reference to the 金 in l. 2. 相 is explained by 质, 'substance,' its opposition to 章, in l. 1, necessitating that meaning;—as Ying-tah points out. 勉勉,--'ever active;' Choo says the expression is equivalent to 不已, 'unceasing.' 纲 denotes 'great measures,' affecting on a large scale, like the great rope which commands the whole of a net; 纪, 'smaller regulations,' which are like the adjustment of threads of silk.

The rhymes are—in st. 1, 橢, 趣 (prop. cat. 4), cat. 3, t. 2: in 2, 王, 璋, cat. 10; 峨, 宜 *, cat. 17: in 3, 楫, 及, cat. 7, t. 3: in 4, 天, 人, cat. 12, t. 1: in 5, 章, 相, 王, 方, cat. 10.

Ode 5. Allusive and narrative. IN PRAISE OF THE VIRTUE OF KING WAN BLESSED BY HIS ANCESTORS, AND RAISED TO THE HIGHEST DIGNITY WITHOUT SEEKING OF HIS OWN. The Preface makes the subject of this piece to be '*the blessing* received from ancestors;' which is not very clear and precise. Nor does the ode itself say positively, who 'the princely man' in it was. Ch'ing thought that the phrase referred to king T'ae and king Ke, Wăn's grandfather and father. Maou wisely says nothing on the point. Yen Ts'an says that it is best here to agree with Choo, and refer the phrase to king Wăn.

St. 1. 旱 is understood to be the name of a hill; but nothing further can be ascertained about it. 麓,—as in the Shoo, II.i.2. The 楛 is described as 'like a thorn-tree, but red.' Its wood is good for making arrow-shafts. Here, as where the phrase has hitherto occurred, Choo, after Maou, defines 岂弟 by 乐易, 'happy and easy.' Acc. to Yen Ts'an, the characters denote 'virtue complete and benevolence ripe, harmony and concord in full accumulation (德盛仁熟,和顺充积之谓).' They seem to convey the idea of one who possesses a natural benevolence and satisfaction, and who is successful without ambition. 干禄,—see Ana. II. xviii. 1. The connection between the first two lines and the last two seems to be this,—that as the foot of the hill was favourable to vegetable growth, so were king Wăn's natural qualities to his distinction and advancement.

二章
瑟彼玉瓚。黄流在中。岂弟君子。福禄攸降。

三章
鸢飞戾天。鱼跃于渊。岂弟君子。遐不作人。

四章
清酒既载。骍牡既备。以享以祀。以介景福。

五章
瑟彼柞棫。民所燎矣。岂弟君子。神所劳矣。

2 Massive is that libation-cup of jade,
With the yellow liquid [sparkling] in it.
Easy and self-possessed was our prince,
The fit recipient of blessing and dignity.

3 The hawk flies up to heaven;
The fishes leap in the deep.
Easy and self-possessed was our prince;—
Did he not exert an influence upon men?

4 His clear spirits are in the vessel;
His red bull is ready;—
To offer, to sacrifice,
To increase his bright happiness.

5 Thick grow the oaks and the *yih*,
Which the people use for fuel.

St. 2. 瑟 is defined here by 缜密貌, 'the app. of being solid and close,' = massive. The 玉瓚 here is the 圭瓚, described under st. 2 of last ode. Choo adds here that the material of the *cup* was of gold. The 'yellow liquid' in it was the herb-flavoured spirits, mentioned in the Shoo, V.xiii. 25. As a cup of such quality was the proper receptacle for those spirits, so was the character of king Wăn such that all blessing must accrue to it (岂弟之 君子必有福禄下其躬，言 以类应; Yen Ts'an).

St. 3. The hawk rises in the sky, and the fishes leap about in the deep,—without an effort;—it is their nature to do so. So there went out an influence from king Wăn, unconsciously to himself. L. 4,—as in st. 4 of last ode.

St. 4. Choo Kung-ts'ëen says, 'When virtue reaches in its influence to men, it is sure also to move spiritual Beings; and its possessor will receive blessing as is here intimated.' The 清 酒 is the same as the 黄流 of st. 2. 载, 'are contained;' *i. e.*, a supply of them is provided in the vessel for them. Choo explains the character by 在尊, 'are in the vase.' The victims for sacrifice, under the Chow dynasty, were red. King Wăn, as being all his life only the lord of Chow, could never have used such a victim; but there is no more difficulty in his being represented as doing so, than in the title of king, and various royal functions, so freely ascribed to him in these odes. The device of Kĕang, that the ode was made for king Woo, on some occasion of his sacrificing, when the duke of Chow reminded him of the virtues of their father, is unnecessary.

St. 5. 瑟 must here ═ 'dense' and 燎 ═ 'to use as fuel.' As natural as it was for the people to take the abundant wood and use it,

六章
莫莫葛藟。施于条枚。岂弟君子。求福不回。

> Easy and self-possessed was our prince,
> Cheered and encouraged by the Spirits.

6 Luxuriant are the dolichos and other creepers,
  Clinging to the branches and stems,
  Easy and self-possessed was our prince,
  Seeking for happiness by no crooked ways.

VI. *Sze chae.*

思齐

一章
思齐大任。文王之母。思媚周姜。京室之妇。大姒嗣

徽音。则百斯男。

1 Pure and reverent was T'ae-jin,
  The mother of king Wăn;
  Loving was she to Chow Këang;—
  A wife becoming the House of Chow.
  T'ae-sze inherited her excellent fame,
  And from her came a hundred sons.

so natural was it for spiritual Beings to bless a man of king Wăn's character. 劳＝慰抚, 'to soothe and encourage.'

St. 6. 莫莫,—nearly as in I.i.II.2. 葛藟,—as in I.i.IV. 条枚,—as in I.i.X.1. 回＝邪, 'crooked,' 'perverse.' Creepers naturally lay hold of trees, and as natural was it for king Wăn to get to the height of dignity which he attained.

The rhymes are—in st.1, 济, 弟, cat.15, t. 2: in 2, 中, 降, cat.9: in 3, 天, 渊, 人, cat.12, t.1: in 4, 载, 备 *, 祀, 福 *, cat. 1, t.3: in 5, 燎, 劳, cat.2: in 6, 枚, 回, cat. 15, t.1.

Ode. 6. Narrative. THE VIRTUE OF KING WAN AND ITS WONDERFUL EFFECTS; WITH THE EXCELLENT CHARACTER OF HIS MOTHER AND WIFE. From st.1 we are led to expect that the subject of the piece will be the two ladies T'ae-jin and T'ae-sze; but there is barely a reference

to the second in the other four stanzas. King Wăn is no doubt the subject of them, though his name does not occur. The critics all resent the view that the virtue of Wăn was derived from his mother and wife, though that is not an unnatural inference from the relation there would seem to be between st.1 and those that follow. Ying-tah arranges the piece in 4 stanzas of 6 lines each, but he mentions that there was an old view, held by Maou, that it consisted of five, 2 of 6 lines, and 3 of 4. This is now adopted, and, apparently, on good grounds;—see Foo Kwang, *in loc.*

St.1. The 思, in ll.1,3, is regarded by Choo as the initial particle; and this view has superseded that of K'ang-shing, who gives the term the meaning of—'constantly thoughtful.' 齐,—read *chae*, with the meaning I have given. 大任,—see on II.2. 媚＝爱, 'to love;'— comp. in I.xi.II.1. 周姜 is 大姜, the 姜女 of III.2. She is here called 周姜, as having married the lord of Chow. 京 in l.4 is explained by Choo, after K'ang-shing, by

二章
惠于宗公。神罔时怨。神罔时恫。刑于寡妻。至于兄
弟。以御于家邦。

三章
雍雍在宫。肃肃在庙。不显亦临。无射亦保。

四章
肆戎疾不殄。烈假不瑕。不闻亦式。不谏亦入。

2　He conformed to the example of his ancestors,
　　And their Spirits had no occasion for complaint.
　　Their Spirits had no occasion for dissatisfaction,
　　And his example acted on his wife,
　　Extended to his brethren,
　　And was felt by all the clans and States.

3　Full of harmony was he in his palace;
　　Full of reverence in the ancestral temple.
　　Out of sight he still felt as under inspection;
　　Unweariedly he maintained [his virtue].

4　Though he could not prevent [some] great calamities,
　　His brightness and magnanimity were without stain.

周　Maou makes it = 王, 'royal:' but the meaning comes to the same thing. The whole line belongs to T'ae-jin, and = 称 其 为 周 室 之 妇, —as in the translation. T'ae-sze was the wife of king Wǎn, so celebrated in the 1st Bk. of Pt. 1. 徽 = 美, 'admirable.' The 斯 in l. 6 = the descriptive 其. We are not, of course, to suppose that T'ae-sze had 100 sons. She had ten, we are told; and her freedom from jealousy so encouraged the fruitfulness of the harem, that all the sons born in it are ascribed to her. See on I. i. V. In the Tso-chuen we have reference to at least eighteen sons of king Wǎn. St. 2. This and the stanzas that follow have king Wǎn for their subject. 惠 = 顺, 'to accord with;'—a not uncommon meaning of the term. 宗 公 = 宗 庙 先 公, 'the former dukes of the ancestral temple;' i.e., his ancestors to whom Wǎn offered sacrifice. 时 in ll. 2, 3 = 是, the substantive verb. 恫 = 痛, 'to be pained by.' Ll. 4—6 are quoted by Mencius, I. Pt. i VII. 12, where we have his view of the meaning. 刑 = 法; here, 'to give a pattern to.' T'ae-sze is called his 寡 妻,—a designa-

tion of the wife of a State, akin to the 寡 小 君, mentioned by Confucius, Ana. XVI. xiv. Choo, after Maou, takes 御 = 迓, = 迎. I prefer Ch'ing's view of it, as = 治, 'to rule.'

St. 3. Yung-yung indicates the 'greatness of Wǎn's harmony (和 之 至),' and suh-suh, the 'greatness of his reverence (敬 之 至).' 不 显 = 人 不 见 之 时, 'when he was unseen.' 亦 临 = 亦 若 有 临 之 者, —as in the translation. See the 'Doctrine of the Mean,' ch. XV., which many of the critics refer to here. L. 4. 射,—i.q. 致, = 厌, 'to weary.' The idea found in the line is that king Wǎn never relaxed in his maintenance of his virtue. It was not only when circumstances called for an effort that he sustained himself; but he did the same when no effort was necessary. As Yen Ts'an says, 无 厌 之 时, 践 履 已 熟, 而 亦 自 保 守, 悠 久 无 疆.

St. 4. L. 1,—comp. the 1st l. of III. 8. 戎 = 大, 'great;' 疾 = 难, 'calamities.' These

五章
肆成人有德。小子有造。古之人无斁。誉髦斯士。

Without previous instruction he did what was right;
Without admonition, he went on [in the path of goodness].
5 So, grown up men became virtuous [through him],
And young men made [constant] attainments.
[Our] ancient prince never felt weariness,
And from him were the fame and eminence of his officers.

VII. *Hwang e.*

皇矣

一章
皇矣上帝。临下有赫。监观四方。求民之莫。维此二

1   Great is God,
Beholding this lower world in majesty.
He surveyed the four quarters [of the kingdom],
Seeking for some one to give settlement to the people.

two words are understood by all of Wǎn's imprisonment at one time by the last Shang sovereign, and other troubles of his early life; and I take them as the subject of 殄 = 绝, 'to be prevented.' 烈 = 光, 'brightness.' 假, = 大; must be here a noun,—as in the translation. 式 = 法, 'what is according to law or right.' Choo expands ll. 3, 4:—虽 事 之 无 所 前 闻 者 而 亦 无 不 合 于 法 度，虽 无 谏 诤 之 者，而 亦 未 尝 不 入 于 善，传 (*i.e.*, 毛 传) 所 谓 性 与 天 合 是 也，

St 5. 成 人, is a designation of men after they are 'capped,' and 小 子 denotes those who are not old enough for that ceremony. 古 之 人 is taken of king Wǎn. Leu Tsoo-k'een observes that it is not more strange to find him thus spoken of than that Yaou and Shun should be similarly designated in the Books of Yu and Hëa. 誉 and 髦 = 'to make famous,' 'to make eminent.'

The rhymes are—in st. 1, 母*, 妇*, cat. 1, t. 2; 音, 男*, cat. 7, t. 1: in 2, 公, 恫, 邦, cat. 9; ? 妻, 弟 : in 3, 庙, 保 (prop. cat. 3), cat. 2: in 4, 瑕*, 人 (prop. cat. 7), cat. 5. t. 2: in 5, 造 (prop. cat. 3), 士, cat. 1, t. 2. It is generally held that there are no rhymes in these two last stanzas, and Twan-she is obliged to resort to a violent poetic license to make any out.

Ode 7. Narrative. SHOWING THE RISE OF THE HOUSE OF CHOW TO THE SOVEREIGNTY OF THE KINGDOM THROUGH THE FAVOUR OF GOD. THE CASES AND ACHIEVEMENTS OF KING T'AE, KING KE, AND ESPECIALLY OF KING WAN.
St. 1. Ll. 1,2 are about equivalent to II.4, l. 1, and other places, expressive of God's govt. of men's affairs. 皇 = 大, 'great.' 临 = 视, 'to see,'—with the idea of 'overseeing.' 下 = 下 土, 'the lower world,'—as in II.v. I. 1, *et al.* 有 赫 expresses the intelligence and strictness of the divine regard. Ll.4,5 express the object of God in a special survey of of China, which the writer has in mind. He wished the happiness of the people, which is secured by the government of their rulers:—

国。其政不获。维彼四国。爰究爰度。上帝耆之。憎

其式廓。乃眷西顾。此维与宅。

二章
作之屏之。其菑其翳。修之平之。其灌其栵。启之辟

Those two [earlier] dynasties
Had failed to satisfy Him with their government;
So throughout the various States,
He sought and considered,
For one on which he might confer the rule.
Hating all the great [States],
He turned His kind regards on the west,
And there gave a settlement [to king T'ae].

2   [King T'ae] raised up and removed
The dead trunks, and the fallen trees.

and a governor was now wanted. 莫,—as in II. v. IV. 4, = 定, 'to settle,' 'establishment;' here, 'one who should give settlement to.' 四方 is the four quarters of the kingdom; *i. e*, all the States of it. Ll. 5,6 show how the necessity for the appointment of a new ruler had arisen. Both Maou and Choo take 二国 of the two previous dynasties of Shang and Hëa;—as in the Shoo, V. xii. 18. This view is much preferable to that of Ch'ing, by which by the 'two *kwoh*' we are to understand the Shang sovereign of the kingdom and the marquis of the State of Ts'ung (殷纣崇侯). Perhaps, the best translation of 不获 would be—'had proved failures.' Choo explains the phrase by 失其道; Ch'ing, by 不得于天心; Këang, by 不得于天. Ll. 7—12 tell us the result of the divine inspection of the rulers of the States. Only in the west was one found worthy to be the father of kings. 四国 in l. 7 = 四方 in l. 3. It is not worth while to discuss the difft. view of Ch'ing. We need not translate 爰 in l. 8. If we do, then I should render—'here...there.' Ll. 9, 10 have greatly perplexed the critics. Maou and Ch'ing both take 耆 in the sense of 老; here = 'to prolong their lives.' On Ch'ing's view, God, in his forbearance, long spared Show and the lord of Ts'ung, giving them space for repentance and amendment. Choo takes 耆 as = 致, 'to bring to,'—a meaning which Maou himself assigns to the character in Part IV. This view I

have adopted, but I am unable to follow Choo in his dealing with l. 10. As it stands, he does not understand it; and therefore he changes 憎, 'to hate,' into 增, 'to increase,' and takes 式廓 as = 规模, 'plans,' measurements.' Thus the line would mean that when God met with a ruler of whom He approved as fit to be king, he would, as preliminary to the ultimate exaltation of his House, in the first place enlarge his boundaries. Unfortunately, the ode does not stand as Choo proposes it should do. Taking the line as it is, by discarding 式 as a mere particle, we get the meaning of it which I have given, and which is fully sanctioned by Këang Ping-chang (天于四方之国,爰究爰度,苟能安斯民者,则以大命致之,而憎恶此强大之国,不能安民,且以残民也,乃,云云). In l. 11, 眷 = 眷然, 'kindly.' Both this line and the next are to be referred to the time of king T'ae, instead of that of king Wăn, as Ch'ing thought and Ying-tah makes Maou also to have thought. The K'ang-he editors allow that the superior critical ability of Choo appears here. 此 in l. 12 refers to the territory of K'e-chow; and 与 = 'to give to.' As Choo expands the line, 以此岐周之地,与太王为居宅也.

St. 2 must all be interpreted of king T'ae; and ll. 1—8 are descriptive of the work he accomplished in bringing the territory of K'e-chow

之。其檉其椐。攘之剔之。其檿其柘。帝遷明德。串

夷載路。天立厥配。受命既固。

三章
帝省其山。柞棫斯拔。松柏斯兌。帝作邦作對。自大

He dressed and regulated
The bushy °clumps, and the [tangled] rows.
He opened up and cleared
The tamarix trees, and the stave-trees.
He hewed and thinned
The mountain-mulberry trees.
God having brought about the removal thither of this intelli-
gent ruler,
The Kwan hordes fled away.
Heaven raised up a helpmeet for him,
And the appointment he had received was made sure.

3 God surveyed the hills,
Where the oaks and *yih* were thinned,
And paths made through the firs and cypresses.

under cultivation. Ll. 1, 2. 作＝拔起,‘to raise up,’ referring to the ‘fallen trees’ in l. 2; 屛＝去, ‘to remove,’ referring to the ‘dead trunks.’ It is the necessity of the rhyme which makes the writer mention the 蓍 (＝木立死者) before the 翳 (＝木自斃者) 之, here and below, may be taken as＝‘them,’ —in app. with the lines that follow. L. 5. 灌,—as in I. i. II. 1. Maou understands 栵 of a particular tree,—a kind of chestnut; but Choo takes it as＝行生者, ‘trees growing in rows.’ And he must be correct, as we cannot understand any particular tree by 灌. The dict. distinguishes between the two meanings of the term, giving Maou's account of it under the pronunciation *leeh*, and Choo's under *le*. Ll. 5, 6. 启 and 辟, both mean ‘to open;’ *i.e.* by clearing away and thinning (芟除). 檉 is called in the Urh-ya the 河柳, or ‘river willow;’ but there is no doubt that the tree is the *tamarix Sinensis*. I have translated 椐 from the principal use to which it is put. Williams calls it—‘a tree found in Ho-nan, used for whip-handles and old men's walking staves.’ Yen

Sze-koo describes it as ‘like a bamboo, growing in joints 8 or 9 cubits long, and 3 or 4 inches in circumference, fit as it grows for walking sticks, without any cutting or forming.’ It is called 灵寿木, ‘the tree of longevity;’—from this use which it serves. The staves are common enough in the hands of old men, and in the market. I doubt Yen-she's account of it as being like a bamboo. Ll. 7, 8. 攘剔, ‘to bare and to scrape,’ denote the process of thinning. 檿 and 柘 both denote varieties of the wild or mountain mulberry tree (山桑). L. 9. 明德 is explained as＝明德之君,—as in the translation; and 遷 of the providence of God in removing king T'ae from Pin to Chow. Choo says that he does not understand l. 10; but he refers to Ch'ing's view of it, according to which 串夷 *i. q.* 混夷 in III. 8. Then 載路＝满路, ‘all the way,’ expressive of the completeness of the rout and flight of the barbarians;—comp. on III. 8, ll. 5, 6. L. 9. By 配 is intended T'ae Këang, the wife of king T'ae.

St. 3 continues to trace the history of the house of Chow, from king T'ae, through king Ke, gradually converging to king Wăn, who,

伯王季。维此王季。因心则友。则友其兄。则笃其

庆。载锡之光。受禄无丧。奄有四方。

四章
维此王季。帝度其心。貊其德音。其德克明。克明克

God, who had raised the State, raised up a proper ruler for it;—
From the time of T'ae-pih and king Ke [this was done].
Now this king Ke
In his heart was full of brotherly duty.
Full of duty to his elder brother,
He gave himself the more to promote the prosperity [of the country],
And secured to him the glory [of his act].
He accepted his dignity, and did not lose it,
And [ere long his family] possessed the whole kingdom.

4　This king Ke
　　Was gifted by God with the power of judgment,
　　So that the fame of his virtue silently grew.
　　His virtue was highly intelligent;—
　　Highly intelligent and of rare discrimination;

indeed, is in the writer's mind all through it. Ll. 1–3. Comp. III. 8, ll. 3, 4. 省＝省 视, 'to survey.' Ch'ing explains it by 善, 'to approve;' but that idea is not in the term itself. Ll. 4, 5. 对＝当, 'a match,' *i. e.*, one equal to the rule of the State. King Wǎn is intended by the term; and l. 5 intimates that this was determined before there was any likelihood of his becoming the ruler even of Chow. T'ae-pih was the eldest son of king T'ae, and king Ke was, perhaps, only the third (季). The succession ought to have devolved on the former; but seeing the sage virtues of Ke's son, Ch'ang (afterwards king Wǎn), and that T'ae wanted the succession to come to him, he withdrew from Chow altogether, and left the State to Ke;—see on Ana. VIII. i. Ll. 6—11 speak of king Ke in his relation to his elder brother. He accepted his act without any failure of his own duty to him, and by his own improvement of it, he made his brother more glorious through it. 因 心 is explained as＝非 勉 强, 'without effort.' His feeling of brotherly duty was simply the natural instinct of his heart. Having accepted the act, it only made him the more earnest to promote the good of the State (益 修 其 德，以 厚 周 家 之 庆), and thus he made his brother glorious by showing what advantages accrued from his resignation (与 其 兄 以 让 德 之 光，犹 曰 彰 其 知 人 之 明，不 为 徒 让 耳). We cannot translate the two 则 nor 载; but must take the three as expletive particles. 丧 in l. 11＝失, 'to lose.' L. 12 was accomplished only in the time of Ke's grandson, king Woo. Choo observes that the meaning of 奄 is something between 忽 and 遂, 'suddenly' and 'accordingly.'

St. 4 goes on to describe the virtue of king Ke, down to l. 9, when king Wǎn is mentioned by name. All the rest of the piece is occupied with him and his achievements. L. 2. 度 is defined by 能 度 物 制 义, 'the ability to estimate things and determine what is right

类。克长克君。王此大邦。克顺克比。比于文王。其

德靡悔。既受帝祉。施于孙子。

五章
帝谓文王。无然畔援。无然歆羡。诞先登于岸。密人

Able to lead, able to rule,—
To rule over this great country;
Rendering a cordial submission, effecting a cordial union.
When [the sway] came to king Wăn,
His virtue left nothing to be dissatisfied with.
He received the blessing of God,
And it was extended to his descendants.

5   God said to king Wăn,
     'Be not like those who reject this and cling to that;
     Be not like those who are ruled by their likings and desires;'
     So he grandly ascended before others to the height [of virtue].
     The people of Meih were disobedient,

in reference to them;' but the term has here a *hiphil* force, and the meaning is what I have given. L. 3. 貌＝静, 'still.' In the Tso-chuen and Le Ke the character appears as 莫, which has that meaning. Ll. 4, 5. 明＝察 是 非, 'to examine truth and error;' 类 ＝分 善 恶, 'to distinguish between good and evil.' L. 6. 长 refers to Ke's ability to be a leader of men, and especially of the princes of the States over which he was a kind of president; 君, to his possession of the virtues of a ruler in his relation to the people. L. 7. 王,— 'to be king over.' This is said from the point of view in the time of king Ching. L. 8 refers to Ke's maintenance of his own loyal duty to the dyn. of Shang, and his making all the States under his own presidency loyal also.—See a narrative of Tso-she, under the 28th year of duke Ch'aou, in which the whole of this stanza is quoted, and explained. Some of the definitions of the terms are different from what I have given. Each critic assumes a liberty to himself in this respect. The stanza, moreover, is quoted by Tso-she with 文 in the first line, instead of 季; but l. 10 seems to show that that must be a mistake.

Ll. 9—12. 比 于 ＝至 于, coming to.' 比 is found in this sense both in the Analects

and in Mencius. 靡 悔,—' was without repentance;' *i. e.*, was complete, there was nothing wanting, nothing wrong about it, to occasion regret to himself or others. 施,—as in I.i.II. By 孙 子, king Woo is, probably, specially intended.

St. 5 records the operations of Wăn against a state called Meih, prefaced by some account of his character. The statement in l.1, that 'God spake to king Wăn,' vexes the critics, and they find in the language simply an intimation that Wăn's conduct was 'in accordance with the will of Heaven.' I am not prepared to object to that view of the meaning; but it is plain that the writer, in giving such a form to his meaning, must have conceived of God as a personal Being, knowing men's hearts and able to influence them. The critics impose on themselves by the manner in which they interchange and play with the terms—帝 and 天. 无 然 ＝不 可 如 此, 'don't be thus.' 畔 ＝离 畔, 'to separate from;' 援,—'to hold with the hand,' 'to cling to;' 歆 denotes 'desire,' proceeding from within; 羡, 'desire,' directed to what is without. Choo Shen ingeniously defines the four characters thus :— 畔 者 疏 而 离 之；援 者, 亲 而 附 之 也； 歆 者, 欲 之 动 乎 中；羡 者, 心

不恭。敢距大邦。侵阮徂共。王赫斯怒。爰整其旅。

以按徂旅。以笃于周祜。以对于天下。

六章
依其在京。侵自阮疆。陟我高冈。无矢我陵。我陵我

阿。无饮我泉。我泉我池。度其鲜原。居岐之阳。在

Daring to oppose our great country,
And invaded Yuen, marching to Kung.
The king rose majestic in his wrath;
He marshalled his troops,
To stop the invading foes;
To consolidate the prosperity of Chow;
To meet [the expectations of] all under heaven.

6 He remained quietly in the capital;
But [his troops] went on from the borders of Yuen.
They ascended our lofty ridges,
And [the enemy] arrayed no forces on our hills,
On our hills, small or large,
Nor drank at our springs,
Our springs or our pools.
He then determined the finest of the plains,
And settled on the south of K'e,

之慕乎外也. 诞 is an initial particle. 岸 is taken by Choo as = 'the highest point of virtue.' Maou simply defines it by 高位, 'a high position.'

Ll. 5—12. Meih or Meih-seu (密须) was a State, ruled by K'eihs (姞),—in the pres. Tsing-ning Chow (静宁州), dep. of P'ing-lëang (平凉), Kan-suh. L. 7. We must take 密人 as the subject of 侵, 'to make an incursion into,' 'to invade.' Yuen was a State adjacent to Meih,—in the pres. King Chow (泾州), dep. P'ing-lëang; and Kung must have been a place or district in it. Ch'ing strangely took Yuen, Tsoo, and Kung as all the names of States,—an error which has crept into many accounts that we meet with of Wǎn's

achievements. 斯 = 其, intensifying the descriptive force of 怒. 爰 is the particle. 按 = 遏, 'to stop.' 徂旅 is the forces of Meih, marching on Kung. 笃 = 厚. The best word I can think of for it is—'to consolidate.' 对 = 答, 'to respond to.'

St. 6. It is hardly possible to determine the meaning of l. 1. Choo takes 依 as = 安貌, 'tranquil-like,' and 京 as the capital of Chow, explaining the whole line as in the translation. Këang prefers to take it of the people of Yuen, now delivered from their enemies, and giving their adherence to king Wǎn, 'as if they had been in the capital of Chow.' A couple of pages would not suffice to state and discuss the different views on a point which is in itself unimportant. L. 2 is descriptive of the movements of

渭之将。万邦之方。下民之王。

七章
帝谓文王。予怀明德。不大声以色。不长夏以革。不
识不知。顺帝之则。帝谓文王。询尔仇方。同尔兄
弟。以尔钩援。与尔临冲。以伐崇墉。

On the side of the Wei;
The centre of all the States,
The resort of the lower people.

7   God said to king Wăn,
‘I am pleased with your intelligent virtue,
Not loudly proclaimed nor pourtrayed,
Without extravagance or changeableness,
Without consciousness of effort on your part,
In accordance with the pattern of God.’
God said to king Wăn,
‘Take measures against the country of your foes.
Along with your brethren,
Get ready your scaling ladders,

Wăn’s forces;—whether he was with them or not. They invaded Meih. Ll. 3—7 intimate their complete success. They met with no opposition. The hills and springs which they passed became, as it were, theirs. 矢 = 陈, ‘to marshal troops.’ 陵 and 阿, in contrast as here, denote smaller hills and larger. Ll. 8, 9 are generally understood of a temporary change which Wăn made of his capital. Choo takes 鲜, after Ch‘ing, in the sense of 善, ‘good.’ Maou takes it differently,—as a designation of small hills lying between large ones; others will have it that 鲜原 was simply the name of a place. The name of the city where Wăn is said to have established himself for a time was Ch‘ing (程 邑). Ying-tah says it was not far from the capital of king T‘ae; and as it here appears on the south of mount K‘e, we are not to think of Fung, which was 300 le to the south-east of that hill. Ll. 10—12. 将 = 侧, ‘the side.’ 方 = 乡, ‘the point to which all the States turned.’ 王 is here i. q. 往, ‘to go to.’ —万 邦 皆 向 慕 之，下 民 皆 归 往 之.

Stt. 7, 8 describe Wăn’s subjugation of Ts‘ung as 5, 6 did that of Meih; and we have, as there, the achievement prefaced by an account of his great qualities. In st. 7, l.1, 怀 = 眷 念, ‘to think kindly of.’ In ll. 2, 3, 以 must be taken as = 与, ‘and,’ or.’ Wăn’s virtue had no great voice or colour; i. e., it was unostentatious. Choo allows that he does not understand 夏 革. There seems no difficulty with 革，—变 革, ‘to change,’ ‘changing;’ and as 夏 often means ‘great,’ Leu Tsoo-k‘een proposes to take it here in the sense of 侈大, ‘extravagant.’ 不 长 = ‘without prolongation of,’ ‘without nourishing, or encouraging.’ Kĕang brings out, substantially, the same meaning, by taking 夏 as = ‘fervour of spirit,’ from the use of the term for ‘summer.’ In ll. 7—12 we have a commission from God to Wăn to attack the State of Ts‘ung,—in the pres. dis. of Hoo (鄂), dep. Se-gan. Acc. to Sze-ma Ts‘een, Hoo the marquis of Ts‘ung, slandered the lord of Chow, who was president of the States in the west, to Show,

八章

临冲闲闲。崇墉言言。执讯连连。攸馘安安。是类是
祃。是致是附。四方以无侮。临冲茀茀。崇墉仡仡。
是伐是肆。是绝是忽。四方以无拂。

> And your engines of onfall and assault,
> To attack the walls of Ts'ung.'

8 The engines of onfall and assault were gently plied,
  Against the walls of Ts'ung high and great;
  Captives for the question were brought in one after another;
  The left ears [of the slain] were taken leisurely.
  He sacrificed to God, and to the Father of war,
  Thus seeking to induce submission;
  And throughout the kingdom none dared to insult him.
  The engines of onfall and assault were vigorously plied,
  Against the walls of Ts'ung very strong;
  He attacked it, and let loose all his forces;
  He extinguished [its sacrifices], and made an end of its existence;
  And throughout the kingdom none dared to oppose him.

and our hero was put in prison. His friends effected his deliverance by presenting to the tyrant beautiful women, fine horses, and other remarkable and valuable things, and he was reinstated in the West with more than his former powers. Three years afterwards, he attacked the marquis of Ts'ung. 询 = 谋, 'to consult about,' 'take measures against.' 仇方 = 仇国, 'hostile States.' 兄弟, 'brethren,' must denote here the chiefs of the States with which Wăn was in alliance, or of which he had the presidency. That they should be thus denominated is insisted on as one proof that Wăn never had in his life-time the title of king. 钩援,—'hooked grapplers.' These may be called *scaling ladders.* 临 and 冲 were engines employed in sieges. They are elsewhere spoken of as 'carriages,' which may only mean that they were moved about on wheels. The *lin* was raised, I apprehend, to an equal height with the walls, or perhaps, a greater height (在上临下者), while the *ch'ung* was employed in assaults upon the walls, affording protection to those who attempted to mine them or break through them. 墉 = 城, 'the wall.'

St. 8 describes the siege of the capital of Ts'ung, at first prosecuted without much vigour, the chief of Chow wishing to win it to submission; but finally ending with its utter overthrow. Ll. 1—7. 闲闲 = 徐缓, expressing the slowness and want of vigour characterizing the first employment of the engines. 言言 = 高大, 'high and great.' 执讯,—see II. i. VIII. 6, *et al.* 连连 = 'come, one after another.' 攸馘,—'those whose left ears were cut off,' or 'the cutting off of left ears.' When prisoners refused to submit, they were put to death, and their left ears cut off. 安

VIII. *Ling t'ae.*

灵台

一章

经始灵台。经之营之。庶民攻之。不日成之。经始勿

亟。庶民子来。

1   When he planned the commencement of the marvellous tower,
     He planned it, and defined it;
     And the people in crowds undertook the work,
     And in no time completed it.
     When he planned the commencement, [he said], 'Be not in a
        hurry;'
     But the people came as if they were his children.

安一'went on leisurely.' 类 is descriptive of a sacrifice to God, at the commencement of the expedition; 祃, of a sacrifice offered, on their arrival at the scene of warfare, to the Father of war. Choo says that this last sacrifice was offered to Hwang-te and Ch'e-yew (黄帝及蚩尤), whom we find engaged in hostilities far back in the mythical era of Chinese history. L. 6 expresses the object of Wăn in these religious services, and in his reluctant prosecution of the war. 致=致其至, 'to induce them to come to him;' 附=使之来附, 'to make them come and submit.' L. 7 tells the effect on the States generally; but Ts'ung itself still held out.

Ll. 8—12. 茀茀 expresses the vigour with which the engines were now plied; 仡仡, the strength of the walls; 肆,— as in II. 8; 绝=殄其祀, 'to abolish its sacrifices;' 忽=灭其国, 'to extinguish the State.'

The rhymes are—in st. 1, 赫*, 莫, 获*, 度, 廓, 宅*, cat. 5, t. 3: in 2, 翳, 枊, cat. 15, t. 3; 椐, 柘*, 路, 固, cat. 5, t. 1: in 3, 拔, 兑, 对, 季, 季, cat. 15, t. 3; 兄, 庆*, 光, 丧, 方, cat. 10: in 4, 心, 音, cat. 7, t. 1; 类, 比, cat. 15, t. 3; 悔*, 祉, 子, cat. 1, t. 2: in 5, 援, 羡, 岸, cat. 14; 恭, 邦, 共, cat. 9; 怒, 旅, 旅, 祜, 下, cat. 5, t. 2: in 6, 京*, 疆, 冈, cat. 10; 阿, 池*, cat. 17; 阳, 将, 方, 王, cat. 10: in 7, 德, 色, 革*, 则, cat. 1, t. 3; 王, 方, cat.

10; 冲, 墉, cat. 9: in 8, 闲, 言, 连, 安, cat. 14; 祃 (prop. cat. 5), 附*, 侮*, cat. 4, t. 2; 茀, 仡, 肆, 忽, 拂, cat. 5, t. 3.

Ode 8. Narrative. THE JOY OF THE PEOPLE IN THE GROWING OPULENCE AND DIGNITY OF KING WĂN. This ode must be referred to the time, when the chief of Chow moved his capital to Fung, after the overthrow of the State of Ts'ung, *i.e.*, to B. C. 1,135, according to the standard Chronology, and only one year before his death. The tower, the park, the pond, and the hall of music were all in connection with Fung,—in the pres. district of Hoo, dep. Se-gan, Shen-se. See ode X. 2.

St. 1. 经 is here defined by 度, 'to measure out;' 营, in l. 2, by 表, 'to mark out.' But in II. vi. I. 3, viii. X. 1, we have 经营, together, as here, meaning 'to plan and build.' 始 in ll. 1, 4, must be taken as a verb, 'to begin,' 'to make a commencement with.' It is difficult to determine the exact meaning of 灵, as applied to the tower, park, and pond. Some take it in the sense of 'royal,' as Fuh K'ëen and Pan Koo; and, no doubt, the towers of the kings of Chow, supposed to be built for astronomical and meteorological purposes, as well as for pleasure, were subsequently called *ling*, while the similar structures of the feudal princes were simply called *kwan-t'ae* (观台), or 'towers of observation.' But Wăn was only a feudal prince when the tower in the text was made; and we may conclude that its name was subsequently extended to the towers of his descendants. Ch'ing thought the name had a reference to the transforming influence that went forth from Wăn, as with a spiritual efficaciousness (文王化行, 似神之精明, 故以名). Choo finds in it an allusion to

二章
王在灵囿。麀鹿攸伏。麀鹿濯濯。白鸟翯翯。王在灵

沼。于牣鱼跃。

三章
虡业维枞。贲鼓维镛。于论鼓钟。于乐辟雍。

四章
于论鼓钟。于乐辟雍。鼍鼓逢逢。矇瞍奏公。

2　The king was in the marvellous park,
　　Where the does were lying down,—
　　The does, so sleek and fat;
　　With the white birds glistening.
　　The king was by the marvellous pond;—
　　How full was it of fishes leaping about!

3　On his posts was the toothed face-board, high and strong,
　　With the large drums and bells.
　　In what unison were their sounds!
　　What joy was there in the hall with its circlet of water!

4　In what unison sounded the drums and bells!
　　What joy was there in the hall with its circlet of water!
　　The lizard-skin drums rolled harmonious,
　　As the blind musicians performed their parts.

the rapidity with which the tower rose, as if it had been the work of Spirits (言 其 倏 然 而 成, 如 神 灵 之 所 为. See Mencius' account of it in I. Pt. i. II. 3. I am inclined to agree with Këang, who takes it simply as= 异, 'marvellous,' a name of admiration, the exact force of which we cannot determine. 攻 = 作, 'to make,' 'to address one's-self to.' 不 日 = 不 多 日, 'in a few days,' 'very soon.' Before 勿 亟 we must understand 'the king said,' or something to that effect (文 王 心 恐 烦 民, 戒 令 勿 亟). 子 来,—'came as sons,' i. e., as sons hastening without being called, to labour for their father.
St. 2. 'The park,' says Choo, 'was at the foot of the tower,'—the tower would be in the park; and also the pond in l. 5. 麀 was the name for the female of the deer; the male was called 麚. 麀 鹿 together, here = 'does;' not— 'does and stags.' Their lying down is mention-

ed as a proof of their feeling of enjoyment and security. 攸 = 所. It is here our 'where.' 濯 濯 = 肥 泽 貌,—as in the translation; so, 翯 翯 = 洁 白 貌. 于, pronounced woo, is a particle of exclamation, as in II. i. V. 2, et al. 牣 = 满, 'to be full.'
Stt. 3, 4 tell how the chief of Chow surrounded himself in Fung with the appliances of music and other festal celebrations, in addition to his tower and park. L. 1, st. 3, is descriptive of the frames on which were suspended various drums and bells. The upright posts were named 虡. That character denotes a fabulous animal, with a deer's head and a serpent's body, and I suppose the feet of the posts were carved to resemble it. The posts were connected by a cross beam (called 枞), from which the instruments were hung, and over this was a face-board, gaily painted, and with its edges cut like the teeth of a saw. This was called 业 (枞 上 大 版; 刻 之 捷 业 如 锯 齿 者 也); and the teeth rose straight and strong, like

IX. *Hëa Woo.*

下武

一章

下武維周。世有哲王。三后在天。王配于京。

1　Successors tread in the steps [of their predecessors] in our Chow.
For generations there had been wise kings;
The three sovereigns were in heaven;
And king [Woo] was their worthy successor in his capital.

so many *ts'ung* trees standing in a row. The 維
in l. 1 may be considered = 是, the substantive verb, but that in l. 2 = 與, 'and;'—see
Wang Yin-che *in voc.* 賁 = 大, 'great.'
Choo says, 'The great drum was 8 cubits long;
4 cubits in diameter at the ends, a third more at
the middle.' 鏞 = 大鐘, 'a great bell.'
于—as in last st. 論 = 倫, 'attuned,' 'sounding in unison (言得其倫理).' 辟 =
璧, the round jade-symbol of rank, with a
square hole in the centre. 雍 was the name of
a building attached to the royal court, called a
school or gymnasium (天子之學), where
archery and other arts were taught to the cadets
of the royal House. Around it was a circular
pool; and the whole thing resembled a *peih*,
with a pavilion rising in the centre of it. Attached to the courts of the States was a similar
building, but the water formed only a semicircle
in front of it (泮宮). Such a building the
chief of Chow had erected in his park. Here he
enjoyed his music; and the form of it served as
a pattern to his royal descendants. In st. 4, l. 3,
鼉,—see the 'Doctrine of the Mean,' XXVI. 9.
The skin of this iguana was used in making
drums. 逢逢 is defined by 和, 'to be
harmonious.' The music masters and musicians
during the Chow dynasty are always spoken of
as blind. The loss of the sense of seeing makes
the blind more acute of ear; and hence blind
persons were chosen for those positions. 'Persons having the pupil, and yet not seeing, were
called *mung*; when they had not the pupil, they
were called *sow*.' 公 = 事, 'business,' 'part.'

The rhymes are—in st. 1, 營, 成, cat. 11;
呕, 来, cat. 1, t. 3: in 2, 圉 *, 伏 *, *ib.;*
濯 *, 鼛 *, 沼, 躍 *, cat. 2: in 3, 枞, 鏞,
鐘, 雍, cat. 9: in 4, 鐘, 雍, 逢, 公, *ib.*

Ode 9. Narrative. IN PRAISE OF KING WOO,
WALKING IN THE WAYS OF HIS FOREFATHERS,
AND BY HIS FILIAL PIETY SECURING THE THRONE
TO HIMSELF AND HIS POSTERITY. Nowhere in

the ode is Woo expressly mentioned as the
subject of it; but the common consent of the
critics in referring it to him is not to be questioned. The 'king' in st. 1, is evidently one standing
in close proximity to the three sovereigns of Chow
who were in heaven. This excludes the idea
that it is king Wän who is spoken of; and to
no sovereign subsequent to Woo can it be referred with any degree of probability.
St. 1. L. 1 has been a great stumbling-block
to the critics. Choo says that he does not understand the 下, and goes on to accept the view
of some other scholar, that the 下 is a mistake
for 文. The meaning of the line will thus be,
that Wän and Woo were the founders of Chow
(文王武王实造周也). But Choo
allows that Wän must be one of the 'three
sovereigns' in l. 3, and the K'ang-he editors say
that the mention of him also in l. 1 is a needless
repetition. They might have said that the
sentiment of the two lines is thus contradictory.
We cannot admit the conjecture that 下 should
be 文, nor that of Luh Tih-ming, who would
read 大; and must fall back on the 'chiseling'
of the old school. Maou adopts from the Urh-
ya a meaning of 武 as = 继, 'to continue;'
but he says nothing on 下. This is supplied
by K'ang-shing, who makes 下 here equivalent
to 后, 'subsequent,' 'future;' and we get the
idea of the line which I have given in the translation (后人能继先祖者,维有
周家最大). This view appears to be
confirmed by the words of Confucius in the
'Doctrine of the Mean,' XVIII. 2,—武王缵
大王,王季,文王之绪. The 'wise
kings' of l. 2 and the 'three sovereigns' of l. 3
are not to be taken of different individuals. Both
expressions are to be understood of the kings T'ae,
Ke, and Wän. All three of them are said to be in
heaven, which is said only of king Wän in I. 1. The
expression, simple enough to a Christian reader,
is to the Chinese critics full of perplexity; and
where their ideas are utterly confused, it is impossible they should express themselves clearly.
'This matter,' says Choo, 'is mysterious and

二章
王配于京。世德作求。永言配命。成王之孚。

三章
成王之孚。下土之式。永言孝思。孝思维则。

四章
媚兹一人。应侯顺德。永言孝思。昭哉嗣服。

2　King [Woo] was their worthy successor in his capital,
　　Rousing himself to seek for the hereditary virtue,
　　Always striving to accord with the will [of Heaven];
　　And thus he secured the confidence due to a king.

3　He secured the confidence due to a king,
　　And became the pattern of all below him.
　　Ever thinking how to be filial,
　　His filial mind was the model [which he supplied].

4　Men loved him, the One man,
　　And responded [to his example] with a docile virtue.
　　Ever thinking how to be filial,
　　He brilliantly continued the doings [of his fathers].

difficult to speak about. When it is said that king Wăn is ascending on the left and the right of God, if we insist that the language implies that king Wăn is really on the left and the right of God, and that there really is God as He is fashioned in the idol so-called in the world, that certainly is an error; but as the Sages have thus expressed themselves, there is this principle.' Of what he really means by—'there is this principle,' I have never been able to get a distinct hold. The 'king' in l 4 must be understood of Woo; the 'capital' is Haou (镐; see on the Shoo, V.iii. 1), to which Woo is said to have moved in B.C. 1,133, the year after Wăn's death. 配＝对, 'to match.' The term must be understood of Woo in relation to his predecessors, as their worthy successor.

St. 2. L. 1, it will be seen, is a repetition of the last line of st. 1; and so, in most of the stanzas below. This is a peculiarity of style, which we have already met with in other odes of this Book. 世德 is the virtue exemplified by the 'three sovereigns' of st. 1, by one after another. 作＝起, 'to rise,' 'to rouse one's self.' 求 has its usual meaning,—'to seek for.' I like this construction of l. 2 better than another advocated by Wang Taou, who takes 作 as—

the substantive verb, or 'to play the part of,' and 求＝匹, as if were the 述, of I. i. I. 1. L. 3,—as l. 3 in I. 6. Here, and below, 言 is merely the particle. L. 4. 成王之孚＝成王者之信于天下, 'produced —completed—in all under heaven the confidence to be reposed in a king.' The people had wished before that a chief of Chow might be the lord of them all; they now doubted no longer that Fah was the king they longed for; and so they carried him on to the throne.

St. 3. Both 式 and 则 have the meaning of 法, 'to be a law or pattern.' 下土,—as in II.v.I. 1, et al. Its use here enables us to determine definitely its signification as meaning 'the lower people,' or all subject to the royal sway, the multitudes, high and low, whose well-being God entrusts to the 'One man.' Woo's 'filial thoughts' were about how he could approve himself worthy of his forefathers. See Mencius' quotation of ll. 3,4, in V. Pt.i. IV. 3, and the turn he gives to them.

St. 4, L.1 here does not repeat the concluding line of st. 3;—'because,' acc. to Foo Kwang, 'this line is the sequel of stt. 2,3, and not of 3 only.' 媚＝爱, 'to love,'—as in VI. 1. 兹

五章
昭兹来许。绳其祖武。于万斯年。受天之祜。

六章
受天之祜。四方来贺。于万斯年。不遐有佐。

5　Brilliantly! and his posterity,
　　Continuing to walk in the steps of their forefather,
　　For myriads of years,
　　Will receive the blessing of Heaven.

6　They will receive the blessing of Heaven,
　　And from the four quarters [of the kingdom] will felicitations
　　　　come to them.
　　For myriads of years,
　　Will there not be their helpers?

X.　*Wăn wang yëw shing.*

文王有声

一章
文王有声。遹骏厥声。遹求厥宁。遹观厥成。文王烝哉。

1　King Wăn is famous;
　　Yea, he is very famous.
　　What he sought was the repose [of the people];
　　What he saw was the completion [of his work].
　　A sovereign true was king Wăn!

一 此, 'this,' *i. e.*, him, king Woo. 一 人,—
'the One man,' a common designation of the old
kings and modern emperors of China. L.2 may
be taken either of the people, as I have done, or of
king Woo;—in the latter case of his 'docile virtue,'
i. e., his filial piety. In either case, 侯 is the
particle, = 维. Yen Ts'an adopts the construction which I have followed:— 天 下 媚
爱 于 武 王, 而 应 之 以 顺 德,
谓 天 下 化 之 也. In l. 4, 服 = 事,
as in II. iii. III. 3, the 'things' being the ways
of his fathers by which they laid the foundation
of the prosperity of their House.
St. 5. L. 1 takes up the first half of l. 4 in
st. 4; and the 兹 here = the 哉 there. 来 =
后 世, 'coming, or after ages;' meaning Woo's
posterity. Choo says that 许 = 所; but the
common meaning of 所 will not suit the passage. Sometimes 所, however, is merely a

particle, and 许 is here nothing more. So, Yen
Ts'an (许, 语 助 也). In l. 2, 绳 = 继,
'to continue;' 武 = 迹, foot-prints.' In l. 3,
and the corresponding line of st. 6, 斯 is a mere
expletive.
St. 6 tells how all the States would for myriads
of years rejoice in the sway of the House of
Chow, and support it against all competitors.
不 遐 = 何 不.
The rhymes are—in st.1, 王, 京 *, cat. 10:
in 2, 求, 孚 *, cat. 3, t. 1: in 3, 式, 则: cat.
1, t. 3: in 4, 德, 服 *, *ib.*: in 5, 许, 武, 祜,
cat. 5, t. 2: in 6, 贺, 佐, cat. 17.

Ode 10. Narrative to the last stanza, which
is perhaps allusive. THE PRAISE OF KING WAN
AND KING WOO:—HOW THE FORMER DISPLAYED
HIS MILITARY PROWESS ONLY TO SECURE THE
TRANQUILLITY OF THE PEOPLE; HOW THIS AP-
PEARED IN THE BUILDING OF FUNG AS HIS

二章
文王受命。有此武功。既伐于崇。作邑于丰。文王烝哉。

三章
筑城伊淢。作丰伊匹。匪棘其欲。遹追来孝。王后

烝哉。

2　King Wăn received the appointment [of Heaven],
　　And achieved his martial success.
　　Having overthrown Ts'ung,
　　He fixed his [capital] city in Fung.
　　A sovereign true was king Wăn!

3　He repaired the walls along the [old] moat:
　　His establishing himself in Fung was according to [the pattern
　　　　of his forefathers],
　　It was not that he was in haste to gratify his wishes;—

CAPITAL CITY; AND HOW THE LATTER ENTERED, IN HIS CAPITAL OF HAOU, INTO THE SOVEREIGNTY OF THE KINGDOM WITH THE SINCERE GOOD WILL OF ALL THE PEOPLE.

S1. 声＝名誉, 'fame.' Choo says that he does not understand 遹, but thinks it may be the same as 聿, an initial particle. Wang Yin-che has shown, with an abundance of evidence, that 欥, 聿, 遹 and 曰, are all particles which are constantly interchanged. Yet they are not mere expletives, nor initial particles, acc. to him, but have a certain conjunctional force. Maou and Ch'ing explain 聿 and 遹, now by 遂, now by 述, and now by 自. Wang condemns all this, and adheres to the account of 欥 in the Shwoh-wăn as 诠词, meaning probably, 'an explanatory conjunction.' The translator, however, cannot always translate the terms; and when he does translate them, he is obliged to vary his renderings. 骏＝大, 'great.' Ll. 3, 4 give the ground of Wăn's great fame. It arose from his 武功, or 'martial merit,' mentioned in st. 2;—he saw the entire success of his enterprizes, and he undertook them, not from love of war, but to secure the repose of the people. We must either neglect the two 厥 altogether in translating, or supplement the lines as I have done. L. 5. Both Maou and Choo take 烝 in the sense of 君, a ruler,' i.e., one who showed himself capable of ruling. 'It is a term,' says Kĕang, 'of admiration and praise.'

St. 2. L. 1 may be taken generally, with reference to the divine favour and destination regarding Wăn, or specifically, with reference to

the orders he got to attack Ts'ung;—see VII. 7. I prefer the former view. L. 4. On VII. 6 it has been said that many of the critics think that Wăn, after the overthrow of Yung, removed his father's capital to a place called Ch'ing; here we have him making another move, about a hundred miles further east from mount K'e. 作邑 is with Choo, and most other scholars, ＝徙都, 'he removed his capital.' They believe that Fung, under a different name, had been the capital of Ts'ung, and that Wăn now moved to it, simply making what repairs on it were necessary for his purpose. This view is, probably, correct; and it is strongly in confirmation of it that we find nothing about the divinations which should have preceded so important a step as the building of a new capital city. He only changed the name from Ts'ung to Fung, with reference to the Fung-water, which was not far off.

St. 3. The moving of his capital to Fung was a great step towards vindicating the sovereignty of the kingdom for the House of Chow; but this stanza is intended to show that Wăn took the step without any such motive. L. 1. The Shwoh-wăn defines 淢 by 疾流, 'a rapid current;' but the critics are all agreed to take the character as ＝洫, which, indeed, was the reading of Han Ying. Now the account of 洫 in the Shwoh-wăn is, that it was the name of the ditch embracing a space of ten le square, ten cubits deep, and as many wide. On this view of the term, Wăn must have built a new city, with such a ditch for a moat, and the surrounding wall, ten le long on every side. Much better is it to take 洫 as meaning 'a moat,' without reference to its depth and width. The dict. gives this as the 2d meaning of the term (城池). 筑城 will then mean that he

四章
王公伊濯。维丰之垣。四方攸同。王后维翰。王后

烝哉。

五章
丰水东注。维禹之绩。四方攸同。皇王维辟。皇王

烝哉。

It was to show the filial duty which had come down to him.
A sovereign true was [our] royal prince!

4   His royal merit was brightly displayed,
    By those walls of Fung.
    There were collected [the sympathies of the people of] the
        four quarters,
    Who regarded the royal prince as their protector.
    A sovereign true was [our] royal prince!

5   The Fung-water flowed on to the east [of the city],
    Through the meritorious labour of Yu.
    There were collected [the sympathies of the people of] the
        four quarters,
    Who would have the great king as their ruler.
    A sovereign true was the great king!

repaired the walls of Ts'ung, damaged by his siege of it; and the whole line must be rendered as in the translation. 伊, and in 1.2, = 维 L. 2 is very obscure. 匹 = 称, 'to be corresponding to.' Choo makes the whole line to = 其作邑居，亦称其城，而不侈大, 'the buildings which he made were also in proportion to the size of the walls, and not extravagantly large.' Këang's view is = 其作丰邑而迁都，与公刘之迁豳，太王之迁岐，相配合焉, 'his making the city of Fung, and removing his capital to it, corresponded to Kung-lëw's removal to Pin, and king T'ae's removal to K'e.' Either of these views is preferable to that of Yen Ts'an, after K'ang-shing, 其作丰邑之制度，唯其称而已，谓称上公之制，已所宜为，不务侈大也, 'the dimensions of which he built Fung were what were befitting; i. e., befitting his rank as a high duke, what he

ought to have, without any attempt at extravagance.' I have adopted the view of Këang. L. 3. 棘 = 急, 'to be earnest,' i. e., to be in a hurry to gratify his own wishes. L. 4. 追,— 'to go back upon the past;' here = to repeat the past in the present. As Këang has it, 直追公刘太王以来一段爱护斯民，恢宏前绪之孝思，而继述之耳.
St. 4 tells how the new capital intensified and increased the devotion of the people to king Wăn and his House. This appears especially in the title 王后, 'royal sovereign,' which is brought on from st. 3. In l. 1. 公 = 功, 'meritorious service;' 濯, = 著明, 'to be displayed brightly.' L. 4. 翰,—as in II.vii.I.3.
St. 5. The ode now turns to king Woo, whose title rises to 皇王, or 'the great king.' Soo Ch'eh says, 皇，大也，武王之王业益大矣，故称皇王焉, '皇 means

六章
镐京辟雍。自西自东。自南自北。无思不服。皇王
烝哉。

七章
考卜维王。宅是镐京。维龟正之。武王成之。武王
烝哉。

八章
丰水有芑。武王岂不仕。诒厥孙谋。以燕翼子。武王
烝哉。

6 In the capital of Haou he built his hall with its circlet of water;
From the west to the east,
From the south to the north,
There was not a thought but did him homage.
A sovereign true was the great king!

7 He examined and divined, did the king,
About settling in the capital of Haou.
The tortoise-shell decided the site,
And king Woo completed the city.
A sovereign true was king Woo!

8 By the Fung-water grows the white millet;—
Did not king Woo show wisdom in his employment of officers?
He would leave his plans to his descendants,
And secure comfort and support to his son.
A sovereign true was king Woo!

great. The royal possession of king Woo became still greater *than that of Wăn*; and therefore he is styled "the great king." Choo says that 皇王 is the designation of him who possesses all under heaven. The Fung-water lay between Wăn's capital of Fung and Woo's of Haou, having the former on the west and the latter on the east. It went on in a north-east direction to the Wei, merged in which it pursued its course to the Ho. L. 1 must evidently be referred to Haou; but the special significance of the terms 东注 does not appear. 注 is appropriate to the course of a stream flowing towards a larger one, or to the sea. L. 2 is a reference to the labour of Yu on the waters, as described with much exaggeration in the Shoo. 辟 in l. 4 = 君, 'ruler.'

St. 6. In l. 1 there would still seem to be a reference to the character of Woo, as really peaceful, notwithstanding his taking up arms against the dyu. of Shang, and overthrowing it. His building the *peih yung* (see on VIII. 3) was an indication of it. Ll. 2—4 describe the sincerity with which the whole people accorded their homage to him.

St. 7. Haou was built by Woo, and hence we have the account of his divining about the site and the undertaking, while nothing of the sort is recorded of Wăn in regard to Fung. 考 = 稽, 'to examine;' *i. e.*, Woo cast the whole thing over in his own mind in the first place. 宅 = 居, 'to reside in,' 'to make his residence.' 正 = 决, to 'determine.' In l. 5 we have the title of *Woo*, or 'martial,' given to king Fah after his death, and showing that the composition of the piece cannot, at the earliest, be placed before the time of king Ching.

St. 8. Both Maou and Choo understand by 苣 a kind of succory; but it is better, to take it, with Yen Ts'an and Këang, as the name of a valuable grain, 'a kind of white millet,' as Williams calls it (白 粱 粟). We shall meet with it again, certainly in this sense. 仕 = 官, 'officers,' or 'to employ as officers.' About the Fung grew this grain, and it suggests to the writer the idea of all the men of ability whom Woo collected around him. 诒 = 传, 'to hand down.' L. 4 = 燕 安 羽 翼 其 子, 'to give soothing comfort and be as wings to his son.' His plan for his descendants would first take effect in the person of his son.

The rhymes are—in st. 1, 声, 声, 宁, 成. cat. 11: in 2, 功, 崇, 丰, cat. 9: in 3, 减 (prop. cat. 1), 匹, cat. 12, t. 1; 欲, 孝 *, cat. 3, t. 2: in 4, 垣, 翰, cat. 14: in 5, 绩, 辟, cat. 16, t. 3: in 6, 雍, 东, cat. 9; 北, 服 *, cat. 1, t. 3: in 7, 王, 京 *, cat. 10; 正, 成, cat. 11: in 8, 苣, 仕, 谋 *, 子, cat. 1, t. 2: and in all the stanzas 烝. cat. 6.

BOOK II.   DECADE OF SHANG MIN.

I.   *Shăng min.*

生民之什三之二

生民

一章

厥初生民。时维姜嫄。生民如何。克禋克祀。以弗无子。履帝武敏歆。攸介攸止。载震载夙。载生载育。时维后稷。

1   The first birth of [our] people
    Was from Këang Yuen.
    How did she give birth to [our] people?
    She had presented a pure offering and sacrificed,
    That her childlessness might be taken away.
    She then trod on a toe-print made by God, and was moved,
    In the large place where she rested.
    She became pregnant; she dwelt retired;
    She gave birth to, and nourished [a son],
    Who was How-tseih.

TITLE OF THE BOOK.—生民之什，三之二, 'The Decade of Shang-min; Book II. of Part III.'

Ode 1.   Narrative.   THE LEGEND OF HOW-TSEIH:—HIS CONCEPTION; HIS BIRTH; THE PERILS OF HIS INFANCY; HIS BOYISH HABITS OF AGRICULTURE; HIS SUBSEQUENT METHODS OF AGRICULTURE, AND HIS FOUNDING OF SACRIFICES; THE HONOURS OF SACRIFICE PAID TO HIM BY THE HOUSE OF CHOW.   Choo says he does not know on what occasion this ode was intended to be sung, but thinks it may have been used after the great border sacrifice, when the flesh of the victims was distributed among the high officers who had taken part in it.   Evidently, as the Preface says, the piece was designed to do honour to How-tseih as the founder to whom the princes of the House of Chow traced their lineage.   After they obtained the sovereignty of the kingdom, he was made 'the assessor of Heaven (配 天)' at the border sacrifice;—the one man by whom the benevolent intention of the supreme Power for the nourishment of the people by means of the fruits of the earth had been realized.   Këang Ping-chang, trying to exhaust the idea of the author in the composition, makes out that his final aim was to impress on king Ching the truth that the prosperity of the dynasty was only to be secured by its promotion of husbandry.—As to the division of the stanzas, Maou made the 3d to consist of 8 lines, and the 4th of 10; Choo, on the contrary, made the 3d of 10 lines, and the 4th of 8. The rhyme is better made out by this arrangement. The 8 stanzas consist of 10 lines and 8 alternately; and all but the first and last commence with the character 誕.

St. 1. L. 1. 厥 is here simply ═ our definite article. 民, 'people,' is not to be taken generally, but with reference to the people of Chow,—the members of the House or family, which came in process of time to the sovereignty of the kingdom. In l. 2, 时 (and in l. 10)═ 是, ' to be;' or the demonstrative pronoun. We can hardly be said to know anything more about Këang Yuen, the mother of How-tseih, than what we are told in the She. It is assumed that she was a daughter of the House of T'ae (有邰氏女), which traced its lineage up to Shin-nung in præhistoric times, and that her name was Yuen. That she was married, and had been so for some time without any child, we infer from l.5; but who her husband was, it is impossible to say. As the Chow surname was Ke (姬), he must have been one of the descendants of Hwang-te. Indeed, Maou makes him to have been the emperor K'uh, the commencement of whose rule is placed in B.C. 2,431, so that Tseih or K'e (that was his name, and Tseih was only a title of office; see on l.10) must have been a brother of Yaou. This view has the sanction of Sze-ma Ts'ëen, Lëw Hin, Pan Koo, Këa Kwei, Ma Yung, Fuh K'ëen, Wang Suh, Hwang-foo Meih, and others. But on this view, it is strange that we should have nothing in the Shoo about the relation between Yaou and K'e; and more strange, that we should find K'e, after the death of Yaou, when he must have been considerably over 100 years old, still in active employment under Shun. Choo follows the view of Ch'ing K'ang-shing, that Këang Yuen was not the wife of K'uh, but only of one of his descendants in the time of Yaou, between whom and K'uh Ch'ing believed there had been no fewer than nine reigns (为高莘之 世妃). The truth is that we must be content to be ignorant as to who the lady's husband was, and put the question on one side, according to the Chinese canon, as 'a doubtful matter (阙疑).' L. 4,—see II.vi.VIII. 4. We need not translate the 克, but had better take it as giving emphasis to the verbs. To whom it was that Këang offered sacrifice we are not told. Maou says it was a custom in ancient times, when the swallow made its appearance, to offer a great border sacrifice, with the first Matchmaker as the assessor of Heaven in it, and that the son of Heaven went himself to it,

attended by his wife, and all the ladies of the harem. At the altar honours were paid to those of the ladies who were in a state of pregnancy, and a bow and arrows were presented to them,—as a sort of auspice that they would give birth to sons. Choo accepts this account; but Kêang Ping-chang has shown that such a ceremony was never heard of till Leu Puh-wei (吕不韦; Ts'in dynasty) invented it; and it would not answer, moreover, the exigency of the stanza, for Këang here sacrifices to have her childlessness taken away (弗═去). The impression we receive from the text is that she offered—to God, we may presume—a sacrifice, all alone, by herself, for that object.

Ll. 6, 7 have occasioned, and still occasion, infinite perplexity to the Chinese critics. Fierce war is waged on the meaning of 帝, of 敏, and of 歆. 1st. Does 歆 belong to l.6 or to l.7? One of these lines must have 5 characters, whereas all the others in the stanza have only 4. 敏 rhyming with 祀, 子, and 止, we might conclude that it terminates l. 6; but we have often found the rhyme resting in these odes on the penultimate term. And the analogy of 攸介攸止, in II. vi. VII. 1, where those 4 characters form a line, is in favour of their doing the same here. I make l. 6 therefore, terminate with 歆. 2d. To whom is 帝 to be referred? The term, acc. to Choo, who follows Ch'ing, ═ 上帝, 'God.' Maou on the contrary held that 帝 here meant 'emperor,' and that Këang's husband, the emperor K'uh, is intended by it. But there is not another instance in the classic of 帝 having this meaning, whereas its occurrence in the sense of 'God' is very frequent. 3d. How are we to understand 敏 and 歆? Maou takes the former term in the sense of 疾, 'to be rapid,' or 'active,' and understands it of Këang Yuen, who followed the emperor to the altar, and was very alert in assisting him at the sacrifice. Then he defines 歆 by 飨, 'to enjoy the offering,' so that the meaning is that God, or some other Spirit who was sacrificed to, accepted the lady's sacrifice, and blessed her. He goes on to say that 介 in l. 7 ═ 大, 'great,' or 'to make great,' and 止 ═ 福禄所止, 'the place (or the individual) from which blessing and dignity rested.' As Ying-tah expands Maou's view:—禋祀郊禖之时,其夫高 莘氏帝率与俱行,姜嫄随帝 之后,践履帝迹,行事敬而敏 疾,故为神歆飨,神既飨其祭,

二章
诞弥厥月。先生如达。不坼不副。无菑无害。以赫厥

灵。上帝不宁。不康禋祀。居然生子。

2   When she had fulfilled her months,
    Her first-born son [came forth] like a lamb.
    There was no bursting, nor rending,
    No injury, no hurt;—
    Showing how wonderful he would be.
    Did not God give her the comfort?
    Had He not accepted her pure offering and sacrifice,
    So that thus easily she brought forth her son?

则 爱 而 祐 之, 于 是 为 天 神 所 美 大, 为 福 禄 所 依 止. All this confusion and perplexity of exegesis I must reject. It has been mentioned above that l. 4 occurs previously in II. vi. VII. 1, and I do not see how any other meaning can be got out of the words than what I have given to them both there and here. Coming now to the interpretation adopted by K'ang-shing and Choo, it is certainly much simpler, and there is really nothing to say against it but the marvellousness of the circumstance. 敏 is taken in the sense of 拇, 'the great toe;' which rests on the authority of the Urh-ya. 歆 is in the sense of 动, 'to be moved.' K'ang-shing says the print of the foot was so large that Këang Yuen merely trod upon the toe; but Yen Ts'an, adopting his view of 帝, joins 敏 with 歆, bringing out the meaning,—'and was immediately moved.' Evidently, this statement is not history, but legend. The wrath of Këang Ping-chang at it need only provoke a smile, nor need we have recourse to Yen Ts'an's doctrine of anthropomorphism. 'When we read,' he says 'that Heaven sees, or that God hears, we are not to infer that Heaven has eyes, or that God has ears.' Still the instance in the text is different from such expressions. The writer would convey by it the ideas that the conception of Howtseih was præternatural, and that it took place in the manner described. There is an analogous legend about the birth of the ancestor of the House of Shang, and Sze-ma Ts'ëen gives to a dragon the paternity of the first emperor of the Han dynasty.

Ll. 8—10. 载 is the particle. 震 = 有 身, 'to be pregnant.' The character occurs repeatedly in the Tso-chuen in this sense. I can make no meaning out of 夙, understood in its usual signification of 早, 'early in the morning,' 'early;' to which Maou here adheres. Choo, after Ch'ing, explains it here by 肃, the meaning of which must be what I have given in the translation. In l. 10, 后 稷,—see on the Shoo, II. i. 18. The two characters are evidently used here as equivalent to a name. They did not belong to the child, until he had grown up, and was appointed minister of Agriculture, and lord of T'ae. His proper name, it has been mentioned, was K'e (弃).

St. 2 is occupied with the birth of the præternaturally conceived child without any trouble or pain to the mother. 诞, here and in stt. 3—7 below, is simply an initial particle. 弥 = 终, 'to finish,' or 'to be finished.' 先 生 = 首 生, 'first born;' 达 is the name for 'a lamb' (the Shwoh-wăn calls it 小 羊). Ll. 3 and 4 make it plain that the point of the comparison in l. 2 is the ease of the birth. 坼 and 副 are synonyms, = 裂, 'to tear,' 'to be torn.' 菑 is pronounced like 灾, and with the meaning of that term. 赫 = 显, 'to manifest.' 厥 灵 is to be referred to the child. Ll. 6,7 may be translated interrogatively, and are equivalent to strong affirmations. We must understand that Këang Yuen is the object of 宁, 'to give repose, or comfort to.' 康 = 安 享, 'to enjoy tranquilly,' 'to accept.' 居 然 = 徒 然, 'with ease;'—compare the use of 居 in II. vii. X. 3.

三章

诞寘之隘巷。牛羊腓字之。诞寘之平林。会伐平林。

诞寘之寒冰。鸟覆翼之。鸟乃去矣。后稷呱矣。实覃

实讦。厥声载路。

四章

诞实匍匐。克岐克嶷。以就口食。艺之荏菽。荏菽旆

3 He was placed in a narrow lane,
But the sheep and oxen protected him with loving care.
He was placed in a wide forest,
Where he was met with by the wood-cutters.
He was placed on the cold ice,
And a bird screened and supported him with its wings.
When the bird went away,
How-tseih began to wail.
His cry was long and loud,
So that his voice filled the whole way.

4 When he was able to crawl,
He looked majestic and intelligent.
When he was able to feed himself,
He fell to planting large beans.
The beans grew luxuriantly;

St. 3,—the dangers of How-tseih's infancy. It does not appear from the ode who it was that exposed the child to the various perils here mentioned. Maou supposed that it was the father, the emperor K'uh. Ch'ing, on the contrary, not holding that Këang Yuen was the wife of K'uh, makes her to have been the party, and assumes that her object was not to get rid of the child, but to show still more clearly what a marvellous gift from heaven he was. I have purposely translated 寘 之 by 'he was placed,' so as to leave the matter in the uncertainty in which we find it. Choo takes 腓 = 芘, 'to protect;'—as in II. i. VII. 5; and it is as well to follow here the analogy of that passage, though Maou's 腓 = 避, 'to avoid,' would suit the line quite as well. 字 = 爱, 'to love,' 'to care for.' 平 林 = 林 之 在 平 地 者, 'a forest on level ground.' 会 = 值, 'he met with,' or 'it

happened that.' It is implied, though not expressed, that the wood-cutters took the child up, and preserved it. 鸟 may be either singular or plural; but the critics all say it was 'a large bird (大 鸟),' who covered the child above with one wing, and supported it beneath with the other (翼 = 藉). 呱 = 啼 声, 'the sound of wailing.' 覃 = 长, 'long;' 讦 = 大, 'great.' 载 路 = 满 路, as in the translation. Compare the same phrase in i. VII. 2.
St. 4,—the marvellous development of the agricultural faculty in him when he was a mere boy. 匍 匐,—as in I. iii. X. 4. The 实 = 寔 = 是, 'to be;' but we can hardly translate it. Choo makes 岐 嶷 = 峻 茂 之 状, 'majestic-looking;' Maou, = 'intelligent.' 口 食, both by Maou and Choo, is taken as = 自

誧。禾役襚襚。麻麦幪幪。瓜瓞唪唪。

五章

诞后稷之穑。有相之道。茀厥丰草。种之黄茂。实方
实苞。实种实褎。实发实秀。实坚实好。实颖实栗。
即有邰家室。

His rows of paddy shot up beautifully;
His hemp and wheat grew strong and close;
His gourds yielded abundantly.

5   The husbandry of How-tseih
Proceeded on the plan of helping [the growth].
Having cleared away the thick grass,
He sowed the ground with the yellow cereals.
He managed the living grain, till it was ready to burst;
Then he used it as seed, and it sprang up;
It grew and came into ear;
It became strong and good;
It hung down, every grain complete;—
And thus he was appointed lord of T'ae.

能 食, 'was able to eat himself,' *i.e.*, was 6 or 7 years old. Accepting this, 以 就 must = 及 至, 'and when he came to.' 及 is one of the meanings of 以 given by Wang Yin-che. L. 4. 艺 = 树, 'to plant.' The 之 loses its meaning in the verb;—'he planted it,'=he planted. 荏 菽 = 大 豆, 'large beans.' 誧誧,—see II. i. VIII. 2. The boy's bean plants sprang up, and grew like flags waving in the wind. And he did not take beans only in hand. 役 = 行 列, 'rows.' He introduced, it would appear, the practice of planting paddy out in rows. 襚 襚 = 苗 美 好 之 貌, 'the appearance of the growing plant looking beautiful.' 幪 幪 = 'luxuriant and dense.' 瓜 瓞,—as in i. III. 1. 唪 唪 = 多 实, 'yielding much fruit.'

St. 5 introduces us to the young man, whose qualities had recommended him to the notice of Yaou, as we may infer from the Shoo, so that he had been appointed minister of Agriculture. He

was not yet lord of T'ae, and it is a question therefore whether the 后 稷 should not go together, simply as the title of that office (后 稷, 农 官 名; Këang Ping-chang). Ll. 1, 2 tell us the general principle which distinguished his husbandry from that of others. 穑, 'to reap,' has here the general meaning of 'the art of husbandry.' 相 = 助 'to assist.' 'The growth of the grain,' says Këang, 'depends on the seasons given by heaven and the nourishment given by the earth; but How-tseih added to these the complete and wise application of human labour and skill.' L. 3 relates to his preparation of the ground for the seed. 茀 = 治, 'to regulate,' 'to manage;' meaning here, 'to clear away.' 黄 茂, 'yellow luxuriances,' is a denomination of the cereals. The next 5 lines tell of his management of the seed, and the richness of his produce. The 种 in l. 6 seems to necessitate this view, for it is better to take 实 种 as in the translation, than to say with Yen Ts'an, after Ch'ing, that 种 denotes the grow-

六章
诞降嘉种。维秬维秠。维穈维芑。恒之秬秠。是获是
亩。恒之穈芑。是任是负。以归肇祀。

6 He gave his people the beautiful grains:—
　·The black millet, and the double-kernelled;
　The tall red, and the white.
　They planted extensively the black and the double-kernelled,
　Which were reaped and stacked on the ground.
　They planted extensively the tall red and the white,

ing up of each kind of plant, without any admixture of other sorts (生 不 杂). We must then understand l. 5 of K‘e's management of the seed, fostering its germinating quality before he committed it to the soil; and we cannot take 方 as in II. vi. VIII. 2, where it denotes the grain in its sheath, about to show itself in the ear. Choo here explains it by 房, as in that other passage; but with the meaning of 'the living germ enclosed in the visible grain as its house.' Then 苞 is the grain with that germ in a state of development, ready to burst out. Choo says, 方, 房也, 苞, 甲而未拆也, on which Choo Kung-ts‘een observes, 生意藏于其中, 是为房也, 生意蓄而欲泄, 是为甲, 甲者草木之仁也, 拆, 则破其种而出之矣. The other terms describe the gradual and successful growth of the plants. 颖 is the heavy ear of the full grain hanging down with its own weight; and 栗, the fullness of each separate grain (栗 不 秕 也). The several 实 can only be explained by 是 or 惟. Këang says that they denote how K‘e had the way of bringing about the results described in the terms that follow (数 实 字 便 有 道 在). L. 8. 'Then he had the House of T‘ae.' This is understood as saying that because of his merits as minister of Agriculture, K‘e was invested with the principality of T‘ae,—in the pres. dis. of Woo-kung (武 功), K‘ëen Chow (乾 州), Shen-se. His mother is said to have been a daughter of that State. Perhaps the ruling chief was displaced, or removed to some other principality. At any rate, somehow, K‘e was made lord of T‘ae.

St. 6 shows us K‘e in his govt. of T‘ae teaching his people the art of agriculture and methods of sacrifice. 降 = 'to send down,' 'to confer.' The expression is strong, and indicates that the people of T‘ae had before K‘e's time been unacquainted with agriculture, or acquainted with it only very imperfectly. 秬 is 'the black millet (黑 黍),' and 秠, a variety of that, the husk of which is said to contain two grains (一 秠 二 米 者). 穈 and 芑 are also two large-grained millets, or varieties of *holcus*, the former red (赤 粱 粟), and the other white (白 粱 粟). It is most likely that these four plants are merely specified by way of illustration, and that the writer meant his readers to understand that it was K‘e who first introduced the cultivation of the cereals. We can find a reason for the specification of them in the fact that the black millets were used in making the spirits which were employed in sacrifices, and the red and white for offerings. L. 4 恒 (*kăng*) = 遍, 'every where,' 'extensively:' meaning that these millets were planted extensively. L. 5. 是 亩, 'were acred,' = 栖 之 于 亩, 'were stacked on the ground.' L. 7. 任 is 'to carry on the the shoulders;' 负, 'on the back.' Choo observes that the processes in l. 3 are to be extended to the black millets, and those in l. 5 to the red and white. It is a case of what is called 互 文. L. 8. 肇 = 始, 'first.' The grain was carried home 以 供 始 祭 之 事, 'to supply the sacrifices which How-tseih first instituted.' Maou thinks that Yaou had conferred on K‘e the privilege of offering the great sacrifices to Heaven; but this is very unlikely, and it could not be said that K‘e founded those sacrifices. The meaning must be that K‘e instituted the sacrifices of the ancestral temple, or at least so developed them that he

七章

诞我祀如何。或舂或揄。或簸或蹂。释之叟叟。烝之

浮浮。载谋载惟。取萧祭脂。取羝以軷。载燔载烈。

以兴嗣岁。

> Which were carried on their shoulders and backs,
> Home for the sacrifices which he founded.

7　And how as to our sacrifices [to him]?
　　Some hull [the grain]; some take it from the mortar;
　　Some sift it; some tread it.
　　It is rattling in the dishes;
　　It is distilled, and the steam floats about.
　　We consult; we observe the rites of purification;
　　We take southernwood and offer it with the fat;
　　We sacrifice a ram to the Spirit of the path;
　　We offer roast flesh and broiled:—
　　And thus introduce the coming year.

might be called the founder of them, just as he was the founder of husbandry, though we cannot suppose that before him men had not made imperfect attempts to draw their food from the earth.

St. 7 must be referred to the ancestral sacrifices of the kings of Chow, when they did special honour to How-tseih as the founder of their line; and it should be translated in the present tense. The 我, therefore, in l.1, is specially applicable, as Ping-chang says, to any monarch of the dyn. of Chow,—the king reigning, whenever the ode was sung. Ll.2—5 describe the preparation of the grain for the offerings, and for distillation, with the process of distillation. But we must not suppose that these things were done at the time of the sacrifice;—they had been previously performed, and the 或 intimates that there were men appointed for each operation. 舂 expresses the 'hulling' of the grain; 揄, 'the scooping of the grain, so hulled, out of the mortar (抒=曰);' 簸, 'the sifting of it.' 蹂 is the 'treading' of the grain out of the ears (蹂, 以 脱 其 穗); but why this operation should be mentioned last, I cannot tell, unless it be to indicate, as Choo seems to say, that there was in this way kept up a constant supply for the hullers. 释 = 淅, 'to wash the grain,' which had thus been cleaned; 叟 叟 give the sound of the grains in the dish as they

were washed. 烝,—'to distil;' 浮 浮 show us the vapour floating about in the process of distillation.

L. 6 refers to the formal observances and solemn thoughtfulness preparatory to the sacrifices. 谋, 'to consult,' belongs to the divining for the day, and the selection of the officers to take part in the service (卜 日, 择 士); 惟 = 思, 'to think' belongs to the fasting, vigils, &c. (斋 戒, 具, 修). L. 7 = 萧 合 祭 牲 之 脂, 熱 之, 'we take southernwood, and burn it along with the fat of the victims.' This filled the ancestral temple with fragrance. L.8. 羝 = 牡 羊, 'a ram.' 軷 was the name for a sacrifice offered to the Spirits of the road on setting out on a journey; but from the mention of it here, we must conclude that it was used also in connection with the services of the ancestral temple. In the Le Ke it is spoken of as offered in the first month of winter (月 令; 孟 冬 其 祀 行). In l.9, 烈 = 炙, 'to broil,' which we have often met with in connection with 燔. The flesh, thus roasted or broiled, was offered to the personator of the dead. L.10 shows that all the services of the ancestral temple, through the honour done to How-tseih in them, were intended to remind the kings of Chow that on an atten-

八章.

卬盛于豆。于豆于登。其香始升。上帝居歆。胡臭亶

时。后稷肇祀。庶无罪悔。以迄于今。

8   We load the stands with the offerings,
The stands both of wood and of earthenware.
As soon as the fragrance ascends,
God, well pleased, smells the sweet savour.
Fragrant is it, and in its due season!
How-tseih founded the sacrifice,
And no one, we presume, has given occasion for blame or regret
    in regard to it,
Down to the present day.

II.   Hing wei.

行苇

一章

敦彼行苇。牛羊勿践履。方苞方体。维叶泥泥。戚戚

1   In thick patches are those rushes, springing by the way (-side);
Let not the cattle and sheep trample them.
Anon they will burst up; anon they will be completely formed,
With their leaves soft and glossy.

tion to agriculture depended the permanence of their dynasty. 嗣岁,—'the inheriting year,' *i. e.*, the coming year, which it was hoped would inherit the fruitfulness of the past.

St. 8 is understood as relating, briefly, to the great border sacrifice to God, where How-tseih was introduced as His assessor. 卬＝我, as in I. iii. IX. 4. 盛 ='to fill in the appropriate offerings.' The 登 was a vessel, shaped like the 豆, but made of earthenware, used to contain the soup, or water in which flesh had been boiled;—in those early days without any addition of vegetables or spices. L. 4. 居＝安, 'tranquilly,' 'well pleased.' 歆＝食气, 'to eat—*i.e.*, to smell—the savour.' L. 5. 胡＝何, 'how,' and 亶＝诚, 'truly.' We may take these two terms as imparting the force of admiration to the 臭 and 时. I prefer this to understanding a 但, 'only,' after 胡.—'How

is it fragrant only? It is also truly seasonable.' Ll. 7,8 may be understood as saying that the lords of Chow, and especially the kings of the dynasty, had been most careful to observe the sacrifice to How-tseih in connection with their other grand sacrifices, thereby keeping up their recognition of the importance of agriculture, and furnishing an example to their successors in all the future.

The rhymes are—in st. 1, 民, 嫄 (prop. cat. 14), cat. 12, t. 1; 祀 子, 敏 *, 止, cat. 1, t. 2; 夙, 育, 稷 (prop. cat. 1), cat. 3, t. 3: in 2, 月, 达. 害, cat. 15, t. 3; 灵, 宁, cat. 11; 祀, 子, cat. 1, t. 2: in 3, 字, 翼, *ib.*; 林, 林, cat. 7, t. 1; 去, 呱, 讦, 路, cat. 5, t. 1: in 4, 匐, 嶷, 食, cat. 1, t. 3; 旆, 穟, cat. 15, t. 3; 幪, 唪, cat. 9: in 5, 道 *, 草 *, 茂 *, 苞 *, 褎, 秀, 好 *, cat. 3, t. 2; 栗, 室, cat. 12, t. 3: in 6, 秠 *, 芑 *, 秠 *, 亩 *, 芑, 负 *, 祀, cat. 1, t. 2: in 7, 揄

兄弟。莫远具尔。或肆之筵。或授之几。

二章

肆筵设席。授几有缉御。或献或酢。洗爵奠斝。醓醢

以荐。或燔或炙。嘉殽脾臄。或歌或咢。

Closely related are brethren ;—
Let none be absent, let all be near.
For some there are spread mats ;
For some there are given stools [besides].

2　The mats are spread, and a second one above ;
The stools are given, and there are plenty of servants.
[The guests] are pledged, and they pledge [the host] in return ;
He rinses the cup, and the guests put theirs down.
Sauces and pickles are brought in,
With roast meat and broiled.

(prop. cat. 4), 蹂, 叟, 浮, cat. 3, t. 1 ; 惟, 脂, cat. 15, t. 1 ; 轼, 烈, 岁, *ib.*, t. 3 : in 8, 登, 升, cat. 6 ; 歆, 今, cat. 7, t. 1 ; 时, 祀, 悔 *, cat. 1, t. 2.

Ode 2. Allusive and narrative. A FESTAL ODE, CELEBRATING SOME ENTERTAINMENT GIVEN BY THE KING TO HIS RELATIVES, WITH THE TRIAL OF ARCHERY AFTER THE FEAST ; CELEBRATING ESPECIALLY THE HONOUR DONE ON SUCH OCCASIONS TO THE AGED. Choo inclines to the view that the feast here described was given at the conclusion of the sacrificial services in the ancestral temple. Before his time, the commentators considered that it had no connection with any sacrifices, but was designed simply to show how the good kings of Chow cultivated the friendly affection of the princes, their relatives, and behaved with courtesy especially to the old. The K'ang-he editors remark that there is no evidence that the trial of archery formed part of the feasts which were given after sacrifices. It does not seem to be worth while to discuss this point at large.

St. 1. 苇,—as in I. v. VII. 1, *et al.* They are called here 行苇, 'reeds by the way,' meaning, says Këang, 'the paths along the ditches in the fields.' 敦 *(twan)* = 聚貌, 'the app. of being collected together.' The line shows us the reeds just appearing, in a mass, above the ground. The 方 in l. 3 = 'now ;' and redoubled, it has the significancy given in the translation. 苞, in st. 5 of last ode, is used of the germ ready to burst from the seed ; here of the young shoot going on to develope itself. 体 = 成

形, 'to complete its form,' *i. e.*, appear as the fully formed reed. 泥泥 = 柔泽貌, as in the translation. In the reeds growing up densely from a common root we have an emblem of brothers all sprung from the same ancestor ; and in plants developing so finely, when preserved from injury, an emblem of the happy fellowships of consanguinity, when nothing is allowed to interfere with mutual confidence and good feeling. 戚戚 = 亲, 'near,' 'affectionate.' Maou defines the expression by 内相亲, 'mutual internal affection.' 莫 = 勿 of l. 2. 具 = 俱, as often. 尔 = 迩, 'to be near.' In ll. 7, 8 the 'brothers' appear assembled at the king's feast, and while the young are only provided with mats to sit on, the old have stools (几) given them in addition, on which they can lean. 肆 = 陈, 'to spread,' 筵,—see on II. vii. VI. 1.

St. 2. 设席 = 重席, 'the redoubling of the mat.' K'ung Ying-tah says, 'When, after it has been said that the mats are spread, it is added that a mat is placed (设席), we know that there were two mats, as in the line 下莞上簟 of II. iv. V. 6.' 缉 = 续, 'to continue ;' 御 = 侍, 'to wait on,' 'attendants.' 缉御 means that there were many attendants, one to succeed another in waiting. This attention was shown especially to the old. Ll. 3, 4. The spirits were first presented to the guests, and each man drank his cup. This was called

三章
敦弓既坚。四鍭既钧。舍矢既均。序宾以贤。敦弓既
句。既挟四鍭。四鍭如树。序宾以不侮。

Excellent provisions there are [also] of tripe and cheek;
With singing to lutes, and with drums.

3   The ornamented bows are strong,
      And the four arrows are all balanced.
      They discharge the arrows, and all hit,
      And the guests are arranged according to their skill.
      The ornamented bows are drawn full,
      And the four arrows are grasped in the hand.
      They go straight to the mark as if planted in it,
      And the guests are arranged by the humble propriety of their
          demeanour.

献. Then the representative of the guests presented a cup to the host, who drank it. This was called 酢. The host then rinsed his cup, and those of the guests were refilled; but instead of drinking them immediately, they put them down for the present (奠之不举). In this way the feast was opened. There is no difference in meaning between 爵 and 罍. The former was the name for a cup under the Chow dynasty; the latter was the name used under the Yin. The 或⋯或, here, and in l. 6,= our 'both...and.' L. 5. 醓醢 = the brine of meat minced small and pickled. There was this 'to present,' that it might be eaten with, and give a relish to, the viands. 脾, 'the stomach;' here = tripe. 臄 = 口上肉, 'the flesh above the mouth,'=cheek. 歌, as has been already observed, is used of singing to the accompaniment of stringed instruments; 咢 is the drum without singing.

St. 3. After feasting, the guests repair to the archery ground. 敦, here read t'eaou,= 画, 'ornamented.' The bows, we saw on II. iii. I. were lacquered, but it would appear that further ornament, in the way of painting, was added. Yen Ts'an says this was only the case with the royal bows, and that the term is used here as the trial described took place at court. The point is unimportant. L. 2. 鍭 is a name for

the arrows with reference to their steel points. They are said to be 'balanced (钧),' because a perfect arrow had its centre of gravity at one third of its whole length from the steel head. L. 4. Choo explains 均 by 皆中, 'all hit;' but that can only mean that all hit the target, not that all hit it in the centre, or equally near the centre, for l. 5 shows that they were arranged according to the skill which they had shown. 均, 'to be level or equal,' would seem to imply that all were equally successful, which cannot be the case. 贤 = 'superiority.' This is a not infrequent use of the character. Choo says the meaning of it here is 射多中.

Ll. 5—8 tell how a further distinction was made among the successful competitors, according to the manner in which they conducted themselves towards those who were unsuccessful. 不侮 in l. 8 = 'showing no insolence;—不以中病不中者. In this matter the adjudication must have been very difficult, and it would be very easy to put on an appearance of complaisance and humility. 句 = 彀, 'to draw a bow to the full.' L. 6 does not imply that the four arrows were held in the hand at the same time. As Ying-tah says, from the E Le, the arrows were stuck in the girdle, and the archer took them out with his right hand, one after the other, fitted them to the string, drew the bow, and discharged them. 如树 describes

四章
曾孙维主。酒醴维醹。酌以大斗。以祈黄耇。黄耇台
背。以引以翼。寿考维祺。以介景福。

4   The distant descendant presides over the feast;
His sweet spirits are strong.
He fills their cups from a measure,
And prays for the hoary old [among his guests];—
That with hoary age and wrinkled back,
They may lead on one another [to virtue], and support one
     another [in it];
That so their old age may be blessed,
And their bright happiness [ever] increased.

III.   Ke tsuy.

既醉
一章
既醉以酒。既饱以德。君子万年。介尔景福。

1   You have made us drink to the full of your spirits;
You have satiated us with your kindness,
May you enjoy, O our lord, myriads of years!
May your bright happiness [ever] be increased!

the arrows sticking in the mark, straight and firm, as if they had been carefully and leisurely planted in it (如手就树之，言贯革而坚正). The archers are all spoken of as 'guests,' as being at the time the king's guests; and in st. 4 he is mentioned as the 主 or 'host.'

St. 4. I suppose that, after the archery, they all returned again to the feast, which the king brought to a conclusion with the ceremony here described, doing special honour to the aged among the guests. 曾孙—as in II.vi.VI., et al. 醴,—as in II.iii.VI.4; 酒醴 must here be taken together, = 'sweet spirits.' 醹＝厚, 'strong.' L. 3 intimates the generosity of the king's treatment of his aged guests, filling their cups with no stinting hand. The shape of the 斗 I do not know;—the handle of it is said to have been 3 feet in length. With this the king drew the spirits from a large vase, and filled the cups,—perhaps more than once. The Preface and the old school make a pause at l. 4, under-

standing that the 祈 intimates that the king here begged the old guests to tell him the results of their experience. Then ll.5—8 tell how those venerable men, having done so, ' to lead him on and support him in a virtuous course,' concluded by wishing for him old age and increasing happiness. Choo, on the other hand, takes the whole as in the translation. The K'ang-he editors say that both interpretations are allowable. Only one of them, however, can be the correct one; and I have no hesitation in preferring the view of Choo. 黄耇, 'yellow age,' means old age marked by hoar hair. 耇,—see on VI. ii. VII 5. 台 is used for 鲐, the name of a fish, remarkable for the spots and wrinkles of its skin, to which it is supposed the skin of old people gets a resemblance. The different 以 seem to imply a reference in the speaker's mind to the spirits, which, by nourishing the old age of the guests, would help them to realize the things which the king desired for them. 祺＝吉, 'auspicious,' 'happy.'

The four stanzas of the ode, as now edited, appear in Maou as seven;—two of 6 lines each,

二章
既醉以酒。尔殽既将。君子万年。介尔昭明。

三章
昭明有融。高朗令终。令终有俶。公尸嘉告。

2　You have made us drink to the full of your spirits;
　　Your viands were all set out before us.
　　May you enjoy, O our lord, myriads of years!
　　May your bright intelligence [ever] be increased!

3　May your bright intelligence become perfect,
　　High and brilliant, leading to a good end!
　　That good end has [now] its beginning:—
　　The personator of your ancestors announced it in his blessing.

and five of 4. Ch'ing divided them into eight stanzas of 4 lines each. There can be no doubt that the modern arrangement is the most correct.

The rhymes are—in st. 1, 苇, 履, 体, 泥, 弟, 尔, 几, cat. 15, t. 2: in 2, 席 *, 酢, 炙 *, 朦, 罘, cat. 5, t. 3; 御, 罿 *, *ib.* t. 2: in 3, 坚, 钧, 均, 贤, cat. 12, t. 1; 句 *, 鏠, 树 *, 侮 *, cat. 4, t. 2: in 4, 主 *, 醹 *, 斗, 耇, *ib.*; 背, 翼, 福 *, cat. 1, t. 3.

Ode 3. Narrative. RESPONSIVE TO THE LAST:—THE UNCLES AND BRETHREN OF THE KING EXPRESS THEIR SENSE OF HIS KINDNESS, AND THEIR WISHES FOR HIS HAPPINESS, MOSTLY IN THE WORDS IN WHICH THE PERSONATOR OF THE DEAD HAD CONVEYED THE SATISFACTION OF HIS ANCESTORS WITH THE SACRIFICE OFFERED TO THEM, AND PROMISED TO HIM THEIR BLESSING. The position of this ode seems to confirm Choo's view of the preceding as descriptive of a feast given by the king to his relatives at the conclusion of a sacrifice in the ancestral temple. It is plain that such a feast must have preceded the occasion to which this ode was appropriate.

St. 1. It seems best to take 醉 and 饱 as in the translation, understanding 尔 or 王 as the nominative to them. Yen Ts'an says:— 王 既醉我以酒, 既饱我以德 德 is taken in the sense of 恩惠, 'kindness,' referring especially to the abundance of the feast. In l. 3, 君子 refers to the king, as does the 尔 in l. 4. Those two lines are a prayer for the king, and we have to suppose 天, 'Heaven,' as the subject of 介, though we need not express it in the translation. To use again the words of Yen Ts'an, 我无以

报上, 愿其享万年之寿, 而天助尔大福. On l. 3, — 'May you, O king, live for ever!' Le Ch'oo says, 'From antiquity it has been the custom of ministers, in responding to their rulers, to wish that they might receive abundance of happiness. The T'ëen-paou (II.i. VI.) is an ode responsive to the sovereign, and the way in which his kindness is responded to in it is simply a wish for his long continued happiness; and so here, the ministers of king Ching respond to him by wishing for him ten thousand years.'

St. 2. 将,—as in II.vi.V. 6. Choo says that 昭明 is equivalent to 光大, 'bright and large.' But it is better to give to 明 the substantive force of 'intelligence.' Wang Gan-shih explains the two terms by 明德, 'intelligent virtue.'

St. 3. 融 is explained by 明之盛, 'the fullness of intelligence.' The term denotes 'steam or vapour issuing forth,' and hence is used here of intelligence, the manifestation of which cannot be repressed. 朗 (formed also with the same elements in the reverse order) denotes the brilliancy of the intelligence. Choo defines it by 虚明, which we may call 'ethereal intelligence.' 令终 = 善终, 'a good end.' Choo says the phrase is equivalent to the 考终命 in the Shoo, V.iv. 39. But it seems to be here more than we understand by a good end, and to characterize not the end of his life merely, but of all his undertakings, their issues being perpetuated in his posterity. L. 3 suggests a thought of caution to the king, that as the end flows from the beginning (俶 = 始), he would best provide for the future by attending to the present. At this point the speaker or speakers seem to be unable to say anything more as from themselves, and go on to quote the language in which the blessing of his ances-

其告维何。笾豆静嘉。朋友攸摄。摄以威仪。

四章

威仪孔时。君子有孝子。孝子不匮。永锡尔类。

五章

4 What was his announcement?
'[The offerings in] your dishes of bamboo and wood are clean
    and fine.
Your friends assisting at the service,
Have done their part with reverent demeanour.

5 'Your reverent demeanour was altogether what the occasion
    required,
And not yours only, but that also of your filial son.
For such filial piety, without ceasing,
There will ever be conferred blessing on you.

tors had been conveyed in the temple. Of the 尸, or their representatives at the sacrifices, I have spoken on II.vi.V. 5, *et al.* The expression 公尸, 'ducal personators,' is somewhat difficult to account for. Choo says that it is an instance of old custom continuing to prevail, even after the princes of Chow had attained to the royal dignity; and nothing less unsatisfactory can be found on the point. 告嘉 = 以善言告之，谓嘏辞也, 'announced in good words, meaning the blessing.' If there were more than one representative of the departed, as I have previously said that each of the ancestors had his personator, it would seem necessary to suppose that one of them, in pronouncing the blessing, spoke for himself and all the others.

St. 4. From l. 2 to the end of the ode we seem to have the words of blessing; and this st. gives some grounds of it. 笾豆,—as in I. xv. V. 2, *et al.* 静嘉 = 清洁而美, 'pure and admirable.' This predicate must be understood of the contents of the dishes. As Yen Ts'an says, 汝笾豆所盛之物，洁静而嘉美. By the 'friends' are intended the various officers who had taken part in the sacrificial services. 摄 has the meaning of 佐 'to assist,' and also of 捡 'to repress,' 'to exercise self-discipline,' and the critics combine them here, which does not seem to be necessary.

St. 5 The 威仪 here must be understood of the king himself, or it may belong to him and his son, carrying on l. 1 to 2. Maou, indeed, and Ch'ing continue to interpret the phrase of the assisting officers, of whom also they understand the 2d line, as saying that they were superior men, who possessed the virtues of 'filial sons.' But we may be sure that their interpretation is wrong. The Spirits of the dead had not sufficient interest in those officers that they should thus dwell upon them; and 君子 is here, as in stt. 1, 2, appropriate to the king, while the 'filial son,' would be his eldest son, who, we know, took a certain part in the services in the ancestral temple. 时 = 'in season,' 'what the seasons required.' I take 有 as if it were 又, = 'and.' Leu Tsoo-k'ëen seems to me to have caught the meaning of l. 3 better than any of the other critics. He understands it of the king and his son, who had both shown themselves so filial (君子既孝，而嗣子又孝，其孝可谓源源不竭矣). Right was it that his ancestors should confer on the king all kinds of blessing (类 = 善). —I may mention another view of the stanza, given by a P'ang Chih-chung (彭执中; at the end of the Sung dyn.):—'From his reverent demeanour so entirely what the occasion required, it might be seen with what filial duty king Ching sacrificed to his ancestors. It was proper that he should have a filial son coming after him; yea, that filial sons should appear for ever in his line, generation after generation, for that Heaven should grant kings thus to follow one another of the same character was in the order of nature and reason.' See the 'Collected Comments,' *in loc.* A similar view did on my first study of the stanza occur to myself, but I concluded that the one given in the translation was preferable.

六章
其类维何。室家之壶。君子万年。永锡祚胤。

七章
其胤维何。天被尔禄。君子万年。景命有仆。

八章
其仆维何。厘尔女士。厘尔女士。从以孙子。

6   'What will the blessings be?
    That along the passages of your palace
    You shall move for ten thousand years;
    And there will be granted to you for ever dignity and posterity.

7   'How as to your posterity?
    Heaven invests you with your dignity,
    Yea for ten thousand years,
    The bright appointment is attached to your person.

8   'How will it be attached?
    There is given you a heroic wife.
    There is given you a heroic wife,
    And from her shall come [the line of] descendants.'

St. 6. 壶 is explained as 宫中之巷, 'the lanes or passages of the palace.' Then we must take ll. 2 and 3 together, and there comes out the meaning that the king should have a long and undisturbed life in the quiet of the apartments of his palace. As Foo Kwang expands the passage,—所谓善者如何, 则云使尔居于深远严密之宫室，无有外虞. This is, perhaps, the most likely of the various interpretations that have been proposed. I much prefer it to the view of Yen Ts'an, who says that as the passages of the palace were the means of egress, l. 2 intimates that from king Ching in his palace a transforming influence should go out over the whole kingdom, and, if it were so, he would deserve to live for ten thousand years. L. 4. 祚 = 福禄, 'happiness and dignities;' but it is difficult to see what more there is in this than is intimated in the two previous lines. 胤 = 子孙, 'posterity,' 'descendants.'

St. 7. 被 (3d tone) = 覆, 'to cover over.' 仆 = 附 or 属, 'to be attached to,' 'to belong to.' The 1st line would seem to be here out of place, for the other lines seem to say nothing about the king's posterity, unless it be that the fact of the appointment of Heaven being attached to his person secured the same also for them.

St. 8. 厘 = 予, 'to give.' 女士 = 女之有士行者, 'a lady [or ladies] having the conduct of an officer.' As it appears, from st. 4, that the king had already a son, ll. 2, 3 must be translated in the present, or in the present-complete tense. 从 = 随, 'and thereon.' We must understand 锡 after it, and 以 is then = 'with,' or, as Julien calls it, the sign of the accusative case.

[It must be confessed that the above communication from the Spiritual world is not a little difficult to construe. We are obliged to have recourse to 'chiseling,' to make out the sense and sequence of the utterance.]

The rhymes are—in st. 1, 德, 福 *, cat. 1, t. 3: in 2, 将, 明 *, cat. 10: in 3, 融, 终, cat. 9; 俶, 告 *, cat. 3, t. 3: in 4, 何, 嘉; 仪 *, cat. 17: in 5, 时, 子, cat. 1, t. 2; 匮, 类, cat. 15, t. 3: in 6, 壶, 年, 胤, cat. 12, t. 1: in 7, 禄, 仆, cat. 3, t. 3: in 8, 士, 士, 子, cat. 1, t. 2.

IV. *Hoo e.*

凫鹥

一章

凫鹥在泾。公尸来燕来宁。尔酒既清。尔殽既馨。公
尸燕饮。福禄来成。

二章

凫鹥在沙。公尸来燕来宜。尔酒既多。尔殽既嘉。公

1 The wild-ducks and widgeons are on the King;
   The personators of your ancestors feast and are happy.
   Your spirits are clear,
   Your viands are fragrant;
   The personators of your ancestors feast and drink;—
   Their happiness and dignity are made complete.

2 The wild ducks and widgeons are on the sand;
   The personators of the dead enjoy the feast, their appropriate
   tribute.

Ode 4. Allusive. AN ODE, APPROPRIATE TO THE FEAST GIVEN TO THE PERSONATORS OF THE DEPARTED, ON THE DAY AFTER THE SACRIFICE IN THE ANCESTRAL TEMPLE. There was a supplementary repetition of the sacrifices on the day succeeding the more solemn service (See the note on the name of Book IX. in the Shoo, Pt. IV.), at the close of which all who had acted as the representatives or personators of the Spirits on the preceding day were feasted, as they had not been at the feast with which it had been wound up. Choo says that the materials of the feast were the remains of the sacrifice of the day before, warmed up again. The 公尸, 'personators of the king's ancestors,' seem to make it plain enough that the previous sacrifice had been that in the ancestral temple, and so say both Maou and Choo. Ching K'ang-shing, however, led away by the language of what is regarded as the supplementary and unauthorized sentences in the Preface, would extend it to all other sacrifices as well; but the K'ang-he editors rightly condemn his view. Choo and the old interpreters agree generally in the interpretation of the stanzas, till they come to the last line, which Choo understands of the personators of the dead, and the others of the king who was feasting them, making it express the blessing which the Spirits would give him. Without saying that Choo's view is wrong, the imperial editors speak rather in favour of the other; but Choo's construction is the more natural, and I cannot see why it should be rejected.

Ll. 1, 2, in all the stanzas. 凫, 'the wild duck,'—as in I. vii. VIII. 1. The 鹥 cannot so readily be determined. Choo explains it by 鸥, 'gulls;' but the difficulty with me is the assigning the King, so far away from the sea, as if it

were the proper habitat of such birds. Maou calls it 凫属, 'a kind of wild duck;' so also Luk Tëen, who adds that 'the *hoo* is fond of diving, while the *e* prefers to float in the water, and hence one name of it is the *gow* (汓).' I am inclined to think therefore that the *e* may be the widgeon, of which it is an acknowledged peculiarity that it does not willingly dive. These birds are represented first as on the King,—upon which Yen Ts'an says, 'The Wei (渭), flowing eastwards, first receives the Fung (丰), and afterwards the King. The Fung enters the Wei from the south, and the King from the north-west. King Wăn resided in Fung, on the west of the river so named, so that it was necessary to cross it before reaching the King. King Woo resided in Haou on the east of the Fung, and was therefore not far from the King.' In consequence of the nearness of the capital to the King, the allusion is made of the birds upon that stream. The 'sands' in st. 2, and the 'islets' in st. 3, would be on its banks and in its channel. 潀 in st. 4 would be where some smaller river flowed into it (小水入大水曰潀); and 亹 (read *mun*) is a gorge, where the stream flows between its banks rising high, and narrowing the channel. In all these places the birds felt at home, and enjoyed themselves; and so the reference to them serves to introduce the parties feasted,—in a situation where they might relax from the gravity of the preceding day, and be happy.

L. 2. 宁 is understood of the quiet happiness of the mind (宁，以心之安言)；宜

尸燕饮。福禄来为。

三章
凫鹥在渚。公尸来燕来处。尔酒既湑。尔殽伊脯。公

尸燕饮。福禄来下。

四章
凫鹥在潨。公尸来燕来宗。既燕于宗。福禄攸降。公

尸燕饮。福禄来崇。

      Your spirits are abundant,
      Your viands are good;
      The personators of your ancestors feast and drink;—
      Happiness and dignity lend them their aids.

3   The wild ducks and widgeons are on the islets;
      The personators of your ancestors feast and enjoy themselves.
      Your spirits are strained,
      Your viands are in slices;
      The personators of your ancestors feast and drink;—
      Happiness and dignity descend on them.

4   The wild ducks and widgeons are where the waters meet;
      The personators of your ancestors feast, and are honoured.
      The feast is spread in the ancestral temple,
      The place where happiness and dignity descend.
      The personators of your ancestors feast and drink;—
      Their happiness and dignity are at the highest point.

= to be treated as they ought to be (宜者
称是燕也); 处 = 得其所安也,
'to find the place in which they could happily
rest;' 宗 = 尊, 'to be honoured;' 熏熏 =
和悦貌, 'the app. of harmony and pleasure;'
in which for the time they rested.
  Ll. 3, 4, in all the stt., are addressed to the
entertainer, i. e., in the present case, to the king,
praising him for the abundance and quality of
the provisions of the feast. 馨 = 'very fragrant (香之远闻);' 湑,—as in II i. V. 3;

伊脯 occasion some difficulty; but 伊 is
evidently = 既 in l. 3, nothing more than the
维 by which it is ordinarily defined. 脯
denotes long pieces of dried or preserved meat,
and why the writer should have described the
viands as consisting of them, I can conceive no
reason but that he wanted a rhyme. He goes
on to speak, in st. 4, of the feast as given in
the ancestral temple, the place of dignity and
honour (攸 = 所), and in st. 5, returns to the
spirits as 欣欣 or 'delicious.' 芬芬,—
as in II. vi. VI. 6.

五章

凫鹥在亹。公尸来止熏熏。旨酒欣欣。燔炙芬芬。公
尸燕饮。无有后艰。

5　The wild ducks and widgeons are in the gorge;
　　The personators of your ancestors rest, full of complacency.
　　Your fine spirits are delicious,
　　Your flesh, roast and broiled, is fragrant;
　　The personators of your ancestors feast and drink;—
　　No troubles shall be theirs after this.

V. *Këa loh.*

假乐

一章.

假乐君子。显显令德。宜民宜人。受禄于天。保右命
之。自天申之。

1　Of [our] admirable, amiable, sovereign
　　Most illustrious is the excellent virtue.
　　He orders rightly the people, orders rightly the officers,
　　And receives his dignity from heaven,
　　Which protects and helps him, and [confirms] his appointment,
　　By repeated acts of renewal from heaven.

Ll. 5, 6 belong to the guests, l. 6 telling, or auspicing the advantages accruing to them from being feasted by the king. 福禄, 'happiness and dignity or emolument,' are expressive of the honour so done to them. 成＝成就, 'to be complete;' or, as the 'Complete Digest' has it, 完全无缺；为 is taken in the sense of 助, 'to aid (福禄不来助其身乎);' 崇＝积而高大, 'accumulated so as to be high and large.'
I have said in the introductory note that l. 6 is referred by the old school to the person of the king. Thus Yen Ts'an expands it in st. 1 to 神以福禄来成汝, 'The Spirits will come and bestow in complete degree happiness and emolument on you;' meaning by the *you* king Ching. But l. 5 is in the 3d person, and there is no indication in the text that there is any change of person in l. 6.

The rhymes are—in st. 1, 泾, 宁, 清, 馨, 成, cat. 11: in 2, 沙, 宜 *, 多, 嘉, 为 *,

cat. 17: in 3, 渚, 处, 湑, 脯, 下 *, cat. 5, t. 2: in 4, 漤, 宗, 宗, 降, 崇, cat. 9: in 5, 亹 *, 熏, 欣, 芬, 艰 *, cat. 13.

Ode 5. Narrative. IN PRAISE OF SOME KING, WHOSE VIRTUE SECURED TO HIM THE FAVOUR OF HEAVEN; AUSPICING FOR HIM ALL HAPPINESS, AND ESPECIALLY A LINE OF DISTINGUISHED POSTERITY. PROBABLY, THE RESPONSE OF THE PERSONATORS OF THE DEPARTED TO THE PREVIOUS ODE. The Preface and the old school say that the king here is king Ching; but of this there is no evidence.

St. 1 is quoted in the 'Doctrine of the Mean,' XVII. 4, with 嘉 instead of 假, and so the passage appears twice in the Tso-chuen. We may conclude therefore that 嘉 is the proper reading; and L. 1＝我可嘉可乐之君子,—as in the translation, the king under whom the piece was composed being intended by 君子. L. 2 is taken as the key-note of

二章 干禄百福。子孙千亿。穆穆皇皇。宜君宜王。不愆不忘。率由旧章。

三章 威仪抑抑。德音秩秩。无怨无恶。率由群匹。受福无疆。四方之纲。

2 [So] does he seek for the emoluments of dignity, [and obtain] all blessings,—
Thousands and hundreds of thousands of descendants,
Of reverent virtue and admirable character,
Fit to be rulers [of States], fit to be king,
Erring in nothing, forgetful of nothing,
Observing and following the old statutes.

3 [May they] manifest all self-restraint in deportment,
And their virtuous fame be without fail!
Without resentments, without dislikes,
[May they] give free course to [the good among] the officers,
Receiving blessing without limit,
And regulating all within the four quarters [of the kingdom]!

the ode, the excellent virtue, so illustrious, being what secured the favour of Heaven. The evidence of the virtue appears in l. 3; 宜 is an active verb, meaning 'to order aright,' 'to do what is befitting in reference to;'—as in I. i. VI., II. i. IV. 8, *et al* When 民 and 人 are contrasted, as here, 人 denotes officers of the govt. (在位者). L. 4. 禄 is here the royal dignity, with all its emoluments. And this line is amplified in the two that succeed. Ch'ing, indeed, supposes that the king is the subject of these lines, and that they describe his dealing with his officers,—the 人 of l. 4, favouring them and giving them appointments; but his view has deservedly fallen into neglect. It is Heaven, no doubt, which is spoken of;—comp. st. 6 in i. II. In the 'Doctrine of the Mean,' we have 佑 for 右, showing that the meaning of the term is 'to aid.' 命 must mean 'to confirm the appointment,' which the king already enjoyed. 申 = 重, 'to repeat,' *i. e.* to renew the appointment so that it should go down from the king to his descendants.

St. 2. Choo says that ll. 1, 2 contain a wish that the king's descendants may be many, and ll. 3—6, a wish that they may be worthy. L. 1, —comp. i. V. 1. The meaning is that the way in which the king sought for his dignity, by the display of illustrious virtue, was such as to bring with it all other blessings (王者干禄而得百福；本上文令德受禄而言). I agree with Choo, after Ch'ing, in referring l. 3 and those that follow to the king's descendants, and not, with Yen Ts'an and others, to the king himself. 穆穆 is defined in the Urh-ya by 敬, 'to be reverent,' and 皇皇 by 美, 'to be admirable.' 宜 has a diff. meaning from that in st. 1, and here='fit to be.' 君 = 诸侯, 'princes of States.' The eldest son would always be king; the others would rule over States. 愆 = 过, 'to err.' 率由 = 循从, 'to observe and follow.' 'The old statutes' are the rules and laws of the ancient good kings.

St. 3 is also to be interpreted of the 子孙, or descendants of the king. L. 1. 抑抑,—as in II. vii. VI. 3. L. 2. 德音 is taken by Choo as in the translation,—a meaning of the phrase which we have often met with. Others, as Yen Ts'an, give 音 here the sense of 言语, 'words.' 秩秩,—as in I. xi. III. 3, *et al.*,= 有

四章

之纲之纪。燕及朋友。百辟卿士。媚于天子。不解于

位。民之攸墍。

4 Regulating all, and determining each point,
   Giving repose to his friends,
   All the princes and ministers
   Will love the son of Heaven.
   Not idly occupying his office,
   The people will find rest in him.

VI. *Kung Lëw.*

公刘

一章

笃公刘。匪居匪康。乃场乃疆。乃积乃仓。乃裹糇粮。

1 Of generous devotion to the people was duke Lëw.
   Unable to rest or take his ease [where he was],
   He divided and subdivided the country into fields;
   He stored up the produce in the fields and in barns;

序 有 常, 'orderly and permanent.' L 3 may be taken actively, as in the translation. So, Choo; but he says also that some understand it passively,—'without giving occasion for resentment or dislike.' L. 4. 匹 = 类, 'the fellows,' or 'compeers,' meaning the various officers who might be regarded as equally deserving. The meaning of 率 由 is not quite different from that of the same phrase in last st., but we cannot translate it in the same way. Ke Pun says, '率 由 旧 章 means—to imitate his ancestors; 率 由 群 匹 means—to honour the worthy.' L. 6. 纲,—as in i.IV.5.

St. 4 continues the good wishes for the king's descendants, and, principally, for the king of the time being among his descendants. L. 1. On 纲 纪 see i. IV. 5. I do not know well what account to give of the two 之. Possibly, the 之 纲 at the end of st. 3 may have suggested this order of the terms; but the more likely solution of the difficulty is that the line reads as it stands, instead of 纲 之 纪 之 , the writer wishing to get 纪 as a rhyme with 友, 士, and 子, below. L. 2. 燕 = 安, 'to give repose to.' 朋 友, 'friends,' is used for the ministers of the court, and members of the

royal family. As Choo expands ll. 1,2,—君 能 纲 纪 四 方, 而 臣 下 赖 之 以 安. Ll. 3, 4. By 百 辟 are intended the feudal princes (诸 侯), and by 卿 士, the high ministers of the court (群 臣). 媚,— 'to love;' as in i. VI. 1, *et al.* Ll. 5,6. 解 = 惰, 'to be idle.' 墍 = 息, 'to rest,' which meaning, we saw, is given to the term by many in I. iii. X. 6.

The rhymes are—in st. 1, 子, 德, cat. 1, t. 3; 人, 天. 命 *, 申, cat. 12, t. 1: in 2, 福 *, 亿, cat. 1, t. 3; 皇, 王, 忘, 章, cat. 10: in 3. 抑 *, 秩, 匹, cat. 12, t. 3: 疆, 纲, cat. 10: in 4, 纪, 友 *, 士, 子, cat. 1, t. 2; 位, 墍, cat. 15, t. 3.

Ode 6. Narrative. THE STORY OF DUKE LEW:—HOW HE MADE HIS FIRST SETTLEMENT IN PIN, BUILDING THERE, LAYING OUT THE GROUND, FORMING ARMIES, ARRANGING FOR A REVENUE, TILL PIN BECAME TOO SMALL FOR ALL HIS PEOPLE. I call this the story of duke Lëw, instead of legend, as in the case of How-tseih, because the events told in it are not of the same marvellous character. There probably is an element of history in those events; but, when we com-

于橐于囊。思辑用光。弓矢斯张。干戈戚扬。爰方
启行。

> He tied up dried meat and grain,
> In bottomless bags and in sacks;—
> That he might hold [the people] together, and glorify [his tribe].
> Then with bows and arrows all ready,
> With shields and spears, and axes, large and small,
> He commenced his march.

pare what is related here of his doings and of the growth of Pin with the intimations as to the condition of the settlement and the people in the time of T'an-foo, as we have them in ode III. of the first Book, it is evident that what we have here are mainly pictures of fancy, and not the relations of history. Who shall gather out the grains of ore from the rubbish in which they are imbedded? The composition of the ode is ascribed in the Preface to duke K'ang of Shaou,—the famous Shih of the Shoo (see on V. xii., *et al.*). He made it, we are told, for king Ching, when he was about to undertake the duties of the govt., to admonish the young monarch, and remind him of the devotion to the people, and to the business of the people, which characterized his great ancestor.

St. 1. L. 1. 公 ='duke;' 刘 is the name. I suppose that the title precedes the other term, because *that* is the name and not the honorary epithet. The case is analogous to that of 古公亶父, 'the ancient duke, T'an-foo.' Lëw was not a duke, but his descendants honoured him as such, the title of king not being carried up by the duke of Chow beyond the grandfather of Wăn. I have translated 篤 by 'of generous devotion to the people,' that being the meaning given to the term here by all the critics. In itself, it = 厚, 'generous,' 'magnanimous,' 'of large heart and mind.' Very early it was applied to Lëw;—see the Shoo, V. iii. 5.

The whole stanza is descriptive of the commencement of Lëw's migration into the territory of Pin. But where did he migrate from? Acc. to Maou, he was living previously in T'ae, the principality with which How-tseih, as we saw on I. 5, was invested by Yaou; and was driven out of it in a time when the rule of Hëa was in great disorder. This is contrary, however, to the generally received view, which I have given on the title of Book I., Pt. I. According to that, Puh-chueh, the grandfather of Lëw, was obliged to fly from the Hëa or Middle Kingdom of that time altogether, and take refuge among the wild tribes of the north and west. Puh-chueh again is said to have been the son of How-tseih, so that Lëw was his great-grandson. This could not be, if the standard chronology is anything

nearly correct in fixing the settlement of Pin in B.C. 1,796. It places K'e's investiture with T'ae in B.C. 2,276, so that from him to his great-grandson, a period of 480 years elapsed, during which there had been the reigns of Shun, and of Yu and 16 of his descendants, besides an interregnum of 40 years. I must believe—if belief at all can be spoken of in such a case—that one of K'e's descendants had taken refuge among the uncivilized people in the west, not far from Pin, and that Lëw, one of *his* descendants again, came forth from among them, moving in the direction of the east, towards the end of the Hëa dynasty.

L. 2,= 不敢宁居, 'He did not dare to dwell at ease.' It thus appears that Lëw did not change his place in consequence of any pressure from without, as T'an-foo did subsequently. It appears further, that wherever he was previously, whether in T'ae, or among some tribe of the west, he was himself a considerable chief, who had advanced from the nomadic to the agricultural condition. His movement was the result, probably, of a restless and ambitious disposition, which required a larger sphere, and in which a principle of benevolence held sway. L. 3. Here and below, 乃 (= 迺) is used as in i. I. iii. 4. We can hardly translate it, but it =our 'and so.' 场 and 疆,—as in II. vi. VI. 3, 4; only the terms have here the force of verbs.

L. 4 积 (read *tsze*) and 仓 are in the same way used as verbs, the former term denoting stacks in the open air. L. 5. 糇 ='flesh dried,' and 粮 ='grain prepared for use.' L. 6. The terms here are translated after the definitions of Choo. Maou makes the difference between the two articles to be simply that the *t'oh* is 'small,' and the *nang* 'large.' Ho K'ëae says the grain was carried in the *nang*, and the other provisions in the *t'oh* fastened round the waist. For l. 7, Choo gives 思以辑和其民人,而显光其国家, 'thinking hereby to keep together in harmony his people and officers, and to distinguish his State and its clans.' But such terms are too magniloquent for Lëw and his circumstances. Evidently, 思

二章
笃公刘。于胥斯原。既庶既繁。既顺乃宣。而无永
叹。陟则在巘。复降在原。何以舟之。维玉及瑶。鞞
琫容刀。

2   Of generous devotion to the people was duke Lëw.
He had surveyed the plain [where he was settled];
[The people] were numerous and crowded;
In sympathy with them, he made proclamation [of his con-
    templated measure],
And there were no perpetual sighings about it.
He ascended to the hill-tops;
He descended again to the plains.
What was it that he carried at his girdle?
Pieces of jade, and *yaou* gems,
And his ornamented scabbard with its sword.

and 用 are no more than our 'to' of the in-
finitive mood. L. 8. See on II. vii. VI. 1. It is
still more plain here that 张 has the sense of
'being prepared,' 'being made ready.' L. 9. 戚
= 斧, 'an axe,' *i. e.*, in the connection, 'a battle
axe;' 扬 = 钺, a weapon of the same description, but larger. L. 9. 爰 = 于 是, 'hereon.'
方 = 始 'to begin.' 启 行, — 'to commence
the march.'
    St. 2 is generally taken as descriptive of the
state of things on the arrival in Pin; but it has
been felt that ll. 3 and 4 were hardly predicable
of the numbers and condition of the people at
first, nor, indeed, consistent with the progress
of the settlement as described in the stanzas
below.   I agree therefore with Këang Ping-
chang in referring this stanza to the state of
things in the earlier site, when Lëw had determined on the removal (上 文 言 可 以 启
行，而 所 以 必 迁 之 故，尚 未 说
出，故 此 章 补 叙 之).
    L. 2. 于 is the particle. 胥 = 相, 'to
look at,' 'to survey.' It is necessary to give 胥
this meaning here, though it is not found in the
dictionary. 斯 原, 'this plain,' as if the 斯
were used in opposition to the 彼 in the next
st.,—the old site which the writer has now immediately in view, in distinction from the new
one. L. 3. 庶 and 繁 are synonyms, signi-

fying the number of the inhabitants. L. 4. The
乃 after 既 indicates that the action of the
second verb was a consequence of what is stated
by the first.   The meaning of 顺 and 宣
given in the translation is adapted to the view
of the whole stanza which I have adopted
from Këang Ping-chang. He expands the
line:—于 是 顺 民 之 情, 宣 布
迁 国 之 令. L. 5. There was of course
some dissatisfaction among the people, because
of the trouble of removal; but it did not last
long. Ll. 6—10 refer to the labours of Lëw in
going over his old territory, before determining
on the migration, to see if he could in any way
escape the necessity of such a movement. Why
he marched about in the style described, and
why his doing so should be mentioned particularly, it is difficult to say. The critics imagine
it was to show how he disliked the mean and
rude dress of the wild people around them;—
we may rather suppose that it was to attract and
please his people by the display. Ll. 6, 7. 'He
ascended and was on the hill-tops; he descended
and again was in the plains.' I cannot conceive
where Lacharme found any authority for his
version of these lines:—*Montes ascendit, nec
deerant qui montium verticem incolerent; in valles
descendit, ubi erant incolæ.* 巘 = 山 顶, 'hill-
tops.' Luh Tih-ming says that some copies
read 甗, and the word is accordingly defined
in the dict. as 'a hill like a boiler;' *i. e.*, accord-

三章

笃公刘。逝彼百泉。瞻彼溥原。乃陟南冈。乃觏于

京。京师之野。于时处处。于时庐旅。于时言言。于

时语语。

3   Of generous devotion to the people was duke Lëw.
     He went there to [the place of] the hundred springs,
     And saw [around him] the wide plain.
     He ascended the ridge on the south,
     And looked at a large [level] height,
     A height affording space for multitudes.
     Here was room to dwell in;
     Here might booths be built for strangers;
     Here he told out his mind;
     Here he entered on deliberations.

ing to Ying-tah, 'large above and small below.' This I do not understand. L. 8. 舟 is used in the sense of 带, 'to carry at the girdle.' L. 9. 瑶,—as in I. v. X. 2. L. 10. 鞞琫,—see on II. vi. IX. 2. I can only take 容刀 as='containing the sword.' The more common view is that the characters=容饰之刀, 'the ornamented sword;' but Choo also gives the other construction (谓鞞琫之中, 容此刀耳).

St. 3 shows us duke Lëw now, certainly, in Pin, selecting the site, we can hardly say for his capital, but where he fixed his own head-quarters as the chief of his tribe. Ll. 2, 3. Where the 'hundred springs' were has not been determined. Some refer them, I think correctly, to the pres. dis. of San-shwuy (三水) in Pin Chow. Too Yëw (杜佑; of the T'ang dyn.) thought the name remained in the district of Pih-ts'euen of the T'ang dyn.; but that would carry us away from Pin altogether to the dep. of Ping-lëang (平凉), in Kan-suh. 溥=大, 'large.'—Here were two requisites for forming a settlement;—a large plain, and plenty of water. Ll. 4—6. 觏=见, 'to see.' 京 in l. 5 must evidently have the force of a substantive, and therefore Choo explains it by 高邱, 'a lofty height.' The first meaning of the term given in the dict. is 大, 'great;' the second is from the Urh-ya,—'the very highest mound or hill.' A hill would in those days be the most

suitable place for a chief to take up his residence on. L. 6 is difficult. Choo says on 京师,—高邱而众居, 'a high hill, where all could dwell.' But what can we make of the 野, which gives us the idea of a tract of comparatively level and uncultivated country? 京师 came afterwards to have the significance of 'a capital city, the residence of the son of Heaven;' but that meaning of the terms was given us from this line, and we cannot here translate—'the country about the capital.' I can only take the line as in apposition with 京 in l. 5, and suppose that it means—'a height which also afforded room for multitudes.'—The author of the 'Essence and Flower of the She' takes 京 as merely another name for the great plain of l. 3, and supports his view by the application to it of 野; but in this way there is no advance in the narrative. Ll. 7—10. 时 = 是; 于时,'—here.' 处处='he built places to dwell in,' i. e., for himself and his people; 庐旅 = 'he made booths or huts for strangers,' i. e., for people of other tribes who came to join them (旅 = 宾旅). In illustration of this, Këang adduces a statement of Maou, that 'when Lëw removed to Pin, eighteen States followed him!' 言 and 语 are distinguished as in the translation (直言曰言, 论难曰语).

四章

笃公刘。于京斯依。跄跄济济。俾筵俾几。既登乃

依。乃造其曹。执豕于牢。酌之用匏。食之饮之。君

之宗之。

五章

笃公刘。既溥既长。既景乃冈。相其阴阳。观其流

4　Of generous devotion to the people was duke Lëw.
When he had found rest on the height,
With his officers all in dignified order,
He caused mats to be spread, with stools upon them;
And they took their places on the mats and leaned on the stools.
He had sent to the herds,
And taken a pig from the pen.
He poured out his spirits into calabashes;
And so he gave them to eat and to drink,
Acknowledged by them as ruler, and honoured.

5　Of generous devotion to the people was duke Lëw.
[His territory] being now broad and long,
He determined the points of the heavens by means of the
shadows; and then, ascending the ridges,

In st. 4 we have an account of the feast given by Lëw when he took possession of his quarters on the chosen site. L. 2 is to be taken of Lëw as now resting (依＝安) on the height. The 斯 has the force of the descriptive 其. L. 2 is taken of his officers or principal men presenting themselves to him in formal and dignified manner (群臣有威仪貌);—see II.vi.V. 2. L. 4,—see on II. 1. L. 5. 登＝登筵, 'to go up upon the mats;' 依＝依几, 'to lean upon the stools.' In this line the force of 乃 after 既 is very clear. L. 6. 造＝就, 'to go to.' This does not imply that Lëw had gone himself for the pig, any more than the 俾 in 4 implies that he himself had placed the mats and stools. We must translate 造 in the past complete tense. Maou defines 曹 by 群, 'herds;' Choo, better, by 群牧之处, 'the place of the shepherds.' It is strange that Williams does not give this meaning of the term. L. 7. 牢,—'an enclosure for feeding cattle.' L. 8＝用匏为爵, 'they used calabashes for cups.' L. 10, upon the analogy of l. 9, would indicate something that Lëw did for his guests, as if he had assumed to them all the relation of ruler, and then divided them into clans, with individuals among them to be their Heads. But we cannot suppose him to have entered, at such a feast as is described, on such important matters; nor was the tribe in a sufficiently advanced state for them. I must suppose therefore that the guests are the subjects of 君 and 宗. So Ch'ing Heuen (群臣从, 而君之尊之).

St. 5 shows us the duke laying out his territory for permanent occupation and cultivation, making provision for a revenue, and some other arrangements. L. 2. 溥 indicates the extent from east to west; 长, the extent from north to south. L. 3. 景 (ying),—'a shadow;' here used as a verb, meaning 'to examine the shadows made by the sun.' The object of this operation was to determine exactly the four cardinal points (考日景以正四方). L. 4.

泉。其军三单。度其隰原。彻田为粮。度其夕阳。幽

居允荒。

六章
笃公刘。于豳斯馆。涉渭为乱取厉取锻。止基乃理。

He surveyed the light and the shade,
Viewing [also] the [course of the] streams and springs.
His armies were three troops;
He measured the marshes and plains;
He fixed the revenue on the system of common cultivation of
the fields;
He measured also the fields west of the hills;
And the settlement of Pin became truly great.

6   Of generous devotion to the people was duke Lëw.
Having settled in temporary lodging houses in Pin,
He crossed the Wei by means of boats,
And gathered whetstones and iron.
When his settlement was fixed, and all boundaries defined,

阴阳,—'the dark and the bright;' meaning, probably, the lie of the country with reference to the hills. Ying-tah says, 'The country south of a hill is *yang*; that north of it is *yin*. But by broad valleys and large streams the climate differs as hot and cold, and the fields are adapted for the cultivation of different things; and therefore he made that survey.' Lacharme has endeavoured to put most of this into his translation:—'*monticulum conscendit, unde in subjectas terras patebat aspectus, quas vidit alias calori solis apricas, alias calori solis minus pervias.*' L. 5. The object of this inspection was, it is supposed, to determine how the fields should be laid out,—in what direction they should be made to lie. Choo says that he does not understand l. 6, and makes no reference to any attempts of others to explain it, showing that he considered them all to be unsatisfactory. So, indeed, they are. Eminently absurd is Maou's view that the line is descriptive of the march to Pin in three bodies, the women and children inside, guarded by the armed men against any surprise or attack. This would belong to stanza 1. I cannot understand why any mention at all should be made of armies here. Ll.7,8 go together, the measuring of the wet grounds and the plains being preparatory to the laying out of the ground. 彻田;—see Mencius, III. Pt. i. III. 6—13. The words mean to assign the fields on the principle of common (彻) labour. Choo says here, 'The fields forming a *tsing* (一井) amounted to 900 acres

(亩); and each of 8 families had 100 acres for itself, leaving 100 acres for the govt., which were cultivated by the 8 families in common.' The Chow system of cultivating the govt. fields by common labour took its rise from this, and the duke of Chow did no more than fully develope the system. 粮 is used in the sense of 'taxes paid in kind.' L. 9. All the critics explain 夕阳, after Maou, by 山西, 'the country lying west of a hill.' Of course this would receive the rays of the sun in the evening, while that on the east of the hill would be in the shade. Lëw, it is supposed, turned his attention to the land on the west of the hills of Pin, to find room for the increasing numbers of his people. L. 10. 允=信, 'truly;' —as often. 荒=大, 'great.'

St. 6 treats of the increase of the people and their territory. L. 2 seems to have reference to the first arrival in the district, when Lëw made temporary lodging homes for himself and his followers (始来未定居之时). Këang, however, will have it that the line has reference to the provision made for fresh arrivals. L.3.—'He crossed the Wei, making a ferry.' 乱 is used in this sense in the Shoo, III. i. Pt. i. 70. L. 4 厉 (now written with 石 at the side) = 砥, 'a whetstone;' 锻 = 铁,

爰众爰有。夹其皇涧。溯其过涧。止旅乃密。芮鞫之即。

The people became numerous and prosperous,
Occupying both sides of the Hwang valley,
And pushing on up that of Kwo;
And as the population became dense,
They went on to the country beyond the Juy.

VII. *Hëung choh.*

泂酌

一章

泂酌彼行潦。挹彼注兹。可以餴饎。岂弟君子。民之

父母。

1　Take the pool-water from a distance;
　Draw it into one vessel and let it flow to another,
　And it may be used to steam rice or millet.
　[How much more should] the happy and courteous sovereign
　Be the parent of the people!

'iron.' These two things are found, it is said, abundantly in the hills south of the Wei. They would want them in Pin for building their houses (if they did build any), and for their implements of agriculture. Ll. 5, 6. 止 = 居, 'their dwellings;' 基 = 定, 'to be settled;' 理,—as in i. III. 4 (既 止 居 于 此, 乃 疆 理 其 田 野). 众 and 有 express the increase in the number of the people and in their resources. Ll. 7, 8. 涧,—'a stream in a valley;' here = a valley. 皇 and 过 are the names of two valleys. 夹, 'to squeeze,' gives us the idea of their occupying the two sides of the valley of Hwang, and 溯, that of their pushing up that of Kwo, beginning at its mouth. Ll. 9, 10. 旅, here = 众, 'all,' 'multitudes;' different from the meaning of the term in st. 3. 止 旅 乃 密 = 所 止 之 众, 乃 日 益 密。 芮 (or with 水 at the side) is the name of a stream, rising on the north-west of mount Woo (吴 山), and flowing east till it joins the King. 鞫 = 水 外, 'the country beyond a river.' 即 = 就, 'to go to.' The term stands at the end for the sake of the rhyme. The line, as ex-

panded by Choo, is—乃 复 即 芮 鞫 而 居 之.

The rhymes are—in st. 1. 康, 疆, 仓, 粮, 囊, 光, 张, 扬, 行 *, cat. 10: in 2, 原, 繁 *, 宣, 叹, 巘, 原, cat. 14; 舟 (prop. cat. 3), 瑶, 刀, cat. 2: in 3, 泉, 原, cat. 14; 冈, 京 *, cat. 10; 野 *, 处, 旅, 语, cat. 5, t. 2: in 4, 依, 济, 几, 依, cat. 15, t. 2; 曹 *, 牢 *, 匏 *, cat. 3, t. 1; 饮, (prop. cat. 7), 宗, cat. 9: in 5, 长, 冈, 阳, cat. 10; 泉, 单, 原, cat. 14; 粮, 阳, 荒, cat. 10: in 6, 馆, 乱, 锻, cat. 14; 理, 有 *, cat. 1, t. 2; 泂, 涧, cat. 14; 密, 即 *, cat. 12, t. 3.

Ode 7. Allusive. THE MOST UNLIKELY THINGS MAY BY HUMAN INGENUITY BE MADE USEFUL; HOW MUCH MORE SHOULD A SOVEREIGN FULFILL THE DUTIES OF HIS POSITION. This piece, like the last, and also the one that follows, are attributed to the duke of Shaou, as made by him for the admonition of king Ching.

Ll. 1—3, in all the stanzas. 行 潦,—as in I. ii. IV. 1. Both Maou and Choo define the terms by 流 潦; but they only mean by that

二章

洞酌彼行潦。挹彼注兹。可以濯罍。岂弟君子。民之

攸归。

三章

洞酌彼行潦。挹彼注兹。可以濯溉。岂弟君子。民之

攸塈。

2   Take the pool-water from a distance;
     Draw it into one vessel and let it flow to another,
     And it may be used to wash a [spirit-] vase.
     [How much more should] the happy and courteous sovereign
     Be the centre of attraction to the people!

3   Take the pool-water from a distance;
     Draw it into one vessel and let it flow to another,
     And it may be used for all purposes of cleansing.
     [How much more should] the happy and courteous sovereign
     Be the centre of rest to the people!

expression the rain which has *flowed into* pools on the road (道 上 雨 水 流 聚)。 酌 and 挹 have here the same meaning—'to lade out,' as the 'Amplification of the Meaning of the She (诗 经 衍 义)' says, 酌 与 挹 无 二 意, 盖 挹 即 酌 也, *i.e.*, the lading out (挹) and the pouring out (酌) indicate here the same thing. In this way l. 2 is an amplification and explanation of l. 1. 洞＝远, 'distant,' 'from a distance.' I do not see what this specification of the pools as at a distance adds to the meaning. By 彼 and 兹, 'that and this,' we are to understand two vessels, which perform the part of filters. I have seen such an arrangement often in Chinese houses. 注 ＝'so as to flow into (＝引).' Medhurst says, '挹 注,—'to transfer liquids from one vessel to another.' 馈 is 'to steam rice;' specially indicating, acc. to the critics, one point in the operation,—the throwing in a fresh quantity of water, when the first has all been steamed off. 馏 is 'to steam millet.' This signification is given in the dictionary (炊 黍 稷 曰 馏); and it gives a much better and simpler meaning than that of 酒 食, to which this passage is referred. 濯 罍,—'to wash a jar;' see on I.

i. III. 2, II. v. VIII. 3. 濯 溉,—'to wash and cleanse.' I do not see that we are to find in l. 3 any reference to sacrifices,—with many of the critics. The terms are quite general. Pool-water purified may be used in sacrifice as for other purposes. That is all we can say.

Ll. 4, 5. By 君子 is intended the 'sovereign' generally. There is a lesson in the ode for Ching, but he is not specially intended by the phrase. 岂 弟,—as in I. v., *et al.* The lines of st. 1 are quoted in the Le Ke, XXIX. 28, and enlarged on as if by Confucius, with rather a different meaning; but we there read 凯 弟, and the former term indicates, it is said, the sovereign's efforts to teach the people, and the latter, the satisfaction and repose which he gives them (凯 以 强 教 之, 弟 以 说 安 之). I prefer to keep to the usual meaning of the terms in the She. 攸 归,—'he to whom the people turn,' around whom they collect. 攸 塈,—'he in whom the people rest;' 塈,—as in V. 4.

     The rhymes are—in st. 1, 馏, 子, 母*, cat. 1, t. 2: in 2, 罍, 归, cat. 15, t. 1: in 3, 溉*, 塈, *ib.*, t. 3. The 兹 and the 子, in the difft. stanzas may be considered to rhyme with themselves.

VIII.   *K'euen o.*

卷阿

一章.

有卷者阿。飘风自南。岂弟君子。来游来歌。以矢

其音。

二章.

伴奂尔游矣。优游尔休矣。岂弟君子。俾尔弥尔性。

1   Into the recesses of the large mound
    Came the wind whirling from the south.
    There was [our] happy, courteous sovereign,
    Rambling and singing;
    And I took occasion to give forth my notes.

2   'Full of spirits you ramble;
    Full of satisfaction you rest.
    O happy and courteous sovereign,

Ode. 8.   Narrative, with allusive portions. ADDRESSED BY THE DUKE OF SHAOU TO KING CHING, DESIRING FOR HIM LONG PROSPERITY, AND CONGRATULATING HIM, IN ORDER TO ADMONISH HIM, ON THE HAPPINESS OF HIS PEOPLE, AND THE NUMBER OF HIS ADMIRABLE OFFICERS. Choo agrees with Maou and his school in accepting the statement of the Preface, which assigns the ode, like the two that precede, to the duke of Shaou, for the admonition of king Ching; but there his agreement with them ends. To myself the admonitory element in the piece is very doubtful; and I see only the complacency of an old statesman in his young sovereign, his joy in his prosperity, and his auspice of, and wishes for, its continuance. The diff't. views of the schools will appear in the notes.

St. 1. 阿,—as in II. iii. II. 1. 卷＝曲, 'a bend,' or recess in the hill. 者,—as in II. v. VIII. 1, *et al.* 飘风 is here merely 'a whirling wind,' not 'a whirlwind.' Its coming from the south indicates its genial nature. L. 3,—as in the prec. ode; and 君子 referring to the king. 来＝是,—as in Ode IV., *et al.* In l. 5, the writer, *i.e.*, the duke of Shaou, speaks of himself. 矢＝陈, 'to set forth.' The term, we have seen, is used of the marshalling of troops; here it is applied to the giving out or utterance of the notes of a song (陈 出 其 声音). The 以,—'and thereupon;'—'I take the opportunity.' The duke, we are to suppose, was walking with the king on some breezy height, and entering into the spirit of the young monarch's delight, he responded to his song with one of his own. On this view the stanza is narrative. Maou took the first two

lines as allusive, and l. 3, as referring not to the king, but to superior men, the 吉 士 of st. 7. The indented mound, with its recesses penetrated by the south wind, appeared to him to introduce the king attended by his officers, communicating their lessons to him in songs. Ch'ing again took ll. 1,2, as metaphorical, intimating that as the indented mound welcomed the genial wind into its recesses, so should the king by humility and courtesy encourage the resort to himself of officers able to give him good counsel and effective assistance to his government. Leu Tsook'een thinks we cannot get at the full meaning of the stanza, till we recognize in it all the three elements,—narrative, allusive, and metaphorical! There can be no doubt it is simply narrative. I cannot understand how Këang Ping-chang, accepting Choo's view of it, as 'not to be changed,' should yet hesitate at his interpreting l. 3 of the king.

St. 2. 伴奂 and 优游 must be synonymous, or nearly so. Choo explains them together by 闲暇, 'at ease and leisure.' Maou explains the first two terms by 广 大, 有 文 章, 'wide, large, and elegant.' I have followed the definitions of Tsow Ts'euen (邹泉 ; Ming dyn.):— 有精神舒展 之意, 有启居自适之意. Ll 4,5. There is a difficulty, on Choo's view, to find a subject for 俾; but it is not, to my mind, nearly so great as that in referring 尔 to the king, and l. 3 away from him. The simplest way is to look on the term as expressive of a wish in the duke's mind, without any very definite object:—'May it be given to you to'.........

似先公酉矣。

三章
尔土宇昄章。亦孔之厚矣。岂弟君子。俾尔弥尔性。

百神尔主矣。

四章
尔受命长矣。茀禄尔康矣。岂弟君子。俾尔弥尔性。

纯嘏尔常矣。

> May you fulfill your years,
> And end them like your ancestors!

3 'Your territory is great and glorious,
   And perfectly secure.
   O happy and courteous sovereign,
   May you fulfill your years,
   As the host of all the Spirits!

4 'You have received the appointment long-acknowledged,
   With peace around your happiness and dignity.
   O happy and courteous sovereign,
   May you fulfill your years,
   With pure happiness your constant possession!

This is the view of Yaou Shun-muh (姚 舜 牧; Ming dyn.):—天 保 三 俾 尔, 是 天 赋 畀, 此 三 俾 尔, 是 人 所 注 望, 皆 忠 臣 望 君 之 辞, 'In the T'een-paou (II.i.VI.) 俾 尔 occurs thrice, with reference to Heaven as the Giver; here we have the same characters also occurring thrice, as expressive of human expectation:—both the desire of a faithful minister for his sovereign.' 弥=终, 'to complete,' 'to fulfill.' Both Maou and Choo take 性 in the sense of 命, 'the appointed time,' or 'life.' Others will have it to mean the whole of the nature, as formed for virtue. 先 公,—'the former dukes;' but evidently all the king's ancestors, both the early dukes and the later kings, are intended. 酉=终, 'end.' They had a good and famous end. Such might the king have! St. 3. 土 宇 = 'the country and all in it,' —lit., the country with its roofs or shelter.

昄 章 = 大 明,—as in the translation. Some would read 版 for 昄, and 版 章 would mean 'population tablets, or lists;' but it was hardly worth Choo's while to mention this view. In l.2, 亦 and 之 are both expletives. L. 4 = 百 神 以 尔 为 主, 'all the Spirits regarding you as their host.' Ying-tah says, 'He who possesses all under the sky sacrifices to all the Spirits, and thus the son of Heaven is, indeed, the host of them all.'

St. 4. 长 in st. 1 describes the appointment of Heaven to the sovereignty of the kingdom 'as long vested in the princes of Chow. 茀, and 嘏 in l.5, both = 福, 'happiness.' The throne had come to Ching with abounding tranquillity (康 = 大 平 无 事); and the speaker wishes in l.5 that he might always possess it in the same condition (常 享 此 太 平 之 茀 禄).

五章

有冯有翼。有孝有德。以引以翼。岂弟君子。四方

为则。

六章

颙颙卬卬。如圭如璋。令闻令望。岂弟君子。四方

为纲。

七章

凤凰于飞。翙翙其羽。亦集爰止。蔼蔼王多吉士。

维君子使。媚于天子。

5 'You have helpers and supporters,
　Men of filial piety and of virtue,
　To lead you on, and act as wings to you,
　[So that], O happy and courteous sovereign,
　You are a pattern to the four quarters [of the kingdom].

6 'Full of dignity and majesty [are they],
　Like a jade-mace [in its purity],
　The subject of praise, the contemplation of hope.
　O happy and courteous sovereign,
　[Through them] the four quarters [of the kingdom] are guided
　　by you.

7 'The male and female phœnix fly about,
　Their wings rustling,
　While they settle in their proper resting place.
　Many are your admirable officers, O king,
　Ready to be employed by you,
　Loving you, the son of Heaven.

St. 5. Choo says that from this stanza to the end, the piece sets forth how the happiness spoken of thus far was to be realized,—by means of wise and loyal counsellors. I do not see, however, so much of admonition as of congratulation in the verses. Ll. 1, 2 give the attributes of the king's 'admirable officers.' 冯＝恃, or 依, 'to rely' or 'lean upon;' 有冯＝有可为依者, 'there are those who may serve to you for reliance.' Similarly 有翼, 有德, 有孝 are to be construed. The 以 in l. 3 = 'fitted thereby to.'…. L. 5 = 四方以为则, 'the four quarters take you as their pattern.'

St. 6. Choo and the critics of his school understand ll. 1—3 of the king,—what he was through the aid of the advisers referred to in the prec. stanza. It seems to me better to take them still of those advisers. L. 1 speaks of their majestic appearance (体貌尊严); l. 2, of the purity of their virtue (德性纯洁); l. 3, of the general appreciation of them. L. 5 = 四方以为纲, 'the four quarters take you as their stay and regulator.' 纲,— see on i. IV. 5, et al.

Stt. 7, 8. 凤凰,—as in the Shco, II. iv. 9. 翙翙 are intended to give the sound of their wings. 亦集爰止＝集于其所

八章

凤凰于飞。翔翔其羽。亦傅于天。蔼蔼王多吉人。维

君子命。媚于庶人。

九章

凤凰鸣矣。于彼高冈。梧桐生矣。于彼朝阳。菶菶萋

萋。雝雝喈喈。

十章

君子之车。既庶且多。君子之马。既闲且驰。矢诗不

8　'The male and female phœnix fly about,
　　Their wings rustling,
　　As they soar up to heaven.
　　Many are your admirable officers, O king,
　　Waiting for your commands,
　　And loving the multitudes of the people.

9　'The male and female phœnix give out their notes,
　　On that lofty ridge.
　　The dryandras grow,
　　On those eastern slopes.
　　They grow luxuriantly;
　　And harmoniously the notes resound.

10　'Your carriages, O sovereign,
　　Are many, many.

止,—as in the translation. 傅,—as in II. vii. X. 3. Ll. 1—3 are supposed to be allusive, serving to introduce the officers spoken of in 4—6. Of course it was all imagination about such fabulous birds making their appearance. Ll. 4—6. 蔼蔼 is explained by 众多, 'many.' 君子, 王, 天子 all, evidently, refer to the king. I do not see how, with 君子 thus used here, it can be taken differently elsewhere in the piece. 吉人＝吉士, 人 taking the place of 士 merely for the sake of the rhyme. Compare 吉士 in I. ii. XII. 1, though the phrase is used there with a very different application. 媚＝爱, 'to love.' We have met with the character in this signification repeatedly. 维君子使 (or 命)＝维君子之所使 (所命).

St. 9 is metaphorical of the prosperity of the kingdom, or allusive, if we take it in connection with the next st. Choo Shen (朱善) says that l. 1 is metaphorical of the abundance of men of virtue and talents; l. 2, of the court; l. 3, of the worthy sovereign; and l. 4, of the brilliant time. The woo-t'ung is the dryandra cordifolia, of which various wonders are related. See Medhurst's dictionary on 桐. The phœnix, it is said, will rest only on this tree. 朝阳 is the opposite of 夕阳 in VI. 5. The east catches the 'morning' beams and is then bright; the west is bright 'in the evening' with the light of the setting sun. L. 5 describes the luxuriant growth of the dryandras, and l. 6 the notes of the phœnixes.

St. 10. 闲＝闲习, 'trained and exercised;' 驰 must have the significancy of 'fleet.' 矢

多。维以遂歌。

Your horses, O sovereign,
Are well trained and fleet.
I have made my few verses,
In prolongation of your song.'

IX. *Min laou.*

民劳

一章
民亦劳止。汔可小康。惠此中国。以绥四方。无纵诡

随。以谨无良。式遏寇虐。憯不畏明。柔远能迩。以

定我王。

1 The people indeed are heavily burdened,
But perhaps a little ease may be got for them.
Let us cherish this centre of the kingdom,
To secure the repose of the four quarters of it.
Let us give no indulgence to the wily and obsequious,
In order to make the unconscientious careful,
And to repress robbers and oppressors,
Who have no fear of the clear will [of Heaven].
Then let us show kindness to those who are distant,
And help those who are near;—
Thus establishing [the throne of] our king.

as in st. 1. 遂＝继, 'to continue.' We have 赓 歌 with the same meaning in the Shoo, II. iv. 11.

The rhymes are—in st. 1, 阿, 歌, cat. 17; 南*, 音, cat. 7, t. 1: in 2, 游, 休, 酋, cat. 3, t. 1: in 3, 厚, 主*, cat. 4, t. 2: in 4, 长, 康, 常, cat. 10: in 5, 翼, 德, 翼, 则, cat. 1, t. 3: in 6, 印, 章, 望, 纲, cat. 10: in 7, 止, 士, 使, 子, cat. 1, t. 2: in 8, 天, 人, 命*, 人, cat. 12, t. 1: in 9, 鸣, 生, cat. 11; 冈, 阳, cat. 10; 萋, 喈, cat. 15, t. 1: in 10, 车*, 马*, cat. 5 (?); 多, 驰*, 多, 歌, cat. 17.

Ode. 9. Narrative. IN A TIME OF DISORDER AND SUFFERING, SOME OFFICER OF DISTINCTION CALLS UPON HIS FELLOWS TO JOIN WITH HIM TO EFFECT A REFORMATION IN THE CAPITAL, AND PUT AWAY THE PARTIES, ESPECIALLY FLATTERING PARASITES, WHO WERE THE CAUSE OF THE PREVAILING MISERY. The Preface assigns the composition of the piece to duke Muh of Shaou, (召穆公), a descendant of duke K'ang, to whom the three preceding odes are ascribed. It further says that he made it to reprehend king Le (刺厉王),—to whose time also are assigned the next ode and the first five of the 3d Book. This then is the first of the 'Major Odes of the Kingdom, Degenerate (变大雅).' Choo agrees with the Preface as to the date of the piece; but he says that it cannot be said to have been addressed directly to the king. Evi-

二章
民亦劳止。汔可小休。惠此中国。以为民逑。无纵诡
随。以谨惛恢。式遏寇虐。无俾民忧。无弃尔劳。以
为王休。

三章
民亦劳止。汔可小息。惠此京师。以绥四国。无纵诡
随。以谨罔极。式遏寇虐。无俾作慝。敬慎威仪。以

2 The people indeed are heavily burdened,
But perhaps a little rest may be got for them.
Let us cherish this centre of the kingdom,
And make it a gathering-place for the people.
Let us give no indulgence to the wily and obsequious,
In order to make the noisy braggarts careful,
And to repress robbers and oppressors;—
So the people shall not have such sorrow.
Do not cast away your [former] service,
But secure the quiet of the king.

3 The people indeed are heavily burdened,
But perhaps a little relief may be got for them.
Let us cherish this capital,
To secure the repose of the States in the four quarters.
Let us give no indulgence to the wily and obsequious,
To make careful those who set no limit to themselves,
And to repress robbers and oppressors,
Not allowing them to act out their evil.

dently it was written by a minister for one or more of his associates; and the reprehending of the king is an idea needlessly tacked on to it.

Ll. 1, 2, in all the stt. Perhaps 亦, as well as 止, should be treated as a mere expletive; I have ventured to translate 亦 by 'indeed,' on the authority of Këang, who says that it is here =甚. 劳=劳弊, 'wearied and worn out.' 汔 is defined by 几, 危, 近, and 期 giving us the ideas of 'perhaps,' 'nearly' with the faint intimation of a wish or half-hope that the thing could be done. 康, 休, 愒, 息, and

安, are all closely allied in meaning,—as in the translation. The 'Complete Digest,' in the first stanza gives:—彼 中 外 之 民, 其 劳 甚 矣, 今 虽 未 能 遽 跻 于 咸 亨 之 域, 庶 几 其 可 以 小 康 矣.

Ll. 3, 4. 惠,—'to show kindness to.' By 中国 is not intended 'the middle State,' but 京师, 'the capital,' or centre of the kingdom, which, indeed, takes its place in st. 3. 四 方

近有德。

四章
民亦劳止。汔可小愒。惠此中国。俾民忧泄。无纵诡

随。以谨丑厉。式遏寇虐。无俾正败。戎虽小子。而

式弘大。

五章
民亦劳止。汔可小安。惠此中国。国无有残。无纵诡

随。以谨缱绻。式遏寇虐。无俾正反。王欲玉女。

Then let us be reverently careful of our demeanour,
To cultivate association with the virtuous.

4　The people indeed are heavily burdened,
But perhaps a little repose may be got for them.
Let us cherish this centre of the kingdom,
That the sorrow of the people may be dispelled.
Let us give no indulgence to the wily and obsequious,
In order to make the multitudes of the evil careful,
And to repress robbers and oppressors,
So that the right shall not be overthrown.
Though you may be [but as] little children,
Your work is vast and great.

5　The people indeed are heavily burdened,
But perhaps a little tranquillity may be got for them.
Let us cherish this centre of the kingdom,
That it may not everywhere suffer such wounds.
Let us give no indulgence to the wily and obsequious,
In order to make the parasites careful,

means all the States in the four quarters of the kingdom (诸夏), or the whole of the kingdom generally, not excluding the territory of the royal domain. So, 四国 in st. 3, and 国 alone in st. 5. In st. 2. 逮 = 聚, 'to collect,' 'the place where they gather (中国者, 民之所聚也).' In st. 3, 泄 = 去 or 散, 'to be removed, or dispersed.' In st. 5, 国无有残 = 'so that throughout the kingdom there may not be the suffering of injury.' As

the 'Essence and Flower of the She' has it,—

惠中国, 则国人无复有被残害者耳.

Ll. 5, 6.　无 is best taken as the imperative 毋. By 诡随, 'deceitful following,' is intended wily men, obsequiously following those from whom or through whom they expected to gain advantage. We must suppose that deceitful flatterers of the king were in the writer's view in the first instance, but the expression need not be confined to his parasites only.

是用大谏。

And to repress robbers and oppressors,
So that the right shall not be reversed.
The king wishes to hold you as [sceptres of] jade,
And therefore I thus strongly admonish you.

纵,—'to connive at,' 'to give indulgence to.' 谨 means 'to be reverent or careful;' here used in a *hiphil* sense, 'to make careful.' One definition of it in the dict. is 严禁, 'sternly to repress,' which would suit very well here. Choo explains it, much in the same way, by 敛束. 无良＝无良心之人, 'men without conscience;'—those parasites and others. They are described in st. 2 as 惽恀, which Maou explains by 大乱, 'men guilty of great disorders,' and Choo, after Ch'ing, by 欢哗, 'braggadocios.' In st. 3, they are 罔极, 'men who set no limits to their evil conduct;' in 4, the 丑厉, 'the crowd of the furiously wicked;' and in 5, the 缱绻. These last terms mean 'inseparably connected,' and are to be understood of men who attached themselves with parasitic clinging to their ruler (小人之固结其君者).

Ll. 7, 8, are a further effect to follow from the course recommended in l. 5, and 式 may have its meaning of 用 ＝ 以, 'to,' 'and thereby.' The same parties are here described as 'robbers and oppressors,' and they are exhibited, in l. 8 of st. 1, as being without any awe of 'what is clear,' *i. e.*, the will of Heaven as to human duty. 憯 ＝ 曾, as in II.iv.VII.1, IX.3. Choo explains 明 by 天之明命. In stt. 2, 3, 5, l. 8, the 无 is not imperative, but, ＝'so as not to,' 'so that not.' In st. 3, 慝 ＝ 恶, 'wickedness;' 作慝,—'to act out their wickedness.' The 'Complete Digest' says:—不使其播恶于众 In stt. 4, 5, 正败 is 'the right injured (败 ＝ 坏);' and 正反, 'the right reversed or overturned,'—a more serious thing, good taken for evil, and evil for good.

Ll. 9, 10 are directly to the party or parties whom the writer had in view. 柔远 is the rule for treating foreigners or people from a distance;—see Confucius' use of the phrase in the 'Doctrine of the Mean,' XX. 12. Yen Ts'an says that by 远 here is intended the E and the Teih (夷狄), *i. e.*, foreigners generally; and this meaning fits in very well with the relations subsisting at the time between China and the tribes about it. 迩, 'the near,' will then be the people of China itself. I venture to give to 能 here the meaning of 助, 'to help,' 'to give ability to.' Choo explains, it by 顺习, 'to deal with them according to sympathy.'

In st. 2, the 'service' would be that of the ministers addressed, and of their fathers and ancestors. Choo takes 休 in l. 10 as ＝ 美; but I do not see why we should depart from the meaning of the term in l. 2. In st. 3, 以近有德,—'to approach the virtuous,' *i. e.*, to cultivate association with them. In st. 4, 戎 ＝ 汝, 'you.' I cannot construe it, as Maou does, with the meaning of 大, 'great.' 小子,—'a little child;' but the expression is common in the Shoo, used by the king of himself, and applied by him to ministers and princes whom he is addressing. It does not necessarily imply youth. Confucius used to address his disciples by it. 式 must here have the full meaning of 用, 'to use,' ＝ the service you do. In st. 5, 玉 ＝ 'to count precious,' 'to make much of.'

The rhymes are—in st. 1, 康, 方, 良, 明*, 王, cat. 10: in 2, 休, 述, 恀 (prop. cat. 5), 忧, 休, cat. 3, t. 1: in 3, 息, 国, 极, 慝, 德, cat. 1, t. 3: in 4, 愒, 泄, 厉, 败, 大, cat. 15, t. 3: in 5, 安, 残, 绻, 反, 谏, cat. 14.

X. *Pan.*

板

一章

上帝板板。下民卒瘅。出话不然。为犹不远。靡圣管

管。不实于亶。犹之未远。是用大谏。

1　God has reversed [His usual course of procedure],
　　And the lower people are full of distress.
　　The words which you utter are not right;
　　The plans which you form are not far-reaching.
　　As there are not sages, you think you have no guidance;
　　You have no reality in your sincerity.
　　[Thus] your plans do not reach far,
　　And I therefore strongly admonish you.

Ode 10. Narrative. AN OFFICER OF EXPERIENCE MOURNS OVER THE PREVAILING MISERY; COMPLAINS OF THE WANT OF SYMPATHY WITH HIM SHOWN BY OTHER OFFICERS, ADMONISHES THEM, AND SETS FORTH THE DUTY REQUIRED OF THEM, ESPECIALLY IN THE ANGRY MOOD IN WHICH IT MIGHT SEEM THAT HEAVEN WAS. The Preface makes this ode, like the last, one of censure addressed to king Le, but the internal evidence requires us here also to assign it to an officer addressing other officers on the disorder into which public affairs had fallen. The Preface also ascribes it to the 'earl of Fan,' on which we can only say that there was a State of that name in the royal domain, and that we find, in the Ch'un Ts'ëw, long after king Le, an earl of it sent from the court on a mission to Loo.

St. 1. The Urh-ya defines 板板 by 僻, 'to be depraved,' 'to be partial.' Maou and Choo, however, take the characters in the sense of 反, 'to reverse,' 'to act contrary to;' with the meaning which I have given (反其常 道). The consequence of this unusual course pursued by God is stated in l. 2. The lower people are His peculiar care, but it might be supposed, from the condition in which they then were, that they were the objects of his aversion. 卒 = 尽, 'entirely;' 瘅 = 病, 'to be in distress.' Nothing could be farther from the truth than this, and that the writer well knew; but by this way of presenting the disorder and misery that prevailed, he seeks to convey his strong impression of it. Maou says that God is here a designation of the king, which is entirely wrong; but his meaning, perhaps, was not more than that of Yen Ts'an, who says that the writer did not wish to blame the king directly, and therefore attributed the state of things to God. I believe that the correct explanation of the language is what I have given. It prepared

the writer's way for all that he had to urge on his associates;—as both he and they believed that calamities from God were signs of His anger at the remissness of govt., and at crimes, especially of the king. L. 3. The subject of 出 is the comrades of the writer, who do not appear directly till st. 3; we must, however, express it now,—'you.' 然, a verb,—'to be right,' 'accordant with reason (合理).' L. 4. 犹 = 谋, 'counsels,' or 'plans;'—as often. L. 5. 靡圣,—'there are not sages;' i. e., you think there are now no sages. Then 管 管 indicates the consequence of this thought as seen in the conduct of the officers, talking and advising as occurred to themselves. Choo, after Maou, explains this phrase by 无所依 据, 'being without anything to rely on.' Ch'ing gives for it 以心自恣, 'you yield to the erring thoughts of your own minds.' How the characters come to have this meaning, I cannot tell. Wang Taou would read 官 with 心 at the bottom, on the authority of the dictionary Kwang-yun (广韵). L. 5. But not only did the officers think they were left to their own resources; they had no reality in their professions of sincerity. 亶 = 诚, 'sincerity.' Yen Ts'an expands the line—矫诬诈伪，不 实于为诚信，而伪为诚信. Ll. 7, 8 give the reason of the writer's composing the ode. The affliction of the time might be ascribed to God; but the real cause of it was in the neglect of their duties by those who should

二章
天之方难。无然宪宪。天之方蹶。无然泄泄。辞之辑

矣。民之洽矣。辞之怿矣。民之莫矣。

三章
我虽异事。及尔同僚。我即尔谋。听我嚣嚣。我言维

服。勿以为笑。先民有言。询于刍荛。

2 Heaven is now sending down calamities;—
Do not be so complacent.
Heaven is now producing such movements;—
Do not be so indifferent.
If your words were harmonious,
The people would become united.
If your words were gentle and kind,
The people would be settled.

3 Though my duties are different from yours,
I am your fellow-servant.
I come to advise with you,
And you hear me with contemptuous indifference.
My words are about the [present urgent] affairs;—
Do not think them matter for laughter.

have been the wise advisers of the king and directors of his govt. The 之 in l. 7 carries that line on to the next, intimating that the want of foresight in the plans was what moved the writer to give his admonition.

St. 2. L. 1. Here and below, 方 = 今, 'now.' 难 = 降难, 'to send down calamities.' L. 2. 无然,—as in i. VII. 5. 宪宪 = 欣欣, 'to be complacent;' almost, 'to be joyful.' L. 3. 蹶 = 动, 'to be moving,' with reference to the unrest and excitement which was everywhere abroad. L. 4. 泄泄 is said to be equivalent to 沓沓 in Men. IV. Pt. i. I. 11, 12. It has the meaning of being remiss and indifferent (弛缓之意). In ll. 5—8, 之 is simply an expletive. 辞 refers to the speeches—advices and plans—of the ministers. 辑 = 和 'to be harmonious,' meaning, I suppose, if the ministers were of one accord among themselves; 怿 = 悦, 'to be of a pleasant character,' what the

people would like. Some make the harmony to be accordance with reason. But the view which I have given is more natural. Yen Ts'an says:—

戒之以言论之间，宜相和协，……庶几合谋并智，可以措民于安耳. 洽 合, 'to be united;' 莫 = 定, 'to be settled.'

St. 3. The writer complains of the way in which he himself and his advice were treated by the other officers, and warns them against the course which they pursued. L. 1. 异事, —'have a difft. service,' = 不同职. L. 2. 及尔,—as in II. v. V. 7. 僚 = 官, 'an officer;' 同寮, = 'official comrades:'—the writer and those whom he was addressing were all, in common, servants of the king. Ll. 3, 4. 即 = 就, 'to come or go to' 嚣嚣 expresses 'the app. of insolent self-sufficiency.' Ll. 5, 6. 服 = 事, meaning the urgent 'affairs' which demanded their immediate attention. Yen Ts'an prefers the meaning of 服 = 行, 'to do,' so

四章
天之方虐。无然谑谑。老夫灌灌。小子蹻蹻。匪我言

耄。尔用忧谑。多将熇熇。不可救药。

五章
天之方懠。无为夸毗。威仪卒迷。善人载尸。民之方

The ancients had a saying:—
'Consult the grass and firewood-gatherers.'

4   Heaven is now exercising oppression;—
Do not in such a way make a mock of things.
An old man, [I speak] with entire sincerity;
But you, my juniors, are full of pride.
It is not that my words are those of age,
But you make a joke of what is sad.
But the troubles will multiply like flames,
Till they are beyond help or remedy.

5   Heaven is now displaying its anger;—
Do not be either boastful or flattering,
Utterly departing from all propriety of demeanour,

that the line='My words are practical,'—may be carried into effect. Ll. 7, 8. 先民,—as in II. v. I. 4, meaning ancient men of worth and eminence. 刍荛,—as 刍荛者, in Mencius, I. Pt. II. ii. 2. If ancient worthies thought that persons in such mean employments were to be consulted, surely the advice of the writer deserved to be taken into account by his comrades.

St. 4. L. 2. 谑,—'to make sport of in an insolent way;' and the repetition of the character expresses 'the app. of doing this,' or expresses the action of the verb emphatically. Ll. 3, 4. 老夫 is the writer's designation of himself as 'an old fellow,' in contrast with the other officers who were 小子, as in st. 4 of the prec. ode. They might not be what we call young, but they were his juniors. 灌灌 is explained by 款款, 'the app. of being sincere.' That was probably the original text,—in the old form of the character. 蹻蹻 is defined by 骄貌, 'the app. of being proud.' 蹻 means 'to raise the feet high in walking,'—to have a haughty gait. Ll. 5, 6. 匪—'it is not that'...;

as often. 用 = 以, 'to take to be.'—'You take what is sad to be matter of insolent jest.' Ll. 7, 8. The subject of these lines is to be found in the 忧 of l. 6,—the troubles and sorrows which were so abounding. 熇熇 = 炽盛, 'to be blazing.' L. 8='Cannot be cured, are beyond the reach of medicine.'

St. 5. L. 1. 懠 = 怒, 'to be angry.' Maou explains 夸毗 together by 体柔人, meaning, apparently, 'to present a soft and obsequious appearance to others.' Such is the meaning of the characters given in the Urh-ya. But this does not suit the 夸, which means 大, 'great;' although the dict., after giving this definition, subjoins, in illustration, the phrase in the text with the above explanation of it. Choo therefore gave to each of the characters its own meaning,—as in the translation, and has been followed by Yen Ts'an (小人之于人,不以大言夸之,则以谀言毗之). L. 3. It is difficult to say whose behaviour the writer meant to speak

殿屎。则莫我敢葵。丧乱蔑资。曾莫惠我师。

六章
天之牖民。如壎如篪。如璋如圭。如取如携。携无曰益。牖民孔易。民之多辟。无自立辟。

Till good men are reduced to personators of the dead.
The people now sigh and groan,
And we dare not examine [into the causes of their trouble].
The ruin and disorder are exhausting all their means of living,
And we show no kindness to our multitudes.

6   Heaven enlightens the people,
As the bamboo flute responds to the porcelain whistle;
As two half maces form a whole one;
As you take a thing, and bring it away in your hand,
Bringing it away without any more ado.
The enlightenment of the people is very easy.
They have [now] many perversities;—
Do not you set up your perversity [before them].

of here. Yen Ts'an refers it to the behaviour of all classes of the people (众人之威仪). In l. 4, 载 is the particle, having, however, a faint meaning, as a sort of copula. Good men reduced to the semblance of personators of the dead were good for nothing, could only eat and drink. L. 5. All the critics follow the Urh-ya in explaining *tëen-he* by 呻吟, as in the translation. The Shwoh-wăn quotes the line as 念 and 尸, with 口 at the side. L. 6. The 我, which is the subject of 敢 (the adv. 莫 standing before it according to a common usage with negatives), must be taken of the writer and the officers he was admonishing,—of the ministers of the king generally. 葵 is used for 揆,—as in II.vii. VIII. 5. L. 7. Choo takes 资 as *i. q.* 咨, 'ah!' 'alas!;' but this seems to me a most unnatural construction; nor is there any necessity for it. 资 denotes 'necessaries,' the means of living; 蔑 (=无) 资, the want of, or the extinction of, the necessaries of life. In l. 8, 师 = 众, meaning the

multitudes of the people. The writer calls them 'our multitudes,' to indicate the claim which they had on the superior classes.

St. 6 seems to say that Heaven had so attuned the mind to virtue, that if good example were set before the people, they would certainly and readily follow it. L. 1. 牖, 'a window,' or 'an opening in a wall,' is here used as a verb, ='to enlighten,'—to let light into the mind as surely as a window lets light into a house. L. 2. 壎 and 篪,—see on II.v. V. 7. These two instruments were played together; and when the whistle gave the note, the flute immediately took it up. So would the people respond to the presentation to them of what was right. L. 3. The *chang*, we have seen was a half mace. Two *chang*, put together, would form a *kwei*, or a whole mace. As surely might the people be brought into accord with what was right. L. 4. You take a thing, and bring it away in your hand,—there is no difficulty. As easily might the people be led. On the analogy of ll. 2,3 what is denoted by 携 must be consequent on what is denoted by 取; hence those critics are wrong who find two illustrations in the line, like Yen Ts'an (如往取物之必得，如手携物之必从). L. 5 sets

七章

价人维藩。大师维垣。大邦维屏。大宗维翰。怀德维

宁。宗子维城。无俾城坏。无独斯畏。

八章

敬天之怒。无敢戏豫。敬天之渝。无敢驰驱。昊天曰

明。及尔出王。昊天曰旦。及尔游衍。

7   Good men are a fence;
     The multitudes of the people are a wall;
     Great States are screens;
     Great Families are buttresses;
     The cherishing of virtue secures repose;
     The circle of [the king's] Relatives is a fortified wall.
     We must not let the fortified wall get destroyed;
     We must not let him solitary be consumed with terrors.

8   Revere the anger of Heaven,
     And presume not to make sport or be idle.
     Revere the changing moods of Heaven,
     And presume not to drive about [at your pleasure].
     Great Heaven is intelligent,
     And is with you in all your goings.
     Great Heaven is clear-seeing,
     And is with you in your wanderings and indulgences.

forth the ease with which the action of l. 4 is accomplished. The 曰 is the particle. 无益,—'without anything more;' i. e., no additional effort is required (无所费). The enlightenment of the people being thus easy, they yielding so readily to the impression of their superiors, the lesson in ll. 7,8 naturally follows. 辟＝邪, 'perversity.' 无＝毋, 'do not.'

St. 7. The statements here made would seem to be what the writer considered to be great truths, which should lie at the basis of 'far-reaching plans.' In harmony with our general view of the ode, 无俾 must be taken as in the translation—counsel given to all the king's ministers. L. 1. Maou explains 价 by 善, 'good ;' Choo, by 大, 'great,' adding 大

德之人, 'men of great virtue,' which makes his account of the character the same as Maou's. 藩＝篱, 'a fence. L. 2. 大师, 'the great multitudes,'＝百姓之众, 'the multitude of the people.' 垣,—'a wall;' but not a fortified wall. L. 3. 大邦 are the great feudal States, which were supposed to serve as 'screens' to the royal domain. L. 4. 大宗＝强族 'the strong Clans (Choo),' or 巨室, 'the great Houses (Wang Gan-shih).' The dict. explains the character with reference to this passage, by 同姓, 'all of the same surname.' 翰,—as in in i. X.4, et al. L.6. 宗子 is explained by Choo as the dict. explains 宗 alone,— 同宗; but the 宗 must here be taken of those of the same surname as the king, and the phrase has the meaning in the translation. 城 —'the fortified wall surrounding a city.' Those six lines are plainly coordinate; and I cannot conceive why many of the critics separate 5 and 6 from the others;—especially strange seems the view advocated by Këang, that 宗子 denotes the king himself. The overthrow of the wall in l. 7 must be extended to the ruin of all the other bulwarks of the throne. If the king were so left alone, every calamity which he could fear would come upon him, This, I conceive, is the meaning of l. 8. 斯 =the descriptive 其.

St. 8 sends home all that precedes by impressing it on the officers that they were always subject to the inspection of Heaven. L. 2. 豫 = 逸 豫, 'to be idle.' L. 3. 渝 = 变, 'changes.' L. 4. 驰 驱,—'to drive furiously about.' Maou explains the phrase by 自 恣, 'to follow one's own passions.' In ll. 5 and 7, 曰 has the force of the copula; 明 and 旦 both mean 'bright;' =intelligent. In ll. 6, 8, 及 尔,—as in st. 3: here,— 天 及 尔, 'Heaven and you.' 王 = 往; 出 王 = 出 入 往 来, 'goes out and in, goes and comes. 衍 = 溢, 'to overflow;' nearly=our 'to be dissipated.'

The rhymes are—in st. 1, 板, 瘅 *, 然, 远, 管, 亶, 远, 谏, cat. 14: in 2, 难, 宪, ib.; 蹶, 泄, cat. 15, t. 3; 辑, 洽 *, cat. 7, t. 3; 怿 *, 莫, cat. 5, t. 3: in 3, 僚, 嚣, 笑, 荛, cat. 2: in 4, 虐 *, 谑 *, 蹻 *, 毫, 谑 *, 熇 *, 药 *, ib.: in 5, 忏, 毗, 迷, 尸, 屎, 葵, 资, 师, cat. 15, t. 1: in 6, 篪, 圭 *, 携 *, cat. 16, t. 1: 益, 易, 辟, 辟, ib., t. 3: in 7, 藩, 垣, 翰, cat. 14; 屏, 宁, 城, cat. 11; 坏, 畏, cat. 15, t. 1: in 8, 怒, 豫, cat. 5, t. 2; 渝 *, 驱 *, cat. 4, t. 1; 明 *, 王, cat. 10; 旦, 衍, cat. 14.

BOOK III.   DECADE OF TANG.

I.   *Tang.*

荡之什三之三

荡

一章

荡荡上帝。下民之辟。疾威上帝。其命多辟。天生烝
民。其命匪谌。靡不有初。鲜克有终。

1 How vast is God,
The ruler of men below!
How arrayed in terrors is God,
With many things irregular in His ordinations!
Heaven gave birth to the multitudes of the people,
But the nature it confers is not to be depended on.
All are [good] at first,
But few prove themselves to be so at the last.

TITLE OF THE BOOK. 荡之什,三之二, 'The Decade of Tang; Book III. of Part III.' But though this Book is called a decade like the others, it really contains eleven odes. The critics say nothing, so far as I know, on the anomaly. It only shows that the division of the last three Parts into Decades was a device later than the time of the compilation assigned to Confucius.

Ode 1. Narrative. WARNINGS ADDRESSED TO KING LE ON THE ISSUES OF THE COURSE WHICH HE WAS PURSUING, SHOWING THAT THE MISERIES OF THE TIME AND THE IMMINENT DANGER OF RUIN WERE TO BE ATTRIBUTED, NOT TO HEAVEN, BUT TO HIMSELF AND HIS MINISTERS. The Preface assigns this ode, like the 9th of last Book, to duke Muh of Shaou. The structure of it is peculiar, for, after the first stanza, we have king Wăn introduced, delivering his warnings to Show, the last king of the Shang dynasty. They are put into Wăn's mouth, in the hope that Le, if, indeed, he was the monarch whom the writer had in view, would transfer the figure of Show to himself, and alter his course so as to avoid a similar ruin. The matter of the ode would suit only Le and Yëw of all the kings of Chow within the period embraced by the She. The following summary of the kings previous to Le, given by Këang Ping-chang, is sufficiently illustrative:—' After Ching and K'ang came king Ch'aou, who went on an expedition to the south from which he did not return; king Muh, who drove about in his chariot wishing to go over all under the sky; king Kung, who extinguished the State of Meih; king E, who smote the dog-Jung; and king E, who changed the forms of audience. These four kings were all chargeable with a loss of virtue, but the consequences of their conduct were not any great detriment to the royal House. When king Le, however, came to the throne, by his violent oppressions, his neglect of good men, his employment of mean creatures, his disannulling the old statutes and laws, his drunkenness, and the fierceness of his will, the dynasty was brought into imminent peril; and this it was which so much grieved duke Muh.'

St. 1. The object of this stanza seems to be to show that whatever miseries might prevail, and be ignorantly ascribed to the Supreme Ruler, they were in reality owing to men's not fulfilling the law of Heaven inscribed on their hearts; and this general statement is preliminary to the particular case of king Le, as set forth in the other stanzas under the figure of Show of Shang. Maou's view of the stanza was that by God king Le really was intended; and so the writer, while blaspheming God, was in reality only blaspheming the king. It is not necessary to take up his view of the lines and phrases in detail; for even the critics of his own school, such as Yen and Këang, have abandoned it in whole or in part.

二章
文王曰咨。咨女殷商。曾是强御。曾是掊克。曾是在
位。曾是在服。天降滔德。女兴是力。

三章
文王曰咨。咨女殷商。而秉义类。强御多怼。流言以

2　King Wăn said, ‘Alas!
　　Alas! you [sovereign of] Yin-shang,
　　That you should have such violently oppressive ministers,
　　That you should have such extortionate exactors,
　　That you should have them in offices,
　　That you should have them in the conduct of affairs!
　　Heaven made them with their insolent dispositions,
　　But it is you who employ them, and give them strength.’

3　King Wăn said, ‘Alas!
　　Alas! you [sovereign of] Yin-shang,

Ll. 1,2. 荡 荡 give the idea of greatness or vastness（广大之貌）. 辟＝君, ‘ruler.’ 下 民,--‘the lower people;’ but in such passages as this, the phrase is equivalent to ‘the men of this lower world,’ as in the translation. Ll. 3,4. 疾 威,--as in II.iv.X. 1, et al. If God were, indeed, the ruler of this world, how was it that He could ever appear in His government, as if arrayed with terrors? This is the question to which we have the writer's answer in ll.5–8. 辟,--as in st. 6 of last ode, ＝ 僻. 命 must be taken of the acts of the king, considered as done under the ordering of God; or we may refer it, more generally, to the evil doings that everywhere abounded, with the same reference. Yen Ts‘an says, 疾 威 者 王 所 为, 而 天 实 命 之. Ll. 5,6. 凭＝众, ‘all,’ ‘the multitudes of.’ 命 must here be taken of the nature conferred by Heaven,—as in the commencing words of the ‘Doctrine of the Mean,’—天 命 之 谓 性. 谌 ＝ 信, ‘to be believed,’ ‘to be trusted.’ Ll. 7,8. 靡 不, ‘not, or none, but,’ ＝ every one, all. ‘All have the beginning;’ i. e., all men have at first the good nature conferred by Heaven. L. 8 ＝ ‘But few are able to have the end,’ i. e., to preserve the same good nature to the last. Yen Ts‘an says, ‘In their beginning all are good, but in the end few are good. Men do violence to, and abandon, themselves;—it is not Heaven that makes them do so.’ I need not enter here into any argument on these incautious utterances.

St 2. Ll.1,2. 咨 ＝ 嗟, ‘alas!’ 殷 商,—as in i.II. 2, et al. By ‘you, Yin-shang,’ is intended Show or Chow, the last sovereign of the Yin or Shang dynasty. Ll.3–6. The force of the 曾 is, I think, given exactly in the translation. Këang makes it equivalent to a question,—何 乃 有 是 人, 何 乃 用 是 人, ‘How is it that you have and employ these men?’ 强 御,—lit., ‘strong opponents,’ meaning violent oppressors（暴 虐 之 臣）. 掊 克,—as in Men. VI. Pt.ii.VII. 2. The Urh-ya explains the phrase by 聚 敛, ‘tax-gatherers.’ It is difficult to fix the meaning of the 克. Perhaps, the two characters, as I have said in Mencius, ＝ ‘grasping and able.’ 服 ＝ 事, ‘affairs;’ 在 服 ＝ ‘in the conduct of affairs.’ L. 7. 滔, ‘waters overflowing,’ gives us the idea of the insolence of the men; and 德 has the general signification of ‘conduct or disposition.’ The dict. quotes the pass. under 慆. The whole line ＝ 天 降 是 滔 慢 凶 德 之 人, ‘Heaven sent down these men of evil character, so insolent.’ L. 8 兴 ＝ 使 之 居 位, ‘put them into office.’ 力 is used as a verb,＝ ‘to give strength to.’ 是 ＝ 实, with little more meaning than our , and indeed.’

St. 3. Ll. 3—6. 而 ＝ 汝, ‘you.’ 秉, ‘to hold fast;’ here ＝ 用, ‘to employ.’ 义 ＝ 善,

对。寇攘式内。侯作侯祝。靡届靡究。

四章
文王曰咨。咨女殷商。女炰烋于中国。敛怨以为德。

不明尔德。时无背无侧。尔德不明。以无陪无卿。

> You ought to employ such as are good,
> But [you employ instead] violent oppressors, who cause many
>   dissatisfactions.
> They respond to you with baseless stories,
> And [thus] robbers and thieves are in your court.
> Thence come oaths and curses,
> Without limit, without end.'

4   King Wăn said, 'Alas!
> Alas! you [sovereign of] Yin-shang,
> You show a strong fierce will in the centre of the kingdom,
> And consider the contracting of enmities a proof of virtue.
> All unintelligent are you of your [proper] virtue,
> And so you have no [good] men behind you, nor by your side.

'good;' 义 类,—'officers of the good class.' 当, 'ought,' is understood before 秉; and 乃用, 'but you use.' before l. 2. Only in this way can any satisfactory meaning be got out of the lines, unless we construe, with Këang, 秉 in the past tense:—'You used good men, but these violent oppressors, with their great hatred, brought false stories to you about them,' &c. But such a sentiment is foreign to the character of the ode. 愬 = 怨, 'to murmur,' 'to resent.' The 多 愬 indicates, in my view, the resentments which the king's officers awakened, rather than those which they indulged. So, the expression is in better harmony with the whole stanza. L. 5 tells how the ministers imposed on the king, and in l. 6 we have the consequence. 寇 implies the employment of violence;—'robbers.' 式 is by some here explained by 用, 'to be employed.' It is little more than an expletive particle, with perhaps the force of the copula. 内 = 王朝, 'the court.' Ll. 7, 8 tell us the consequence of such a state of things. 侯 is the particle. Choo says that

作 is read as 诅, and with the meaning of that character,—'to curse;' synonymous with 祝. But this does not seem necessary. The reduplication of the 侯 only serves to eke out the line, which = 侯作祝诅, 'they go on cursing.' 届 = 极, 'limit.' 究 = 穷 or 已, 'stopping,' 'coming to an end.'

St. 4 attributes the disorders to the king's own example. L. 3. 炰 烋 (we find quotations of the line with 咆 烋, and 咆 哮) are defined by 气 健 貌, 'the app. of a strong temper,' i. e., of a violent and self-confident will. I take 中 国 as in ii. IX. L. 4 is well expanded by Choo— 多 为 可 怨 之 事,而 自 以 为 德, 'you do many things calculated to excite enmity, and yet you yourself consider them to be virtuous.' Ll. 5, 7 have the same meaning, the order of the characters being varied for the sake of the rhyme. Ll. 6. 8. 时 = 是 = 于 是, 'thus.' 背 and 侧, 'behind and on your side.'

五章
文王曰咨。咨女殷商。天不湎尔以酒。不义从式。既
愆尔止。靡明靡晦。式号式呼。俾昼作夜。
六章
文王曰咨。咨女殷商。如蜩如螗。如沸如羹。小大近

Without any intelligence of your [proper] virtue,
You have no [good] intimate adviser nor minister.'

5　King Wăn said, 'Alas!
Alas! you [sovereign of] Yin-shang,
It is not Heaven that flushes your face with spirits,
So that you follow what is evil and imitate it.
You go wrong in all your conduct;
You make no distinction between the light and the darkness;
But amid clamour and shouting,
You turn the day into night.'

6　King Wăn said, 'Alas!
Alas! you [sovereign of] Yin-shang,
[All round you] is like the noise of cicadas,
Or like the bubbling of boiling soup.
Affairs, great and small, are approaching to ruin;

are understood to refer to smaller officers, such as might attend on the king's person; 陪 (＝貳, 'associate') and 卿, to the great ministers of the govt.

St. 5 affirms more strongly that the root of all prevailing misery and disorder was in the king himself, and specifies his drunkenness. Ll. 3, 4. Choo defines 湎 by 饮 酒 变 色, 'drinking till the colour is changed,' i.e., till the face is flushed. 不 义 从 式 is a natural sequence of this drunkenness, ＝ 惟 不 义 之 事 是 从 而 法 (or 用) 之. Ch'ing took l. 4 as＝不 宜 从 而 法 行 之, 'you ought not to follow and imitate them,' —that is, men who drink to excess. It is strange that Wang Taou should prefer this exegesis.

L. 5. 止＝容 止, 'demeanour;'—the whole of the conduct and bearing. L. 6. The redoubled 靡 like the redoubled 无, means 'without reference to,' 'without consideration of.' L. 7. 式,—redoubled, as often, and merely the particle. L. 8. we speak of 'turning night into day.' Here the day is turned into the night. Excesses, only common in darkness, were committed openly.

St. 6. Ll. 3, 4 are taken by Choo as embleming the confusion and disorder that everywhere prevailed. This is preferable to Yen Ts'an's reference of them to the drunken orgies of the prec. stanza. 蜩 we have met with already, as the cicada, or broad locust; 螗 is an insect of the same kind. 如 沸 如 羹, 'like bubbling, like soup,' ＝ 如 羹 之 沸, as in the translation. The repetition of the 如, separating

丧。人尚乎由行。内奰于中国。覃及鬼方。

七章
文王曰咨。咨女殷商。匪上帝不时。殷不用旧。虽无

老成人。尚有典刑。曾是莫听。大命以倾。

八章
文王曰咨。咨女殷商。人亦有言。颠沛之揭。枝叶未

And still you [and your creatures] go on in this course.
Indignation is rife against you here in the Middle kingdom,
And extends to the demon regions.'

7　King Wăn said, 'Alas!
Alas! you [sovereign of] Yin-shang,
It is not God that has caused this evil time,
But it arises from Yin's not using the old [ways].
Although you have not old experienced men,
There are still the ancient statutes and laws.
But you will not listen to them,
And so your great appointment is being overthrown.'

8　King Wăn said, 'Alas!
Alas! you [sovereign of] Yin-shang,
People have a saying,

the difft. words of a line, which go together to constitute one idea, is a peculiarity of the ancient poetical style, common enough in the odes, and especially in this Book. L. 6. 人 is the designation of the king and his creatures (君臣; Këang); 尚,—'still;' the 乎 is merely an expletive, or we may say that 尚乎＝尚且,'still.' 由行＝由此而行,'to pursue this course.' Maou's construction of 尚 as ＝上, and 人尚＝居人上, meaning the king as dwelling—placed—above the people is inadmissible. Ll. 7, 8. The opposition of 中国 and 鬼方 makes us take the former expression of the kingdom at large,—all the States. What region or regions the 'demon lands' were we cannot tell. Maou explains the phrase by 远方, 'distant quarters.' In the Yih the same name occurs, and Kaou-tsung (in the 13th cent. B.C.) is said to have attacked

the country. It could not be very distant from China, but still it was beyond it. It is strange that the custom of calling foreigners *demons*, still everywhere prevalent in China, should have the sanction of the She, and of this high antiquity. 奰＝怒, 'to be the object of anger.' 覃＝延, 'to extend to.'

St. 7. L. 3＝非上帝为此不善之时,—as in the translation. 不 may be taken as an adjective, qualifying the 时. L. 4. 殷,—like 殷商, meaning the king of Yin. L. 6. 典,—'canons,' the instructions and general lessons of former kings (先王之训典); 刑＝法, 'laws.' L. 8. 倾＝倾覆, 'to be overturned.'

St. 8. L. 3. 颠沛,—see on Ana. IV. v. 3. 揭,—'to be raised,' *i. e.*, so that the roots are

有害。本实先拨。殷鉴不远。在夏后之世。

"When a tree falls utterly,
While its branches and leaves are yet uninjured,
It must first have been uprooted."
The beacon of Yin is not far-distant;—
It is in the age of the [last] sovereign of Hëa.'

II. *Yih.*

抑

一章

抑抑威仪。维德之隅。人亦有言。靡哲不愚。

1   An outward demeanour, cautious and grave,
Is an indication of the [inward] virtue.
People have the saying,
'There is no wise man who is not [also] stupid.'

seen. Ll. 4, 5 show that it is the fall of a tree which is spoken of;—拨 ='to uproot.' I do not understand Choo, when he says that the character is equivalent to 绝. 殷鉴,—'what Yin has to look at;'=the beacon of Yin. The last sovereign of Hëa was the tyrant Këeh. In these two concluding lines is the moral of the ode. King Le was to look to Show as his beacon, as Show had been warned to look to Këeh.

The rhymes are—in st. 1, 帝 *, 辟, 帝, 辟, cat. 16, t. 3; 谌 (prop. cat. 7), 终, cat. 9: in 2, 克, 服 *, 德, 力, cat. 1, t. 3: in 3, 类, 怼, 对, 内, cat. 15, t. 3; 祝, 究, cat. 3, t. 2: in 4, 国, 德, 德, 侧, cat. 1, t. 3; 明 *, 卿 *, cat. 10: in 5, 式, 止, 晦 *, cat. 1, t. 2; 呼, 夜 *, cat. 5, t. 1: in 6, 蟠, 羹 *, 丧, 行 *, 方, cat. 10: in 7, 时, 旧 *, cat. 1, t. 2; 刑, 听, 倾, cat. 11: in 8, 揭, 害, 拨, 世, cat. 15, t. 3. Also 咨, cat. 15, t. 1; and 商, cat. 10, in stt. 2–8, rhyme with themselves.

Ode 2. Narrative excepting st. 9, which is allusive. CONTAINING VARIOUS COUNSELS WHICH DUKE WOO OF WEI MADE TO ADMONISH HIM-SELF, WHEN HE WAS OVER HIS NINETIETH YEAR ; —ESPECIALLY ON THE DUTY OF A RULER TO BE CAREFUL OF HIS OUTWARD DEMEANOUR, AND TO RECEIVE WITH DOCILITY INSTRUCTIONS DELIVER-ED TO HIM. Ode VI. of the 7th Book of last Part is also attributed, we saw, to the same duke Woo, and there is a remarkable similarity in the structure and in many of the phrases of the two pieces. Especially do there appear in both the duty of attending to the outward deportment, and the way in which that is liable to be disordered by drunkenness. The authority for attributing this ode to duke Woo is the statement of the Preface, and an article in the 'Narratives of the States (国语，楚语，上, art. 6).' The article relates how Woo, at the age of 95, insisted on all his ministers and officers being instant, in season and out of sea-son, to admonish him on his conduct, and con-cludes by saying that he made the 'warnings in the E to admonish himself (作懿戒以自儆).' The E is taken as only another name for *Yih*. It is added that after his death he was styled 'the Intelligent and Sage duke Woo.' One would hope that the incident related of him on the 1st ode of Bk. IV., Pt. I. is not true.

But the Preface says that the ode was made by duke Woo, not only to admonish himself, but also to reprehend king Le. Now, Woo be-came marquis of Wei in B. C. 811, fully 16 years after the death of Le. His rule lasted for 55 years. This ode must have been made near the close of it;—the composition therefore must be dated considerably more than half a century from Le's reign. Unless there were in it very clear indications of its referring to Le and his times, we ought not to accept the statement of the Preface. But there are no such indications. The school of Maou, coming to the study of the piece with a foregone conclusion, try, indeed, to make them out; but the whole is much more naturally explained on the view that it was simply for Woo's own admonition. It is clear to my mind that king Le was dragged into the piece to account for its place in the Ya, supposed to contain only Odes of the Kingdom.

庶人之愚。亦职维疾。哲人之愚。亦维斯戻。
二章
无竞维人。四方其训之。有觉德行。四国顺之。讦谟
定命。远犹辰告。敬慎威仪。维民之则。

The stupidity of the ordinary man
Is determined by his [natural] defects.
The stupidity of the wise man
Is from his doing violence [to his natural character].

2　What is most powerful is the being the man;—
In all quarters [of the State] men are influenced by it.
To an upright virtuous conduct,
All in the four quarters of the State render obedient homage.
With great counsels and determinate orders,
With far-reaching plans and timely announcements,
And with reverent care of his outward demeanour,
One will become the pattern of the people.

St. 1. *The relation of the outward demeanour to inward virtue. The difft. stupidities of difft. people.* L. 1,—as in II. vii. VI. 3. L. 2. 隅 is defined by 廉角, 'a corner or angle.' Evidently it is used here in the sense which I have given it. The demeanour is the outcome or indication of the inward character. L. 4. 哲 = 知, 'wise men. The line = 无有哲而不愚者,哲而自戕其所守,则为愚矣,—as in the translation. The line is a sort of key-note to the piece. The writer will not acknowledge the sentiment. The wise man ought not to become the stupid. Ll. 6, 8. 疾 is used nearly as in Ana. XVII. xvi. of a natural failing or defect. 职 = 主, as in I. x. I., *et al.*; here, 'to be determined by.' 戾 = 反, 'to go contrary, do violence, to.' 斯戻,—'the going contrary to;' 斯 = the descriptive 其. Both 亦 and 维 have to be disregarded in making out the meaning.

St. 2. *The power of a man, playing the man in a high position, to influence others.* Ll. 1, 2. 竞 = 强, 'to be strong.' The line = 莫 强 乎 人, according to the analogy of the 'Doctrine of the Mean,' I. 3,— 莫 见 乎 隐, &c. Yen Ts'an refers to 莫 强, in Mencius, I. Pt.i. V. 1. Literally, we might render—'There is nothing strong, only man.' By 人 we are to understand 'being the man,' realizing all his ideal,—as Choo says, 能 尽 人 道, 'being able to complete his humanity.' The old school, misled by their reference of the ode to king Le, take 得 人, 'getting men,' as getting proper men to fill all the offices of govt. 训 之 = 以 之 为 训, 'take such an one as instructor.' Ll. 3, 4. Maou defines 觉 by 直, 'straight-forward,' 'upright;' Choo, by 直大, 'upright and great.' 四 方 in l. 2 and 四 国 in l. 4 must be taken as synonyms. Ll. 5—8. 讦 = 大, 'great;' 'great plans' are not concerned about one's own person or affairs. 定 命, 'determined orders,' are orders based on principle, and not varying with circumstances. 辰 告, 'timely announcements,' are those given out at the proper season, whenever they ought to be made public, or are required.

三章

其在于今。兴迷乱于政。颠覆厥德。荒湛于酒。女虽

湛乐从。弗念厥绍。罔敷求先王。克共明刑。

四章

肆皇天弗尚。如彼泉流。无沦胥以亡。夙兴夜寐。洒

埽廷内。维民之章。修尔车马。弓矢戎兵。用戒戎作。

3   As for the circumstances of the present time,
You are bent on error and confusion in your government.
Your virtue is subverted;
You are besotted by drink.
Although you thus pursue nothing but pleasure,
How is it you do not think of your relation to the past,
And do not widely study the former kings,
That you might hold fast their wise laws?

4   Shall not those whom great Heaven does not approve of,
Surely as the waters flow from a spring,
Sink down together to ruin?
Rise early and go to bed late,
Sprinkle and sweep your court-yard;—

In st. 3 the admonitions become sharp, and personal. We need not suppose that duke Woo was really guilty of the things here charged upon him; but he chose to be addressed in this style, that he might be the more put upon his guard against them. Much of the piece must be taken in the same way. Ll. 1, 2 The 兴 here occasions a good deal of difficulty, and we can hardly tell what to make of it. Yen Ts'an is the only critic, so far as I have observed, who makes the first line terminate with it, so that the meaning is—'As for the things under our present ruler, him who has now risen to the throne;'—with reference to king Le. But how could a composition written more than 50 years after Le's death speak of him as the king *now?* Even those of Maou's school who end the line with 今 interpret it of Le, unconscious of the anachronism they fall into. It might seem that by pointing as Yen Ts'an does, we get 兴 to rhyme with 政, but the characters belong to different categories. Choo follows Ch'ing in explaining 兴 by 尚 or 尊尚, 'to give honour to;' but this seems to require the construction of the lines that follow, which Ch'ing adopts:—'You give honour—*i. e.*, office—to those

who introduce error into the govt.,' &c. The translation shows the meaning I have ventured to give to the term. L. 4. 湛,—read as, and = 耽, 'lustful pleasure,' and 'to be addicted to pleasure.' In construing l. 5, we have to understand a 是 before 从;—'although it is addiction to pleasure which you follow.' Ll. 6—8 have their meaning brought out by means of an interrogation. 厥绍,—'your connection;' *i. e.*, your relation by your descent to your worthy ancestors (所承之绪). 共 (2d tone) is defined by 执, 'to hold fast.'

St. 4 Here again the meaning of ll. 1—3 has to be brought out interrogatively. 肆,—as in i. III. 8, VI. 4, 5. It is defined by 故, 'therefore;' but we can hardly translate it. Choo explains 弗尚 by 厌弃之, 'dislikes and casts them away.' Literally the characters = 'does not esteem or honour.' As surely as the water flows in a stream from the spring, so would such persons sink together, under the displeasure of Heaven, to ruin. 沦 = 陷, 'to

用遏蛮方。

五章
质尔人民。谨尔侯度。用戒不虞。慎尔出话。敬尔威

仪。无不柔嘉。白圭之玷。尚可磨也。斯言之玷。不

可为也。

So as to be a pattern to the people.
Have in good order your chariots and horses,
Your bows and arrows, and [other] weapons of war;—
To be prepared for warlike action,
To keep at a distance [the hordes of] the South.

5　Perfect what concerns your officers and people;
Be careful of your duties as a prince [of the kingdom];—
To be prepared for unforeseen dangers.
Be cautious of what you say;
Be reverentially careful of your outward demeanour;
In all things be mild and correct.
A flaw in a mace of white jade
May be ground away;
But for a flaw in speech
Nothing can be done.

sink down;' 胥 = 相, 'together;' 以 = 'and thereby.' L. 5. 廷内 or 庭内,—'the court-yard, and what is inside of it.' 'The line,' it is observed, 'seems to say nothing forcible, but it includes the putting away of slander and of venery, the despising of wealth, and setting a high price on virtue.' L. 6. 章 = 表, 'a signal.' L. 8. 遏 = 远, 'to keep at a distance.' As Yen Ts'an says, 用此以遏远蛮方, 使之不敢来侵.

St 5. L. 1. 质 is defined by 成 and 定, 成 probably being understood in the sense of 平, 'to pacify,' 'to reduce to a state of order.' In the 'Flower and Essence of the She,' however, it is said that 质 has all the meaning which I

have given it in the translation (质者平治民成就之义). 人, as distin-guished from 民,—'men in office.'

L. 2 should be decisive against any reference of the ode to king Le. 尔侯度 = 'the measures or rules which you, as one of the princes of the kingdom, should observe (诸侯所守之法度).' L. 8 不虞 is a common ex-pression for 'sudden emergencies,'—dangers that had not been foreseen, or specially provided for. L. 6. 柔 = 柔顺, 'mild.' See a proof of the value Confucius set on ll. 7—10, in the Ana., XI. v. 斯言,—'this word;' — any word. 玷,—'a flaw,' 'a defect.' 不可为 = 不可修为, 'cannot be repaired,' i. e., cannot be remedied.

六章.
无易由言。无曰苟矣。莫扪朕舌。言不可逝矣。无言

不仇。无德不报。惠于朋友。庶民小子。子孙绳绳。

万民靡不承。

七章
视尔友君子。辑柔尔颜。不遐有愆。相在尔室。尚不

6   Do not speak lightly;—your words are your own:—
    Do not say, 'This is of little importance.'
    No one can hold my tongue for me;
    Words are not to be cast away.
    Every word finds its answer;
    Every good deed has its recompense.
    If you are gracious among your friends,
    And to the people, as if they were your children,
    Your descendants will continue in unbroken line,
    And all the people will surely be obedient to you.

7   Looked at in friendly intercourse with superior men,
    You make your countenance harmonious and mild;—
    Anxious not to do anything wrong.
    Looked at in your chamber,

St. 6. *On the importance of being careful of one's words.* L.1. We have the same characters in II.v.III. 8; but the force of 由 言 is here more apparent; or, at least, they may have a meaning quite applicable here and justifiable, that does not present itself in the former passage. Yen Ts'an explains the phrase by 自 由 之 言, 'words from one's self,'—which are one's own. L. 2 is to be taken with reference to the speech;—'Do not say that what you utter is of little importance.' Ll. 3,4. 扪 = 持, 'to hold.' 逝 = 去, 'to go.' Words once spoken go away from the utterer, and cannot be recalled. Ll. 5,6. 仇 = 答, 'to be responded to;'—synonymous with 报. Ll. 7—10 give an illustration of what is here said. 惠 will be kindness shown both in word and deed. The 'friends' are the ruler's ministers and great officers, with whom he was in the habit of associating. Yen Ts'an expands l. 8 into—下 及 庶 民 与 其 小 子, but

I cannot suppose that the 小 子 are the children of the people, or any class different from the 庶 民. Twan Ch'ang-woo (段 昌 武; Sung dyn.) says, 此 小 子 止 谓 庶 民, 'The 小 子 here means nothing more than the people.' The translation shows my view of the line. 绳 绳,—as in I.i.V. 2.
St. 7. *Carefulness in speech enforced by spiritual considerations.* Ll. 1—3. 友 君 子 = 友 于 君 子, 'friendly with superior men.' 辑 = 和, 'to be harmonious;' 'to make harmonious;'—as often. L. 3 gives a thought as it passes through the mind of the individual spoken of—'Am I not;—may I not be—doing what is wrong?' 遐 = 何, 'how,' 'why.' Ll. 4,5. Being in the 室 or 'chamber' was a very different thing from being in the society of friends, and a man might think it was not necessary to keep himself under restraint there; but the monitor requires that he should do so. All this is indicated by the 尚   The open court

愧于屋漏。无曰不显。莫予云觏。神之格思。不可度

思。矧可射思。

八章

辟尔为德。俾臧俾嘉。淑慎尔止。不愆于仪。不僭不

贼。鲜不为则。投我以桃。报之以李。彼童而角。实

You ought to be equally free from shame before the light
　　which shines in.
Do not say, 'This place is not public;
No one can see me here.'
The approaches of spiritual Beings
Cannot be calculated [beforehand];
But the more should they not be slighted.

8　O prince, let your practice of virtue
　　Be entirely good and admirable.
　　Watch well over your behaviour,
　　And allow nothing wrong in your demeanour.
　　Committing no excess, doing nothing injurious;—
　　There are few who will not in such a case take you for their
　　　　pattern.
　　When one throws to me a peach,
　　I return to him a plum.

in Chinese houses, to which several roofs converge, which receives the water from them, and serves to admit the light to the rooms below, is called the 屋漏, or 'dripping place of a house.' From the connection of the phrase here, however, with the chamber, I prefer to interpret it of the opening or window in the north-west wall, through which the light was admitted (日 光 所 漏 入). Ll. 6—10. 无 = 毋, imperative; 莫 is indicative, = 'there is none;' 云 is expletive; 思 is the final particle; 度, 'to measure' or 'calculate;' 射 = 致 = 厌, 'to dislike,' 'to be tired of;' 矧 = 'how much more,' or 'how much less,' according to the connection. See ll. 8, 10 quoted in the 'Doctrine of the Mean,' XVI. 4.

St. 8. *The sure issue and influence of virtuous conduct in a ruler.* Ll. 2. 辟 = 君, 'a ruler,' and refers to duke Woo. The 'Complete Di-

gest' remarks that after 尔 we must make a short pause or halt (辟 尔·略 顿), and that the 俾 is emphatic (俾 字 着 力). 辟 is directly addressed to Woo, and must be translated, 'O ruler.' It seems strange that the lines should ever have been construed differently; and yet the old school takes 辟 in the sense of 法, 'a law,' 'to take the law from.' Yen Ts'an says, 'All under the sky take the law from you (*i.e.*, from king Le, supposing the lesson is addressed to him), and your conduct is their pattern; you ought to make them good and admirable!' Ll. 3—6. 淑 = 善, 'well.' 止 = 容 止, 'the behaviour,' generally. 僭 = 差, 'to be in error.' 贼 = 害, 'to injure,' *i.e.*, to be injurious to virtue. L. 6 = 少 不 为 人 所 法 则 者. The 鲜 gives to the line a general force and application; but we can

虹小子。

九章

荏染柔木。言缗之丝。温温恭人。维德之基。其维哲

人。告之话言。顺德之行。其维愚人。覆谓我僭。民

各有心。

十章

于乎小子。未知臧否。匪手携之。言示之事。匪面命

To look for horns on a young ram
Will only weary you, my son.

9　The soft and elastic wood
Can be fitted with the silken string.
The mild and the respectful man
Possesses the foundation of virtue.
There is a wise man;—
I tell him [good] words,
And he yields to them the practice of docile virtue.
There is a stupid man;—
He says on the contrary that my words are not true:—
So different are people's minds.

10　Oh! my son,
When you did not know what was good, and what was not good,

hardly give it in a translation any other reference than to duke Woo.　Ll. 7—10 are illustrations of the truth insisted on, and of the absurdity of expecting the same result in any other way.　L. 9 will be understood by comparing it with l. 12 in the last stanza of II. vii. VI., duke Woo's ode against drunkenness.　虹＝讧, 'to scatter and confuse.'　The 小子, 'little son,' addressed to a man of 95, is dwelt on as showing the earnestness of Woo, and his desire to be kept ever in mind of his duty.

St. 9.　*On docility in receiving good advice.*　Ll. 1—4.　荏染 is defined as 'soft-looking (柔貌),' and 柔, which means 'soft' has here the additional meaning of 'lasting (柔忍之木),' given to it.　缗＝被, 'to cover;' here ＝ to fit with.　Such wood, fitted with the string, becomes a bow,—an article of use and value; and serves with the poet to introduce the idea of the mild and humble man, who has in his qualities the capacity of becoming truly virtuous.　Ll. 5—10.　The 哲 and the 愚 of

st. 1 reappear.　Both Maou and Choo understand the 话 言 of the 'good words of antiquity;'—which does not appear to be necessary.　L.7 is construed by the critics as＝ 顺 其 德 而 行 之, 'acts in accordance with the virtue [in the words], and practises it.'　I prefer the meaning which I have given in the translation,—that the 顺 德 is the wise man's own docile virtue.　L. 10 appears to be a reflection on the two cases which have just been stated.　As Choo puts it,—言 人 心 不 同, 愚 智 相 越 之 远 也.　This is much more natural and simple than to hear in it a remark of the stupid man :—'You think so, but other people may have a different opinion.'　As Yen Ts'an has it,—人 各 有 意 见, 何 得 以 汝 所 见 为 是.

St. 10.　*If people will not learn, it is in consequence of their self-sufficiency.　What is excusable in a child may justly be required from a grown man who has been well taught.　L. 1.　于 (read woo) 乎,*

之。言提其耳。借曰未知。亦既抱子。民之靡盈。谁
夙知而莫成。

十一章

昊天孔昭。我生靡乐。视尔梦梦。我心惨惨。诲尔谆
谆。听我藐藐。匪用为教。覆用为虐。借曰未知。亦
聿既耄。

Not [only] did I lead you on by the hand,
But I showed the difference by appealing to affairs.
Not [only] did I charge you face to face,
But I held you by the ears.
And still perhaps you do not know,
Although you have held a son in your arms.
If people are not self-sufficient,
Who comes [only] to a late maturity after early instruction?

11　Great Heaven is very intelligent,
And I pass my life without pleasure.
When I see you so dark and stupid,
My heart is full of pain.
I taught you with assiduous repetition,
And you listened to me with contempt.
You would not consider me your teacher,
But regarded me as troublesome.

—an exclamation. L. 2 臧否 (p'e)＝'good and evil,' 'right and wrong.' Ll. 3—6 show us the parent teaching the child,—holding him up by the hand, giving him by facts illustrations of his lessons, telling him plainly, face to face, bending down to him, and holding him by the ear, that no instructions may be lost. 匪＝非徒, 'not only.' The two 言 are merely particles. Ll. 7, 8 leave the moral in them to be supplied:—'Now that you are old, and have a son of your own, you ought to know.' Some read the lesson rather differently:—'If still you do not know, you are old, and there is no time to be lost in learning it.' 借＝假, 'suppose,' 'if;' 借曰,—'suppose you say;' or, which I prefer, 曰 may be disregarded, as merely expletive. Ll. 9, 10. 靡盈＝不自盈满, 'not to be full of one's self.' 夙 and 莫 (＝暮).＝'early and late;' in the morning of life, and in its decline.

St. 11. *The lamentation of a father over his son, old and yet stupid.* Ll. 1—4. 昭＝明, 'intelligent,' 'clear-seeing.' 梦梦＝'all-dark, and unintelligent.' 惨惨＝忧貌, 'sad-looking.' Ll. 5, 6. 谆谆 expresses the 'earnestness and frequency' with which the instructions were given; 藐藐, 'the indiffer-

十二章

于乎小子。告尔旧止。听用我谋。庶无大悔。天方艰

难。曰丧厥国。取譬不远。昊天不忒。回遹其德。俾

民大棘。

Still perhaps you do not know;—
But you are very old.

12 Oh! my son,
I have told you the old ways.
Hear and follow my counsels;—
Then shall you have no cause for great regret.
Heaven is now inflicting calamities,
And is destroying the State.
My illustrations are not taken from things remote;—
Great Heaven makes no mistakes.
If you go on to deteriorate in your virtue,
You will bring the people to great distress.

ence and contempt' with which they were received. Ll. 7, 8. 用为＝以为, 'to consider to be;'—you do not regard my words as teaching, which you should welcome, but as an oppression inflicted on you. Ll. 9, 10,—much as 9, 10 in last stanza, only 耄, 'an octogenarian,' or 'a nonogenarian' is a great advance from 已抱子. 亦聿 cannot be translated. They simply fill out the line.

St. 12. *All the previous stanzas are here enforced by a consideration of the consequences of attending to, or neglecting, the lessons given in them.* L. 2. 止 is the final particle. 旧＝旧章, 'the old ways or maxims.' L. 6. 曰 and 厥 can hardly be translated. The former has the force of our 'to-wit.' L. 7. The 'illustrations' are understood of the confirmation which might be adduced from instances in the past of the consequences of wrong-doing;—like the instance in the concluding lines of ode I. 忒＝差, 'to fall into error.' 回遹＝邪僻, 'perverse and evil;' here used actively as a verb. 棘＝急, 'urgent;' *i. e.*, urgent distress. Ch'ing gives 大困急 for 大棘.

The rhymes are—in st. 1, 隅 *, 愚 *, repeated thrice) cat. 4, t. 1; 疾 (prop. cat. 12),

戾, cat. 15, t. 3: in 2, 训, 顺, cat. 13; 告 (prop. cat. 3), 则, cat. 1, t. 3: in 3, 政, 刑, cat. 11; 酒, 绍 (prop. cat. 2), cat. 3, t. 2: in 4, 尚, 亡, 章, 兵 *, 方, cat. 10; 寐, 内, cat. 15, t. 3: in 5, 度, 虞, cat. 5, t. 1; 仪 *, 嘉, 磨, 为 *, cat. 17; 玷, 玷, cat. 7, t. 1: in 6, 舌, 逝, cat. 15, t. 3; 苟 (prop. cat. 4), 仇, 报 *, cat. 3, t. 2; 友 *, 子, cat. 1, t. 2; 绳, 承, cat. 6; in 7, 颜, 愆, cat. 14; 漏, 觏, cat. 4, t. 2; 格 *, 度, 射 *, cat. 5, t. 3: in 8, 嘉, 仪 *, cat. 17; 贼, 则, cat. 1, t. 3; 李, 子, *ib.*, t. 2: in 9, 丝, 基, *ib.*, t. 1; 言, 行 (prop. cat. 10), cat. 14; 僭, 心, cat. 7, t. 1: in 10, 子, 否, 事. 耳, 子, cat. 1, t. 2; 盈, 成. cat. 11: in 11, 昭, 乐 *, 惨 (prop. cat. 14; but Twan reads 懆), 蔑 *, 教, 虐 *, 耄, cat. 2: in 12, 子, 止, 悔 *, cat. 1, t. 2; 国, 忒, 德, 棘, *ib.*, t. 3. It will be seen that, in some of the stanzas, the versification is very irregular and defective;—more so, **perhaps, than in any previous** ode.

III.　*Sang yëw.*

桑柔
一章
菀彼桑柔。其下侯旬。捋采其刘。瘼此下民。不殄心
忧。仓兄填兮。倬彼昊天。宁不我矜。

1　Luxuriant is that young mulberry tree,
　　And beneath it wide is the shade;
　　But they will pluck its leaves till it is quite destroyed.
　　The distress inflicted on these [multitudes of the] people,
　　Is an unceasing sorrow to my heart;—
　　My commiseration fills [my breast].
　　O thou bright and great Heaven,
　　Shouldest thou not have compassion on us?

Ode 3. Metaphorical, narrative, and allusive. THE EARL OF JUY MOURNS OVER THE MISERY AND DISORDER OF THE TIMES, WITH A VIEW TO REPREHEND THE MISGOVERNMENT OF KING LE,—ESPECIALLY HIS OPPRESSIONS AND LISTENING TO BAD COUNSELLORS. The piece itself says nothing about the earl of Juy as its author; but the statement rests not only on the authority of the Preface, but also on the Tso-chuen. An earl of Juy is mentioned in the Shoo, V. xxii., and others subsequently occur in history. Tso-she, under the 1st year of duke Wǎn, quotes the first line of st. 12, as from the ode of Lëang-foo of Juy (芮 良 夫 之 诗). The difficulty of a translator is to determine in what tenses he will render many of the verbs. In st. 7 we have a point of time indicated clearly enough in the statement that—'Heaven has extinguished or put an end to the king.' This is universally explained of the dethronement (in effect) of Le in B.C. 841. The people then rose *en masse* against him, irritated by his long-continued oppressions; and he only saved his life by flying to Che (彘), in the pres. Hoh-chow (霍 州), dep. P'ing-yang, Shan-se. There he remained till he died in 827. In the meantime the govt. was carried on by the dukes of Shaou and Chow, the period of their administration being known as 共 和, which may, perhaps, be translated 'Mutual Harmony,'—an important chronological era in Chinese history. The piece then would be composed sometime during that period; and much of it, after st. 7, is interpreted by Këang with a special reference to the two loyal dukes, faithful at once to the House of Chow and to the people. I thought of translating stt. 1—6 in the past tense, and from 8 to 16 in the present; but the whole is given as if it were equally passing immediately under the writer's eye, and if he had anywhere those dukes in view, his allusions to them are too indistinct to

justify a translator in giving them prominence. I have used, therefore, the present tense throughout. The ode was composed, I suppose, immediately after Le's dethronement, and he is before the writer throughout as the cause of the suffering which so greatly distressed and depressed him.

St. 1. Ll. 1—3, 菀,—as in II. iv. VIII. 7, *et al.* 桑 柔 = 柔 桑, 'a soft, *i. e.*, a young mulberry tree.' The characters are inverted for the sake of the rhyme. 其 下, 'beneath it,' = the shade afforded by it. 侯 is the particle, = 维. 旬 is defined by 遍,—'wide.' 捋,—as in I. xv. II. 3; comp. also I. i. VIII. 2. 刘 = 残, 'to lacerate and destroy.' The 其 刘 places the stript tree before us as in a picture. These three lines are metaphorical of the flourishing kingdom which was now brought to the verge of ruin. Ll. 4—6. 瘼,—as in II. v. X. 2. 殄 = 绝, 'to come to an end.' 仓 兄 mean 'commiseration (悲 闵 之 意);'—equivalent to the same characters with 心 at the side. Maou took them differently; but we need not take up his interpretation of them, nor that of 填, which he explained by 久, 'long-continued;'—a meaning which it elsewhere has. Choo says that he does not himself know what to make of this last character; but the view given in the translation is sufficiently natural and simple. It is from Hoo Yih-kwei (胡 一 桂; Yuen dyn.) who says 填, 满 也, 积 也, 仓 兄 填 兮, 言 悲 闵 积 满 于 中 之 意. In ll. 7, 8, the writer

二章
四牡骙骙。旐旟有翩。乱生不夷。靡国不泯。民靡有

黎。具祸以烬。於乎有哀。国步斯频。

三章
国步蔑资。天不我将。靡所止疑。云徂何往。君子实

2 The four steeds [gallop about], eager and strong;
The tortoise-and-serpent and the falcon banners fly about.
Disorder grows, and no peace can be secured.
Every State is being ruined;
There are no black heads among the people;
All are reduced to ashes, [as it were], by calamity.
Oh! alas!
The doom of the kingdom hurries on.

3 There is nothing to arrest the doom of the kingdom;
Heaven does not nourish us.
There is no place in which to stop securely;
There is no place to which to go.

appeals to Heaven. 倬 = 明貌, 'bright-looking;'—see in i. IV. 4. 宁 = 何, 'how,' 'why.'

St. 2. *The consequences of the king's misgovernment in the wars and desolation everywhere prevailing.* Ll. 1,2 give us a picture of an army on its march. L. 1,—see II. iii. III. 1. L. 2,—see II. i. VIII; 2. 有翩 give 'the app. of the banners flying in the wind.' L. 3 describes the effects of the constant strife. 夷 = 平, apparently used as a verb,—'to be pacified;' 泯 = 灭, 'to be extinguished,' 'to be ruined.' 黎 is used in the sense of 'black-headed,' and l. 4 gives a very graphic picture of the times, when the young and able-bodied of the people were slain or absent on distant expeditions, so that only old and gray-headed people were to be seen (斯时丁壮尽行·国中之民未有黎首). Maou tries to construe 黎 in the sense of 齐, so that the line = 'The people are disordered.' Yen Ts'an takes it as = 众,—'The people are few.' Choo's interpretation seems to bring its own evidence with it. 具 = 俱, 'all.' 祸, 'calamity,' has here the force of a verb in the passive,—'to be *calamitized*,' if we could say so.

以烬 = 'so as to be reduced to ashes.' In ll. 7,8, the writer makes his moan, as if he felt that it was of no use again appealing to Heaven. 有哀 = 'alas!' 'it is deplorable.' 步 is used much as in II. viii. V. 2. It is defined here, in the same way, by 运 = 'revolution,' 'doom,' 'fate.' 频 = 急, 'urgent.' 斯 = the graphic 其.

St. 3. *The same subject, with an indication of the writer's view that the misery was all owing to the king's neglect of the men who would give him peaceful counsels.* L. 1. 蔑资,—much as in II. xiii. X. 5. Choo here construes 资 as there, = 'alas!'; but still more unnaturally. The writer says that 'the fate of the kingdom has nothing to rely on (国运困穷,无所资赖). L. 2. 将 = 养, 'to nourish.' L. 3. Both Maou and Choo define 疑 here by 定, 'established,' 'sure;' and it is found in the dictionary in that sense, with the pronunciation *ying*; though here it is commonly read as *yih*, which also is given in the dict. with a kindred signification. L. 4. 云 is the initial particle; though we might also construe it here as = 'to say.' 徂 and 往 can hardly be distinguished in

维。秉心无竞。谁生厉阶。至今为梗。

四章

忧心殷殷。念我土宇。我生不辰。逢天僤怒。自西徂

东。靡所定处。多我觏痻。孔棘我圉。

Superior men are the bonds [of the social state],
Allowing no love of strife in their hearts.
Who reared the steps of the dissatisfaction,
Which has reached the present distress?

4　The grief of my heart is extreme,
And I dwell on [the condition of] our territory.
I was born at an unhappy time,
To meet with the severe anger of Heaven.
From the west to the east,
There is no quiet place of abiding.
Many are the distresses I meet with;
Very urgent is the trouble on our borders.

meaning—'If we would go, where can we go to (云往耳，而果何所往也).' Ll. 5, 6 are hard to construe. Maou says nothing at all on l. 5. Ch'ing understood by 君子 the princes of the States. Yen Ts'an refers it to king Le (指厉王), and this seems also to have been the view of Choo, who says, 然非君子之有争心也，谁实为此祸阶使至今为病乎. But they both refrain from giving any explanation of the 维; which, evidently, has here a distinct verbal force of its own. The key to the true meaning is found in II. iv. VII. 3, where 维 = 持, 'to hold together.' Then 君子 will mean the good and able men in whose hands the govt. should have been (执政之君子，实宜维持国家); and l. 6 indicates the ruling principle of their character and course,—seeking peace and pursuing it, so as to maintain order. But such men were not in favour with the king; and he is intended in ll. 7, 8, laying the stair-steps of evil (厉 = 恶), by

his neglect and discouragement of them. 梗 = 病, 'distress,' 'misery.'

St. 4. *The writer continues to dwell on the misery of the country, and his own sadness in the contemplation of it.* 殷殷,—as in II. iv. VIII. 12. 土宇,—as in ii. VIII. 3. Choo, indeed, here defines 土 by 乡, 'village,' and 宇 (after Maou) by 居, 'dwelling,' or 'residence;' but I prefer to take the terms as in the former passage,—more generally. Choo's view was the same, probably, as that of Ying-tah, that the writer was an officer engaged in the conduct of an expedition of the east, and that, in this l. 2, he is thinking of home; but I do not see that we are required by anything in the verses to take such a view. 不辰 = 不时, 'an unpropitious time.' 僤 = 厚, 'great.' Another reading is 亶. L. 5 seems to me equivalent merely to 'from the west (where the capital was) to the east;' i.e., all through the kingdom. 痻 = 病, 'to be afflicted,' 'distress.' 圉 is defined by 边 and 垂, 'borders.' The distress not only prevailed in the kingdom, but beyond. The rude tribes

五章

为谋为毖。乱况斯削。告尔忧恤。诲尔序爵。谁能执

热。逝不以濯。其何能淑。载胥及溺。

六章

如彼溯风。亦孔之僾。民有肃心。荓云不逮。好是稼

5 You have your counsels; you employ caution;
But the disorder grows and dismemberments ensue.
I tell you the subjects for anxiety;
I instruct you how to distinguish the orders of men.
Who can hold anything hot?
Must he not dip it [first] in water?
How can you [by your method] bring a good state of things
    about?
You [and your advisers] will sink together in ruin.

6 [The state of things] is like going in the teeth of the wind,
Which makes one quite breathless.
Some have a mind to go forward,
But they are made to think it is of no use to do so.

were pressing on the borders; but this does not necessarily imply that the writer was serving there.

In st. 5 the writer addresses himself directly to the king, who is intended by the 尔, 'you.' We have to understand an 尔, as the subject of the 为 in l. 1. 毖＝慎, 'to be careful,' 'caution.' Some take the 1st 为 as＝'to form,' 'to make,' and the 2d as＝以 为, 'to take to be,' 'to think;' but they are evidently co-ordinate (王岂不谋且慎哉). The king's plans, however, were radically bad, and their consequences were evil. 况＝滋, 'to increase;' 斯 削,－斯＝则, or with little more force than 而, 'and (而 国 日 削).' In ll. 3, 4 the writer says he had told the king what matters should occasion him the most anxiety, and how he could remedy the disorder prevailing only by the use of the proper men. 序 爵＝次 序 贤 能 之 爵, 'to arrange in an orderly way the rank of the worthy and able.' Ts'aou Suy-chung says, 'Outside the royal domain were the dukes, marquises, earls, viscounts, and barons; about the court were the koo, the kung, and all the various officers:—these had the rank. In arranging the individuals,

those of ability and virtue should have been placed in high positions for the conduct of affairs, and those of a difft. style, in low positions, simply to receive orders; those who achieved merit should have been advanced, and those who did not so, should have been dismissed.' Ll. 5—8. A heated substance would only injure him who handled it incautiously; and the king's measures could only lead himself and others to ruin;—see ll. 5, 6 quoted by Mencius, IV. Pt. i. VII. 6, where the meaning is plain; but still I am puzzled with l. 6. 逝, indeed, is merely the initial particle, like 载 in l. 8; but I have ventured to take a new view of 不 以 濯. Nearly all the critics suppose them to mean—'without dipping the hand in water.' But to dip the hands in water will not be of much service in laying hold of a heated substance; whereas, if the substance be put in the water and cooled, it may then be handled. I verily believe this is the meaning; but the utmost Wang Taou will allow to it, is that it may be proposed as a new view (可 备 一 说). The Tso-chuen, under the 31st year of duke Sëang, quotes the passage rather in accordance with my view.

St. 6. *But those who might have been effectual advisers and helpers to the king had been forced hopelessly to retire from the public service.* Ll. 1, 2. 溯 风 is 'going against, in the teeth of, the wind.' To do so produces breathlessness (僾

稸。力民代食。稼穑维宝。代食维好。

七章
天降丧乱。灭我立王。降此蟊贼。稼穑卒痒。哀恫中

国。具赘卒荒。靡有旅力。以念穹苍。

They attach themselves to husbandry,
And labour like the people instead of eating [the bread of
office].
Their sowing and reaping are precious to them;
They love this substitute for [official] emolument.

7　Heaven is sending down death and disorder,
And has put an end to our king.
It is sending down those devourers of the grain,
So that the husbandry is all in evil case.
All is in peril and going to ruin;
I have no strength [to do anything],
And think of [the Power in] the azure vault.

— 嗢, 'difficulty in breathing'). Thus a strong opposing wind acts on men's breath; and similarly did the king's oppressive govt. act on men's minds. L. 3 is assigned to men who would take service if they could do any good. 民 is equivalent to 人,—meaning men of worth (民 犹 人 也, 指 贤 人). 肃 = 进, 'to advance;' i. e., to enter on public employment. L. 4. 荓 = 使, 'to cause.' It is best to take it in the passive:—Such men are made to say, 'We cannot do anything (皆 使 之 曰, 世 乱 也, 非 吾 所 能 及 也).' Ll. 5—8. Such men, dispirited, take to farmers, and are happier than if they had struggled on for office. 力 民 代 食 = 尽 力 农 民 之 事 以 代 禄 食, 'They put forth their strength on the business of husbandmen to be a substitute for an official provision.' 宝,—'to be precious.' — 爱, 'to prize,' or 'love.'

St. 7. I have observed in the introductory note that, in ll 1, 2 here, there seems to be an allusion to the casting out of king Le, and his flight to Che. In no other way can l. 2 be explained so naturally. I agree therefore in taking 灭, with Choo, as in the past-complete tense, rather than with Yen Ts'an, in the future, as if the writer were speaking of the issue to which things were tending. 我 立 王,—'the king whom we had established.' Le would succeed according to the testament of his father; but the ministers would carry that into execution. Ll. 3, 4 indicate famine as another evil following in the wake of many others, so that those who had taken to husbandry would hardly find a living by it. 蟊 贼—see in II. vi. VIII. 2. 痒,—see in II. iv. VIII. 1. 卒 = 尽, 'altogether,' 'entirely.' Ll. 5, 6. 哀 恫,—a compound exclamation;—'alas! alas!' 具 = 俱, 'all together;' 赘 gives us the idea of 'repetition,' 'one thing as connected with another.' Ll. 7, 8. 旅 力,—as in II. vi. I. 3; but the idea is here simply that of 'strength,' or 'ability.' 穹 苍, 'the concave azure,' is a name for heaven, =our azure vault. The 'Flower and Essence of the She' expands these lines well:— 斯 时 曾 无 有 竭 力 于 朝, 忧 念 上 天

八章
维此惠君。民人所瞻。秉心宣犹。考慎其相。维彼不
顺。自独俾臧。自有肺肠。俾民卒狂。
九章
瞻彼中林。牲牲其鹿。朋友已谮。不胥以谷。人亦有
言。进退维谷。

8 Here is a good and righteous ruler,
Who is looked up to by the people and by all;—
He keeps his heart, and his plans are formed on mature deli-
beration,
Searching carefully for helpers.
There is one who has no such character,
But reckons only his own views to be good;—
He holds only to his own thoughts,
And causes the people to be distracted.

9 Look into the middle of that forest,
At the herds of deer roaming together.
[But here] friends are insincere,
And do not help one another in what is good.
People have the saying,
'To go forwards or backwards is alike impracticable.'

之降灾也，盖念穹苍，则必求
所以挽回天意矣.

St. 8. *Two pictures;—the good and thoughtful ruler, and the wayward.* Këang contends that by the good ruler here are intended the two loyal ministers,—the dukes of Shaou and Chow. But I cannot agree with him. If such had been the writer's intention, he would have indicated it more clearly. The former picture is of what king Lë ought to have been; the latter, of what he was. 惠 in l.1 is defined by its opposite 不 顺；in l.5, 惠 = 顺 理 , 'to act in accordance with reason and principle.' In l.3, the 'keeping the heart' is expressive of impartiality,—even justice. 宣 = 遍；—the plans are formed after mature consideration, and large advice. 考,—'to examine;' with reference to the care with which he looks out for advisers；慎,—'to be cautious;' with reference

to the care with which he employs them. In l.6, 俾 = 以 为 , 'to consider, or allow, to be.' L.7, 肺 肠 , 'lungs and intestines;'—comp. 心 腹 肾 肠 in the Shoo, IV.vii. Pt. iii. 3. L. 8. 卒,—as in the prec. st.

St. 9. *An instance of the disorder of the times in the faithlessness of friends.* L.2 牲 牲 represents the deer as 'numerous and moving together.' Comp. 诜 诜 in I. i. V. 1. L.3. 谮 = 不 信 , 'not true,' faithless.' L.4 = 不 相 与 以 善 道 , 'They do not associate together in good ways;'—the intercourse of friends was not like the intercourse of deer. This is an instance of what is called 反 兴, 'allusion by contrast.' L.6. 谷 is explained by 穷, 'to be reduced to the last degree,'=to be impracticable.

十章
维此圣人。瞻言百里。维彼愚人。覆狂以喜。匪言不
能。胡斯畏忌。

十一章
维此良人。弗求弗迪。维彼忍心。是顾是复。民之贪
乱。宁为荼毒。

十二章
大风有隧。有空大谷。维此良人。作为式谷。维彼不
顺。征以中垢。

10   Here is a wise man;—
His views and words reach to a hundred *le*.
There is a stupid man;—
He on the contrary rejoices in his madness.
It is not that I could not speak [all this];—
How is it I was withheld by my fear?

11   Here is a good man,
But he is not sought out nor employed.
There is a hard-hearted man,
And he is thought of and promoted once and again.
The people [in consequence] desire disorder,
And find enjoyment in bitter, poisonous ways.

12   Great winds have a path;—
They come from the large empty valleys.
Here is a good man,
Whose doings will be good.
There is a man unobservant of the right,
Whose goings will be according to his inward filthiness.

St. 10. *The wise man and the stupid;*—two classes of the king's advisers. Ll. 1,2 indicate the foresight of the wise man. Choo says, 圣人 炳 于 几 先, 所 视 而 言 者, 无 远 而 不 察. The king's advisers were of the stupid and reckless class. The writer could have warned the king against them; but he was restrained by his fear of his violence.

St. 11. *The good man and the cruel; and the consequence of the king's giving all his favour to the latter.* 迪 = 进, meaning to advance to office, and to employ. 复 = 重, 'to repeat.' The meaning is as in the translation. The people became like the officers whom the king maintained over them. 宁 = 甘, 'pleased,' 'to find it sweet.' 荼,—see on I. iii. VIII. 2. Choo says, 'The t'oo is a bitter vegetable, whose taste is bitter, and its juice is acrid, and injurious to life; hence it is called 荼毒.'

St. 12. *The good man and the unprincipled act each according to his nature.* 隧 = 道, 'the way,' or 'path.' Great winds come out from the hollow valleys. There is, as it were, their birth-place. 式 is defined by 用, 'to use;' but it is really nothing more than the copula. Choo says he does not understand l. 6; but is

十三章

大风有隧。贪人败类。听言则对。诵言如醉。匪用其

良。覆俾我悖。

十四章

嗟尔朋友。予岂不知而作。如彼飞虫。时亦弋获。既

之阴女。反予来赫。

13 Great winds have a path;—
The covetous men try to subvert their peers.
I would speak, if he would hear my words,
But I can [only] croon them over as if I were drunk.
He will not employ the good,
And on the contrary causes me [such] distress.

14 Ah! my friends,
Is it in ignorance that I make [this ode]?
[But it may happen] as in the case of a bird on the wing,
Which sometimes is hit and caught.
I go to do you good,
But you become the more incensed against me.

willing to accept 征 as = 行, 'to go,' = to do. If we assent to this, then there should be no difficulty with the 中. Its most natural meaning is what I have given (中垢者, 由中而发于外也). Wang Taou says there is probably an error of the text in 征. This is very likely.

St. 13. Choo says that 败类 is equivalent to 圮族 in the Shoo, I. 11, which we may admit. Ll. 3, 4 are very variously construed; but the view which I have given of them is as likely as any. 对 here is not 'to answer,' but 'to speak to,' to take the initiative. 诵言,—'to croon one's words to one's self.' Choo Kung-ts'een says, 无可与语,故自诵其言耳,诵言犹云独语也. 悖 (or with 言 at the side) = 乱, 'disorder,' 'confusion.' I think the writer must be referring to his own state of mind as indicated in l. 4. Wang Taou, however, takes 我 as = 我民, in which cases 悖 would be expressive of the general disorder that prevailed.

Sze-ma Ts'een, in his account of king Le, says that in his 30th year his chief favourite was a duke E of Yung (荣夷公), and that Lëang-foo of Juy remonstrated with him on the ground of E's well known covetousness and greed;— but without effect. It may be therefore that he is specially intended by the 贪人 of this stanza.

St. 14. By the 'friends,' whom the writer addresses in this stanza, we are to understand the evil ministers of the king. We need not suppose that the name is ironical;—he would fain be their friend, if they would only allow him to be so. The meaning of l. 2 is, that he knew what reception his sentiments were likely to meet with. He goes on to say, in ll. 3, 4, that, notwithstanding, he might do some good:—as birds on the wing are generally missed, yet sometimes one is brought down (岂无一二或中者乎). 虫 is used here as = 鸟, 'a bird;' —it is often employed not of insects merely, but of all living creatures. 弋,—see on Ana. VII. xxvi; 弋获 = 射中, 'to shoot and hit.' Ll. 5, 6 are an expostulation. 之 is taken as = 往, 'to go,' in consequence of the 来 in l. 6. 阴 (in 3d tone),—'to afford shelter to,' = to

十五章
民之罔极。职凉善背。为民不利。如云不克。民之回

遹。职竞用力。

十六章
民之未戾。职盗为寇。凉曰不可。覆背善詈。虽曰匪

予。既作尔歌。

15　The unlimited disorder of the people
　　Is owing to those hypocrites, skilful to prevaricate.
　　They work out the injury of the people,
　　As if their efforts were not equal to it.
　　The depravity of the people
　　Is brought about by their strenuous endeavours.

16　That the people are unsettled
　　Is owing to the robbers that prey on them.
　　Hypocritical, they say 'These men will not do;'
　　But when their backs are turned, they show their skill in re-
　　viling [the good].
　　Although you say, 'We did not do this,'
　　I have made this song about you.

benefit (as if there were 艹 at the top). 赫＝ 'to be angry with (加赫然之怒于已).' Choo mentions, with a measure of approbation, a view of these two lines, taking 阴 with its usual meaning and tone:—'I went and privately told you my views, and yet you say on the contrary that I came to terrify you (赫＝吓).'

St. 15. With ll. 1, 5 comp. ll. 5, 6 of st. 11. 职 in ll. 2, 6,—with the meaning which we have often found, and which is explained by 主 and 专, meaning—'to be owing to,' 'to be determined by.' Choo says he does not understand 凉 in l. 2; but he gives Maou's explanation of it by 薄, with reference to the 'light, bad ways' of those in office; and Ch'ing's by 谅＝信, 'to be true.' He approves of the latter, but manipulates it himself into 'hypocrites (名为直谅).' 善背＝工为反覆,—as in the translation. 云 in l. 4 is the particle intermediate. 回遹,—as in II. 12. 职竞用力＝亦由此辈专竞用力而然也;—the 职竞 are construed together.

St. 16. 戾＝定, 'to settle,'—as in II. iv. X. 2. 职,—as in the prec. stanza. So with 凉 in l. 3.—'They hypocritically say that small men will not do to be in office; but when their backs are turned from you, they show their skill in speaking evil to revile superior men.' So Choo says on ll. 3, 4. On ll. 5, 6, his words are, 'But these men gloss themselves over, and think that they did not speak so; but I have made this song [about them]:—I know the truth; the thing is evident and cannot be concealed (然其人又自文饰,以为此非我言也,则我已作尔歌矣,言得其情,且事已著明,不可掩覆也).' It is not worth the space to discuss other interpretations. On 匪予 Hoo Yih-kwei says, 是不认过之词, 'It is a refusal to acknowledge their fault.' 作尔歌＝已作此诗而歌汝之行, 'I have made this ode, and sung your conduct.'

The rhymes are—in st. 1, 柔, 刘, 忧, cat. 3, t. 1; 旬, 民, 填, 天, 矜 *, cat. 12, t. 1: in 2, 骙, 夷, 黎, 哀 *, cat. 15, t. 1; 翩 *,

IV. *Yun han.*

云汉
一章
倬彼云汉。昭回于天。王曰於乎。何辜今之人。天降
丧乱。饥馑荐臻。靡神不举。靡爱斯牲。圭璧既卒。

1 Bright was that milky way,
Shining and revolving in the sky.
The king said, 'Oh!
What crime is chargeable on us now,
That Heaven [thus] sends down death and disorder?
Famine comes again and again.

泯, 烬, 频, cat. 12, t. 1 : in 3, 资, 疑 (prop. cat. 1), 维, 阶, cat. 15, t. 1; 将, 往, 竞 *, 梗 *, cat. 10 : in 4, 殷, 辰 *, 东 (prop. cat. 9), 瘼, cat. 13; 宇, 怒, 处, 圉, cat. 5, t. 2 : in 5, 悖 *, 恤 *, 热 (prop. cat. 15), cat. 12, t. 3; 削, 爵 *, 濯 *, 溺 *, cat. 2 : in 6, 风 *, 心, cat. 7, t. 1; 瘝, 逮, cat. 15, t. 3; 穑, 食, cat. 1, t. 3; 宝 *, 好 *, cat. 3, t. 2 : in 7, 王, 瘅, 荒, 苍, cat. 10; 贼, 国, 力, cat. 1, t. 3 : in 8, 瞻 (prop. cat. 8), 相, 臧, 肠, 狂, cat. 10 : in 9, 林, 谮, cat. 7, t. 1; 麃, 穀, 谷, cat. 3, t. 3 : in 10, 人 人, cat. 12, t. 1; 里, 喜, 能 *, 忌, cat. 1, t. 2 : in 11, 迪 *, 复, 毒, cat. 3, t. 3 : in 12, 谷, 穀, 垢 (prop. cat. 4), *ib.*: in 13, 隧, 类, 对, 醉, 悖, cat. 15, t. 3 : in 14, 作 *, 获 *, 赫 *, cat. 5, t. 3 : in 15, 极, 背 *, 克, 力, cat. 1, t. 3 : in 16, 寇 (prop. cat. 4), 可, 罟 *, 歌, cat. 17.

Ode 4. Narrative. KING SEUEN, ON OCCASION OF A GREAT DROUGHT, EXPOSTULATES WITH GOD AND ALL THE SPIRITS, WHO MIGHT BE EXPECTED TO SUCCOUR HIM AND HIS PEOPLE, ASKS THEM WHEREFORE THEY WERE CONTENDING WITH HIM, AND DETAILS THE MEASURES HE HAD TAKEN, AND WAS STILL TAKING, FOR THE REMOVAL OF THE CALAMITY. King Seuen does not occur by name in the ode, though it is ascribed in st. 1 to a king; and all critics accept the statement of the Preface that it was made, in admiration of Seuen, by Jing Shuh (仍叔),—a great officer, we may presume, of the court. It is mentioned in the Ch'un Ts'ëw, under the 5th year of duke Hwan (B. C. 706), that the king sent the son of

Jing Shuh on a mission to the court of Loo; and this, it is supposed, was the son of the writer of this ode. This is just possible; but Seuen's accession is placed in B. C. 876, and his great death in B. C. 781. Jing Shuh may have been the standing appellation of the Head of the family. At what year in Seuen's reign the drought occurred, and whether it extended over a series of years, we cannot ascertain. The 'Bamboo Books' refer it to the 21st year of king Le, and say that it continued on to his death in Che, and that then, on the restoration of his son (king Seuen) by the two regents, there ensued a great rain. Hwang-poo Meih refers it to the end of Seuen's reign, as a judgment for the errors into which he then fell. The standard chronology places it in B. C. 821,—Seuen's 6th year. This point must be left undetermined. As Këang says, 疏以宣王遭旱, 早晚及旱年多少, 经传无文, 当阙之是也。 St. 1. Ll. 1, 2 are introductory, and must be translated in the past tense. The author would have us think of the king gazing at night on the sky, to see if there were any indications of coming rain. As there were none, he gave vent to his feelings in the verses that follow. 云汉,—as in i. IV. 4. Ts'aou Suy-chung says, 'The appearance of the Han in the sky is like a cloud, and yet it is not a cloud;—hence it is called "The cloudy Han!"' I do not think, however, the name means anything more than 'the Han in the clouds.' What the Han was on the face of the earth, that the Milky Way was in the sky. 昭 = 光, 'bright;' 回 = 转, 'turning,' 'revolving.' Këang observes that l. 4 is not to be understood as spoken murmuringly;—the king really wished to know what offence he and his people were chargeable with. L. 6. 饥馑,—see on II. iv. X. 1. 荐,—*i. q.* 荐, 'to occur repeatedly;' 臻 = 至, 'to come.' The phrase denotes that the drought had not been of one year only (言非一岁之旱). The 举

宁莫我听。

二章
旱既大甚。蕴隆虫虫。不殄禋祀。自郊徂宫。上下奠
瘗。靡神不宗。后稷不克。上帝不临。耗斁下土。宁
丁我躬。

There is no victim I have grudged;
Our maces and other tokens are exhausted:—
How is it that I am not heard?

2　'The drought is excessive;
Its fervours become more and more tormenting.
I have not ceased offering pure sacrifices;
From the border altars I have gone to the ancestral temple.
To the [Powers] above and below I have presented my offer-
　　ings and then buried them:—
There is no Spirit whom I have not honoured.
How-tseih is not equal to the occasion;
God does not come to us.

in l. 7 has a pregnant meaning,—舉而祭之 'to take up and sacrifice to.' Choo illustrates the line by referring to a custom, in times of great calamity, of sacrificing to all Spirits, even searching out sacrifices that had fallen into disuse, and reviving them. L. 8. 爱＝'to grudge,'—as often. 斯牲,—any victims. L. 9. We have in the Shoo, V. vi. an instance of the use of the *peih* and *kwei* in sacrificing;—see on pp. 4, 8. All such symbols in the royal tressury had been used on this occasion. 卒＝尽, 'to be used up,' 'to be exhausted.' L. 10. 宁＝何, 'why,' or 'how.' Yen Ts'an remarks that 宁 occurs frequently in this ode, and is explained now by 曾, now by 偏, now by 安 (or 何), and now as expressing a wish. We must not cling tenaciously, he says, to ex-plain it always in the same way, but follow the exigency of each passage. Here again, Këang cautions the reader against finding in the line the language of complaint.

St. 2. L. 1. 大甚 ＝'is too or very exces-sive.' L. 2. The Urh-ya explains 虫虫 (with 火 at the side) by 熏, 'steaming vapour.' Here it denotes the fervent heat;—accumulated (蕴＝蓄 or 积), and very violent (隆＝盛). L. 3＝我禋祀未尝止绝,

'my pure sacrifices have never ceased.' 禋祀,—as in II. vi. VIII. 4. L. 4. 宫＝宗庙, 'the ancestral temple;'—as often. 郊,—'the border altars,' at which Heaven and Earth were sacrificed to; a service, according to Confucius, rendered to God. See the 'Doctrine of the Mean,' XIX. 6. In l. 5, 上 is interpreted of the sacrifice to Heaven, and 下 of that to the Earth. 奠 is the placing of the offerings on the ground (or on the altars) during the sacrifice; 瘗, 'the burying them afterwards in the earth (奠是方祭时事, 瘗是祭毕时事).' The two terms embrace all the articles used in sacrificing;—as Ying-tah says, 礼神之物, 酒, 食, 牲, 玉之属, 'the spirits, the eatables (grain and cakes), the jade-tokens.' The fact that these were all buried at the conclusion of the sacrifice explains the statement in the preceding stanza about the jade-tokens being used up. L. 6. 宗＝尊, 'to honour.' Ll. 7, 8. How-tseih was not able to deliver from the drought (不克); and God, who could have given the help, would not do it. Hence Choo explains 临 by 享, 'to accept the offerings.' I prefer translating the term as I have done. Yen Ts'an says, 不肯临顾

三章
旱既大甚。則不可推。兢兢業業。如霆如雷。周餘黎民。靡有孑遺。昊天上帝。則不我遺。胡不相畏。先祖于摧。

This wasting and ruin of our country,—
Would that it fell [only] on me!

3 The drought is excessive,
And I may not try to excuse myself.
I am full of terror and feel the peril,
Like the clap of thunder or the roll.
Of the remnant of Chow, among the black-haired people,
There will not be half a man left;
Nor will God from His great heaven
Exempt [even] me.
Shall we not mingle our fears together?
[The sacrifices to] my ancestors will be extinguished.

我. Ll. 9, 10., 耗 *i. q.* 耗,—'to waste,' 'to injure;' 敉 = 敗, 'to ruin.' 丁 = 当, 'to light upon.' Choo takes 宁 as in last stanza, = 何; but there seems to be an opposi on between 下 土, meaning the country generally, the people, and 我 躬, the king's own person. I prefer therefore taking 宁 as = 'would that.' Choo himself says that such a construction is not at all unsuitable (或 曰, 与 其 耗 敉 下 土, 宁 使 灾 害 当 我 身 也, 亦 通). It was one of the Soos who first proposed this view.

St. 3. L. 2. Both Maou and Choo define 推 by 去, 'to put away,' 'to remove;' so that the line simply says that the drought could not be removed. The significance of the term, however, is deeper than this. Its primary meaning is 'to push away;' and the king is speaking, I believe, of the responsibility for the calamity,—how he acknowledged it as resting on himself, and did not wish to put it off on any other body (不 可 推 其 过 于 他 人). Compare 王 无 罪 岁, in Men. I. Pt. i. III. 5. In ll. 3, 4 the king is speaking of his own alarm, and not, as Ch'ing says, of that of the people. 兢 兢 =

恐, 'to be afraid;' 业 业 = 危, 'to be or to feel in peril.' L. 4,—as in II. iii. IV. 4. Ll. 5, 6. 周 余 = 周 家 所 余 之 民, 'the people that remain of the House of Chow;'—referring, probably, to the way in which the country had been depopulated in the preceding reign. 孑 = 无 右 臂 貌, 'the app. of a person who has lost the right arm;' and hence it comes to signify 'half a man.' See the remarks of Mencius on the absurdity of taking these lines literally, and the important canon which he lays down for the interpretation of the She (V. Pt. i. IV. 2). As Choo expands it, we must here bring to the interpretation our understanding of the object of the writer, and then we perceive that the king is grieving over the drought, and does not really mean to say that there would be none of the people left. Ll. 7, 8. I cannot take 昊 天 上 帝 otherwise than in the translation. Lacharme makes the two parts of the line in apposition:—'*Augustum cœlum qui est summus rerum dominus et dominator.*' But such an apposition of the personal name and the vague designation of Heaven, especially with the epithet of 'great' attached, is to my mind exceedingly unnatural. 则 in l. 8 has the force of our 'even.' Even the king himself would not be left. The terms are not to be understood as a sort of repetition of ll. 5, 6,—that the people would not be left to him. Ll. 9 10. The king turns, as it were, to his officers and relatives, and calls on them to sympathize with him

四章
旱既大甚。則不可沮。赫赫炎炎。云我无所。大命近

止。靡瞻靡顾。群公先正。則不我助。父母先祖。胡

宁忍予。

五章
旱既大甚。涤涤山川。旱魃为虐。如惔如焚。我心惮

4 'The drought is excessive,
And it cannot be stopped.
More fierce and fiery,
It is leaving me no place.
My end is near;—
I have none to look up to, none to look round to.
The many dukes and their ministers of the past
Give me no help.
O ye parents and [nearer] ancestors,
How can ye bear to see us thus?

5 'The drought is excessive;—
Parched are the hills, and the streams are dried.

in his distress and fears. Ho Këae is the only critic, so far as I have observed, who points out this force of the 相（胡不相畏, 对大夫，君子言之，言我君子，何可不相与畏惧乎）. 摧＝灭, 'to be extinguished.' 于 is the particle. By 'ancestors' being extinguished, he means that their sacrifices would be so,—the greatest calamity which a filial Chinese can conceive (先祖之祀，将自此而灭也). Throughout the Ch'un Ts'ëw, the extinction of a family or a State means the extinction of its sacrifices.

St. 4. L. 2. 沮＝止, 'to be stopped,' L. 3 is descriptive of the fierce blazing heat that accompanied the drought (旱气, 热气). L. 4. Many critics make 云＝皆云, 'all say.' It is, however, merely the initial particle. 我无所,—'I have no place,' i. e., of shelter. The suffering was unendurable. Ll. 5, 6. 大命 occurs in I. 7, meaning 'the great appointment' of Heaven in giving the throne to the House of Chow; but it can hardly have that meaning here, and it is understood to be a designation of death. The 'Complete Digest' says that it must be taken not of the king only,

but of all the people (大命，合天下之人);—which I do not see. 止 is the final particle. Ll. 7, 8 tell us that the king had sacrificed to all the ducal lords of Chow in the early period of the House's history, and their ministers of note;—but without avail. 正 is used of the Heads of official departments (正者长也，先世官之长). Some take 群公 more generally,—of all princes of of States, who had signalized themselves by services to the people and to the kingdom. In ll. 9, 10 the king turns to his parents and his royal ancestors, nearer to him than the dukes of antiquity. He could hardly hope that his father, the oppressive Le, would, in his spirit-state, give him any aid; but we are only to find in his words the expression of natural feeling. Probably it was a regard to the character of Le, which made Ch'ing, and after him Ying-tah, take the 先祖 as kings Wǎn and Woo, and refer the 父母 to them as the parents of the people. In l. 10, Yen Ts'an and some others take 宁, as＝偏, 'partially,' 'what could not have been expected.' In its ordinary meaning of 'how,' it is tautological after 胡.

St. 5. L. 2. 涤涤 indicates the appearance of the hills and streams, as scorched by the

暑。忧心如熏。群公先正。则我不闻。昊天上帝。宁

俾我遁。

六章

旱既大甚。黾勉畏去。胡宁瘨我以旱。憯不知其故。

祈年孔夙。方社不莫。昊天上帝。则不我虞。敬恭明

神。宜无悔怒。

The demon of drought exercises his oppression,
As if scattering flames and fire.
My heart is terrified with the heat;—
My sorrowing heart is as if on fire.
The many dukes and their ministers of the past
Do not hear me.
O God, from Thy great heaven,
Grant me the liberty to withdraw [into retirement]!

6 'The drought is excessive;—
I struggle, and fear to go away.
How is it I am afflicted with this drought?
I cannot ascertain the cause of it.
In praying for a good year I was abundantly early;
I was not late [in sacrificing] to [the Spirits] of the four quarters
   and of the land.
God in the great heaven
Does not consider me.

heat. Maou defines it in the same way as 赫赫 in last st.,—旱气. The hills were parched, and vegetation on them withered; and the streams were dried up. Ll. 3, 4. 魃＝旱神, or 旱鬼, 'the demon of drought. Ying-tah, from 'The Book of Spirits and Prodigies,' gives the following account of him:—'In the southern regions there is a man, two or three cubits in length, with the upper part of his body bare, and his eyes in the top of his head. He runs with the speed of the wind, and is named Poh. In whatever State he appears, there ensues a great drought.' L. 4 is descriptive of the demon's action. 惔＝燎, 'to set on fire.' Ll. 5, 6. 憚＝劳, 'to be burdened with,' or 畏, 'to fear.' 熏,—'to smoke,' 'to steam.'

Ll. 7, 8. Comp. the corresponding lines of last stanza. Ll. 9, 10. 宁 is expressive of a wish. The king supposes that the calamity is owing to himself. As Këang expands the last line, 'If I do not satisfy the mind of Heaven, it were better to let me withdraw, and give place to one more worthy. Let not the multitudes of the people thus suffer on my account.'

St. 6. In this stanza the king ventures to expostulate with God, and to complain because of the calamity that had befallen the country, which he could in no way understand. L. 2. He had expressed a wish that he might retire from the throne; here he says that he was afraid to do so,—lest, apparently, he should thereby be leaving his post of duty. 黾勉 ＝ 'I earnestly exert myself.' Yen Ts'an says, 民命方

七章

旱既大甚。散无友纪。鞫哉庶正。疚哉冢宰。趣马师氏。膳夫左右。靡人不周。无不能止。瞻卬昊天。云

Reverent to the intelligent Spirits,
I ought not to be thus the object of their anger.

7 'The drought is excessive;—
All is dispersion, and the bonds of government are relaxed.
Reduced to extremities are the Heads of departments;
Full of distress are my chief minister,
The master of the horse, the commander of the guards,
The chief cook, and my attendants.
There is no one who has not [tried to] help [the people];
They have not refrained on the ground of being unable.

急，当思救，故亀勉于此. Choo says that he was afraid to go, because he had nowhere to go to（出无所之）. Ll. 3, 4. 胡宁，—as in st. 4. 瘨＝病, 'to distress.' 惨＝曾，—as in II. iv. VII. 1, et al. Ll. 5,6 must be translated in the past tense. They tell what had been the king's practice. The rule was that in the 1st month of spring he should pray to God for a blessing on the labours of the year, and in the 1st month of winter, to the Honoured ones of heaven（天宗,—the sun, moon, and stars）, for a blessing on the year to follow. He had not allowed the season to go by. On l. 6, see II. vi. VII. 2. These were sacrifices of thanksgiving, and the king had not delayed to offer them. Ll. 7—10. As the king had thus eagerly discharged his religious duties, God and all spiritual Beings should be pleased with him, and bless him, instead of dealing with him as they were doing. 虞＝度, 'to consider;' here, ＝ to sympathize with. 悔＝恨, 'to be angry with.'

St. 7. L. 2 is very perplexing. We ask what is the subject of 散, 'to be dispersed;' and it is difficult to tell. Choo says that 友纪 is equivalent to 纪纲, so that 无友纪＝ 'there is no government;' and he mentions the view of some that 友 is a misprint for 有. This seems to me very likely. In the misery and confusion occasioned by the drought, the ordinary duties of govt. were suspended, and 'all was dispersion.' Yen Ts'an and others, after Ch'ing, try to explain the 友 in its ordinary meaning, saying-that 'a ruler considers his

ministers to be his *friends*, with whom he directs the govt. of the kingdom（相与纲纪四方者）, but now, in the exigency of the drought, all their ordinary duties were suspended.' A meaning is thus brought out, the same as Choo's, but the attempt to explain the 友 is very forced. I must prefer taking 友 for 有. Këang would interpret 散 of 'a dispersion of the stores of grain,（指散粟赈济言）;' and though this view derives some support from the meaning given to l. 7, I cannot adopt it in this place. Ll. 3—6. 鞫＝穷, 'to be reduced to extremities.' 正,—as in stt. 4,5, 庶正＝众官之长. 疚＝病, 'to be distressed.' 冢宰, 趣马, 师氏, 膳夫,—see on II. iv. IX. 4. 左右 must be taken generally for the officers who attended on the king's person. Ll. 7,8 are to be taken of the officers mentioned, and generally. Choo expands them,—诸臣无有一人不周救百姓者, 无有自言不能, 而遂止不为也;—as in the translation. 周＝救, 'to save,' 'to help.' Ll. 9,10. 卬,—i. q. 仰, 'to look up to.' 云 is still the particle; 里 is defined by 忧, 'to be sorrowful;' as if it were 悝, which is so explained in the Urh-ya. It is amusing how often almost every word, about which there is any difficulty in these odes, becomes a battle-field of

如何里。

八章

瞻卬昊天。有嘒其星。大夫君子。昭假无赢。大命近

止。无弃尔成。何求为我。以戾庶正。瞻卬昊天。曷

惠其宁。

> I look up to the great heaven;—
> Why am I plunged in this sorrow?

8　'I look up to the great heaven,
　　But its stars sparkle bright.
　　My great officers and excellent men,
　　Ye have drawn near [to Heaven] with reverence with all your
　　　　powers.
　　Death is approaching,
　　But do not cast away what you have done.
　　You are seeking not for me only,
　　But to give rest to all our departments.
　　I look up to the great heaven;—
　　When shall I be favoured with repose?'

different interpretations. Këang takes 里 in the sense of 理, and makes l. 10 — 'In what way ought I to manage (不 知 更 当 如 何 办 理)?' Yen Ts'an takes it in the sense of 居, so that the line='What will become of the people in the fields and villages (田 里 之 间, 将 如 何 乎)?' It seems evident that the view which I have followed is the correct one.

St. 8. The king addresses himself to his officers, and tells them that though they might seem to have done their utmost, and in vain, they must still persevere, and concludes with a final appeal to Heaven. L. 2. 嘒 occurred in I. ii. X., with reference to the stars, meaning 'small-like,' and 嘒嘒 (= 有嘒) has twice occurred, onomatopoetic of the noise made by insects and bells; but neither of these usages suits the exigency of this line. Choo therefore defines the term here by 明 貌, 'bright-looking,' which may be the same, only more clearly expressed, as Maou's account of it,— 众 星 貌, 'the app. of all the stars.' There was nothing in the aspect of the sky to betoken rain. L. 4 has been variously explained, but I content myself with giving the view of Choo, who takes

假 as = 格, 'to come to,' meaning that the officers 'had come to Heaven,' co-operating earnestly with the king in all the services and measures which he had taken to remove or abate the calamity. They had done this until there seemed nothing left which they could do more (无 赢=无 余). Choo's words are— 群 臣 竭 其 精 诚, 而 助 王 以 昭 假 于 天 者 已 无 余 矣. We must give to 昭 the meaning of 'reverently,' 'sincerely.' Ll. 5, 6. The fruitlessness so far of all that had been done might engender a feeling of despair; but the king himself struggles against that, and encourages his officers to do the same. L. 5,— as in st. 4. Ll. 7, 8 remind the officers that it was not the king's interest only which they were seeking. L. 7='Is it that you are seeking [relief] for me only (何 但 求 为 我 之 一 身 而 已)?' 戾=定, 'to settle.' In ll. 9, 10 the king once more turns to Heaven, and begs its favour. 曷 惠 其 宁=何 时 惠 我 以 安 宁 乎, 'When will you favour me with repose?'

The rhymes are—in st. 1, 天, 人, 臻, cat. 12, t. 1; 牲, 听, cat. 11: in 2, 虫, 宫, 宗, 临 (prop. cat. 7) 躬, cat. 9: in 3, 推, 雷,

V. *Sung kaou.*

崧高

一章

崧高维岳。骏极于天。维岳降神。生甫及申。维申及甫。维周之翰。四国于蕃。四方于宣。

1   Grandly lofty are the mountains,
With their large masses reaching to the heavens.
From these mountains was sent down a Spirit,
Who gave birth to [the princes of] Foo and Shin.
Foo and Shin,
Are the support of Chow,
Screens to all the States,
Diffusing [their influence] over the four quarters of the kingdom.

遗，遗，畏，摧，cat. 15, t. 1: in 4, 沮，所，顾，助，祖，予，cat. 5, t. 2: in 5, 川*，焚，熏，闻，遁，cat. 13: in 6, 去，故，莫，虞，怒，cat. 5, t. 1: in 7, 纪，宰，氏 (prop. cat. 16)，右*，止，里，cat. 1, t. 2: in 8, 星，赢，成，正，宁，cat. 11.

Ode 5. Narrative. CELEBRATING THE APPOINTMENT BY KING SEUEN OF A RELATIVE TO BE THE MARQUIS OF SHIN, AND DEFENDER OF THE SOUTHERN BORDER OF THE KINGDOM, WITH THE ARRANGEMENTS MADE FOR HIS ENTERING ON HIS CHARGE. Seuen is not mentioned in the ode, but there is little doubt as to his being the king intended in it. The writer of it was Yin Keih-foo, who appears in II. iii. III. as the commander of an expedition, against the tribes of the Hëen-yun, in the commencement of that monarch's reign. Then in II. viii. III. we have an account of the building of Sëay as the capital of the State, which is also a principal topic in the ode before us. We must accept the date assigned to the piece; but a more important question is whether there had been previously a State of Shin, or whether that part of the country where it lay was now for the first time colonized. None of the Chinese critics have entered seriously on a discussion of this point; but it possesses considerable interest for the inquirer who is anxious to get for himself a definite knowledge of the growth of the kingdom of China. But for the expressions in st. 6 about the chief of Shin's *returning* to the south, I should adopt without hesitation the view that it was now for the first time that the State of Shin was constituted. We have in this ode and II. viii. III. the building and fortifying of Sëay as the capital city, the erection even of the ancestral temple, the laying out of the country

for cultivation, and the removal of the chief's family from the royal domain to it. All these statements point to colonization. If the undertaking was not entirely of that character, it was so to a great extent. Possibly, there may have been a Shin within the limits of the royal domain, south from the capital, the lord of which had done good service, and was in close alliance with the royal House, whom the king now invested with this newly formed principality, to defend the kingdom against the encroachments of the ambitious and restless Man. This would be a better solution of the difficulty than to suppose that there had been a State of Shin, beyond the limits of the royal domain, and that what was now done was to enlarge its territory, and build a new city as its capital in a situation better adapted to the exigencies of the time. Those, however, who adopt this view place the older capital in the present dis. of Nan-yang in the dept. of the same name, Ho-nan, while Sëay was in Tang Chow, in the same dept;—See, however, the notes on st. 6.—The movement which the ode celebrates with so much eclat did not turn out happily. King Seuen's son, Yëw, married a daughter of the House of Shin, a daughter probably of the chief mentioned here, and made her his queen. When he degraded her in consequence of his attachment to Paou Sze, her father formed an alliance with the Dog Jung, which issued in the death of Yëw, and the removal of the capital to Loh. Subsequently, Shin proved but a very ineffectual barrier against the tribes that were banded together under the rule of Ts'oo, and was extinguished and absorbed by that growing state during the period of the Ch'un Ts'ëw. I may add further here that in the history of the connection between the kings Seuen and Yëw and the House of Shin we have an illustration of how one-sided is the Chinese rule that individuals of the same surname shall not intermarry. This might seem to preclude the marriage of cousins; but it does so only in the male

二章

疊疊申伯。王缵之事。于邑于谢。南国是式。王命召

伯。定申伯之宅。登是南邦。世执其功。

2   Full of activity is the chief of Shin,
    And the king would employ him to continue the services [of
        his fathers],
    With his capital in Sëay,
    Where he should be a pattern to the States of the south.
    The king gave charge to the earl of Shaou,
    To arrange all about the residence of the chief of Shin,
    Where he should do what was necessary for the regions of
        the south,
    And where his posterity might maintain his merit.

line. King Seuen's mother was a Këang, and his son's wife was also a Këang. Husband and wife must have been very closely related by consanguinity.

St. 1. Ll. 1,—4. A mountain large and high is called 崧 ; and the largest of such mountains again are called 岳 (or 嶽); and the Shoo opens with a 'chief of the four mountains,' as the principal minister of Yaou:—see on the Shoo, I. 11. From this distant personage was descended the great family that boasted the surname of Këang, branches of which, in the time of Chow, ruled over the States of Ts'e, (齐), Heu (许), Shin (申), and Leu (吕) or Foo (甫). The four great mountains, or the Spirits presiding over them, were supposed to have a special interest in it, and hence are here said to have sent down a Spirit or Spirits which caused the birth of the princes of Shin and Foo, whom the writer of the ode had in his mind's eye. On the 3d line, 'The mountains sent down spirits,' Hwang Ch'un (黄 樿, Sung dyn.) remarks that it is merely a personification of the poet's fancy, to show how High Heaven had a mind to revive the fortunes of Chow, and that we need not trouble ourselves about whether there were such Spirits or not (惟 岳 降 神, 乃 诗 人 形 容 之 辞, 以 见 上 天 兴 周 之 意, 不 必 泥 其 有 无 也). By 申 and 甫 we must understand the princes of those States. There can be no doubt that by 申 is intended the 申 伯 of the ode, and as we know that 申 was a marquisate, I have translated these characters by the Chief of Shin, with

reference to the authority which we must suppose was given to the marquis over the States of the south generally. Choo supposes that 甫 indicates the marquis of Leu or Foo, to whom we owe the 27th Book of the 5th Part of the Shoo,—a prince of the time of king Muh, anterior to Seuen by nearly two centuries. A contemporary of the marquis of Shin must be intended, a descendant of that previous worthy, who had rendered important service to Seuen. Very absurd is the view of Yen Ts'an, that the person intended was Chung Shan-foo, who was the chief minister to Seuen. This interpretation is traceable to a comment of Ch'ing on the Le Ke, XXVI. 8, where the stanza is quoted. But we know from other sources that that Chung Shan-foo was not a Këang at all;—Sss on the next ode.

Ll. 5—8. 翰,—as in II. vii. I. 3, et al. The 于 in ll. 7, 8, and also in l. 4, st. 6, is the preposition, = 於, 'in,' 'at,' &c., the order of the characters being inverted for the sake of euphony. So says Wang Yin-che, the great Authority upon the particles. His words are:— 于, 於 也, 常 语 也, 亦 有 于 句 中 倒 用 者; and then he adduces the above three instances from this ode. 蕃,—as in ii. X. 8, 'a screen.' 宣=宣 其 德 泽, —as in the translation.

St. 2. Ll. 1—4. 疊 疊,—as in i. I. 2. Choo, indeed, says the phrase is used differently in the two places, but I cannot see the difference 缵 = 继, 'to continue.' It is used here with hiphil force. The king would have him continue his services in a new sphere (王 使 之 继).

三章

王命申伯。式是南邦。因是谢人。以作尔庸。王命召
伯。彻申伯土田。王命傅御。迁其私人。

3　The king gave charge to the chief of Shin,
'Be a pattern to the regions of the south,
And by means of those people of Sëay,
Proceed to display your merit.'
The king gave charge to the earl of Shaou,
To make the statutory definition of the territory and fields of
　　the chief of Shin.
The king gave charge to the chief's steward
To remove the members of his family to the spot.

事 refers to the services he had already rendered to the throne. I much prefer this to Choo's view of it as 'the services of his forefathers (先世之事).' 邑 is here used in the sense of 'a capital city,' as in i. X. 2, and the single term = the 作邑 there. The two 于 have to be disregarded, though there is a plausibility in Ying-tah's explanation of the first by 往, 'to go to,' and the second as the preposition. 式 = 'to give a pattern to (使诸侯以为法).' Ch'in P'ang-fei remarks that, in this 4th line, we have the commission of the marquis to take the leadership of the southern States (命为州牧).

Ll. 5,—8. 召伯,—see on II. viii. III. It is supposed that the earl of Shaou was minister of Works, and that on him devolved the duty of arranging the details of every new apportionment of territory. He was also, we may suppose, one of the *kung* at the court; but all this does not affect the translation of 伯 by 'earl.' 定宅, 'to settle the residences,' must mean to do all that was necessary to be done, as described in st. 4, for the chief of Shin's taking up his residence in Sëay. Ll. 7,8 refer to what he should do when settled there. 登 is defined by 成, 'complete.' Yen Ts'an tries in vain to bring out a suitable meaning from the ordinary acceptation of the term,—'to ascend.' L. 8 identifies him with his descendants.

St. 3. Ll. 1—4. L. 2. = l. 4 of last stanza. L. 3. Sëay was to be the centre of the State. The city and the country round it would be more thickly peopled than other parts; and there the chief should lay the foundations of his influence, which should thence go forth. 因 simply = 'by means of.' 作 = 奋起, 'to put forth vigorously,' 'to display.' 庸 = 功, 'merit,' or 'service.' Maou absurdly interprets the term as if it were 墉, = 城, 'walls.'

Ll. 5—8. 彻土田,—comp. 彻田, in ii. VI. 5, where duke Lëw does for himself what the earl of Shaou is here told to do for Shin. The terms mean to lay out the land on the principle of mutual cultivation, so that a fixed revenue might be made sure for the chief. L. 7. By 傅御, 'master and manager,' we are to understand, probably, the steward or principal officer of the marquis's household in Haou. So Choo takes the terms;—申伯家臣之长. Then 私人, 'private men,' will be all the members of the household, the whole family, rather than 家臣, 'the officers of it,' as Maou explains the phrase. As the 'Complete Digest' expands ll. 7, 8, 私人不迁, 无以遂燕居之乐, 王又命申伯之傅御迁其私人, 而室家之欢, 自是安矣, 'While his family was not removed to his new residence, the chief could not enjoy his domestic bliss, and the king further ordered his principal officer to convey the household to Sëay.' The only difficulty in my mind is that I do not see why the king should have given orders for this;—was it not competent for the chief himself to do so?

四章
申伯之功。召伯是营。有俶其城。寝庙既成。既成藐

藐。王锡申伯。四牡蹻蹻。钩膺濯濯。

五章
王遣申伯。路车乘马。我图尔居。莫如南土。锡尔介

圭。以作尔宝。往近王舅。南土是保。

4   Of the services of the chief of Shin,
    The foundation was laid by the earl of Shaou,
    Who built first the walls [of his city],
    And then completed his ancestral temple.
    When the temple was completed, wide and grand,
    The king conferred on the chief of Shin
    Four noble steeds,
    With their hooks for the trappings of the breast-bands, glittering bright.

5   The king sent away the chief of Shin,
    With a carriage of state and its team of horses.
    'I have consulted about your residence,
    That it had best be fixed in the South.'
    I confer on you a great sceptre,
    As the symbol of your dignity.

St. 4. Ll.1—4 tell us how the earl of Shaou accomplished part of the charge committed to him. The critics will nearly all of them have it, that l.1 relates to the chief of Shin's occupancy of Sëay, so that 功 is merely = 事, 'affair;' and then 营 in l. 2 is 'the building of that city.' But I must take 功 with a higher and more general meaning. The line is a proleptical description by his friend, Yin Keih-foo, of the services which the chief in his new sphere would render to Chow; and of which the foundation was laid by the earl of Shaou in fulfilling the commission given to him by the king. 俶 = 始, 'commencement.' 城, — 'walls;' i. e., the walls of Sëay. 寝庙, together, — 'the ancestral temple;' as in II. v. IV. 4.

Ll. 5—8. We are to suppose that news of the completion of Sëay has been sent to the court, and the king dispatches the new marquis to his fief. 藐藐 describes the appearance of the temple as deep and solemn (深貌). 蹻蹻 = 壮貌, 'strong-looking;'—comp. the same phrase in ii. X. 4. 钩膺,—as in II. iii. IV. 1. 濯濯 = 光明貌, 'bright-looking.' These steeds with their equipments were tokens of the royal favour, usually granted on occasions of investiture. The subject is continued in the next stanza.

St. 5. St. 2. The state-carriage here would be one adorned with ivory, as being conferred on a prince of a different surname from the royal House;—See on II. vii. VIII, 1. The team was that described in prec. stanza. Ll. 3, 4. 图 refers to the thought and consideration with which the king had determined on placing his relative as the chief of Shin in the South. That quarter of the kingdom required his presence and services more than any other. Ll. 5, 6. 圭 was the jade-token of rank, which the princes of States held as the emblem of their dignity, and which they carried with them when they appeared at court. I do not know that we are to find any special meaning in the adjunct of 介 = 大, 'great,' with which the kwei is mentioned here.

六章
申伯信迈。王饯于郿。申伯还南。谢于诚归。王命召
伯。彻申伯土疆。以峙其粻。式遄其行。

七章
申伯番番。既入于谢。徒御啴啴。周邦咸喜。戎有良

Go, my uncle,
And protect the country of the South.'

6　The chief of Shin took his departure,
And the king gave him a parting feast in Mei.
Then the chief of Shin returned, [and proceeded] to the south,
And found himself at last in Sëay.
The king had given charge to the earl of Shaou,
To make the statutory division of the lands,
And to lay up stores of provisions,
That the progress of the chief might be accelerated.

7　Martial-like, the chief of Shin
Entered into Sëay.

If it were merely the token of a marquis, it would be the 信圭; if the marquis of Shin, as chief of the South, ranked above an ordinary marquis, it may have been the 桓圭, proper to a duke; —some even say the 镇圭, which was proper to the king himself. 宝＝瑞, in the Shoo, II. i. 7, meaning 'a symbol of rank.' Ll. 7, 3. 近 is used here merely as a particle, ＝ 其 in the line which we have often met with,—彼其之子. 近 is probably a mistake for 迈, which is an obsolete synonym of that 其;—see Wang Yin-che on 其 (read 记). 王舅, 'king's uncle,'＝my uncle. We thus know that king Seuen's mother must have been a Këang, and that the chief of Shin was her brother. [The 舅 here ＝ 舅氏 in I. xi. IX., where I have inadvertently translated the terms by 'mother's nephew,' instead of 'mother's brother.' Lacharme is correct in rendering them there, as 舅 here, by 'avunculus.' Ch'ung-urh was duke Hëen's son, and not his grandson.]

St. 6. Ll. 1—4. I have said in the introductory note, that the 还 and 旧 here seem to point to the chief's having previously been settled in the south. A closer study of these lines, however,

enables us to explain the terms without our being obliged to draw such a conclusion from them. The king gave a parting feast to the chief in Mei, the name of which still remains in one of the districts, dep. Fung-ts'ëang. It lay west from the capital Haou, and as Ying-tăh observes, 'The way from Haou to Shin did not lie through Mei. The king was then on a visit of inspection to K'e-chow, and so it was that he gave his charge and the parting-feast to the chief in Mei, who immediately after returned to Haou (还旧于镐), and thence proceeded to Shin.' Thus the 还南 does not refer to the chief of Shin's having been formerly in the south; and 旧 need not have any more meaning than I have given it in the translation. 迈＝行, 'to go,' 'to proceed.' 信 and 诚 intimate that the king had detained him once and again (以见王之数留, 疑于行之不果故也). 饯,—see in I. iii. XIV. Ll. 5—8. When the chief was once on the way, there was nothing to detain him, as all previous preparations had been made for his journey. L. 6,—as l. 6 of st. 3. 峙＝积, or 聚, 'to accumulate,' or 'store up.' 粻＝粮,—'provisions.' 式 is the initial particle. 遄＝速, 'to hasten.'

翰。不显申伯。王之元舅。文武是宪。

八章
申伯之德。柔惠且直。揉此万邦。闻于四国。吉甫作

诵。其诗孔硕。其风肆好。以赠申伯。

His footmen and charioteers were numerous,
And throughout the regions of Chow all rejoiced.
'You have got a good support:—
Very distinguished is the chief of Shin,
The great uncle of the king,
The pattern of the officers, both civil and military.'

8　The virtue of the chief of Shin
Is mild, and regulated, and upright.
He will keep all these countries in order,
And be famed throughout the kingdom.
[I], Keih-foo, made this song
An ode of great excellence,
Of influence good,
To present to the chief of Shin.

St. 7. Ll. 1—4. 番 番 = 武 勇 貌, 'martial-looking;'—compare the same characters in
the Shoo, V. xxx. 5, where K'ung Gan-kwoh
would interpret them in the same way. 嘽
嘽,—as in II. iii. IV. 4. 周 邦, 'the regions
of Chow,'= 周 人, 'the people of Chow.' In
ll. 5—8 we have the people of Chow congratulating one another—with little cause, as it turned out—on the security which they might now
feel with regard to their southern borders.
戎 = 汝, 'you;'—as in ii. IX. 4. 不 显,—
as in i. I. 1, et al. 宪 = 法, 'to afford a pattern to.' Some take the term as='to take a
pattern from,' as if the line='Taking the kings
Wăn and Woo as his pattern;' but this does not
suit the connection so well.
　St. 8. The author of the ode gives expression
to his appreciation of his friend, and his hopes
of his doing great things in the south. He
shows also that he had a sufficiently good
opinion of his own composition. Ll. 1—4. 惠

= 顺, as in III.8, et al.; meaning that the chief's
virtue was regulated, so as to be in accordance
with reason and principle. 'It contained,' says
Yen Ts'an, 'the elements of mild docility, and
stout straight-forwardness, the union of which is
necessary to make virtue complete.' Choo explains 揉 by 治, and Ch'ing by 顺;='to
rule,' 'to keep in obedience.' The dict. gives
the character with this meaning in the 1st tone.
The 2d tone gives a better meaning,—'to make
what is crooked straight.' Ll. 5—8. 诵,—as
in II. iv. VII. 10; with reference to the piece as
intended to be sung. Choo defines 风 by 声,
'sound,' or 'notes.' I must think the meaning
of the term here is 'influence.' 'It was sufficient,' says Yen Ts'an, 'to affect and move the
good in men's hearts.'
　The rhymes are—in st. 1, 天, 神, 申, cat.
12, t. 1; 翰, 蕃, 宣 cat. 14: in 2, 事, 式,
cat. 1, t. 2; 伯 *, 宅 *, cat. 5, t. 3; 邦, 功,

VI. *Ching min.*

烝民
一章
天生烝民。有物有則。民之秉彝。好是懿德。天監有
周。昭假于下。保茲天子。生仲山甫。

1   Heaven, in giving birth to the multitudes of the people,
To every faculty and relationship annexed its law.
The people possess this normal nature,
And they [consequently] love its normal virtue.
Heaven beheld the ruler of Chow,
Brilliantly affecting it by his conduct below;
And to maintain him, its Son,
Gave birth to Chung Shan-foo.

cat. 9: in 3, 邦, 庸, *ib.*; 田, 人, cat. 12, t. 1: iu 4, 營, 城, 成, cat. 11; 藐 *, 蹺 *, 濯 *, cat. 2: in 5, 馬 *, 士, cat. 5, t. 2; 宝 *, 保 *, cat. 3, t. 2: in 6, 郿, 归, cat. 15, t. 1; 疆, 粻, 行 *, cat. 10: in 7, 番 *, 嘽, 翰, 憲, cat. 14: in 8, 德, 直, 国, cat. 1, t. 3; 碩 *, 伯 *, cat. 5, t. 3.

Ode 6. Narrative. CELEBRATING THE VIR-TUES OF CHUNG SHAN-FOO, WHO APPEARS TO HAVE BEEN THE PRINCIPAL MINISTER OF KING SEUEN, AND HIS DESPATCH TO THE EAST, TO FORTIFY THE CAPITAL OF THE STATE OF TS'E. Like the pre-ceding ode, this was also made by Yin Keih-foo, to present to his friend on his departure from the court.

St. 1. Ll. 1—4 would in themselves be diffi-cult to interpret, but we get an idea of the meaning, which has been attached to them from a very early time, by Mencius' quotation of them in support of his doctrine of the goodness of hu-man nature, and the remarks on them which he attributes to Confucius;—see Mencius, V. Pt. i. VI. 8. 烝 = 众, 'all;' and 烝 民, 'all the people,'= mankind generally. 有 物 有 則, —'there are things, and there are their laws (則 = 法).' But the 'things' must be under-stood of what belongs to the human constitu-tion; and the critics interpret the term most generally, with reference to all man's bodily faculties and all the relationships of society. Every faculty has its function to fulfil, and every relationship its duty to discharge. The function and the duty are the laws which the human being has to observe;—the seeing clear-ly, for instance, with the eyes, and hearing distinctly with the ears; the maintenance of righteousness between ruler and minister, and

of affection between parent and child. This is the normal nature called 彝 in l. 3, and else-where denominated 常 性 and 恒 性. 秉, I think, must = 'to be endowed with.' In l. 4 the 'admirable virtue' is the nature fulfilling the various laws of its constitution. The student may find the following sentences of Chin Tih-sëw interesting:— 則者, 准 則 之 谓, 一 定 而 不 可 易 也. 彝 而 言 秉 者, 浑 然 一 理, 具 于 吾 心. 不 可 移 夺, 若 秉 执 然, 为 其 有 此, 故 于 美 德, 无 不 知 好 之 者, 仁 义 忠 孝, 所 谓 美 德 也, 人 无 贤 愚, 莫 不 好 之 也.

Ll. 5—8. 监 = 视, 'to see.' 有 周 = 'the ruler of Chow;' the same as 'the Son of Heaven' in l. 7. 昭 假 于 下, = 昭 假, as in IV. 8, l. 4, denoting the effect of king Seuen's charac-ter and conduct of his govt. on Heaven, their immediate effect being 'below,' on the multi-tudes of the people. Thus the line= 明 明 在 下, 赫 赫 在 上, in i. II. 1. As Choo Kung-tsëen says, 明 德 在 下, 而 感 格 于 天. The connection between these lines, and those that precede seems to be this,—that Heaven produces all men with the good nature there described; but on occasions it produces others with virtue and powers peculiar to them-selves. Such an occasion was presented to the case of king Seuen, and therefore, to mark its appreciation of him, and for his help, it now produced Chung Shan-foo. So, the critics ge-nerally. As Wang Chih (王 质 ; Sung dyn.)

二章
仲山甫之德。柔嘉维则。令仪令色。小心翼翼。古训
是式。威仪是力。天子是若。明命使赋。
三章
王命仲山甫。式是百辟。缵戎祖考。王躬是保。出纳

2   The virtue of Chung Shan-foo
     Is mild and admirable, according as it ought to be.
     Good is his deportment; good his looks;
     The lessons of antiquity are his law;
     He is strenuously attentive to his deportment.
     In full accord with the Son of Heaven,
     He is employed to spread abroad his bright decrees.

3   The king gave charge to Chung Shan-foo:—
     'Be a pattern to all the princes;
     Continue [the services of] your ancestors.
     You have to protect the royal person;

says, 民 之 秉 彝 好 德, 盖 其 常 稟, 然 天 有 特 为 时 而 生 者, 则 与 常 稟 不 同, 所 谓 出 乎 其 类, 拔 乎 其 萃 者. To the same effect Yen Ts'an:—天 眷 宣 王, 为 生 贤 佐 也. As to the personage, whose birth is thus specially ascribed to Heaven, both Maou and Choo say that the three characters 仲 山 甫 were his designation. This does not seem quite accurate. He was a descendant of king T'ae, styled Yu-chung (虞 仲), whom king Seuen, because of his merits appointed marquis of Fan (樊 侯), when he adopted 仲 as his 氏 or clan name. His surname of course was Ke (姬); and Shan-foo was his designation. After a time, the State of Fan lapsed again to Chow, and another family received it as its appanage, taking the surname of Fan. Such is the account given, after much research, by Wang Taou. The dict. appears to be wrong in saying that Fan became the surname of Shan-foo's descendants.

St. 2,—the virtue of Chung Shan-foo. L. 2. 维 则 is to be referred back to 有 则 in the last stanza. His virtue mild and admirable, was according to the law for it;—we might translate —'was normal.' As Lou says, 'If the mildness had gone beyond that standard, it would have been weakness.' L. 3. We must construe

令 with a *hiphil* force. As the 'Essence and Flower of the She' expands the 令 仪,—外 则 令 善 其 容 止. L. 5. By 古 训, 'ancient lessons,' we must understand the rules and maxims of the former sage kings. 式 = 法, 'to take as the law,' 'to imitate.' L. 6. 力 is used as a verb, = 勉, 'to be strenuous with.' L. 7. 若 = 顺, 'to be in accordance with.' King and minister were drawn together by a mutual sympathy and a common aim. L. 8. 明 命, 'the brilliant orders,' belong to the king. 赋 = 布, 'to spread abroad;' meaning to make known, and carry into execution.

St. 3. L. 1. When the king gave the charge to Shan-foo, which is contained in ll. 2—8, we cannot tell. I apprehend it is merely the writer's way of indicating the important functions with which his hero was entrusted. L. 2. 式 = 'to give law, be a pattern, to.' 百 辟 = all the princes of the States. From this line it is inferred that Shan-foo was king Seuen's chief minister (冢 宰, 总 领 诸 侯). L. 3. 戎 = 汝, 'you;'—as in st. 7. of prec. ode. From l. 4. it is inferred that with the office of chief minister Shan-foo united that of Grand-guardian (大 保), which latter Choo thinks may have been hereditary in his family. L. 5.

王命。王之喉舌。赋政于外。四方爰发。

四章
肃肃王命。仲山甫将之。邦国若否。仲山甫明之。既

明且哲。以保其身。夙夜匪解。以事一人。

五章
人亦有言。柔则茹之。刚则吐之。维仲山甫。柔亦不

> Give out the royal decrees, and report on them.
> Be the king's throat and tongue;
> Spread his government abroad,
> So that in all quarters it shall be responded to.'

4　Most dignified was the king's charge,
　And Chung Shan-foo carries it into execution.
　In the States, the princes, be they good or bad,
　Are clearly distinguished by Chung Shan-foo.
　Intelligent is he and wise,
　Protecting his own person;
　Never idle, day or night,
　In the service of the One man.

5　The people have a saying:—
　'The soft is devoured,
　And the hard is ejected from the mouth.'
　But Chung Shan-foo

is understood as in the translation. 王命＝明命 of last st.; 出 is to receive the king's decrees and send them forth (承而布之); 纳 is to report again to the king on the progress and effects of these (行而复之). L. 1. 'Throat and tongue'＝mouth-piece. l. 8. 发＝起而应之, 'to rise and respond to.' 爰, —'hereon.' The king expresses the issue, as if it were already an accomplished fact.

St. 4. Ll. 1, 2. 肃肃＝严, 'grave,' 'dignified.' 将＝奉行, 'to carry into execution.' Ll. 3, 4. 若＝顺, 'obedient.' 若否＝臧 否, 'good or bad.' By the 'States' we are to understand the princes of them. 明＝辨而明之, 'to distinguish clearly.' Ll. 5—8. 明 and 哲 are distinguished as the quality of wisdom (哲) and the manifestation of it (明者哲之发, 哲者明之实).

St. 5. The virtue of Shan-foo is here shown to have nothing feeble in its mildness, but to be equally characterized by gentleness and firmness. People generally eat readily what is soft, and cast out of their mouths what is hard for the teeth; and so a bad minister will oppress those who cannot resist, and keep away from those whom it would be dangerous to meddle with.

茹。刚亦不吐。不侮矜寡。不畏强御。

六章

人亦有言。德輶如毛。民鲜克举之。我仪图之。维仲

山甫举之。爱莫助之。衮职有阙。维仲山甫补之。

七章

仲山甫出祖。四牡业业。征夫捷捷。每怀靡及。四牡

Does not devour the soft,
Nor eject the powerful.
He does not insult the poor or the widow;
He does not fear the strong or the oppressive.

6   The people have a saying:—
'Virtue is light as a hair,
But few are able to lift it.'
When I think of the matter,
It is only Chung Shan-foo that can lift it.
I love him, but can do nothing to help him.
Any defects in the king's duties
Are supplied by Chung Shan-foo.

7   Chung Shan-foo went forth, having sacrificed to the Spirit of
the road.
His four steeds were strong;

But it was not so with Shan-foo. 茹 = 食, 'to eat.' Choo explains it by 纳, 'to receive,' 'to take in;' which hardly seems necessary. 矜, —as in II.viii.X.2, 'wifeless.' But wifeless men and widows are mentioned merely as specimens of the helpless classes, which might be safely insulted, but which Shan-foo did not insult. 强 御,—as in I.2,3.

St. 6. Keih-foo exalts here to the utmost the virtue of his friend. Ll. 2, 3. Virtue ought to be light and easy of practice, as it is that for which man was made; but alas! few people are actually virtuous. This a common saying of those times attested. 輶 = 轻, 'to be light.' Ll. 3,—5. 仪 = 度, 'to estimate,' 'to calculate.' It is much better to take the term thus, than to try to keep the meaning of 匹, 'mate,'

'comrade,' which 仪 sometimes has. Ch'ing did so; and Yen Ts'an, after him, says, 'I examine, and among my comrades there is none but Chung Shan-foo who can lift up the hair of virtue.' L. 5 says that he would be glad to help Shan-foo, but his virtue was complete without any help. Ll. 7, 8. 衮,—see on I. xv. VI. 1. By 衮 职 we must understand 'the duties of the king,' i.e., of him who wore the 衮 dress.

We come at last, in st. 7, to the occasion on which the ode was made, the despatch of Chung Shan-foo by the king to fortify the principal city of Ts'e. We must suppose that the city was the capital of Ts'e, for if it had been any other, it would have been mentioned more particularly. We have, however, no record in history of the transaction. In the 20th year of king Le, B.C.858, duke Hёen of Ts'e moved his capital to Lin-tsze (临 菑); but we can hardly suppose that it

彭彭。八鸾锵锵。王命仲山甫。城彼东方。

八章
四牡骙骙。八鸾喈喈。仲山甫徂齐。式遄其归。吉甫

作诵。穆如清风。仲山甫永怀。以慰其心。

His men were alert;
He was always anxious lest he should not be equal to his
　　commission;
His steeds went on without stopping,
To the tinkling of their eight bells.
The king had given charge to Chung Shan-foo,
To fortify the city there in the east.

8　With his four steeds so strong,
And their eight bells, all tinkling,
Chung Shan-foo proceeded to Ts'e;—
And he will soon return.
I, Yin Keih-foo, have made this song:—
May it enter like a quiet wind,
Among the constant anxieties of Chung Shan-foo,
To soothe his mind!

had remained unfortified for so long a time,—perhaps half a century. There had been many troubles in Ts'e, and the fortifications of its capital may have been in need of repair. L. 1. 祖 was the name for a sacrifice to the Spirit of roads, at the commencement of a journey or expedition. It would be of little use trying to ascertain what ancient personage was sacrificed to as such. L. 2,—as in II. i. VII. 4. L. 3. 征 夫,—as in II. vii. X. 2, 3. 捷捷,= 疾貌, expressing the rapidity with which they marched;—comp. the same phrase in II. v. VI. 4. L. 4 = 常恐不及事也. It may be referred either to Shan-foo, or to his men, whom he animated with his own spirit. L. 5,—as in i. II. 8. L. 6. Comp. l. 4 in II. iii. VIII. 1. 锵 here = 将 there. L. 8. By 东方 we are to understand Ts'e, in the east of the kingdom.

St. 8. L. 1,—as in III. 2. L. 2,—see II. vi. IV. 2. L. 4. Comp. l. 8 in V. 6. The line may be taken as a wish, or indicatively as in the translation, and expressing Keih-foo's confidence in his friend's ability to accomplish speedily the object of his mission. L. 5,—as in VI. 8. L. 6. It is difficult to translate the 穆, which Choo defines by 深长, 'deep and long.' Evidently it is intended to characterize the influence which the ode should have on Shan-foo, like that of a clear and quiet wind on external nature.

The rhymes are—in st. 1, 则, 德, cat. 1, t. 3; 下 *, 甫, cat. 5, t. 2: in 2, 德, 则, 色, 翼, 式, 力, cat. 1, t. 3; 若 *, 赋, cat. 5, t. 2: in 3, 考 *, 保 *, cat. 3, t. 2; 舌, 外, 发, cat. 15, t. 3. Lines 1, 2 do not rhyme together, nor with any of the others. In 4, 将, 明 *, cat. 10; 身, 人, cat. 12, t. 1: in 5, 茹, 吐,

VII. *Han yih.*

韩奕

一章

奕奕梁山。维禹甸之。有倬其道。韩侯受命。王亲命

之。缵戎祖考。无废朕命。夙夜匪解。虔共尔位。朕

命不易。榦不庭方。以佐戎辟。

1 Very grand is the mountain of Lëang,
Which was made cultivable by Yu.
Bright is the way from it,
[Along which came] the marquis of Han to receive investiture.
The king himself gave the charge:—
'Continue the services of your ancestors;
Let not my charge to you come to nought.
Be diligent, early and late,
And reverently discharge your duties;—
So shall my appointment of you not change.

甫, 茹, 吐, 寡*, 御, cat. 5, t. 2: in 6, 举,
举, 助, 补, *ib.:* in 7, 业, 捷*, 及 (prop.
cat. 7), cat. 8, t. 3; 彭*, 锵, 方, cat. 10: in 8,
骙喈, 齐, 归, cat. 15, t. 1; 风*, 心, cat.
7, t. 1.

Ode 7. Narrative. CELEBRATING THE MAR-
QUIS OF HAN:—HIS INVESTITURE, AND THE
KING'S CHARGE TO HIM; THE GIFTS HE RE-
CEIVED, AND THE PARTING FEAST; HIS MAR-
RIAGE; THE EXCELLENCE OF HIS TERRITORY;
AND HIS SWAY OVER THE REGIONS OF THE
NORTH. The ode is referred by the Preface to
the time of king Seuen, which is not controverted by any of the critics, and the authorship to Yin Keih-foo, but this point is not so
clear. The ode itself does not say it, nor is
there any authority for it independent of the
statement in the Preface. The Han which is
spoken of was a marquisate, held by Kes, sprung
from one of the sons of king Woo. After the
time of king Seuen, it was extinguished by the
State of Tsin, and assigned to one of the ministers of that growing dominion, who took the
clan-name of Han. It subsequently, on the
breaking up of Tsin, after the Ch'un Ts'ëw
period, became one of the seven great States
into which the kingdom was divided,—of much
larger dimensions than the original marquisate
of Han.

St. 1. Ll. 1, 2. 'Mount Lëang,'—see on the
Shoo, III. i. Pt. i. 4. It was considered the
'guardian hill' of Han (韩之镇。 奕奕

is defined by 大, 'great;' but Wang Taou remarks that the reduplication of 奕 here is not
to be taken as setting forth the great size of
the mountain, but as a dignifying description of
it (美大之词). I think he is correct,
and have translated accordingly. 甸=治,
'to regulate.' 治 is the term, in the passage
of the Shoo referred to, applied to Yu's dealing
with mount Lëang, whatever that was, when the
inundation of the Ho was remedied, and the
country around made capable of cultivation.

Ll. 3, 4. The most natural interpretation of
these lines is that the prince of Han, after the
death of his father, came by the regular route
of communication, which was in good condition,
to the capital, to receive the king's confirmation of his succession. Maou, however, refers
the 道, to the method of king Seuen's administration, brilliantly reformed from the disorder
which marked the reign of his father; and
命 he understands of the prince's appointment
to be chief of the regions of the north (侯伯).
To this I cannot agree.

Ll. 5—12 Contain the king's charge to the
new marquis. L. 7. 朕 is the royal 'we' or
'our.' 命 is the appointment of the prince,
and all which was implied in it. 无废='do
not neglect,' 'do not allow to come to nought.'

二章
四牡奕奕。孔修且张。韩侯入觐。以其介圭。入觐

于王。王锡韩侯。淑旗绥章。簟第错衡。玄衮赤

舄。钩膺镂锡。鞹鞃浅幭。鞗革金厄。

Be a support against those princes who do not come to court,
Thus assisting your sovereign.'

2   With his four steeds, all noble,
Very long, and large,
The marquis of Han came to court,
With the large sceptre of his rank;—
He entered and appeared before the king.
The king gave him
A fine dragon-flag, with its feathery ornaments;
A chequered bamboo-screen, and an ornamented yoke;
A dark-coloured robe with the dragons on it, and the red slippers;
The hooks for the trappings of the breast-bands, and the carved
frontlets;

L. 9. 共 = 供, 'to discharge;' 虔 = 敬, 'reverently.' 尔位, 'your position,' = 尔职, 'your duties;' *i.e.*, the duties of your position.' L. 10. 易 = 改, 'to change.' L. 11. Maou takes 庭 = 直, 'straight,'—as in II. vi. VIII. 1. But 不庭 is in the Tso-chuen a denomination of States whose princes did not, as was their duty, present themselves on the regular occasions in the king's court. The new marquis was to prove himself a support of the throne against such leaders of insubordination. This gives 榦 a pregnant signification, = 作桢榦而正之. Choo defines it here simply by 正, 'to correct.' L. 12. The king indicates himself by 辟, here = 'sovereign.'

St. 2. Ll. 1—5 belong to the marquis's presenting himself at court. Ll. 1—2. 奕奕,— much as in st. 1, denoting the splendid app. of his horses. 修 = 长, 'long;' 张 = 大, 'large.' Ll. 3, 4. 觐 = 见, 'to appear before;'— it is the term appropriate to the feudal princes appearing before the king. The 介圭 is here the sceptre belonging to the marquises of

Han,—granted originally by the king; and the prince now brought it with him, that it might be verified at the court, and so vindicate his claim to succeed to the State.

Ll. 6—12 give an enumeration of gifts conferred by the king. The critics say they are mentioned in detail, because the occasion was extraordinary, and king Seuen would show how well he knew to reward loyal duty. L. 7. 旗, —as in II. i. VIII. 3, *et al.* 淑 = 善, 'good;' but we must take the term here as = 'splendid.' So Ch'ing (旗之善色者). By 绥 (in dict, read *juy*) 章 we are to understand the pennon or signal, carried at the top of the staff to which the banner was attached, made of dyed feathers or of ox-tails, as a piece of blazonry (以为表章), and somehow indicative of the rank of him who used it. L. 8. 簟 第,—as in II. iii. IV. 1; 错 衡,—*ib.*, st. 2. L. 9. 玄衮,— as in II. vii. VIII. 1. 赤舄 ;—as in I. xv. XII. 1. L. 10. 钩 膺,—as in V. 4. 'An ornament on the forehead of the horse was called *yang* (马眉上饰曰锡).' It was made of metal,

三章

韓侯出祖。出宿于屠。顯父餞之。清酒百壺。其殽維
何。炰鱉鮮魚。其蔌維何。維筍及蒲。其贈維何。乘
馬路車。籩豆有且。侯氏燕胥。

The leaning-board bound with leather, and a tiger's skin to
   cover it,
The ends of the reins, with their metal rings.

3   When the marquis of Han left the court, he sacrificed to the
      Spirit of the road;
   He went forth, and lodged for the night in Too.
   There Hëen-foo gave him the parting feast;—
   With a hundred vases of clear spirits.
   And what were the viands?
   Roast turtle and fresh fish.
   And what were the vegetables?
   Bamboo sprouts and *poo*.
   And what were the gifts?
   A carriage of state with its team.
   Many were the vessels of sauces and fruits;
   And the other princes [at court] joined in the feast.

engraven or inlaid (鏤). L. 11. 鞃靷,—
the *k'ang* was a cross-board fixed in the the carriage, against which the parties in it might lean,
and for the sake of greater strength it was bound
with leather (橫木可凭者，以鞃
持之，使牢固). 淺 is taken for 虎
皮, 'a tiger's skin,' so called from the shortness
of the hair. This was laid over the leaning
board to cover it (幭). L. 12. 鋚革,—as in
II.ii.IX.4. The 金厄 were metal rings, with
which these ends of the reins were fitted and
ornamented.

St. 3. L. 1. 出 refers to the new marquis's
leaving the capital, on his return to Han. 祖,
—as in VI. 7. L. 2. 屠 must be the name of
some place not far from the capital, where the
marquis halted,—no doubt, in expectation of the
parting feast. Ll. 3 餞,—as in V. 6. Hëen-
foo must have been some noble and high minis-

ter, delegated by the king to preside at the
parting-feast. Some erroneously suppose that
it was given as by himself (奉王命也，
非朋友私餞; Këang). L. 4 is intend-
ed to show on what a large scale it was. L. 6.
炰鱉,—as in II.iii.III.6. L. 7. 蔌 is a
general name for culinary vegetables (菜茹
之总名). L. 8. The 筍, or bamboo
sprouts, are well known as a vegetable; but I
cannot tell what the *poo* were. In the Chow
Le, however, I.v. 61, we find them mentioned
as one of the staple articles for the vegetable
dishes, under the name of 深蒲, which Biot
has translated by 'des pieds de jonc pris au fond
de l'eau.' L. 10. The carriage would be one of
those adorned with metal, as the marquis was
a Ke. L. 11. 且 has given to it here the meaning of 多貌 'the app. of being many.' L.12.
侯氏, 'the princes,' is a designation of the

四章

韩侯取妻。汾王之甥。蹶父之子。韩侯迎止。于蹶之
里。百两彭彭。八鸾锵锵。不显其光。诸娣从之。祁
祁如云。韩侯顾之。烂其盈门。

4   The marquis of Han took to himself a wife,—
A niece of king Fun,
The daughter of Kwei-foo.
The marquis of Han went to receive her,
To the residence of Kwei.
His hundred chariots were in grand array,
The eight bells of each emitting their tinkling;—
Illustrious was the glory [of the occasion].
The virgins, her companions, followed the lady,
Leisurely like a beautiful cloud.
The marquis of Han looked round at them,
Filling the gate with their splendour.

other princes who were at court at the time (觐礼诸侯来朝者之称). I prefer to take 胥 as the final particle, instead of = 相, with 燕胥 for 相胥 on account of the rhyme. Choo mentions both constructions, himself preferring the latter. I think he would also restrict 侯氏 to the marquis of Han, though he explains the phrase as has been done above. The view in the translation however, is quite legitimate. K'ang-shing says, 诸侯在京师未去者,于显父饯之时,皆来相与燕,其笾豆且然．荣其多也。

St. 4.   The marriage of the young prince. To this the marquis seems to have proceeded immediately after his return to Han. It was the rule, indeed, that marriage should follow immediately that a feudal prince had concluded the mourning for his father, and had received the royal sanction to his succession. L. 2. By king Fun we are to understand king Le, who was so styled from the river Fun, which was near Che where he lived so long after he was driven from the throne. One of Le's sisters must have been married to the father of the lady, so that she was his 甥, or niece. Kwei-foo was probably the designation of the father of the lady; or, as Ying-tah says, Kwei may have been his clan name, and Foo the designa-

tion. That he was a minister of the court of Chow is inferred from l. 2 of next stanza. Had he been one of the feudal princes, his State would have been mentioned. His surname, it appears also from next st., was K'eih,—the surname, acc. to tradition, of one of the sons of Hwang-te. Ll. 4—5. 迎 intimates that the marquis went in person to meet his bride. 止 is the final particle. 里 = 居, 'the place of residence.' This was probably the city assigned to Kwei-foo, and would not be far from the capital (必在王城外; Ho K'üe). Ll. 6, 7. 百两,—as in I. ii. I; 彭彭,—as in I. viii. X. 3. L. 7,—as is VII. 7. L. 8,—as in i. II. 5. Ll. 9, 10. 诸娣,—'all the younger sisters.' The bride was accompanied by a younger sister and a cousin;—virgins from the harem of her father. Then two Houses of the same surname sent, each, a young lady with similar suite, to accompany her; so that a feudal prince was said to marry nine ladies at once (诸侯,一娶九女). All these must be included in the 诸女, and might well be said to look like a cloud. Maou defines 祁祁 by 徐靓, 'leisurely and adorned.' The marquis might well look round and admire.

五章

蹶父孔武。靡国不到。为韩姞相攸。莫如韩乐。孔乐

韩土。川泽讦讦。鲂𩶄甫甫。麀鹿噳噳。有熊有罴。

有猫有虎。庆既令居。韩姞燕誉。

六章

溥彼韩城。燕师所完。以先祖受命。因时百蛮。王锡

5   Kwei-foo is very martial,
    And there is no State which he had not visited.
    When he would select a home for Han-k'eih,
    There seemed none so pleasant as Han.
    Very pleasant is the territory of Han,
    With its large streams and meres,
    Full of big bream and tench;
    With its multitudes of deer,
    With its bears and grisly bears;
    With its wild-cats and tigers.
    Glad was he of so admirable a situation,
    And here Han-k'eih found rest and joy.

6   Large is the wall of [the city of] Han,
    Built by the multitudes of Yen.
    As his ancestor had received charge

St. 5. Ll. 1—4. I have referred, on the last stanza, to the evidence these lines supply that Kwei-foo was a high minister of the court, who had been employed on many missions to the different States. He had, evidently, and very properly, taken the opportunity to look out for a good match for his daughter; and Ying-tah is troubled, unnecessarily, to defend him against a charge of violating the established rule that the family or friends of the gentleman must take the initiative. 韩姞 is the daughter,—a *K'eih* originally, and then distinguished from all other *K'eihs* as the wife of the prince of Han.

Ll. 5—10 are descriptive of the pleasantness of Han. 讦讦 and 甫甫 set forth the large size of the rivers and marshes, and of their finny inhabitants. 麀鹿,—see i. VIII. 2; but evidently they give us the idea in this place of 'deer generally.' 噳噳＝众, 'to be in multitudes.' 猫, 'a cat,' is here＝a wild-cat. 'It

seems strange,' says Fan Ch'oo-e (范处义; Sung dyn.). 'that these wild creatures should be mentioned in proof of the pleasantness of the country; but they came into the mind of the poet, and their existence in such numbers showed how the country abounded in woods. Moreover, the skins of the bears could be worn, and their flesh would afford good eating; while the wild cats would destroy the vermin, and the tigers the wild boars which preyed upon the fields!' L. 1 has for its subject Kwei-foo. 庆 (＝喜) 既 ＝ 既庆, the inversion being more euphonious. L. 12. 燕＝安, and 誉＝ 乐,—as in the translation.

St. 6. Ll. 1, 2. 溥＝大, 'to be large.' Yen was the State to which Shih, the duke K'ang of Shaou, was appointed; and it would appear that he had been entrusted with the charge to build and fortify the capital of the principality

韩侯。其追其貊。奄受北国。因以其伯。实墉实壑。

实亩实籍。献其貔皮。赤豹黄罴。

> To preside over all the wild tribes [of that quarter],
> The king [now] gave to the marquis of Han
> The Chuy and the Mih,
> Forthwith to hold the States of the north,
> And to preside over them as their chief;
> Making strong his walls, and deep his moats,
> Laying out his fields, regulating his revenues,
> Presenting his skins of the white fox,
> With those of the red panther and the yellow grisly bear.

VIII. *Këang Han.*

江汉

一章

江汉浮浮。武夫滔滔。匪安匪游。淮夷来求。既出我

1　Large was the volume of the Këang and the Han,
　And the troops advanced like a flowing current.
　There was no resting, no idle wandering;—
　We were seeking for the tribes of the Hwae.

of Han, just as we have seen his descendant appointed by king Seuen to do the same duty for the new State of Shin. Ll. 3, 4. 先祖 will be the first marquis of Han, who received charge not only for the rule of that State, but to be president of the wild tribes beyond it. These are called 'the hundred *Man*,' as being in the Man domain (see the note on the Shoo, III. i. Pt. ii. 22). The 时 = 是, seems to—'certain,' referring to the tribes which more particularly required attention and management in the early time. We are puzzled with the 因, which Ying-tah has endeavoured, successfully it seems to me, to account for, as meaning—'to go on to,' *i.e.*, to go on from Han to regulate those tribes. The 以, 'on the ground of,' is to be carried on to l. 5 and those that follow. L.6. The Chuy, of whom there is no previous mention in any record, and the Mih must have been two tribes, which were now giving trouble. L. 7. 奄 may here be translated 'forthwith.' By 北国 I must understand the wild tribes of the north,

called 'States' by courtesy. L. 8. 因,—as in l. 4. Ll. 9, 10. The 实,—as in ii. I. 5, where see the remark of Këang Ping-chang upon the term. The walls, moats (壑=城 池), fields, and revenues, are those of Han, though I should like to think it was part of the duty of the marquis to promote the civilization of the wild tribes. 亩=治其田亩, 'to manage his fields;' 籍 = 正赋税, 'to adjust his revenues;' meaning that he should attend to the cultivation of the country on the Chow system of mutual aid. Ll. 11,12. 貔 is given in the Urh-ya as 白 狐, 'a white fox.' Other authorities make it a kind of tiger or leopard; some, the white or polar bear. The 皮 must be carried on to l. 12. 豹 is a kind of leopard or panther;—see I. ii. XIV. 1, *et al.* 罴,—as in II.iv. V. 5,6. The author of the Japanese plates says he does not know either of these animals.

车。既设我旟。匪安匪舒。淮夷来铺。

二章
江汉汤汤。武夫洸洸。经营四方。告成于王。四方

既平。王国庶定。时靡有争。王心载宁。

We had sent forth our chariots;
We had displayed our falcon-banners.
There was no resting, no remissness;—
Against the tribes of the Hwae were we marshalled.

2　Large flowed the Këang and the Han,
And grandly martial looked the troops.
The whole country had been reduced to order,
And an announcement of our success had been made to the king.
When the whole country was pacified,

The rhymes are—in st. 1, 甸, 命 *, cat. 12, t. 1；道 *, 考 *, cat. 3, t. 2；解，易，辟，cat. 16, t. 3: in 2, 张，王，章，衡 *，锡，cat. 10；幭 (prop. cat. 15), 厄, cat. 16, t. 3: in 3, 祖，屠，壶，鱼，蒲；车 *，且 *，胥，cat. 5, t. 1: in 4, 子，里, cat. 1, t. 2；彭 *，锵，光, cat. 10；云，门, cat. 13: in 5, 到，乐 *，cat. 2；士，讦，甫，旟，虎, cat. 5, t. 2；居誉 *ib.*, t. 1: in 6, 完，蛮, cat. 14；貊 *，伯 *，壑，籍 *, cat. 5, t. 3；皮 *，罴 *, cat. 17.

Ode 8. Narrative. CELEBRATING AN EXPEDITION AGAINST THE MORE SOUTHERN TRIBES OF THE HWAE, AND THE WORK DONE FOR THE KING IN THEIR COUNTRY, BY HOO, THE EARL OF SHAOU, WITH THE MANNER IN WHICH THE KING REWARDED HIM AND HE RESPONDED TO THE ROYAL FAVOUR. This is another of the odes of king Seuen's time, and the expedition celebrated in it is assigned in the common chronology to the second year of his reign, B. C. 825 (or, counting A. D. as 1, 826). The Preface attributes its composition, as in the case of the prec. ode, to Yin Keih-foo; but the internal evidence of the piece is sufficient to discredit such an authorship. The 我 in st. 1 shows that it was written by some one—one of the officers—in the expedition; and the date of the composition is to be placed at the time indicated in the second stanza, when the army had returned in triumph to the junction of the Këang and the Han. The earl of Shaou who commanded in it is the same whose services at the formation of the State of Shin are commemorated in ode 5.

St. 1. Ll. 1, 2. The mention of the Këang and the Han together indicates to us their point of junction at the present Han-k'ow;—see on the Shoo, III. i. Pt. ii, 8, 9, *et al.* The troops had marched thither from the north, and then pursued their course along the united stream, thus placing themselves on the south of the tribes about the Hwae. It is remarked that they could safely take that decided course, because the tribes of King Chow had previously been reduced to order, as related in II.iii.IV. 浮 浮, describes 'the appearance of the vast volume of the rivers (水 盛 貌)'. 武 夫 is to be taken of the troops of the expedition generally,—all 'warriors.' 滔 滔,—as in I. viii. X. 4. Ll. 3, 4. 安,—'to rest,' to take the thing easily; 游,—'to wander,' to march in a sauntering manner. 来, here and throughout the ode,= 是. So, Wang Yin-che. This view of the character makes the construction simple and easy. The statement that the troops were come *to seek* the enemy strikingly sets forth their ardour. Ll. 5, 6. See II. i. VIII. 2. Ll. 7, 8. 舒 = 宽 舒, 'to be remiss.' 铺 = 陈, 'to marshal,' or to 'be in array.' The Hwae,—see on the Shoo, III. i. Pt. ii. 11.

St. 2. The expedition had been entirely successful, and we must suppose that the army was now returned to the junction of the Këang and the Han, and was halting till an answer should be received from the king to the announcement of the success which had been made. Ll. 1, 2. 汤 汤,—as in I. viii. X. 3. 洸 洸 = 武 貌, 'martial-looking.' Ll. 3, 4 must be translated in the past-complete tense. Ll. 3, 4. The 四 方 refers to all the quarters of the country occupied by the tribes against which the expedition had been sent. 经 营,—'we

三章
江汉之浒。王命召虎。式辟四方。彻我疆土。匪疚匪

棘。王国来极。于疆于理。至于南海。

> The king's State began to feel settled.
> There was then an end of strife,
> And the king's heart was composed.
>
> 3　On the banks of the Këang and the Han,
> The king had given charge to Hoo of Shaou:—
> 'Open up the whole of the country;
> Make the statutory division of my lands there;
> Not to distress the people, nor with urgency,
> But making them conform to the royal state.
> Make the larger and the smaller divisions of the ground,
> As far as the southern sea.'

had planned and built;' *i. e.*, we had reduced it to order, we had done all that could be done for it. 成—'success,' the accomplishment of all that had been intended. Ll. 5, 6. 四方, —as in l. 3. 王国 must be taken, I think, of the royal State, the king's domain. 庶 is defined by 幸. It expresses an auspice very confidently. In l. 7 the writer perhaps expresses himself too strongly, as if, with the pacification of the Hwae tribes, there was an end of strife and confusion throughout the kingdom (其时 靡有叛戾乖争者). 载 is the particle. Yen Ts'an draws a conclusion from this stanza, which can hardly command our assent, that the enemy had submitted without fighting (淮夷望风而服,不待战).

St. 3, it seems to me, must be taken as retrospective. The king's charge in it is not in reply to the announcement of success, but that which had been sent to the general, when the army had reached the junction of the rivers on its forward march. If we do not take it thus, we must suppose that the earl of Shaou had again to return to the country which he had subdued;—of which there is no intimation. We had to take the second stanza of the story of duke Lëw in the same retrospective way. Ll. 1, 2. 浒,— as in I. vi. VII. 1. 虎 was the name of the earl of Shaou; more commonly known by the honorary title given to him, after his death, of duke Muh

(穆公). We are not to think that the king came in person and gave the charge; but that he sent it (非谓宣王临江汉之地而命 之; Ch'in P'ang-fei).' We see from it that the king's object was not so much the subjection of the wild tribes, as the permanent order and settlement of the country. L. 3. 辟,—as in i. VII. 2. L. 4,—comp. l. 6 in V. 3. By the 我 the king asserts it as belonging to himself. The territory had not been assigned to any feudal prince, and he was willing, probably, that the aborigines should continue to occupy it, if they would only acknowledge his authority, and observe his regulations. Ll. 5, 6. The earl was to execute his charge wisely, and with due consideration for the now submissive people. 王 国,—as in prec. stanza. 极 is here defined by 中 and 中 之 表, 'that which is exactly in the centre,' 'that which will serve as a standard rule.' Such rule the royal lands would afford. L. 6,—comp. l. 3 in i. III. 4. 于 can be regarded no more than 乃 there. The only difference in the lines is that here we must use the imperative, instead of the indicative. There is no necessity to take 于 = 往, as Këang does. 'The southern sea' indicates the sea about the mouth of the Këang and north of it to the Hwae. We have a memorable note of the idea of the geography of his kingdom possessed by king Seuen.

四章

王命召虎。来旬来宣。文武受命。召公维翰。无曰予小子。召公是似。肇敏戎公。用锡尔祉。

五章

厘尔圭瓒。秬鬯一卣。告于文人。锡山土田。于周受命。自召祖命。虎拜稽首。天子万年。

4   The king gave charge to Hoo of Shaou:—
    'You have everywhere diffused [and carried out my orders).
    When Wăn and Woo received their appointment,
    The duke of Shaou was their strong support.
    You do not [only] have a regard to me the little child,
    But you try to resemble that duke of Shaou.
    You have commenced and earnestly displayed your merit;
    And I will make you happy.

5   'I give you a large libation-cup of jade,
    And a jar of herb-flavoured spirits from the black millet.
    I have made announcement to the accomplished one,
    And confer on you hills, lands, and fields.
    In [K'e-]chow shall you receive investiture,
    According as your ancestor received his.'
    Hoo bowed with his head to the ground, [and said],
    'May the Son of Heaven live for ever!'

In stt. 4, 5 we seem to have the reply of the king to the announcement of success. I cannot agree with Këang in regarding st. 4 as merely a continuation of the charge in st. 3 (与 上 章 皆 一 时 事). Even he and the others who take the same view are obliged to find in st. 5 the reward conferred on the victorious leader; but these two stanzas are connected together. The 王 命 of l. 1 in 4 extends to l. 6 in 5. The 命 may be used with reference to any royal communication. In st. 4, the second and other lines, on the view of the whole which I adopt, must be taken indicatively. 旬, — as in III. 1. 宣 = 布, 'to spread abroad;' i. e., the orders which he had received from the king. Ll. 3, 4. The 文 武 are kings Wăn and Woo; and the 召 公 is the great Shih, duke K'ang,

the founder of the House, who was one of their principal supporters. 翰 = 榦, as in II. vii. I. 3, et al. Ll. 5, 6 are intended to depreciate the king himself and exalt the earl. The king was not to be compared with Wăn and Woo, but Hoo was a true descendant of Shih. Ll. 7, 8. 戎 公 = 汝 功, 'your meritorious service.' 用 = 以, 'thereon,' 'therefore.' The happiness which the king would give is that detailed in st. 5. l. 1. 厘 = 赐, 'to give;' as in ii. III.

8. 圭 瓒 is the same as 玉 瓒, in i. V. 2; —see the notes there, and on i. IV. 2. L. 2. Comp. in the Shoo, V. xiii. 25. The cup and the spirits would be used by the earl in sacrificing in his ancestral temple. But there were more substantial rewards for him in the shape of an increase of territory,—hills and fields (土 田 are taken together). 文 人, 'the accomplish-

六章
虎拜稽首。对扬王休。作召公考。天子万寿。明明天
子。令闻不已。矢其文德。洽此四国。

6　Hoo bowed with his head to the ground,
　　And in response displayed the goodness of the king,
　　And roused himself to maintain the fame of his ancestor.
　　'May the Son of Heaven live for ever!
　　Very intelligent is the Son of Heaven;
　　His good fame shall be without end.
　　Let him display his civil virtues,
　　Till they permeate all quarters of the kingdom.

IX.　Chang woo.

常武
一章
赫赫明明。王命卿士。南仲大祖。大师皇父。整我六

1　Grandly and clearly,
　　The king gave charge to his minister,
　　A descendant of Nan Chung,
　　The Grand-master Hwang-foo:—

ed man' is understood to indicate king Wăn, which is probable from what is said in l. 5, that the earl should be invested with his new possessions in Chow, or the old territory of K'e-chow, in the same manner (自 = 从) as his great ancestor had originally received investiture. Duke K'ang received the principality of Yen, but a branch of the family continued in the royal domain, holding the appanage of Shaou; and it is some increase of this which is promised to Hoo. Ll. 7, 8 tell us how the earl received the communication from the king.

St. 6 contains at greater length the manner in which the earl responded to the king's favour; but it is not likely that ll. 4—8 were spoken at the same time as the last line of st. 5. Rather I should suppose they should be referred to the time of his being invested with the additional territory. L. 2. 对 = 答, 'in response to;' 扬 = 称, 'to declare,' 'to celebrate;' 休 = 美, 'excellent,' without saying what. L. 3 is very enigmatic, and has been construed in very different ways. The view in the translation is that of Yen Ts'an, of which Kĕang Ping-chang approves. 考 = 成, meaning the merit which duke K'ang had achieved in the service

of the kingdom; and Hoo now roused himself to similar duty (功 之 成 者 为 考 也, 作者 振 起 也, 公 言 虎 以 孙 继 祖 敢 不 奋 勉 以 振 起 召 公 之 成 功, 而 不 致 倾 颓). Choo takes the line as meaning that the duke made some vessel to be used in sacrificing to duke K'ang, and engraved on it this stanza, 以 考 其 成 (these 4 characters I cannot make sense of). He then adduces the inscription on an ancient sacrificial vessel of the time of the Chow dynasty, modelled, apparently, from this stanza; but it is not sufficient to justify his construction of the line. Ll. 4—8. The critics all unite in praising the earl for advising the king to display (矢 = 陈) the 'civil virtues' rather than military prowess. 洽,—'to instil into,' 'to imbue.'

The rhymes are—in st. 1, 浮, 滔 *, 游, 求, cat. 3, t. 1; 车 *, 旐, 舒, 铺, cat. 5, t. 1: in 2, 汤, 洸, 方, 王, cat. 10; 平 *,

师。以修我戎。既敬既戒。惠此南国。

二章
王谓尹氏。命程伯休父。左右陈行。戒我师旅。率彼

'Put my six armies in order,
And get ready all my apparatus of war.
Be reverent, be cautious,
That we may give comfort to the States of the south.'

2   The King said to the Head of the Yin clan,
'Give a charge to Hëw-foo, earl of Ch'ing,
To undertake the arrangement of the ranks,
And to warn all my troops.
Along the bank of the Hwae,

定, 争, 宁, cat. 11: in 3, 浒, 虎, 士, cat.
5, t. 2; 棘, 极, cat. 1, t. 3; 理, 海, ib., t. 2:
in 4, 宣, 翰, cat. 14; 子, 似, 祉, cat. 1,
t. 2: in 5, 卣 (prop. cat. 3), 人, 田, 命 *,
命 *, 年, cat. 12, t. 1: in 6, 首, 休, 考 *,
寿, cat. 3, t. 2; 子, 已, cat. 1, t. 2; 德, 国,
ib., t. 3.

Ode 9. Narrative. CELEBRATING AN EXPE-
DITION OF KING SEUEN AGAINST THE MORE
NORTHERN TRIBES OF THE HWAE,—ITS IMPOSING
PROGRESS AND COMPLETE SUCCESS. The Preface ascribes the composition of the piece to
duke Muh of Shaou, the earl Hoo of the preceding ode,—whether correctly or not we cannot
tell. The title—*Chang woo*, 'always martial'—
has occasioned much speculation, as it is not
taken, as is the case with the titles generally,
from any line of the piece. It may be, as Twan
Ch'ang-woo says, that this circumstance shows
that the title possesses a peculiar significancy;
but the attempts to discover it have been unsuccessful. According to the Chinese canon,
阙 之 可 也.
St. 1. *The appointment of a commander-in-chief.*
The king accompanied, we shall find, the expedition in person, but he wisely entrusted the
actual command of the armies to an officer of
experience. L. 1 is appropriate to the orders
of the king, it being considered necessary that
anything emanating from him should be described
in grand terms. L. 2. 卿 士 = 'minister;'
with reference, I think, to the office of Grand-
master, which, it appears from l. 4, was held
by Hwang-foo, who was now appointed commander-in-chief. He was a descendant, we are
told in l. 3, of Nan Chung, the same who is
celebrated in II. i. VIII., as having done good

service to the State against the Hëen-yun, in
the time of king Wǎn. A minister, styled also
Hwang-foo, is mentioned in II. iv. IX. as a very
bad and dangerous man in the time of Yëw,
Seuen's son and successor. Both character and
years forbid us identifying him with the worthy
in the text; but he may have been his son. Ll.
5—8 contain the charge proper given to the
general, though some critics also include in it
ll. 3, 4. 六 师,—see on i. IV. 3. King Seuen
would take the field with all his forces. The
以 in l. 6 can only have the force of 'and.' 戎
= 兵 器, 'military weapons,' = all the apparatus of war. Ll. 7, 8. The States of the South
are all those in the province of Seu which were
harassed and disturbed by the movements of the
wild tribes that necessitated the expedition. It
was to be conducted specially with a view to
their relief and comfort. We can hardly do
other than translate l. 7 in the imperative mood,
though 既 is the sign of the past tense. The
command is in the substance of the lines rather
than in the form of them. As Ying-tah expands
them, 师 严 器 备, 当 恭 敬 临 之,
又 当 戒 惧 而 处 之, 施 仁 爱 之
心, 于 此 南 方 淮 浦 之 旁 国,
勿 得 暴 掠, 为 民 之 害 也.
St. 2. *The charge to the minister of War.* Ll.
1, 2. 尹 氏,—'*The* Yin,' or the Head of the
Yin clan. This is Yin Keih-foo, author of
several pieces in this Book, and whose own
military services against the Hëen-yun are
commemorated in II. iii. III. He appears here
as the 内 史, 'Recorder of the Interior,' or
secretary to the king, and transmits his orders
to Hëw-foo, earl of Ch'ing, a district in the

淮浦。省此徐土。不留不处。三事就绪。

三章
赫赫业业。有严天子。王舒保作。匪绍匪游。徐方绎

骚。震惊徐方。如雷如霆。徐方震惊。

[We go] to see the land of Seu,
Not delaying [our march], not occupying [the territory],
That the threefold labours [of husbandry] may proceed in
     order.'

3   Full of grandeur and strength,
     The Son of Heaven looked majestic.
     Leisurely and calmly the king advanced,
     Not with his troops in masses, nor in broken lines.
     The region of Seu from stage to stage was moved;
     It shook and was terrified,—the region of Seu.
     As by the roll of thunder or its sudden crash,
     The region of Seu shook and was terrified.

royal domain, near to Fung, who was Seuen's minister of War (司马), and would act in the expedition under Hwang-foo, as second in command. L. 3 陈行,—'to marshal the ranks.' 左右,—'on the left, on the right.' Hёw-foo would assign to the difft. divisions of the forces their several places, and see that they were all in good order. L. 4. 师旅,—as in II. iii. IV. 3, 1. 9. The line here, indeed, is equivalent to that line there. 戒 = 誓告, 'to address in the way of admonition.' The substance of the address would be to enforce what is said in ll. 5—8. 率 = 循, 'to march along.' 淮浦, —'the banks of the Hwae (浦 = 滨).' Along these would be the seat of the war; and on the northern bank of the river, the tribes on the south of it having been dealt with in the expedition celebrated in the prec. ode. L. 6, 省 = 视, or 察, 'to see,' or 'to examine.' The king was confident of success. It would take little more than the presence of his armies to secure the re-establishment of order. L. 7. 留 is explained as 宿兵以镇之, 'stationing troops in the country to overawe it,' and 处 as 迁延不还, 'moving about and protracting

the time without returning.' Choo says he does not understand what the 'three businesses' in l. 8 are, but mentions the view which I have given in the translation (三农之事). 就绪,— 'to go on as in a thread.' It was expected that on the plan which was proposed the labours of spring, summer, and autumn might go on without interruption notwithstanding the presence of the armies.

St. 3. *The majestic advance of the king, and awe inspired by it.* Ll. 1, 2. Choo defines 赫 赫 by 显, 'distinguished,' and 业业 by 大, 'great,' or 'grand.' 严 = 威, 'awful dignity.' Ll. 2, 4. Choo does not understand l. 3, but he mentions Maou's definitions of the terms, which I have followed. 舒 = 徐, 'leisurely;' 保 = 安, 'calmly;' 作 = 行, 'to march' (So, Ch'ing). By 王 we must understand the king and his forces. 绍 = 纠紧, 'tied together;' i. e., in masses. 游,—'wandering about;' i. e., in broken lines. The advance was in perfect order. Ll. 5—8. 绎 = 连络, 'in continued and uninterrupted succession.' 骚, 'to be moved and agitated.' L. 7. 震惊,—'to shake with terror.' L. 7,—as in IV. 3.

四章
王奋厥武。如震如怒。进厥虎臣。阚如虓虎。铺敦淮
濆。仍执丑虏。截彼淮浦。王师之所。

五章
王旅啴啴。如飞如翰。如江如汉。如山之苞。如川之
流。绵绵翼翼。不测不克。濯征徐国。

4 The king aroused his warlike energy,
As if he were moved with anger.
He advanced his tiger-like officers,
Looking fierce like raging tigers.
He displayed his masses along the bank of the Hwae,
And forthwith seized a crowd of captives.
Securely kept was the country about the bank of the Hwae,
Occupied by the royal armies.

5 The royal legions were numerous;
[Swift] as if they flew on wings,
[Imposing] as the current of the Këang and the Han;
Firm as a mountain;
Rolling on like a stream;
Continuous and orderly;
Inscrutable, invincible;
Grandly proceeding to set in order the States of Seu.

St. 4. The whole region of Seu was moved and awed by the invading force. This st. tells us how any resistance that was offered was dealt with. L.2=如震雷之怒, 'like the rage of shaking thunder.' Le Ch'oo-e observes that the two substantive words in the line are to be construed together, without reference to the 如 between them, such repetition of a term being merely one of the characteristics of the ancient style (一句，虽有两如字，乃古文之一体). Këang observes that the 进, 'to advance,' in l.3 was the work of Hëw-foo. It may have been so; but it suited the poet's purpose to ascribe it to the king. 'The tiger officers' are to be taken of the officers of the army generally (泛言，不止皇父休父). L.4. 阚＝奋怒之貌,

'the app. of being furiously angry.' 虓 denotes a tiger who has lashed himself into rage. L.5. 铺,—as in VIII.1. 敦＝厚, 'thick.' Choo gives, apparently for 铺敦，厚集其陈,—as in the translation. 濆＝浦, 'a river's banks.' L.7. 仍＝就, 'to come to,'—forthwith. 丑（＝众）虏,—'a crowd of captives.' L.7. 截 denotes 'the appearance of being guarded against all attempts (截，然不可犯之貌).' The king's army was between the seat of trouble and the Hwae. The wild tribes could not cross it, nor receive any succours from the other side.

St. 5 gives a glowing description of the king's army. 啴啴,—as in II.iii.IV.4. L.2 in-

六章
王犹允塞。徐方既来。徐方既同。天子之功。四方既
平。徐方来庭。徐方不回。王曰还归。

6　The king's plans were directed in truth and sincerity,
　　And the region of Seu came [at once to terms];
　　Its [chiefs] were all collected together;—
　　Through the merit of the Son of Heaven.
　　The country was all reduced to order;
　　Its [chiefs] appeared before the king.
　　They would not again change their minds,
　　And the king said, 'Let us return.'

X.　Chen jang.

瞻印

一章
瞻印昊天。则不我惠。孔填不宁。降此大厉。邦靡有

1　I look up to great Heaven,
　　But it shows us no kindness.
　　Very long have we been disquieted,
　　And these great calamities are sent down [upon us].

dicates the rapidity of its march; l. 3, the imposing appearance of its progress; l. 4, its strength and firmness (comp. 苟 in II. iv. V. 1); l. 5, its unbroken advance; l. 6, the continuousness of its lines, and their adjustment (翼 翼,—as in II. i. VII. 5. *et al.*); and l. 7, its invincibility (不 測＝不可知也; 不克＝不可胜 也). L. 8. 濯＝大, 'grandly.' 征 is here ＝正, 'to correct,' 'to set in order.'

St. 6 gives the successful conclusion of the enterprise. L. 1. 犹＝道 'method of procedure.' 允 塞,—'was true and real.' But in what way it was so, the poet does not say. The several 既 seem to denote the rapidity with which the king's plans were crowned with success. The rebellious had come to submission almost before the plans were developed. L. 5. 庭 cannot here be the king's court, but his head-quarters in Seu—his court for the time. L. 5. 回,—'to return.' There had not been time to test the sincerity of their submission, but the

king felt assured that they would not rebel again. Choo and the dict. explain 回 here by 违, 'to disobey.'

The rhymes are—in st. 1, 士 (prop. cat. 1), 祖, 父, 戎 (prop. cat. 9), cat. 5, t. 2; 戒 *, 国, cat. 1, t. 3: in 2, 父, 旅, 浦, 土, 处, 绪, cat. 5, t. 2: in 3, 游, 骚 *, cat. 3, t. 1; 霆, 惊, cat. 11: in 4, 武, 怒, 虎, 虏, 浦, 所, cat. 5, t. 1: in 5, 啴, 翰, 汉, cat. 14; 苟 *, 流, cat. 3, t. 1; 翼, 克, 国, cat. 1, t, 3: in 6, 塞, 来, cat. 1, t. 3; 同, 功, cat. 9; 平 *, 庭, cat. 11; 回, 归, cat. 15, t. 1.

Ode 10. Narrative; but allusive in the last stanza. Tʜᴇ ᴡʀɪᴛᴇʀ ᴅᴇᴘʟᴏʀᴇꜱ ᴛʜᴇ ᴍɪꜱᴇʀʏ ᴀɴᴅ ᴏᴘᴘʀᴇꜱꜱɪᴏɴ ᴛʜᴀᴛ ᴘʀᴇᴠᴀɪʟᴇᴅ, ᴀɴᴅ ɪɴᴛɪᴍᴀᴛᴇꜱ ᴛʜᴀᴛ ᴛʜᴇʏ ᴡᴇʀᴇ ᴄᴀᴜꜱᴇᴅ ʙʏ ᴛʜᴇ ɪɴᴛᴇʀꜰᴇʀᴇɴᴄᴇ ᴏꜰ ᴡᴏᴍᴇɴ ᴀɴᴅ ᴇᴜɴᴜᴄʜꜱ ɪɴ ᴛʜᴇ ɢᴏᴠᴇʀɴᴍᴇɴᴛ. The Preface says that this piece was composed by the earl of Fan against king Yĕw. There can be no doubt, I think, that it belongs to the time of Yĕw, for it will not suit the reign of any

定。士民其瘵。蟊贼蟊疾。靡有夷届。罪罟不收。靡

有夷瘳。

二章
人有土田。女反有之。人有民人。女覆夺之。此宜无

罪。女反收之。彼宜有罪。女覆说之。

> There is nothing settled in the country;
> Officers and people are in distress.
> Through the insects from without and from within,
> There is no peace or limit [to our misery].
> The net of crime is not taken up,
> And there is no peace nor cure [for our state].

2   Men had their ground and fields,
>   But you have them [now].
>   Men had their people and followers,
>   But you have violently taken them from them.
>   Here is one who ought to be held guiltless,

other king; but there is nothing in it to indicate the authorship. We saw that the last ode of the preceding Book was also ascribed to an earl of Fan in the time of king Le. If the note of the Preface be correct, the writer of this ode may have been the son or grandson of the writer of the other.

St. 1. Ll. 1, 2. Comp. ll. 9, 10 in IV. 7, 8. The writer appeals to Heaven, as if the suffering that abounded were caused by it, and then proceeds to indicate and probe the real sources of it;—according to the manner of many of these odes. Ll. 3, 4. Choo, after Maou, takes 填 as = 久, 'for a long time,' and 厉 = 乱, 'disorders;'—as in the translation. Këang suggests another construction which is perhaps preferable, taking 填 in the sense of 塞, 'to be hindered,' 'to be straitened;'—this brings on 天 more clearly as the subject of 降 (天何不惠养我乎, 使我甚抑塞, 不皇宁处也, 而又降此大乱之灾, 云云). Ll. 5, 6. 瘵,—as in II. vii. X. 2, but the signification is here passive. Ll. 7, 8. 蟊贼,—see II. vi. VIII. 2, III. iii. III. 7. The characters are evidently used here metaphorically of some evil ministers of the king; but there is to me a difficulty with 蟊疾, the other two characters in the line. Choo says nothing about them farther than that 疾 is to be taken as = 害, 'to

injure,' so that the line = 'Insect-like they commit insect injury.' Maou and Ch'ing have neither of them anything on the point; but Ying-tah says that 'Maou-tsih denotes insects that injure the grain, and maou-tseih the appearance of their doing so;'—as above. More satisfactory is a view given by Këang from some old writer of the surname Ho (何氏), that 'insects which attack the grain, coming from without, are called tsih, while those that are produced within the grain itself are called tseih (蟊,害苗之虫,自外来曰贼,自内生曰疾).' On this view, the insects from without will be Hwang-foo and other bad ministers of Yëw, and those from within will be represented principally by the queen Paou Sze. 届 = 极, 'limit or end.' 夷 = 平, 'peace,' 'to be pacified.' Ll. 9, 10. By the 'net of crime (罟 = 网)' we are to understand the multitude of penal laws, to whose doom people were exposed. These were never relaxed, never modified. Men were continually exposed to them; they acted as a net, which is never taken up, but is always kept in the water. 瘳,—as in I. vi. XVI. 2.

St. 2. The point of interest here is to determine to whom to refer the 'you;'—whether to the king directly, or to the evil ministers represented by the devouring insects in last stanza. It seems best to refer it to the king, like the 尔 in st. 7. Ll. 1, 3 belong to princes and offi-

三章
哲夫成城。哲妇倾城。懿厥哲妇。为枭为鸱。妇有长
舌。维厉之阶。乱匪降自天。生自妇人。匪教匪诲。
时维妇寺。

四章
鞫人忮忒。谮始竟背。岂曰不极。伊胡为慝。如贾三

But you snare him [in the net of crime].
There is one who ought to be held guilty,
But you let him escape [from it].

3 A wise man builds up the wall [of a city],
But a wise woman overthrows it.
Admirable may be the wise woman,
But she is [no better than] an owl.
A woman with a long tongue
Is [like] a stepping-stone to disorder.
[Disorder] does not come down from heaven;—
It is produced by the woman.
Those from whom come no lessons, no instruction,
Are women and eunuchs.

4 They beat men down, hurtful, deceitful.
Their slanders in the beginning may be falsified in the end,

cers who had received gifts of lands and cities in former reigns. 反 and 覆 =our 'but.' 收 is here defined by 拘, 'to detain,' 'to hook;'— difft. from its meaning in last st. 说, — read as, and with the meaning of, 脱, 'to let escape.'

St. 3 was, no doubt, specially intended for Paou Sze and her creatures in the palace; but the form in which the sentiment is given is much too general. Only a Chinese will agree that it is a bad thing for a woman to be wise. The writer seems to have thought that there was something inherently, essentially, vicious in female nature, so that what were virtues in a man, and instruments of good, became, when possessed by a woman, transmuted into vices and instruments of evil. See the whole stanza translated by Morrison, under the character 城. 夫, 妇 are not here, 'husband and wife,' but man

and woman (男 子, 妇 人). All that Choo says on l. 4 is that kĕaou and ch'e are 'birds with disagreeable voices,' or birds of evil omen. Ch'e is the owl,= 鸱 in I. xii. VI. 2. I apprehend the kĕaou is also an owl, and is only another form of 鸮; but there is no Chinese authority for saying so. The dict. defines it as 'an unfilial bird,' 'a bird which, when grown, eats its mother.' Other accounts of it are given; —see on 流 离 in I. iii. XII. 4. 阶 denotes the steps of a stair or a ladder. L. 9 may be taken either actively, as in the translation; or passively—'Those who are incapable of being taught.' L. 10. 时 = 是, 'these,' 'to be.' 寺 = 奄 人, 'eunuchs.'

St. 4 enlarges on the procedure of the parties spoken of and evil done by them, with the impropriety of letting them have anything to do

倍。君子是识。妇无公事。休其蚕织。

五章
天何以刺。何神不富。舍尔介狄。维予胥忌。不吊不

祥。威仪不类。人之云亡。邦国殄瘁。

But they do not say [that their words were] very wrong;—
[They say],' ' What evil was there in them?'
As if in the three times cent. per cent. of traffic,
A superior man should have any knowledge of it;
So a woman who has nothing to do with public affairs,
Leaves her silk-worms and weaving.

5   Why is it that Heaven is [thus] reproving [you]?
Why is it that the Spirits are not blessing [you]?
You neglect your great barbarian [foes],
And regard me with hatred.
You are regardless of the evil omens [that abound],
And your demeanour is all-unseemly;

with public affairs. L.1. The subject of 鞫
(= 穷, 'to reduce to extremity') is the women
and eunuchs of l. 10, st. 3,—Paou Sze and her
creatures; and 忮 (= 害) 忒 (= 变诈)
are descriptive of their characters. L. 2 竟 =
终, 'in the end.' 背 = 反, 'to be contrary
to.' Ll. 3,4 are not a little perplexing. If we
take the subject of 曰 to be the false slander-
ers, then 岂曰 'do they say?' is equivalent
to—' They do not say.' They do not say that
their words are 不极,—'wrong without
limit;' but they make light of them, as in l. 4
(而反曰是何足为慝 (= 恶)
乎). This is Choo's construction; and though
it is 'chiselling,' nothing better can be made of
the lines. I was inclined to translate according
to the view of the lines given by Këang:—' May
not this be pronounced excessively wrong?
But he (i. e., the king) says on the contrary,
"What is there wrong in it?"' But to justify
this, l.3 should be 岂不曰极, instead of
岂曰不极. Ll.5, 6 present a case which
would be altogether out of reason. 贾,—'a

trader.' 三倍 is a profit *three times* the
amount of the capital. A trader may know
such a thing and seek it; but it is foreign to the
superior man to do so. So ought it to be for a
woman to occupy herself at all with public affairs, leaving her proper duties of rearing silk-
worms and of weaving.
In st.5 the writer addresses the king directly.
In ll. 1,2, 何以 and 何, are equivalents —
'why,' 'how is it.' Maou defines 富, 'to enrich,' by 福, 'to bless.' Without answering
his questions, the writer goes on to expose the
king's errors, which, indeed, supplied the best
answer to them. Ll. 3,4. 介狄;—'the great
Teih.' There must have been at the time a
threatening of trouble from some of the wild
tribes in the north; but the king took no measures against them, while he made the writer,
because of his plain speaking, the special object
of his animosity. We are to conclude that it was
not in this ode only that the author gave expression to his sentiments. 胥 = 相. The
king magnified the author, so as to put himself
on equal terms with him as his adversary. Ll.
5,6 further describe the king's ignorance of the
situation of affairs, and incompetency for it.
吊 = 闵, 'to pity;' 'to regard with compas-

六章
天之降罔。维其优矣。人之云亡。心之忧矣。天之降

罔。维其几矣。人之云亡。心之悲矣。

七章
觱沸槛泉。维其深矣。心之忧矣。宁自今矣。不自

我先。不自我后。藐藐昊天。无不克巩。无忝皇祖。

    [Good] men are going away,
    And the country is sure to go to ruin.

6   Heaven is letting down its net,
    And many [are the calamities in it].
    [Good] men are going away,
    And my heart is sorrowful.
    Heaven is letting down its net,
    And soon [will all be caught in it].
    Good men are going away.
    And my heart is sad.

7   Right from the spring comes the water bubbling,
    Revealing its depth.
    The sorrow of my heart,—
    Is it [only] of to-day?
    Why were these things not before me?
    Or why were they not after me?

sion. 不祥 is expressive of all the calamitous events which were rife, bad in themselves, and ominous of what was worse. 不类 = 不善, 'are not good;' or more generally, 'are not as they ought to be.' Ll. 7,8 tell the consequences, already experienced and impending, of the king's conduct. 人 has to be taken of 善人, 'good men.' 云 is the particle. 亡,—'to disappear,' 'to go away.' 殄瘁 —'to be lacerated and worn with cares.'
  St. 6. Ll. 1, 2. By the net which Heaven is represented as sending down must be understood the calamities continually multiplying, in which the people found themselves involved as in a net.

Then 优,=多, 'to be many.' Yen Ts'an says, 天降祸以为罗网, 多于前, 'Heaven is sending down calamities to act as a net, more numerously than before.' Ll. 5, 6. 几 is taken here in the sense of 近, 'to be near,' or 将及, 'to be close at hand.' 悲 in l. 8 is an advance on the meaning of 忧 in l. 4, as a settled *sadness* is more than a present grief or sorrow.
  St. 7. Ll. 1—4. L. 1,—as in II. vii. VIII. 2. The manner in which the water bubbled up from such a spring was an evidence of its depth; and so the nature of the writer's sorrow showed that it had long been growing. 宁=何, 'how.'

式救尔后。

But mysteriously Great Heaven
Is able to strengthen anything;
Do not disgrace your great ancestors,
And it will save your posterity.

XI. *Shaou min.*

召旻

一章

旻天疾威。天笃降丧。瘨我饥馑。民卒流亡。我居圉
卒荒。

1   Compassionate Heaven is arrayed in angry terrors;
Heaven is indeed sending down ruin,
Afflicting us with famine,
So that the people are all wandering fugitives;—
In the settled regions and on the borders all is desolation.

Ll. 5, 6,—as in II. iv. VIII. 2. Ll. 7, 8. After all, the extremity of the kingdom might prove Heaven's opportunity. 藐藐 is defined by 高远貌, 'the app. of being high and distant;' but the idea which it gives us is that of mysteriousness. 巩=固, 'to strengthen,' 'to make firm.' Ll. 9, 10 are an admonition to king Yĕw, grounded on the writer's faith that all things are possible with Heaven.   L. 9 summons him to repentance, though that is not expressed. 式 is the initial particle, though we might also give to it the meaning of 用 or 以.

The rhymes are—in st. 1. 惠, 厉, 瘵, 届, cat. 15, t. 3; 收, 瘳, cat. 3, t. 1: in 2, 田, 人, cat. 12, t. 1; 夺, 说, cat. 15, t. 3; 罪, 罪, *ib.*, t. 2: in 3, 城, 城, cat. 11; 鸱, 阶, cat. 15. t. 1; 天, 人, cat. 12, t. 1; 海 *, 寺, cat. 1, t. 2: in 4, 忒, 背 *, 极, 臆, 识, 识, cat. 1, t. 3; 倍, 事, *ib.*, t. 2: in 5, 富 *, 忌, *ib.*, 祥, 亡, cat. 10; 类, 瘁, cat. 15, t. 3: in 6, 冈, 亡, 冈, 亡, cat. 10; 优, 忧, cat. 3, t. 1; 几, 悲, cat. 15, t. 1: in 7, 深, 今, cat. 7, t. 1; 后, 巩 (prop. cat. 9), 后, cat. 4, t. 2.

Ode 11. Narrative, all but st. 6, which is perhaps metaphorical. THE WRITER BEMOANS THE MISERY AND RUIN WHICH WERE GOING ON, SHOWING HOW THEY WERE OWING TO THE KING'S EMPLOYMENT OF MEAN AND WORTHLESS CREATURES. The Preface ascribes this piece, like the last, to the earl of Fan; the style is like that of the other, and I believe that the authorship of the two was the same. 'The writer,' says Këang, 'saw that nothing now could be done for the kingdom, and that the honoured capital of Chow was near destruction; but in his loyal and righteous heart he could not cease to hope concerning his sovereign. In the former ode he expresses his wish that the king would not disgrace his great ancestors, and here that he would use such ministers as the duke of Shaou. A filial son will not refrain from giving medicine to his father, though he knows that his disease is incurable, and a loyal minister will still give good advice to his sovereign, though he knows that the kingdom is on the verge of ruin.' The name of the ode seems to be taken from the character 旻 in st. 1, and 召 in st. 7; and it is thus distinguished from the *Seaou-min* of II. v. I.

St. 1. L. 1,—see on II. iii. I. 1.   L. 2. 笃= 厚, 'largely,'—in many and severe ways. L. 3. 瘨,—as in IV. 6. 饥馑,—as in II. iv. X. 1, *et al.* L. 4. 卒=尽, 'entirely.' 流亡,— 'are disappearing as if borne away on a current.'

二章
天降罪罟。蟊贼内讧。昏椓靡共。溃溃回遹。实靖夷

我邦。

三章
皋皋訿訿。曾不知其玷。兢兢业业。孔填不宁。我位

孔贬。

四章
如彼岁旱。草不溃茂。如彼栖苴。我相此邦。无不

2　Heaven sends down its net of crime;—
　　Devouring insects, who weary and confuse men's minds,
　　Ignorant, oppressive, negligent,
　　Breeders of confusion, utterly perverse:—
　　These are the men employed to tranquillize our country.

3　Insolent and slanderous,—
　　[The king] does not know a flaw in them.
　　We, careful and feeling in peril,
　　For long in unrest,
　　Are constantly subjected to degradation.

4　As in a year of drought,
　　The grass not attaining to luxuriance;

L. 5. 罟,—as in III. iv. 居, as opposed to 罝, is explained as 国 中, 'the centre of the kingdom;'—perhaps the capital, or more generally the royal domain and the feudal States (内 而 国 中, 外 而 四 境, 卒 皆 荒 芜 空 虚). 荒, as in the passage just quoted, ='to be desolate.'

St. 2. Ll. 1, 2,—comp. ll. 7, 9 in st. 1 of last ode. 讧,—*i. q.* 虹 in II. 8. The action of these insect-like creatures works 'within,' *i. e.,* I suppose on men's minds. L. 3. Maou and Ch'ing take 昏椓 as a designation for eunuchs; and the passage is referred to in the dict. under the meaning of 'to castrate,' which belongs to 椓. I prefer, however, to take the terms as in the translation (昏 而 不 明, 椓 而 肆 虐). 靡 共 may be taken as in the translation, 共 being=供, 'to discharge one's duty;' or as ='disrespectful,' 共 being=恭. L. 4. 溃 溃=败 乱 其 事, 'ruining and disordering their affairs (So, Fan Ch'oo-e).' 回 遹,

—as in II. 12, *et al.* Thus far these destroyers of the country appear as a pest from Heaven; but l. 5, intimates that it was the king who was the cause of all the misery by employing them. 靖 夷=治 平, 'to regulate and order.'

St. 3. L. 1 is further descriptive of the parties branded in last st. 皋 皋='to be insolent.' Both Maou and Choo agree in this definition of the terms. 訿 訿,—as in II. v. I. 2. L. 3,—as in IV. 3. This and l. 4 are descriptive of the writer and of others like-minded with him. L. 4,—as in st. 1 of last ode. 贬,—'to be degraded.'

St. 4. L. 2. Both Maou and Choo define 溃 here by 遂, as in II. v. I. 4, last line. L. 3. There is a difficulty with 栖 苴. The dict., under the pronunciation *cha,* defines 苴 by 水 中 浮 草, 'grass floating in the water.' If that mean an aquatic grass, then 栖 苴 will denote the same taken from the grass and stuck upon a tree, where of course it will get dry and withered;—and this seems to be the view of the line taken by Choo (栖 苴, 水 中 浮 草, 栖 于 木 上 者, 言 枯 槁 无 润 泽

溃止。

五章

维昔之富不如时。维今之疚不如兹。彼疏斯粺。胡不

自替。职兄斯引。

> As water plants attached to a tree;
> So do I see in this country
> All going to confusion.
>
> 5 The wealth of former days
> Was not like our present condition.
> The distress of the present
> Did not previously reach this degree.
> Those are [like] coarse rice, these are [like] fine;—
> Why do you not retire of yourselves,
> But prolong my anxious sorrow?

也). The dict, however, quotes the gloss of Ying-tah, that 苴 is the name for any withered vegetation.' A withered branch hanging on a tree, and the same fallen into the water, and floating about in it, are equally called 苴.' In l. 5, 止 is the final particle. 溃＝乱;—as in the translation. On the difft meanings of 溃, Yen Ts'an says, 'In I. iii. X. 6, we have 有洸有溃, where 溃 is explained by 怒, "anger;" in II. v. I. 4, we have 是用 不溃于成, where 溃 is explained by 遂, "to succeed in," "to attain to," as in l. 2 of this stanza; in st. 2 of this ode, we have 溃 溃, and here 无不溃止, where the term is explained by 乱, "disorder." On all the instances Hëang-she (项氏; probably Hëang Gan-she 项安世; al. 平甫, al. 容斋; Sung dyn.) observes, "When water is 溃, it breaks forth violently in every direction, hence great anger is 溃怒; great progress is 溃 遂; great disorder is 溃乱:—the same idea underlies each application of the term."' But this **explanation is very lame**, because the term is used without 怒 and the other adjuncts. Këang insists on 败 as the explanation of the term in every instance. Thus l. 2 is with him＝ 'Does not the grass have its luxuriance destroyed?'

St. 5. Ll. 1,2. Choo says that 时＝是, 'this,' having in mind probably the 兹 in l. 4; but I prefer Ch'ing's 时＝今时, 'the present time.' Formerly men who deserved it got wealth, i. e., the emoluments of office; now only worthless creatures were in office. Ll. 3,4. **And** the distress of good men at this time was beyond all precedent. L. 5. 彼,—'those,' referring to the worthless men who enjoyed the favour of the king; 斯,—'these,' referring to the good men who were discountenanced. 疏,— 'coarse,'＝粝, rice that has not been hulled. 粺,—'rice that has been hulled fine,'＝fine. In ll. 6,7, the writer addresses himself to the king's favourites. 替＝废; 自替,—'to retire of themselves.' 职＝'because of this;' compare III. 15,16, and the other places where the character has occurred. 兄＝悦; comp. 仓兄, in III. 1. 引＝长, 'to be prolonged.' 斯 has its descriptive power,—like 其. St. 6. **Choo gives this stanza like the others**

六章
池之竭矣。不云自频。泉之竭矣。不云自中。溥斯害
矣。职兄斯弘。不灾我躬。

七章
昔先王受命。有如召公。日辟国百里。今也日蹙国百
里。於乎哀哉。维今之人。不尚有旧。

6 A pool becomes dry,—
   Is it not because no water comes to it from its banks?
   A spring becomes dry,—
   Is it not because no water rises in it from itself?
   Great is the injury [all about],
   So that my anxious sorrow is increased.
   Will not calamity light on my person?

7 Formerly when the former kings received their appointment,
   There were such ministers as the duke of Shaou,
   Who would in a day enlarge the kingdom a hundred *le*.
   Now it is contracted in a day a hundred *le*.
   Oh! Alas!
   Among the men of the present day,
   Are there not still some with the old virtue?

as narrative (赋); but he allowed on one occasion in conversation that it was better taken as metaphorical.   Ll. 1—4 mention two things, each of which had its cause; and so the cause of the present disorder and threatening ruin might be discovered.   Ll. 2 and 4 must be construed interrogatively, 云 being disregarded as expletive. 频 = 涯, 'banks.' These are mentioned as the feeders of the pool, because through them the water would be conveyed into it; whereas the spring fed itself, 'from its centre.' L. 5. 溥 = 大 or 广, 'great,' 'wide.' 斯 = 'this,' or 'the.' L. 6,—as l. 7 in last stanza. 弘 = 大, 'great.' 灾 = 栽, used as a verb. The whole line is interrogative.

St. 7. Ll. 1, 2. 'The former kings' must be Wǎn and Woo. Kěang without any reason makes 先 王 to be 'the former king,' Seuen, Yěw's father; and the duke of Shaou necessari-

ly becomes duke Muh of the 6th and other odes, instead of duke K'ang,—the famous Shih. Ll. 3, 4 辟 = 开, 'to open up;'—as in VIII. 3. 蹙,—the opposite of 辟, 'to be contracted.' L. 7 is to be construed interrogatively. 尚,— 'still.' 旧 = 旧 德 之 人, 'men of the old virtue.'

The rhymes are—in st. 1, 丧, 亡, 荒, cat. 10: in 2, 讧, 共, 邦, cat. 9: in 3, 玷, 贬, cat. 7, t. 1: in 4 there are no rhymes;—though Twan-she gives us 茂 (prop. cat. 3), 止, cat. 1, t. 2: 5, 富 *, 时, 疚 *, 兹, *ib.*, t. 1; in 6, 中, 弘, 躬, cat. 9. Out of 5 and 6 together, he makes 替 (?) 引, 频 rhyme, cat. 12, t. 1. In 7, 里, 里, 旧 *, cat. 1, t. 2.

THE SHE KING.

PART IV.
ODES OF THE TEMPLE AND THE ALTAR.

BOOK I. SACRIFICIAL ODES OF CHOW.

[i.] THE DECADE OF TS'ING MEAOU.

I. *Ts'ing mëaou.*

诗经

周颂四之一

清庙之什四一之一

清庙

於穆清庙。肃雍显相。济济多士。秉文之德。对越在
天。骏奔走在庙。不显不承。无射于人斯。

Ah! solemn is the ancestral temple in its pure stillness.
Reverent and harmonious were the distinguished assistants;
Great was the number of the officers:—
[All] assiduous followers of the virtue of [king] Wăn.
In response to him in heaven,
Grandly they hurried about in the temple.
Distinguished is he and honoured,
And will never be wearied of among men.

TITLE OF THE PART— 颂 四 , 'Part IV. Odes of the Temple and the Altar.' Choo's definition of 颂 is 宗 庙 之 乐 歌 , 'Songs for the music of the Ancestral Temple;' Këang's, 祭 祀 之 乐 歌 , 'Songs for the music at Sacrifices.' The term 颂 itself means 'to praise (称 颂 成 功 谓 之 颂), so that I have in previous volumes spoken of the odes in this Part as 'Songs of Praise.' In the Great Preface we have:—颂 者 美 盛 德 之 形 容, 以 其 成 功 告 于 神 明 者 也, 'The *Sung* are pieces in admiration of the embodied manifestation of complete virtue, announcing to spiritual Beings their achievement thereof.' This account takes its form from the ancient interchange of the characters 颂 and 容. We find, indeed, in the Dict. *yung* given as the first pronunciation of 颂, with the definition of 貌, 'appearance,' 'form.' As all the pieces cannot be referred to the services of the ancestral temple, I have combined in the name of the Part the definitions of Choo and Këang. Yet there are some odes whose only claim to have anything to do with sacrifices is that they are found in it. Choo adds, in opposition to the older interpreters,

II. *Wei T'ëen che ming.*

维天之命

维天之命。於穆不已。於乎不显。文王之德之纯。 ○

The ordinances of Heaven,—
How deep are they and unintermitting!
And oh! how illustrious
Was the singleness of the virtue of king Wăn!

that of the thirty-one pieces in the *Sung* of Chow, while most were made (or fixed, 定) by the duke of Chow, there are perhaps some among them belonging to the reign of king K'ang, and even of a later date. To the *Sung* of Chow, he says, were annexed the four pieces called the *Sung* of Loo, and the five forming the *Sung* of Shang, because of their analogous character.

TITLE OF THE BOOK, AND OF THIS SECTION OF IT. As this stands in the K'ang-he edition, and was fixed, I suppose, by Choo, we have 周颂, 清庙之什,四之一, 'Book I. of Part IV.; the Decade of Ts'ing-mëaou in the Temple Odes of Choo.' But this ordinary distribution of the different portions of this Part is defective, making five Books, instead of three only:—the odes of Chow; of Loo; and of Shang. Then, as the odes of Chow have been arranged into Decades (with eleven pieces in the last, as in the third Book of Part III.), we have to divide the title of the Book, and that of the Decades; as I have done. The former will be— 周颂 四之一, 'The Sacrificial Odes of Chow; Book I. of Part IV.;' and the latter, 清庙之 什,四一之一, 'Decade of Ts'ing-mëaou; Section I. of Book I., Part IV.'

Ode. 1. Narrative. CELEBRATING THE REVE-RENTIAL MANNER IN WHICH A SACRIFICE TO KING WAN WAS PERFORMED, AND FURTHER PRAISING HIM. Choo agrees with the Preface in assigning the composition of this piece to the time of the sacrifice mentioned in the Shoo, V. xiii. 29, when, the building of Loh being finished, king Ching came to the new city, and offered a red bull to king Wăn, and the same to king Woo. The ode seems to me to have been sung in honour of Wăn after the sacrifice was offered.

L. 1. 於 (*woo*),—the exclamation. 穆 is, with Maou, = 美, 'admirable,' 'elegant;' with Choo,= 深远, 'deep and distant,' 'solemn.' The term is descriptive of the temple, further said to be 清, 'pure,' or as Choo defines the term, 清静, 'pure and still.' Maou and Ch'ing make it applicable rather to the worship or the worshippers in the temple; but why should we depart from the natural and appropriate signification of the line? L. 2 belongs to the

princes of the States who were assembled on the occasion, and assisted (相 =助) the king in the service. 肃 = 敬, 'to be reverent;' 雍 = 和, 'harmonious.' L. 3 belongs to the officers who took part in the service,—in the libations, the prayers, and the various arrangements. 济济 =众, 'numerous;'—as often. I refer l.4 both to the princes and the officers, who are said to be characterized by the same virtues which had marked king Wăn. 文之德 can hardly be 'the virtues of civil life,' but= 文王之德; —as in the translation. Ll. 5, 6. There is an opposition of 在天 and 在庙, the former referring to king Wăn as in heaven, the latter to him as present by his spirit-tablet in the temple. 对,—'responding to,'= 配; 越 is defined by 於. The line is rugged; but it leads us to think of the worshippers as being awed by the thought of king Wăn in his exalted state, and con-sequently being most exact and alert in all their duties in the temple. 骏 is defined by 大 而疾, 'grandly and alertly.' Wang Taou takes 越 as= 扬, a meaning found in the Urh-ya; and 对越, he says, = 对扬 in III. iii. VIII. 8. Ll. 7, 8 indicate the testimony borne by all the service to the virtue of king Wăn. L. 7 must be taken interrogatively, or we may disregard the 不. 承=尊, 'to honour,'; to be honoured.' 射,—as in III. iii. II. 7, *et al.* 斯 is the final particle.

There are no rhymes in the ode. Choo ob-serves that in these odes of Chow, there are many of them that do not rhyme;—a peculiarity which he cannot account for. It is mainly owing to this circumstance, I suppose, that we have no longer the odes divided into 章 or stanzas. They are marked off, however, into 节 or small paragraphs. I have indicated those by a space between them in the translation, and by a ○ in the text.

Ode 2. Narrative. CELEBRATING THE VIR-TUE OF KING WAN AS COMPARABLE TO THAT OF

假以溢我。我其收之。骏惠我文王。曾孙笃之。

How does he [now] show his kindness?
We will receive [his favour],
Striving to be in accord with him, our king Wăn;
And may his remotest descendant be abundantly the same!

III.　　*Wei ts'ing.*

维清

维清缉熙。文王之典。肇禋迄用有成。维周之祯。

Clear, and to be preserved bright,
Are the statutes of king Wăn.
From the first sacrifice [to him],
Till now when they have issued in our complete State,
They have been the happy omen of [the fortunes of] Chow.

HEAVEN, AND LOOKING TO HIM FOR BLESSING IN THE FUTURE. The Preface says that in this ode there is an announcement of the realization of complete peace throughout the kingdom; and Maou and Ch'ing particularize and refine upon this, referring it to a sacrifice to king Wăn by the duke of Chow, when he had completed the statutes for the new dynasty in the sixth year of his regency But neither the ode nor any ancient testimony authorizes a more definite argument of the contents than that which I have given.

Ll. 1, 2. Choo, after Ch'ing, defines 天之命 by 天之道, 'the way of Heaven.' One of the Ch'ings of the Sung dyn., however, discriminates between 天道 and 天命, saying that the former is indicative of what Heaven is in itself (天之自然者), and the latter of what Heaven gives to its creatures (天予万物者). The phrase in the text means, I apprehend, the will and operations of Heaven as seen in nature and providence. 不已＝不息, 'do not rest or cease,' i.e., operate without intermission. Choo's definition is 无穷, 'inexhaustible,' and Maou's, 无极, 'illimitable.' Maou defines 纯 by 大, 'great;' Choo, better, by 不杂, 'unmixed,'—the 'singleness' of the translation, and the 不二 of Ch'ing. See Tsze-sze on the 4 lines in the 'Doctrine of the Mean,' XXVI. 10.

Ll. 5—8. The Tso-chuen, under the 26th year of duke Sëang, quotes l. 5 as 何以恤我, and Choo would adopt that as the correct reading. I have no doubt that it indicates the meaning, and have translated accordingly. Maou takes 假 as ＝嘉 (as in III. ii. V. 1), and 溢＝慎, so that the line＝以嘉美之道戒慎于我; but I can hardly make sense of this. 收＝受, 'to receive; Maou defines it by 聚, 'to collect.' 骏惠＝大顺, 'to be greatly in accord with.' 曾孙＝后王, 'future kings.' Any of the descendants of Wăn, after king Ching, might be so denominated. 笃＝厚, 'generously devoted.' The whole line is expressive of a hope, or prayer, as line 3 expresses the purpose of the writer for himself.

I do not think we are to inquire minutely wherein the accord with king Wăn was, or was to be manifested. As a specimen of how the Chinese critics enlarge on the ode, I subjoin the remarks of Këang-Ping-chang, in his expansion of it:—'The virtue of king Wăn, above and beneath, flows forth equally in the same streams with that of Heaven and Earth. King Wăn is just Heaven;—[as seen] at the present time in the quiet of all the States, the succession of abundant years, gentle winds, sweet rains, the happiness of the people, and the abundance of all natural productions. In whatever way Heaven may show its favour to us, king Wăn will also do the same. We will receive it, and hereby be in great accordance with the

IV. *Lëeh wăn.*

烈文

烈文辟公。锡兹祉福。惠我无疆。子孙保之。无封靡

Ye, brilliant and accomplished princes,
Have conferred on me this happiness.
Your favours to me are without limit,
And my descendants will preserve [the fruits of] them.

ways of king Wăn. To be in accordance with his ways is the same as to be in accordance with the ways of Heaven. And why should we speak only of the present time? His descendants hereafter are sure as well largely to carry out his virtue, and not forget him.'

There are no rhymes.

Ode 3. Narrative. APPROPRIATE AT SOME SACRIFICE TO KING WĂN, AND CELEBRATING HIS STATUTES. According to the Preface, this ode was sung to accompany the performance of the dance of king Wăn, called *Sëang* (奏 象 舞). That dance consisted in going through a number of bodily movements and evolutions, intended to illustrate the style of fighting introduced by Wăn in his various wars, and of which, it is supposed, we have an example in the speech of king Woo at Muh:—'Do not advance more than six or seven steps, and then stop and adjust your ranks. Do not exceed four blows, five blows, six blows, or seven blows; and then stop and adjust your ranks (Shoo, V. ii. 7, 8).' Choo observes, however, that there is no reference in the piece to the dance, and the imperial editors allow this, while at the same time they are very unwilling to give up the view of the Preface, accumulating a great number of authorities in support of it. But the fact is, all we can say about the ode is that it is appropriate to some sacrifice to king Wăn. The 典 is to me irreconcileable with the old view, which takes it in the sense of 法, 'laws,' or ' methods;' meaning the style of fighting which Wăn, it is said, introduced. But the term has a higher meaning than that, and='canons,' ' statutes.' The piece has the appearance of a fragment. As Choo says, 此 诗 疑 有 阙 文.

L. 1. 清 is defined by 清明, 'perspicuous,' ' clear.' The term is indicative, and not, as Choo and many others say, to be taken in the imperative mood. 缉 = 续, 'to continue;' 熙 = 明, 'clear.' These two terms are to be translated as I have done (所 当 缉 熙 者). L. 3 may be taken, as in the translation, of the time when Wăn was first sacrificed to (谓 武 王 有 天 下，始 祀 文 王 以 王 礼 之 时); or, so far as the terms are

concerned, of the time when Wăn himself first offered a particular sacrifice which the writer has in his mind (文 王 受 命，始 祭 天 而 枝 伐 也，周 礼 以 禋 祀 祀 昊 天 上 帝; Ch'ing). I much prefer the former method. 禋,—simply = 祀, ' to sacrifice.' L. 4. 迄 = 至, 'till,' 'down to.' It covers the rest of the line :—' till by the use of them there is completion ;' the meaning being, apparently, what the translation indicates. L. 4. 祯,—'a happy omen.' See on the 'Doctrine of the Mean,' ch. XXIV.

Rhymes are found in 成, 祯, cat. 11; 典 *, 禋 *, cat. 13.

Ode 4. Narrative. A SONG IN PRAISE OF THE PRINCES WHO HAVE ASSISTED AT A SACRIFICE, AND ADMONISHING THEM. The Preface says that this piece was made on the occasion of king Ching's accession to the government, when he thus addressed the princes who had assisted him in the ancestral temple. Choo views it as a piece for general use in the ancestral temple, when the king presented a cup to his assisting guests after they had thrice presented the cup to the representatives of the dead. These two views considerably affect the interpretation of several of the lines. The imperial editors incline to maintain the occasion of the composition as assigned in the Preface. But there is nothing really in the piece to enable an impartial student to give his vote in favour of either view. Kёang Ping-chang, for a wonder, agrees with Choo, saying, 仪 礼，宾 三 献 尸 之 后，主 人 酌 宾，歌 烈 文 在 此 时，盖 先 之 以 载 见 之 诗，而 后 歌 烈 文 也. But in the text of the E.Le there is no mention of the singing this piece.

L. 1. 辟 公 = 诸 侯, ' the feudal princes;' —the 'distinguished assistants' of ode I. 公 has here the general signification of ' prince,' and the phrase='ruling princes.' 烈 = 光, 'brilliant;'—some give it the signification of 'meritorious.' It is certainly most natural to take the princes as the subject of 锡 and 惠 in ll. 2,3; and

于尔邦。维王其崇之。念兹戎功。继序其皇之。○无
竞维人。四方其训之。不显维德。百辟其刑之。於乎
前王不忘。

Be not mercenary nor extravagant in your States,
And the king will honour you.
Thinking of this great service,
He will enlarge the dignity of your successors.

What is most powerful is the being the man;—
Its influence will be felt throughout your States.
What is most distinguished is being virtuous;—
It will secure the imitation of all the princes.
Ah! the former kings are not forgotten!

'the happiness' as referring to the sacrifice which had been performed with their assistance. The 'Essence and Flower of the She,' however, understands 神, 'the Spirits (no doubt, of Wăn and Woo),' who had been sacrificed to, as the nominative to 锡, and the happiness will be the blessing they had pronounced through their representatives (我君臣各竭诚敬之心，神用锡此福祉). Even this is better than Maou's finding the subject of 锡 in king Wăn, and making the 'happiness' to be the States conferred on the princes after the overthrow of the Shang dynasty. By this the 我 is made = 汝! Nothing in exegesis could be more licentious. The antecedent to 之 in l.4 is not clear. I suppose it is to be sought in the 惠 of l.3.

Choo says he does not understand 封 靡 in l.5; but accepts the meaning given in the translation. 封 = 专 利 以 自 封 殖 'Fung means to be entirely devoted to gain to enrich one's self;' 靡 = 汏 侈, 'to be extravagant.' Maou brings out, substantially, the same meanings. The 其 in ll. 6, 8, 10, and 12, as well as that in II.1.6, are referred by Wan Ying-che

to the category of 乃. They are a repetition of the subject, and must be translated by 'will.' In l.7, 戎 = 大, 'great;'—as often. By 'this great service' is intended the assistance the princes had given at the sacrifice. It seems out of the question to understand the words, with Maou and a host of others, of the service which the princes rendered when they gathered round king Woo in his struggle with the last sovereign of Shang. L.8. 继 序 = 以 序 相 继, 'succeeding to one another in order.' The successors of the princes before the king are intended. 皇 = 大, 'to make great.' As Choo expands the line, 使 汝 之 子 孙, 继 序 而 昌 大 之.

Ll.9—12. Compare what was said on III.ii. II. L.13 sends the thoughts of the princes back to kings Wăn and Woo, and they are reminded that by obeying the admonitions now given to them, they would be following out their grand example.

Twan-she gives as rhymes here, 福 (prop. cat. 1), 保 *, cat. 3, t.2; 邦, 崇, 功, 皇 (prop. cat. 10), cat. 9; and 人, 训 (prop. cat. 13), 刑 (prop. cat. 11), cat. 12, t.1. Koo-she, 公, 邦, 崇, 功; and 疆, 皇, 忘. Choo, quite erroneously, 公, 疆.

V.　*T'ëen tsoh*

天作

天作高山。大王荒之。彼作矣。文王康之。彼岨矣
岐。有夷之行。子孙保之。

Heaven made the lofty hill,
And king T'ae brought [the country about] it under cultivation.
He made the commencement with it,
And king Wăn tranquilly [carried on the work],
[Till] that rugged [mount] K'e
Had level roads leading to it.
May their descendants ever preserve it!

Ode 5. Narrative. APPROPRIATE TO A SACRI-FICE TO KING T'AE. The Preface says the piece was used in the seasonal sacrifices to all the former kings and dukes of the House of Chow;—see in II. i. VI. 5. Choo confines it to a sacrifice to king T'ae. The imperial editors allow that both views have their difficulties. As only kings T'ae and Wăn are mentioned in it, why should the Preface extend it to all the ancestors of the House of Chow? As they are both mentioned, why should Choo confine it to king T'ae? They themselves favour the view of the Preface; but there is force in an observation of Choo Kung-ts'ëen, that, as the piece puts forward mount K'e both in the beginning and the end, it is plain it was made for a sacrifice to king T'ae. See the account of T'ae's labours there in III. i. VII.

Ll. 1, 2. By 'the lofty hill' we are evidently to understand mount K'e, and 荒＝治, 'to bring under cultivation.' Maou takes 荒 as＝大, 'to make great;' and seems to take 高山 generally,—'Heaven produces all things that are found on the high hills, but king T'ae by his practice of right ways was able to increase them.' Foo Kwang observes that 'to bring wild desolation (治荒) to order is called 荒, just as the regulation of disorder (治乱) is called 乱.' Ll.3,4. I can only get a meaning out of these lines by referring 彼 to king T'ae, and taking 康＝安, as in the translation. Ch'ing

explains 彼 by 万民, 'all the people;' i. e., all the people dwelling about mount K'e. They set to work and built residences (作宫室) there, so that king Wăn could comfortably occupy it! Ll. 5, 6. Maou read 彼祖矣, making l. 5, and joining 岐 to 有夷之行 as l. 6. But the meaning that can be forced from the lines read so is very inane:—'He, i. e., king Wăn, went away, but by that time there were level roads about K'e;' or, acc. to Ch'ing, 'Those who went there afterwards, did so because the ruler of K'e exercised an easy government;' or, acc. to Këang, 'Although king Wăn moved away from it, yet his govt. of K'e was a model for the practice of a hundred ages.' Choo adopted the reading of 岨 for 祖, which had been proposed by Ch'in Kwoh (沈括; Sung dyn.; earlier than Choo). In a chapter of the Books of the after Han (西南夷传) we find the line as 彼岨者岐. There seems a necessity for altering Maou's reading and arrangement of the lines. 夷＝平, 'level.' 行＝路, 'roads.' L. 7 is to be taken as a wish, or the expression of an assurance. It fared ill with the kings of Chow after they parted with the territory of K'e to the lords of Ts'in.

The rhymes are—荒, 康, 行 *, cat. 10.

VI. *Haou T'ëen yëw shing ming.*

昊天有成命

昊天有成命。二后受之。成王不敢康。夙夜基命宥
密。於缉熙。单厥心。肆其靖之。

Heaven made its determinate appointment,
Which [our] two sovereigns received.
King Ching did not dare to rest idly in it.
But night and day enlarged its foundations by his deep and
　silent virtue.
How did he continue and glorify [his heritage],
Exerting all his heart,
And so securing its tranquillity!

VII. *Wo tsëang.*

我将

我将我享。维羊维牛。维天其右之。○仪式刑文王之

I have brought my offerings,
A ram and a bull.
May Heaven accept them!

Ode 6. Narrative. APPROPRIATE TO A SACRI-
FICE TO KING CHING. The different views which
are taken of this ode depend on the interpretation of the characters 成王 in l. 3. Is 成
the honorary title given to Sung (诵), the son
and successor of king Woo? Or are we to take
them as in the line 成王之孚, in III. i.
IX.. where they mean 'to complete the sincerity befitting a true king?' The old interpreters adopted the affirmative reply to the latter question; Choo, that to the former. With
those consequently the ode was to be sung at
the sacrifice (or sacrifices) to Heaven and Earth;
with Choo, it was to be sung at a sacrifice to
king Ching, and its date must be posterior to
his reign. I have no hesitation in giving in my
adhesion to the view of Choo, which had been
advanced, indeed, before him by Gow-yang Sëw,
and moreover was held in the Ch'un Ts'ëw period
by eminent scholars;—see the 'Narratives of the
States (国语,周语,下, art. 4.).' No stu-
dent, coming to the study of the piece without a
foregone conclusion, would take 成王 as mean-

ing anything but king Ching. When Choo was
asked how he interpreted the same characters differently in III.i.IX., he replied that he was obliged to do so by the context; and Lëw Kin observes,
'In III. i. IX., Choo exposed the error of former
scholars, and showed that the characters 成
王 were not to be taken as the honorary title
of the king Sung. Here he corrected the error
of former scholars, and showed that the same
characters were that king's honorary title.
His determination was correct in each case.'
Ll. 1,2. The 'two sovereigns' are Wăn and
Woo. The appointment of the House of Chow
to the sovereignty of the kingdom had long been
determined on (成=定) by Heaven, but the accomplishment of the divine will took place in their
time. Ll. 3,4. 康=安宁, 'to rest quietly;
accepting, that is, the appointment as an accomplished fact, about which he needed not to give
himself any concern. 基命,—'to found the
appointment;' meaning, here, to strengthen it,
enlarging, as it were, the foundation, so that it
might bear the superincumbent dynasty for

典。日靖四方。伊嘏文王。既右饗之。○我其夙夜。
畏天之威。于時保之。

I imitate and follow and observe the statutes of king Wăn,
Seeking daily to secure the tranquillity of the kingdom.
King Wăn, the Blesser,
Has descended on the right and accepted [the offerings].

Do I not, night and day,
Revere the majesty of Heaven,
Thus to preserve [their favour]?

ages. 宥＝宏深, 'wide and deep;' 密＝静密, 'still.' These two terms seem to be descriptive of the virtue of Ching. Ll. 5—7. L. 5,--see III.l. 1; but both 緝 and 熙 are to be taken as verbs, their object being the inheritance which Ching had received from Wăn and Woo. 單＝盡 or 竭, 'to exert to the utmost.' 肄 may have here the meaning given to it of 故, 'therefore,' 'so that.' 靖＝安, 'to tranquillize,' 'make secure.' There are no rhymes.

Ode 7. Narrative. AN ODE APPROPRIATE TO A SACRIFICE TO KING WAN, ASSOCIATED WITH HEAVEN, IN THE HALL OF AUDIENCE. There is happily an agreement between the schools as to the occasion of this ode. The Preface, indeed, makes no mention of Heaven in its argument of it; but its mention of the Hall of Audience (明堂, 'Brilliant Hall') sufficiently shows the occasion to which it referred. We must suppose that the princes are all assembled at the royal court, and that the king receives them in the famous hall. A sacrifice is there presented by him to God, and with Him is associated king Wăn, the two being the fountain from which, and the channel through which, the sovereignty had come to the House of Chow. It is unnecessary to enter into the controversies on the hall itself, and God as sacrificed to in it, whether to be conceived of as one or as five.

Ll. 1—3. Maou defines 將 by 大, 'great,' 'greatly;' and 享 by 獻, 'to offer,' 'offerings;' but it is much better to take 將＝奉, 'to bring,' 'to present;'—with Ch'ing and Choo. The reduplication of 我 is simply in the style of the She, to which attention has been called repeatedly; and we may regard 享 as under the regimen of 奉,—as in the translation. The

其 in l. 3 gives to it all the force of a prayer. The worshipper does not dare to presume that Heaven will accept the offering, but he asks that it will do so (不敢必也). 右＝尊, 'to honour;' not ＝助, 'to assist.' The offerings were on the left of the Spirit-tablets, so that if God accepted the sacrifice, he would descend and be on the right of the offerings. It has been observed before, that the right was anciently the place of honour.

Ll. 4—7. From Heaven the ode turns to king Wăn, and the worshipper is sure that he does accept the service, rendered to him. Observe the contrast between the 既 of l. 7 and the 其 of l. 3. 儀, 式, and 刑 are all of cognate signification, ＝法, 'to take as the law.' Yen Ts'an observes that the accumulation of the terms is for the sake of emphasis (謂法之不已). 伊 is merely an initial particle. 嘏, ＝'the Blesser (錫福).' Maou's construction,—'We have always received blessing from king Wăn,' comes to the same thing.

Ll. 8—10. 于時＝于是, 'thus.' Some prefer to keep the proper meaning of 時, so that 于時＝'ever.' The antecedent to 之 in 保之 is very differently given. K'angshing makes it the ways of king Wăn (于是得安文王之道). Choo makes it the regard of Heaven and Wăn, as seen in their descending to accept the offerings (以保天與文王所以降鑒之意), and also the appointment by Heaven to the sovereignty (天命可以長保矣).

Rhymes are found in 牛*, 右*, cat. I, t. 1; and in 方, 王, 饗, cat. 10.

VIII. *She mae.*

时迈

时迈其邦。昊天其子之。○实右序有周。薄言震之。

莫不震叠。怀柔百神。及河乔岳。允王维后。○

Now is he making a progress through the States,
May Heaven accept him as its Son!

Truly are the honour and succession come from it to the
House of Chow.
To his movements
All respond with tremulous awe.
He has attracted and given rest to all spiritual Beings,
Even to [the Spirits of] the Ho, and the highest hills.
Truly is the king the sovereign Lord.

Ode 8. Narrative. APPROPRIATE TO KING WOO'S SACRIFICING TO HEAVEN, AND TO THE SPIRITS OF THE HILLS AND RIVERS, ON A PROGRESS THROUGH THE KINGDOM, AFTER THE OVERTHROW OF THE SHANG DYNASTY. Here again there is, happily, an agreement between the schools. The Tso-chuen, under the 12th year of duke Seuen, quotes l. 11 as from a *Sung* of king Woo, and in the Narratives of the States (国语 周语, art. 1) the piece is ascribed to the duke of Chow. No doubt, it was made by the duke, soon after the accession of Woo, for the purpose mentioned in the argument. Of such progresses through the kingdom, the example was set by Shun, as related in the Shoo, II. 8; and they were made an institution of the Chow dynasty. This was not done, however, till the duke of Chow had completed his code of statutes in the reign of king Ching. The Progress in this ode must have been made by Woo in assertion of his being appointed by Heaven to succeed to the rulers of the dynasty of Shang. The difficulty with a translator is as to the person in which he will translate the piece. In l. 14 we have 我, 'I.' The rest is all narrative,—in the 3d person; and I am strongly of opinion that the 'I' is to be taken of the duke of Chow. As he made the piece, he probably also recited it on occasion of the sacrifices, in the hearing of assembled princes. In speaking of Woo throughout as 'the king,' he sufficiently guarded himself against having any designs on the throne, and he could speak of himself as the legislator of the dynasty without presumption. Lacharme seems to have recognized the duke of Chow as the speaker throughout; but the 我 in l. 11 he refers to Woo, introducing, however, an *inquit*, 'he says;' for which I do not see any necessity:

—'*Jam inquit, eo spectant animi totius mei studia, ut virtutem colam.*'

Ll. 1, 2. I prefer to take 时 as = 今时, 'now,' rather than = 以时, with Ying-tah and Choo, so that 时迈 would = 'making the seasonal progress through the States.' This, it seems to me, was a special tour through the kingdom, with a special tentative object in it, to ascertain whether Woo's possession of the throne was acknowledged. 迈, = 行, 'to go,' 'to make a progress through.' 其 is taken as in l. 1 of last ode, giving to the whole line the force of a wish (不敢必也). Heaven's accepting Woo as its Son would be its acknowledgment of him as the holder by its will of the kingdom. As Yen Ts'an says, 有天下曰天子子之谓以周继夏商也.

Ll. 3—8 contain the assertion of the writer, and what he considered the proof, that Woo's occupancy of the throne was acknowledged by Heaven, by men, and by all Spirits. 实 is emphatic, = 'Yes,' 'really.' Then 天 must be understood as the subject of 右 and 序, the former referring to the exaltation of Woo above all the princes (尊于诸侯之上), and the latter to his place as assigned to him in the line of sovereigns of the kingdom (次于帝王之统). 有周 may be 'the House of Chow,' or Woo, the chief of that House. Ll. 4, 5 give the proof of Woo's sovereignty from his

明昭有周。式序在位。载戢干戈。载櫜弓矢。我求懿

德。肆于时夏。允王保之。

Brilliant and illustrious is the House of Chow.
He has regulated the positions of the princes;
He has called in shields and spears;
He has returned to their cases bows and arrows.
I will cultivate admirable virtue,
And display it throughout these great regions:—
Truly will the king preserve the appointment.

IX. *Chih king.*

执竞

执竞武王。无竞维烈。不显成康。上帝是皇。自彼成

The arm of king Woo was full of strength;
Irresistible was his ardour.
Greatly illustrious were Ching and K'ang,
Kinged by God.

influence over all the States, for they must be understood as intended in the writer's mind by the 之 and the 莫不. Choo says, 薄言震之，而四方诸侯莫不震惧. The 1st 震 is active,—expressive of the way in which he moved the States. 叠=惧, 'to be afraid.' 薄言,—as in I. i. VIII. It is of no use trying to translate them. Ll. 6, 7 contain the proof of Woo's sovereignty from his influence on spiritual Beings, *i. e.*, on the Spirits of the rivers and hills throughout the kingdom. We have of course to accept the statement on the word of the writer. 怀 is defined by 来, 'to attract;' 柔, by 安, 'to give rest to.' The Spirits came and accepted his sacrifices; they found rest in Woo as their host. The Ho and the lofty mountains (乔 = 高) are mentioned, because, if their Spirits were satisfied with Woo, those of all other streams and hills, no doubt, were so. L. 8 is the writer's exulting assurance of the triumph of his House. Ll. 9—14 carry out the spirit of l. 8. 式 and the two 载 are particles. L. 10 belongs to Woo's distribution of the fiefs of the kingdom;—see the Shoo, V. iii. 10. 戢 = 聚, 'to collect,' 'to

call in.' 櫜,—as in II. iii. I, 3. A time of peace had been inaugurated. On ll. 12, 13 I have made some observations in the introductory note. I must take them of the duke of Chow speaking of himself, and telling how he would go on to labour for the consolidation of the dynasty, elaborating all its statutes, which should be established throughout the kingdom. 肆 = 陈, 'to diffuse,' 'spread abroad.' 时夏 = 是夏, 'this Hëa,' Hëa being a name for the kingdom, as we find it used in the Shoo II. i. 20, even before the rise of the Hëa dynasty. 保之 = 保天命, 'to preserve the appointment of Heaven.' That had been gained by war; it would be preserved by peace and good government. The characters 肆夏 in l. 13 are sometimes used as the name of the ode. There are no rhymes.

Ode. 9. Narrative. AN ODE APPROPRIATE IN SACRIFICING TO THE KINGS WOO, CHING, AND K'ANG. Here again, in the interpretation of this ode, Choo differs from the Preface, and from Maou and his school. On the place of king Woo in the piece there is no disagreement, but whereas Choo, after Gow-yang Sëw, finds also Ching and K'ang in it, the others restrict it to king Woo alone. Difficulties attach from the text to both views; nor do I accord so

康。奄有四方。斤斤其明。○钟鼓喤喤。磬莞将将。降福穰穰。○降福简简。威仪反反。既醉既饱。福禄来反。

When we consider how Ching and K'ang
Grandly held all within the four quarters [of the kingdom],
How penetrating was their intelligence!

The bells and drums sound in harmony;
The sounding stones and flutes blend their notes;
Abundant blessing is sent down.

Blessing is sent down in large measure;
Careful and exact is all our deportment;
We have drunk, and we have eaten, to the full;
Our happiness and dignity will be prolonged.

readily with Choo as in the interpretation of ode VI. We are obliged to strain the terms 成 and 康 in ll. 3, 5 if we take them as descriptive of king Woo; and on the other hand the predicates in ll. 4, 6 seem extravagant, when taken of Ching and K'ang. The imperial editors say that Choo himself, before he published his great work on the She, held the view of the old interpreters, but they do not say that he was wrong in changing his mind, while yet they think it right to preserve the older interpretation alongside of his more matured one. It is an occasion for the application of the canon,—to put on one side what is doubtful.

Ll. 1—4. The critics are all anxious that l. 1 should be understood of the firm moral purpose of king Woo, maintaining in his heart his strong and unresting will to deliver the kingdom from tyranny, subduing every wrong impulse in himself, and resolute to secure universal good order. The writer, it appears to me, would simply indicate the impression which he had of Woo's vigour and force. With l. 2 comp. l. 9 in ode 4. 烈 = 'ardour.' Maou and Choo take it of the result of that,= 业 and 功 业. There is no difficulty with l. 3, if we take 成 and 康 as meaning the kings who were so styled. If we refer the terms to Woo, then the line='most illustrious was he, who completed his great work and secured its tranquillity.' So says Maou,—一不显乎其成大功而安之. It is difficult to get at Ch'ing's exact idea of the line, but he says,—不显乎其成

安祖考之道. L. 4. 皇 = 君, taken as a verb, 'to establish as ruler or king (上帝之所君). This is much better than Maou's making the term = 美, 'to admire;' which is immediately manipulated by Yingtah into 'to bless.'

Ll. 5—7. Choo says nothing on the 奄 here. Maou explains it by 同, 'together;' where I cannot follow him. The dict. defines it by 大有余, 'grandly and more;' which suits the connection. It could not be said that Ching and K'ang were kings equal to Woo; but, coming, in immediate succession to him, one of them after the other, to the throne, they maintained what he had acquired. They were not without great qualities, which justified their being associated with him in the honours of sacrifice. 斤斤 is defined by 明察 and 明之察, 'clearly examining,' 'the examining of intelligence.'

Ll. 9—10. The writer has done now with the characters and achievement of the kings sacrificed to; and he proceeds to speak of the music at the sacrifice, and the blessing conferred on the worshippers. 喤喤 is here defined by 和, 'to be harmonious,' 'to sound in harmony.' 筦,—i. q. 管, which occurred in I. iii. XVII.2, meaning simply a reed or tube. We shall meet with it hereafter as an instrument of music,—a

X. *Sze wăn.*

思文

思文后稷。克配彼天。立我烝民。莫匪尔极。贻我来

牟。帝命率育。无此疆尔界。陈常于时夏。

O accomplished How-tseih,
Thou didst prove thyself the correlate of Heaven;
Thou didst give grain-food to our multitudes;—
The immense gift of thy goodness.
Thou didst confer on us the wheat and the barley,
Which God appointed for the nourishment of all;
And without distinction of territory or boundary,
The rules of social duty were diffused throughout these great
    regions.

kind of flute; which is its meaning here. 将将 is defined by 集 and 和集, 'to blend harmoniously.' The subject of 降福 must be found, I apprehend, in the Spirits of the kings sacrificed to（此时神降之福）. 穰穰 is defined in the Urh-ya by 福, 'happiness,' or 'blessing;' but we are obliged to take the terms here of the abundance of the blessing. Maou defines them by 众, and Choo, by 多.

Ll. 11.—14. 简简＝大, 'great,' 'in large measure.' 反反,—as in II. vii. VI. 3. L. 13 belongs to the conclusion of the sacrifice, when those engaged in it all drank together by way of fellowship and refreshment. Compare in III. ii. III. 1, though the language there has reference to the feast that followed a sacrifice in the ancestral temple. 来反＝是反. Choo defines 反 by 覆, 'to be redoubled.' The blessing would not be received and then expire. It would keep coming back, and be, as it were, repeated（此福禄反覆，日至而未艾）

The rhymes are— 王, 康, 皇, 方, 明 *, 喤, 将, 穰, cat. 10; 简, 反, 反, cat. 14.

Ode. 10. Narrative. CELEBRATING HOW-TSEIH;—AN ODE APPROPRIATE TO THE BORDER SACRIFICE, WHEN HOW-TSEIH WAS WORSHIPPED AS THE CORRELATE OF GOD. It is not worth while to go into minor controversies on the argument of this ode. There is a sufficient agree-

ment upon it, but in the interpretation of the lines and characters there are, as we shall see, various differences of view. Compare the Legend of How-tseih, in III. iii. I.

Ll. 1, 2.   思 is the initial particle,—as in III. i. VI. i. We can only give 文 the general sense of 'accomplished,' as in the panegyric of Yaou, in the Shoo, I.i.1. 配天, 'to correspond to Heaven,' is to be taken, I think, of the achievements of How-tseih's life, rather than of the place assigned to him at the border sacrifice. Ll. 3, 4. Choo follows Ch'ing in taking 立＝粒, 'to supply with grain-food,' — as in the Shoo, II.iv.1. Then 极＝至, 'the utmost amount;' and the meaning of l. 4 is as given in the translation. Maou says nothing on 立, but he defines 极 by 中, 'the middle,' *i.e.*, the proper Mean of human nature, and this meaning is most unnaturally forced out of the lines:—'Thou didst preserve and establish the *true* life of all people under the sky, so that by thee, How-tseih, we might all get the correct Mean of our nature（存立我天下众民之命使众民无不于尔后稷得其中正，言民赖后稷复其常性）.' Ll. 5, 6. 来 is taken as＝小麦, or 'wheat.' Wang Taou contends that it is merely the particle, or＝是; but 来, when used in that sense, as no doubt it frequently is, is followed by a verb. 牟 (often with 麦 at the side)

一 大 麦, 'barley.' L. 4 says that grain-food was specially designed by God for universal (率 = 遍) nourishment. It was thus by How-tseih that the design of God came to be realized. Ll. 7, 8. I can make nothing of the 尔 in l. 7; and the only one among the critics who has tried to keep in it the sense of 'you,' in his expansion of the passage, is Ch'ing K'ang-shing. His words are— 天 命 以 是 循 存 后 稷 养 天 下 之 功, 而 广 大 其 子 孙 之 国, 无 此 封 竟 于 女, 今 之 经 界 乃 大 有 天 下 ;

but I leave it for others to make out their meaning. I interpret 尔 as if it were 彼, opposed to the 此, and enabling us to explain the whole line as in the translation. 常 = 常 道 'the constant path,' the duties of social life. 时 夏,—as in ode 8. When the people were supplied with food, they could be taught to be virtuous. See Confucius' saying in the Ana. XIII. ix. 4.—This ode is sometimes called the 纳 夏.

A rhyme is found in 稷, 极, cat. 1, t. 3.

BOOK I. THE SACRIFICIAL ODES OF CHOW.

[ii.] THE DECADE OF SHIN KUNG.

I. *Shin-kung.*

臣工之什四一之二

臣工

嗟嗟臣工。敬尔在公。王厘尔成。来咨来茹。○嗟嗟
保介。维莫之春。亦又何求。如何新畬。於皇来牟。
将受厥明。明昭上帝。迄用康年。命我众人。庤乃钱

Ah! Ah! ministers and officers,
Reverently attend to your public duties.
The king has given you perfect rules;—
Consult about them and consider them.

Ah! Ah! ye assistants,
It is now the end of spring;
And what have ye to seek for?
[Only] how to manage the new fields and those of the third
    year.
How beautiful are the wheat and the barley,
Whose bright produce we shall receive!

TITLE OF THE SECTION.—臣 工 之 什，四 一 之 二 , 'The Decade of Shin-kung; Section II. of Book I. of Part. IV.'

Ode 1. Narrative. INSTRUCTIONS GIVEN TO THE OFFICERS OF HUSBANDRY;—PROBABLY AFTER THE SACRIFICE IN THE SPRING TO GOD FOR A GOOD YEAR. According to the Preface, this was an ode sung in the ancestral temple, when the king was sending away the princes who had been at court and assisted him in the spring sacrifice to his ancestors. The imperial editors say that Choo himself at first accepted this view, but afterwards adopted that which I have given above in the first part of the argument,— 'simply because the text only speaks of the business of husbandry (盖 以 经 文 言 农 事 耳).'

They add that later scholars have urged that if Choo's view be correct, the piece should have had its place among the *Ya*, and not among the *Sung.* But on the view of the Preface, the same thing might be urged, so far as the words of the ode themselves are concerned, There is no doubt in my mind that the old view is incorrect. Upon it we have an ode to the princes, and not a word in it is addressed to them. Nothing could be more far-fetched than Maou's method of accounting for this,—that the king chose to address the ministers of the princes, only the better to admonish the princes. Add to this the use of 我 in l. 13; and I do not see how any unprejudiced student of the piece can hold to the account of it in the Preface.

铸。奄观铚艾。

> The bright and glorious God
> Will in them give us a good year.
> Order all our men
> To be provided with their spuds and hoes:—
> Anon we shall see the sickles at work.

Ll. 1—4. The reduplication of 嗟 嗟, 'ah! ah!' is emphatic. 工 = 官, 'an officer.' 臣 工 = 群 臣 百 官, 'all ye ministers, all ye officers;' but we must suppose that only the officers of husbandry are intended. 敬 尔 在 公 = 敬 尔 在 公 之 事,—as in the translation. The meaning is apparent, but how to construe 在 公 is difficult. Comp. 在 御 in I. vii. VIII. 2. 厘 = 赐, 'to give,'—as in III. ii. III. 8, *et al.* I do not see the necessity of taking 王 as = 前 王, 'the former kings.' 成 = 成 法, 'perfect rules.' The redoubled 来 is simply = 是, and is not to be translated 'come.' 咨, — 'to deliberate;' 茹, — as in II. iii. III. 4. 'There would be many things,' says Ts'een T'een-seih (钱 天 锡 ; Ming dyn.), 'such as peculiarities of soil and situation, to be taken into account in the application of the general laws.'

Ll. 5,6. The meaning of 保 介 is quite undetermined, and has to be fixed by the connection. Maou says nothing on the terms. They occur in the Le Ke, IV. i. 13 in connection with the king's praying to God for a blessing on the labours of the year. There the king appears in his carriage, with his plough between the charioteer and a 保 介 ; and Ch'ing explains the phrase as meaning 勇 士, or 车 右, the mailed soldier who sat on the charioteer's right (保 = 衣 and 介 = 甲); and he insists on the same meaning here. But whether he be correct or not in his interpretation of the terms in that passage, such a signification of them is inapplicable here ; and therefore Choo makes them a denomination of the assistant officers of husbandry (农 官 之 副). Even Këang accepts this determination, and argues in favour of it (保 = 安 and 介 = 助). 莫 春, 'late in spring,' *i. e.*, the third month of the season, is to be understood with reference to the Hëa year. Ll. 7,8. L. 7 may also be translated, 'And what more do *we* require of you?' So, the 'Flower and Essence of the She (其 他 又 何 所 求 于 民).' 新 = 新 田, 'new fields;'—see on II. iii. IV. 1; 畬 denotes fields in the third year of their cultivation. A 治 has to be understood before 新 (所 求 者 惟 此 新 畬 之 田, 治 之 如 何 耳). Ll. 9,10. 於 皇 is said by Choo to be 'an exclamation of admiration;' = 於 乎, 美 哉. 来 麦,—as in [i.] X. 明 is taken by Choo as = 明 赐, 'the bright gift:' *i. e.*, of God. But the meaning which I have given is more natural and suitable. Fan Ch'oo-e says, 'The wheat and barley were ripe in summer. In the end of spring they were beginning to ripen. Hence the speaker is led on from the mention of that time to think of them.' Ll. 11,12. 迄 = 至, 'to come to ;' here = our 'will.' 用 = 以, 'by means of the wheat and the barley.' 康 年,—'make the year happy ;' *i. e.*, grant a fruitful year. Ll. 13—15. 众 人, 'all the men,' is, of course, to be taken of the husbandmen, = 甸 徒. 钱 (2d tone) is defined by ts'eaou (兆 with 金 at the side), said by Medhurst to be 'a spade or shovel, a weeder or hoe.' Ts'een T'een-seih says it was used to raise the earth (起 土). The poh was a kind of hoe; the chih, a short reaping-hook or sickle. 奄,—'soon,' 'anon.' 艾 (read e, to distinguish it from the plant gae),—'to cut,' 'to reap.'

Rhymes are found in 工, 公, cat. 9 ; to which we may add 求, 牟, cat. 3, t. 1 ; and 年, 人, cat. 12, t. 1.

II. *E he.*

噫嘻

噫嘻成王。既昭假尔。率时农夫。播厥百谷。骏发尔

私。终三十里。亦服尔耕。十千维耦。

Oh! yes, king Ching
Brightly brought himself near.
Lead your husbandmen
To sow their various kinds of grain,
Going vigorously to work on your private fields,
All over the thirty *le.*
Attend to your ploughing,
With your ten thousand men all in pairs.

Ode 2. Narrative. INSTRUCTIONS TO THE OFFICERS OF HUSBANDRY. PROBABLY, LIKE THE PRECEDING ODE, AFTER SOME SACRIFICE TO GOD FOR A GOOD YEAR. The Preface says that this was an ode sung on the occasions of sacrifice by the king to God, in spring and summer, for a good year. But there is no intimation of sacrifice in it; nor would any one ever have thought of seeking for it but for the place of the ode in this Part of the She. Evidently the piece is of a kindred nature with the preceding one.

Ll. 1, 2. 噫 嘻 form a compound exclamation; but it is not easy to determine its peculiar significance. The dict. says that e is an exclamation 'of pain,' 'of anger,' 'of perplexity;' none of which meanings suits this passage. Maou, again, defines he by 和, and Ying-tah by 敕, with which meanings I cannot construe the line. Yen Sze-koo (T'ang dyn.), however, explains the term as 自 得 之 貌, 'the app. of satisfaction,' or 'self-possession.' So I understand it; and the two together='Oh! yes.' The 成 王 既 昭 假 尔 are all but unmanageable. That 成 王 can only mean king Ching seems clear. Maou gives for the terms—成 是 王 事, which become still more obscure in Ying-tah's expansion of them. Ch'ing makes out the six characters to mean—能 成 周 王 之 功, 其 德 已 著 至 矣, 谓 光 被 四 表, 格 于 上 下. Choo, of course, takes 成 王 correctly, but he says that 昭 假 尔 is like the 格 尔 众 庶 of the Shoo, IV. i. 1, *et al.*; and expands—成 始 置 田 官 而

尝 戒 命 之 也, 'King Ching first appointed officers of the fields, and cautioned and charged them.' This also is quite unsatisfactory. Këang mentions an older view of Choo's—我 之 成 其 王 业 者, 既 昭 假 于 尔 上 帝, 'Our establishment of our royal possession has been brightly approved by Thee, O God.' Këang rightly objects to this, that it introduces confusion into the piece, the 尔 here being referred to God, and those in ll. 5. 7 to the people; and then he gives the view of one of the Soo, of which he himself approves:—天 之 所 以 成 我 王 业 者 既 昭 至 矣, 'The way in which Heaven has established our royal possession has been made brightly to appear;'—taking 尔 simply as= 矣. But to both these views, besides other objections, there applies especially this, that the interpretation of 成 王 is inadmissible. The view which I have adopted in the translation is a modification of one suggested in 'The Flower and Essence of the She.' We are to suppose that king K'ang, in connection with his sacrifice at the border altar, had performed some service at the shrine of king Ching, asking, perhaps, what day would be propitious for the sacrifice (卜 日 于 成 王 之 庙). Then when the sacrifice had gone off happily, and he had assembled the officers of husbandry, he begins his address to them by saying that king Ching had come brightly near, and directed them to a fortunate day. This is the only way in which I can make any sense out of these lines. 尔 is simply= 矣. L. 3. 时= 是, 'these.' L. 4. 百 谷, 'the hundred kinds of grain,'= the various kinds.

III. *Chin loo.*

振鹭

振鹭于飞。于彼西雍。我客戾止。亦有斯容。○在彼
无恶。在此无斁。庶几夙夜。以永终誉。

A flock of egrets is flying,
About the marsh there in the west.
My visitors came,
With an [elegant] carriage like those birds.

There, [in their States], not disliked;
Here, [in Chow], never tired of;—
They are sure, day and night,
To perpetuate their fame.

Ll. 5, 6. 骏发尔私＝大发尔私
田, 'grandly turn up your private fields.' Choo
defines 发 by 耕, 'to plough;' but the term
should be taken more generally. Ch'ing says,
'In the cultivation of the ground, the allotments
of families were separated by a small ditch (遂);
ten allotments, by a larger (沟); a hundred, by
what we may call a brook (洫); a thousand by
a small stream (浍); and ten thousand, by a
river (川). The space occupied by 10,000 families formed a square of a little more than 33 *le*.'
We may suppose that this space is intended by
the round number of 30 *le* in the text. Ch'ing
further says that it constituted a *poo* (一部)
and was under the charge of a special officer.
The mention of the 'private fields' seems to
imply that there were also 'the public fields,'
cultivated by the husbandmen in common on
behalf of the government;—contrary to the view
of Choo, that in the royal domain, in the portion
of it here contemplated, the public revenue
was derived from a different system. As the
people are elsewhere introduced, wishing that
the rain might first fall upon the public fields,
to show their loyalty, the king here speaks only
of the private fields, to show his sympathy and
consideration for the people. Ll. 7, 8. 服 is
here explained by 事, as often; but we must
take it with verbal force, =' to attend to the business of.' 十千＝一万, the ten thousand
holders of the 30 *le*. They were all to be called
forth to labour, in pairs to each plough. Choo
takes the meaning to be that, though so numerous,
they were to work with good will and union of

strength and attention, realizing on a grand
scale the harmony of a single pair of labourers
(万人毕出，并力齐心如合
一耦).
There are no rhymes.

Ode 3. Allusive. CELEBRATING THE REPRE-
SENTATIVES OF THE TWO FORMER DYNASTIES, WHO
HAD COME TO COURT TO ASSIST AT SACRIFICE;—
MAY HAVE BEEN SUNG WHEN THE KING WAS
DISMISSING THEM IN THE ANCESTRAL TEMPLE. The
Preface simply says that in this ode we have
the representatives of the two previous dynasties,
who had come to court to assist at sacrifice (二
王之后来助祭);—to which account
of the piece Choo adds nothing. The larger
argument which I have adopted is taken from
Këang (二王之后来助祭，遣于
庙之乐歌也).
Ll. 1—4. 鹭,—as in I. xii. I. 2, 3. The bird
was prized for the pure white of its plumage, and
its movements were also supposed to be remarkable for their elegance (鹭本洁白，又
善飞舞以为容). 振 is defined by
群飞貌, 'the app. of the egrets flying in a
flock.' 雍 is defined, from the connection, by
泽, 'a marsh or pool.' 'The *loo*,' says Ying-
tah, 'is a water-bird, and hence it could be flying
only to a marsh. This gives us the meaning of
yung. The marsh in question was in the west;
but no stress is to be laid on the 西.' It is
generally held that 西雍 is the pool about

IV. *Fung nëen.*

丰年

丰年多黍多稌。亦有高廪。万亿及秭。为酒为醴。烝
畀祖妣。以洽百礼。降福孔皆。

Abundant is the year, with much millet and much rice;
And we have our high granaries,
With myriads, and hundreds of thousands, and millions [of
　　measures in them];
For spirits and sweet spirits,
To present to our ancestors, male and female,
And to supply all our ceremonies.
The blessings sent down on us are of every kind.

the 辟雍 of III. i. VIII. 3, 4, which, it is said, was in the western suburb of the capital; but this point cannot be determined. Wherever the pool was, the egrets were in their element at it, and so the visitors whom the piece celebrates were in their element at the court of Chow. Those visitors, it is affirmed in the argument, were the representatives of the dynasty of Hëa, from the principality of Ke (杞), and of Shang, from that of Sung. It is of course only from tradition that the term 客 is thus restricted. 戾＝至, 'to come to.' 止 is the final particle. 斯 ＝such. The deportment of the visitors was supposed to be as elegant as the movements of the birds (斯指鷺言), so there is a metaphorical as well as an allusive element in these lines.

Ll. 5—8 are in praise of the two nobles, and contain assurance of the king's confidence in them and good will to them. 在彼, 在此, — 'there,' 'here;' — their own States, and at the court of Chow. 无恶, 无斁＝无有恶之者, 无有厌之者;—as in the translation. 庶几, along with the wish of the king, convey his assurance, that so it would be with them. They would ever conduct themselves so as to deserve the praise which ll. 5. 6 expressed. 永终, together,＝'to perpetuate.' Këang says, 'The rise of the three dynasties was entirely from the appointment of Heaven, without the shadow of partiality displayed in it, The displacement of one arose from such men as Këeh and Show; and the elevation of another from such men as T‘ang and Woo. The descendants of the occupying

and of the displaced Houses stood to one another in the relation of host and guest, without any consciousness of undue exaltation on the part of the former, or of shame on the part of the latter!' But this would require more than mortal virtue on both sides.

The rhymes are—雍, 容, cat. 9, and 恶, 斁*, 夜*, 誉, cat. 5, t. 1.

Ode 4. Narrative. AN ODE OF THANKSGIVING FOR A PLENTIFUL YEAR. Both the Preface and Choo say further that the ode was used at the sacrifices in autumn and winter, and Choo adds that the thanksgiving was to the Father of Husbandry (Shin-nung,—see on II. vi. VII. 2,—the First Husbandman, or How-tseïh), the Spirits of the land and those of the four quarters (方社 ; as also in II. vi VII. 2), &c. But opinions are endlessly divided as to the Spirits who were sacrificed to; and Fan Ch‘oo-e, after enumerating half a dozen conflicting views, concludes by saying that 'the sum of the matter is that it was a piece to be sung at a sacrifice of thanksgiving (要之, 为报祭之乐章).'

L. 1. 稌＝稻, 'paddy or rice.' This line is understood as referring to the grain of the people, that there would be no scarcity in their families, while ll. 2,3 refer specially to the stores of the king. Under millet and rice, we may suppose, all other kinds of grain are comprehended. Ll. 2,3. Choo observes here that 亦 is merely an expletive particle ;—so I have treated it in nearly all cases of its occurrence. 万, without question, means 10,000; and 亿 is most commonly accepted as the name for 100,

V.　*Yëw koo.*

有瞽

有瞽有瞽。在周之庭。○设业设虡。崇牙树羽。应田县鼓。鞉磬柷圉。既备乃奏。箫管备举。○喤喤厥

There are the blind musicians; there are the blind musicians;
In the court of [the temple of] Chow.

There are [the music frames] with their face-boards and posts,
The high toothed-edge [of the former], and the feathers stuck [in the latter];
With the drums, large and small, suspended from them;
And the hand-drums and sounding-stones, the instrument to give the signal for commencing, and the stopper.

000. I must also agree with Kwoh and others in taking 秭 as meaning a million. If we do not take the terms as thus rising in decimal progression, then 亿 will be 10,000 × 10,000 = 100,000,000, and 秭, = 亿 × 亿 = 10,000,000,000,000,000. The latter seems to be the view of Maou and Choo here (数万至万曰亿, 数亿至亿曰秭). The common use of 秭 is as the denomination for a hundred millions. Ll. 5—7. 为, —'to make.' 烝 = 进, 'to set forth;' so that 烝畀 = 'to offer to.' 祖妣, —'grandfather and grandmother,' 妣 taking that meaning from 祖. But we must extend the meaning to ancestors, male and female, generally. 洽 = 备, 'to be provided for.' 百礼, —'all ceremonies;' meaning all sacrifices and feasts whatsoever. L. 8. We must understand a 神, meaning all the Spirits who had been or might be sacrificed to, as the subject of 降. 皆 = 遍, 'universal.' Choo takes the line as in the future tense, which, possibly, is the better construction (而神降之福, 将甚遍也).

The rhymes are—秭, 醴, 妣, 礼, 皆, cat. 15, t. 2.

Ode 5. Narrative. THE BLIND MUSICIANS OF CHOW; THE INSTRUMENTS OF MUSIC; AND THEIR HARMONY. The Preface, which is followed by Choo, says that this piece was made on the occasion of the duke of Chow's completing his instruments of music, and announcing the fact in a grand performance in the temple of king Wǎn.

The critics generally admit that it was not made for any occasion of sacrifice (非祭祀之时所奏).

Ll. 1, 2. 有瞽, —like 矇瞍, in III. i. VIII. 4. The repetition of the phrase serves to denote that the blind musicians were many. In the Chow Le, III. i. 22, the enumeration of these blind musicians gives 2 directors of the 1st rank (大师), 4 of the second (小师), 40 performers of the 1st grade, 100 of the 2d, and 160 of the 3d; with 300 assistants who were possessed of vision. I must say that I am incredulous as to this collection of blind musicians about the court of Chow. 庭, —'a court-yard.' Here we must understand it of the court below the raised hall of the temple of king Wǎn.

Ll. 3—8. All the instruments here were performed on in the open court below the hall. Ll. 3, 4, —see on III. i. VIII. 3. Choo says that the feathers spoken of were stuck or placed (树 = 置) on the teeth of the face-board. More probably they were employed as ornaments for the tops of the posts;—so, the 'Flower and Essence of the She (虡之上角, 置羽为饰).' 应 is generally taken as the name of a small drum, and 田 as that of a large one. 'The *ying* and the *t'ëen* were the suspended drums;' —under the Hëa dynasty, it is said, drums were made with feet on which they stood; under the Shang, they were supported on pillars; the duke of Chow introduced the practice of suspending them from a frame. 鞉, — i. q. 鼗; —see Ana. XVII. ix. 4. The instrument was a small drum, which could be held in the hand, with two ears, or balls attached to it by strings. The balls struck the ends and made music, as the handle was twirled about. 柷 and 圉 did

声。肃雍和鸣。先祖是听。我客戾止。永观厥成。

These being all complete, the music is struck up.
The pan-pipe and the double-flute begin at the same time.

Harmoniously blend their sounds;
In solemn unison they give forth their notes.
Our ancestors will give ear;
Our visitors will be there;—
Long to witness the complete performance.

VI.   *Ts'een.*

潜

猗与漆沮。潜有多鱼。有鳣有鲔。鲦鲿鰋鲤。以享以

祀。以介景福。

Oh! in the Tseih and the Ts'eu,
There are many fish in the warrens;—
Sturgeons, large and snouted,
T'ëaous, yellow-jaws, mudfish, and carp:—
For offerings, for sacrifice,
That our bright happiness may be increased.

not themselves discourse music, but were used to direct the band, the former giving the signal for the performers to commence, the latter for them to stop. The *ch'uh* was a sort of wooden box, with a handle in the top, which moved a cross piece of wood at the bottom, that gave the signal as it struck against the sides. The *yu* was made to resemble a couching tiger, with a toothed ridge upon his back, along which a stick was drawn to give the signal to stop. Another name of it is 敔. Medhurst, under *ch'uh*, has confounded the two instruments together. 奏 = 作乐, 'to make music.' The *sëaou* was a sort of pan-pipe, made on a large scale with 23 tubes of bamboo, or on a smaller, with 16 tubes. 管,—this was a kind of flute. But it was double in structure somehow, so that two were blown together.

Ll. 9—13. Nothing is said in the above lines of the stringed instruments, which were used in the hall above the court, nor is the enumeration complete of all the instruments which were used in the court below. We cannot account for the omissions; but in ll. 9, 10, the writer proclaims the excellence of the performance. 喤 喤,—as in [i.] IX. Comp. the difft. application of 肃雍 in [i.] I. Ll. 11—13 must be taken in the future tense. The 'visitors' are understood, as in ode 3. 成 = 'the complete performance:'—what would take place on grand occasions.

The rhymes are—簧, 虡, 羽, 喜, 圉, 奏 (prop. cat. 4), 举, cat. 5, t. 2; 庭, 声, 鸣, 听, 成, cat. 11.

Ode 6. Narrative. SUNG IN THE LAST MONTH OF WINTER, AND IN SPRING, WHEN THE KING PRESENTED A FISH IN THE ANCESTRAL TEMPLE. This is the argument of the piece given in the Preface, and in which the critics generally concur. In the Le Ke, IV. vi. 49, it is mentioned that the king, in the beginning of winter, gave orders to his chief fisher to commence his duties,

VII. *Yung.*

雍

有来雍雍。至止肃肃。相维辟公。天子穆穆。○於荐

广牡。相予肆祀。假哉皇考。绥予孝子。○宣哲维人。

They come full of harmony;
They are here, in all gravity;—
The princes assisting,
While the Son of Heaven looks profound.

'While I present [this] noble bull,
And they assist me in setting forth the sacrifice,

and went himself to see his operations. He partook of the fish first captured, but first presented one as an offering in the back apartment of the ancestral temple; and in the first month of spring, when the sturgeon began to make their appearance (IV. i. 25), the king presented one in the same place. On these notices the argument in the Preface is constructed; and no doubt, some analogous ceremonies were observed by the kings of Chow. When the fish generally, and then the sturgeon, came into season, choice specimens would be presented to their ancestors, as an act of duty, and an acknowledgment that it was to their favour that the king and the people were indebted for the supplies of food which they received from the waters.

Ll. 1, 2. 猗与 is a compound term of exclamation. 漆沮,—rivers of K'e-chow; the same that are mentioned in II. iii. VI. 1. Some take 潜 here as the verb,=‘to lie hid;’ but both Maou and Choo define the term by 槮, a place constructed of wood, if we can speak of construction in the case, thrown into the water for the comfort of the fish, to afford them warmth, and where they might breed. This meaning of the character is found in the dictionary (鱼之所息谓之潜).

L. 3,—see on I. v. III. 4. We have met with all the names in l. 4 but 鲦, or 白鲦, which is described as ‘a fish, long and narrow.’ Williams thinks it may be a species of *thryssa* or *engraulis*. The ‘increase of happiness’ would come from the Spirits of their ancestors. ‘So offering and sacrificing,’ says Le Hwa, ‘the Spirits would aid them with great happiness (神助之以大福). But we are not to suppose that the Spirits would send down happiness, because of the many fishes that were offered to them. They would do so because of the reverence and sincerity with which they were offered when they were in season.’

The rhymes are—沮, 鱼, cat. 5, t. 1; 鲔, 鲤, 祀, 福 *, cat. 1, t. 2.

Ode 7. Narrative. APPROPRIATE AT A SACRIFICE BY KING WOO TO HIS FATHER WAN. This account of the ode is that given by Choo. According to the Preface, the piece was appropriate to the *te* (禘), or great quinquennial sacrifice offered by the kings of Chow, mentioned in the Analects, III. x., xi., and Ying-tah further thinks that it was made by the duke of Chow for king Ching to celebrate the universal peace which was established throughout the kingdom. Maou also says that the great ancestor contemplated in it was king Wǎn, which seems to me inconsistent with the nature of the *Te* sacrifice. The imperial editors allow that the ode better admits of explanation on Choo's view. There is, in fact, no end of the perplexities and conflicting opinions in the interpretation of the details on the old view, and Choo exercised a wise discretion in departing from it. In Confucius' time the three great families of Loo used this ode in sacrificing in their ancestral temples;—to the great dissatisfaction of the sage (See Ana. III. ii.). They used it at the conclusion of the sacrifice, when the sacrificial vessels and their contents were being removed (以雍彻), and the probability is that it was made at first to be used at that time, and hence we find it called by the name of *ch'eh* (彻) as well as *yung*.—Even on the view of the ode given by Choo, he has some difficulties to dispose of. Ll. 1—4 are plainly narrative, and proceed from an onlooker. The king would never speak of himself in the terms 天子穆穆. Ll. 5—8 are as plainly from the lips of the king, the sacrificer; and so are ll. 13—16. But if ll.9—12 stood alone, we should take them, like ll. 1—4, as descriptive, and translate in the 3d person.

Ll.,—4. Ll. 1,2 are predicates of the princes (辟公,—as in [i.], IV.) assisting in the service. 雍雍 and 肃肃,—as in III. i. VI.3.

文武维后。燕及皇天。克昌厥后。○绥我眉寿。介以
繁祉。既右烈考。亦右文母。

O great and august Father,
Comfort me, your filial son!

'With penetrating wisdom thou did'st play the man,
A sovereign with the gifts both of peace and war,
Giving rest even to great Heaven,
And ensuring prosperity to thy descendants.

'Thou comfortest me with the eyebrows of longevity;
Thou makest me great with manifold blessings.
I offer this sacrifice to my meritorious father,
And to my accomplished mother.'

I can only regard 止 as a particle. Choo says on 穆穆 simply that it is descriptive of the king (天子之容). Ying-tah, after the Urh-ya, finds nothing more in it than the general idea of 美, 'admirable,' 'elegant.' But that does not exhaust its meaning. The 'Complete Digest' expands it into 至和无迹，至敬无声，端默无为. 'Profound' comes nearer it than any one English term I can think of.

Ll.5—8. Here we have king Woo speaking, though there is no indication in the text of any change of person. Ll. 1,2. Choo takes 於 as the exclamation Oh!; and this obliges him to understand that the bull was contributed by the assisting princes (此和敬之诸侯荐大牲以助我之祭事). But the imperial editors observe that there is no evidence that such a thing was ever done by the princes, while there are abundant testimonies as to the victims being provided by the king. The difficulty is altogether avoided by reading 於 with its usual pronunciation, which gives the meaning of the line as in the translation. 肆 = 陈; 肆祀,—'to arrange, set forth, the sacrifice.'

Ll.7,8. 假 = 大, 'great;' we might also take it as = 嘉, 'admirable.' 皇考,—皇, as in III.i. X.5; 考 is 'a deceased father.' 绥,—'to comfort,' 'to give support and settlement to.'

Ll. 9—12 must be translated in the 2d person, though the lines themselves, as I have said, rather indicate the 3d. 维人，维后,—compare the 维人 in [i.] IV., l. 9. 宣 = 通 or 遍, with reference to the comprehensive range and penetration of Wǎn's wisdom. 燕 = 安, 'to give rest to.' Hwang Tso, referring to the statement in III.i. VII.1, that 'God surveyed the four quarters of the kingdom, seeking for some one to give settlement to the people,' adds, 'Thus what Heaven has at heart is the settlement of the people. When they have rest given to them, Heaven is at rest.' 昌 = 盛, with hiphil force, 'to make prosperous.'

Ll. 13—16. 眉寿,—as in II.ii. VII.4. 繁,—'manifold.' 右 = 尊, 'to honour,'—with reference to the sacrifice that had been offered. 烈考,—i. q., 皇考, in l.7. 文母 must be referred to T'ae-sze, the queen of Wǎn. In sacrifices to ancestors, the tablets of their wives were placed in their shrines, so that both shared in the honours of the service.

The rhymes are—雍, 公, cat. 10; 肃, 穆, cat. 3. t. 3; 牡 *, 考 *, ib., t. 2; 祀, 子, cat. 1, t. 2; 人, 天, cat. 12, t. 1; 后, 後, cat. 4, t. 2; 寿, 考 *, cat. 3, t. 2; 祉, 母 *, cat. 1, t. 2.

VIII.　*Tae hëen.*

载见

载见辟王。曰求厥章。龙旗阳阳。和铃央央。鞗革有
鸧。休有烈光。○率见昭考。以孝以享。○以介眉寿。

They appeared before their sovereign king,
To seek from him the rules [they were to observe].
With their dragon-emblazoned banners, flying bright,
The bells on them and their front-boards tinkling,
And with the rings on the ends of the reins glittering,
Admirable was their majesty, and splendour.

He led them to appear before his father shrined on the left,
Where he discharged his filial duty, and presented his offerings;—

Ode 8. Narrative. APPROPRIATE TO AN OCCASION WHEN THE FEUDAL PRINCES WERE ASSISTING KING CHING AT A SACRIFICE TO KING WOO. The Preface and Choo agree so far regarding this ode in that they regard it as having been made with reference to a sacrifice by king Ching in the temple of his father. Wherein they differ is, that the Preface says the sacrifice was on the *first* occasion of the princes making their appearance before the shrine of Woo, while Choo allows no such specification of time in it. Which view we are to adopt depends on the meaning given to the commencing term 载. Is it the initial particle, and untranslateable, as Choo holds? Or has it the meaning of 始, as Maou says, so that l. 1 will mean, 'on the first appearance of the princes at the court of their sovereign?' The character itself will admit of either interpretation of it, and there is nothing in the piece to fix its meaning. The imperial editors give their decision in favour of the view of the Preface, which Choo himself at one time admitted. There was an appropriateness, they say, in king Ching's leading them to the temple of his father, on their first presentation at his court. This I allow, but there would be nothing inappropriate in his doing so on some subsequent occasion as well. The point is one which cannot be positively determined.—The ode, it will be observed, is *about* the sacrifice; but it was not said or sung at the sacrifice. Ll. 1—6. 载, is the initial particle; or=始, 'first,' 'on the first occasion of;'—see above. 见 (read *hëen*)=朝觐, 'to appear at court before the king.' We must understand 辟公, 'the

feudal princes,' as in l. 12, as the subject. 辟王, 'the ruling king,' is of course king Ching. 曰 is not to be translated. Mih-tsze quotes the line with 聿 (尚贤篇). 章=法度, 'laws and rules;' meaning the various regulations which were delivered to the princes when they appeared at court, to be put in force in their own States. Ll. 3—6 all describe the state with which the arrival of the princes at the capital was accompanied. 旗,—as in II.i.VIII. 3. This is the first time we have found the descriptive 龙 along with it. 阳阳 expresses the brilliance of the flags. Bells attached to the front-board of the carriage were called 和; those fixed at the top of the banner-staff, 铃; other bells on the yoke or the horses' bits were called 鸾. 央央 is intended to give the sound made by the bells. From III.iii.VII. 2 we learn that the end of the reins were adorned with metal rings; 有鸧 denotes the glittering appearance which these made. So Ch'ing explains the phrase (金饰貌);—better than Choo's taking it of the sound made by the rings. 休=美 'admirable.'

Ll. 7, 8 have for their subject the king, who, after giving audience to the princes, proceeded to present them, as it were, to the Spirit of his father. 见,—as in l. 1. 昭考 is not to be translated —'his illustrious father.' 昭 has here the

永言保之。思皇多祜。烈文辟公。绥以多福。俾缉熙

于纯嘏。

That he might have granted to him long life,
And ever preserve [his dignity].
Great and many are his blessings.
They are the brilliant and accomplished princes,
Who cheer him with his many sources of happiness,
Enabling him to perpetuate them in their brightness as pure
    blessing.

IX.   *Yëw k'ih.*

有客

有客有客。亦白其马。有萋有且。敦琢其旅。有客宿

The noble visitor! The noble visitor!
Drawn like his ancestors by white horses!
The reverend and dignified,
Polished members of his suite!

technical sense which is explained under chapter 19th of 'The Doctrine of the Mean.' Woo's place in the Ancestral Temple was on the left of the shrine of the great ancestor of the House of Chow.   The reduplication of the 以 might be disregarded.   The offerings were the expression of the king's filial piety.   Ho K'ëae says, 'Hëaou denotes the filial thoughts,—the inward tasking of the mind; hëang denotes the offerings, the outward contribution to the utmost of the ability (孝 者, 孝 思, 内 尽 志 也, 享 者, 献 享, 外 尽 物 也).'

Ll. 9—14.   The subject of 介 will be 神,— the spirit of king Woo, who would respond with blessing to the filial offerings of his son. 言 is the expletive particle.   On the 之, the 'Complete Digest' says, 之 字 指 今 日 言, which I do not understand.   The meaning of l.2 evidently is that king Ching, through the favour of his father, would long preserve his dignity, and all the blessings of his lot.   思 is the initial particle ;—as in the 10th ode of last Decade, et al. 祜=福, 'happiness,' 'blessings.' Ll.12—14, are in compliment to the princes assisting at the sacrifice, intimating that it was to their co-operation that the king was indebted for the favourable answer which would be given to his sacrifice.   This seems to me the only natural or legitimate construction of these lines; and I am surprised that the imperial editors should demur to it, and call attention to Ch'ing's view that l. 13 is to be understood of the blessing which the princes themselves would receive, and not of that which they secured for the king (绥 之 以 多 福, 是 神 安 辟 公 以 多 福, 非 谓 安 孝 子 也). L. 12,—as in ode IV. of last Decade ; 缉 熙,—as in ode VI. of the same.   于 has perhaps the force of 'up to the point of.'   Choo's expansion of l.14 is— 使 我 (but the whole par. is in the 3d person) 得 继 而 明 之, 至 于 纯 嘏 也.

The rhymes are— 王, 章, 阳, 央, 鸧, 光, 享 *, cat. 10; 寿, 保 *, cat. 3, t. 2; 祜, 嘏 *, cat. 5, t. 2.

Ode 9.   Narrative.   CELEBRATING THE DUKE OF SUNG ON ONE OF HIS APPEARANCES AT THE CAPITAL AND ASSISTING AT THE SACRIFICE IN THE ANCESTRAL TEMPLE OF CHOW ;—SHOWING HOW HE WAS ESTEEMED AND CHERISHED BY THE KING.   From ode 3 we may conclude that the visitor here celebrated was the representative

宿。有客信信。言授之縶。以縶其马。○薄言追之。

左右绥之。既有淫威。降福孔夷。

The noble guest will stop [but] a night or two!
The noble guest will stop [but] two nights or four!
Give him ropes
To bind his horses.

I will convoy him [with a parting feast];
I will comfort him in every possible way.
Adorned with such great dignity,
It is very natural that he should be blessed.

of one of the former dynasties, and the mention of his white horse (or horses) is a sufficient substantiation of the tradition in the Preface, that he was the famous viscount of Wei (see the Shoo, IV. xi.), an elder brother, or an uncle, of the last king of the Shang dyn. When the rebellion of that king's son was put down, and the son himself put to death, the viscount of Wei was made duke of Sung, there to continue the sacrifices of the House of Shang. In this ode he is represented as coming to the court of Chow, where he would assist king Ching in the sacrifices in his ancestral temple. Ho K'ëae says, 'The language, like that of ode 3, is all in praise of the guest, but it was sung or recited in the temple ; and therefore it is rightly placed among the *Sung*.' Perhaps there is an indication in it of the temple,—in the last line.

Ll. 1—4. The repetition of the 有客 serves to call attention to the visitor, and to intimate the joy which the sight of him occasioned. K'ëang is the only critic I have met with who finds in it an indication that more than one visitor is indicated by it,—the duke of Sung namely, and his attendants. With the dynasty of Yin white had been the esteemed and sacred colour, as red was with Chow, and hence the duke, as the representative of Yin, had his carriage drawn by white horses. Riding on horseback being a thing not mentioned in the She, we must take 马 in the plural. The use of 白驹 in II. iv. II. may be pleaded in favour of a singular construction of 马 ; but perhaps, in that ode also we ought to take 驹 as plural.

At any rate, the duke of Sung would come to the court of Chow, as the other princes did, in a carriage. Choo says 亦 is merely the initial particle, but I prefer regarding it here, with Soo Ch'eh, as 仍, with all the meaning in the translation. 有萋有且 is descriptive of the 旅 in l. 4, the officers in attendance on the duke. Choo acknowledges that he does not understand 萋且 ; but Maou gives the characters the meaning of 敬慎貌, 'the app. of being reverent and careful.' It is as well to accept this explanation, though given merely because it would suit the connection. Compare 萋斐 in II. v. VI. 1. 敦 (read *tuy*) 琢 is defined by 选择, 'selected.' The characters, no doubt,＝追琢 in III, i. IV. 5, There they are used of metal and jade engraved and chiselled ; here they are metaphorically applied to the officers of Sung. 旅,—'a company ;' here, the suite of the duke.

Ll. 5—8 are indicative of the esteem felt at the court for the duke, and how gladly the king would have detained him. Compare the similar phraseology in II. iv. II. 1, 2. 'To lodge one night in a place is called 宿 ; to lodge two nights is called 信.' The Urh-ya explains the repetition of 宿, as meaning 'to lodge two nights (再宿)' and that of 信 as meaning 'to lodge four nights (四宿)' 言 is merely the expletive particle. The first 縶 ＝ a 'rope ;'

X. *Woo.*

武

於皇武王。无竞维烈。允文文王。克开厥后。嗣武受
之。胜殷遏刘。耆定尔功。

Oh! great wast thou, O king Woo,
Displaying the utmost strength in thy work.
Truly accomplished was king Wăn,
Opening the path for his successors.
Thou did'st receive the inheritance from him;
Thou did'st vanquish Yin, and put a stop to its cruelties;—
Effecting the firm establishment of thy merit.

the second,='to tie or tether.' If his horses
were tied, the duke would be obliged to remain.
Ll. 9—12. The duke would not be stayed,
and here the king tells how he would continue
to show his appreciation of him, when he was
gone. 薄言 is the compound particle with
which we are familiar. 追之 is taken as=
送之, 'I will escort him,' including the giving to him a parting feast. L. 10 has been
taken variously. Choo understands 左右,
' on the left and the right,' as=in every possible
way; and the meaning of the line is as I have
given it in the translation. The construction is
natural and unstrained. Ch'ing understood
左右 of the king's ministers (左右之
臣), who would be present at the feast, and
show their desire for the happiness of the distinguished visitor. The 'Essence and Flower of
the She' adopts this view. Kĕang takes 左右
of the members of the duke's suite, who deserved, as well as their master, to be esteemed and
honoured. L. 11 is referred to the duke of
Sung, the greatest of the feudatories of Chow,
and worthy of his dignity; so that 淫 has the
sense of 大, 'great.' The only critic who takes
a difft. view is Fan Ch'oo-e, who refers the line
to Woo-kăng, on whom the duke of Chow had
dealt the terrors of justice (威), because of his
rebellion (淫). Thus the line contains a warning to the duke of Sung; but this is foreign to
the spirit of the whole piece, to say nothing of
the 'chiselling' of the construction. I said that
in l. 12 there is, perhaps, an indication of the

ode's having been sung in the temple;—before
the shrine of king Woo. The subject of
降福 is not expressed, but 神 may very
well be understood, and the line,='Very easy is
it for thee, O spirit [of my father], to send
down blessing on him.' I have left the meaning, however, indefinite in the translation. 夷
= 易, 'easy,'=natural.
The rhymes are—马*, 旅, 马*, cat. 5, t.
2; 追, 绥, 威, 夷 cat. 15, t. 1.

Ode 10. Narrative. SUNG IN THE ANCESTRAL
TEMPLE TO THE MUSIC REGULATING THE DANCE
IN HONOUR OF THE ACHIEVEMENTS OF KING WOO.
This account of the piece, given in the Preface,
is variously corroborated, and I do not know
that any of the critics have called it in question.
The dance was made by the duke of Chow, and
was supposed to represent in some way the success of Woo's career. Perhaps the brief ode
was sung as a prelude to the dance; or it may
be that the seven lines are only a fragment.
This, indeed, is most likely, as we have several
odes in the next section all referred to the same
occasion. The 尔 in l. 7 has made me use the
second person in the translation throughout.
Ll. 1,2. 於 (woo),—the exclamation. The
structure of l. 2 is like that of 无 竞 惟 人,
which we have met with in III. iii. II., et al.
烈,
—in the sense of 功, 'merit,' 'achievement.'
Nothing could be conceived of grander or
stronger than what Woo had accomplished. Ll.
3,4. But if Woo had reared the superstructure,

Wăn had laid the foundations of it. 开 厥
后,—'opened the future,' *i. e.,* prepared the
way for all that should be done by those who
came after him. Ll. 5—8. 嗣 武,—'inheriting
Woo;' *i. e.,* Woo, as the successor and heir of
Wăn. ' 受 之,—'received it; *i. e.,* all that
Wăn had done. 遏,—to repress;' as in III.ii.
IX. 刘 = 杀, ' to kill;' meaning all the mur-
derous oppression exercised by Show. 耆 =
致, 'to bring about;'—as in III. i. VII. Even
Maou thus explains 耆 here. Fan Ch'oo-e is
again singular in insisting on the usual meaning of the term, as = 老, so that l. 7 is with
him='When thou was old, thou did'st establish
thy merit!'

There are no rhymes.

170

BOOK I. SACRIFICIAL ODES OF CHOW.

[iii.] THE DECADE OF MIN YU SEAOU-TSZE.

I. *Min yu.*

闵予小子之什四一之三

闵予小子

闵予小子。遭家不造。嬛嬛在疚。於乎皇考。永世克孝。○念兹皇祖。陟降庭止。维予小子。夙夜敬止。○於乎皇王。继序思不忘。

Alas for me, who am [as] a little child,
On whom has devolved the unsettled State!
Solitary am I and full of distress.
Oh! my great Father,
All thy life long, thou wast filial.

Thou didst think of my great grandfather,
[Seeing him, as it were,] ascending and descending in the court.
I, the little child,
Day and night will be so reverent.

Oh! ye great kings,
As your successor, I will strive not to forget you.

TITLE OF THE SECTION.—闵予小子之什, 四一之三, 'The Decade of Min yu seaou-tsze; Section III. of Book I., Part IV.' Ode 1. Narrative. APPROPRIATE TO THE YOUNG KING CHING, DECLARING HIS SENTIMENTS IN THE TEMPLE OF HIS FATHER. The Preface says merely that we have here 'the heir-king presenting himself in the ancestral temple (嗣王朝于庙也);' but the common consent of Maou and all the critics is that the king was Ching. The only question is as to the date of the com-position, whether the piece was made for him on his repairing to the temple when the mourning for his father was expired, or after the expiration of the regency of the duke of Chow. Këang supposes that it was made for Ching's regular use (平日朝于庙), so that both these occasions may be embraced in it.

Ll. 1–5. 闵 = 病, 'distress,' 'to be distressed,' so that l.1='Distressed am I, the little child.' 小子 is Ching's humble designation of himself; and is frequently put into his lips in

II. *Fang loh.*

访落

访予落止。率时昭考。於乎悠哉。朕未有艾。将予就
之。继犹判涣。维予小子。未堪家多难。绍庭上下。

I take counsel at the beginning of my [rule],
How I can follow [the example] of my shrined father.
Ah! far-reaching [were his plans],
And I am not yet able to carry them out.
However I endeavour to reach to them,
My continuation of them will still be all-deflected.
I am [but as] a little child,
Unequal to the many difficulties of the State.

the Shoo (*e. g.*, V. vii. 2,9, *et al.*). It may seem appropriate in the lips of him who was only a boy; but elders also employed it. It occurs, for instance, in the Shoo, V. vi.10, used by the duke of Chow of himself. 家＝国 家, which we may translate 'the kingdom.' 造 is defined by 成, which Ying-tah endeavours to explain by saying, 'When there is progressive action, there will be completion in the end; hence 造＝成 (有所造为，终必成就，故造犹成也).' Whether there be a reference to any special calamities in l. 2 we cannot tell; but compare king Ching's complaint in the Shoo, V. vii.1. 嬛,—*i. q.*, 茕. The redoubled character gives the idea of being solitary and unsupported (孤独). 疚,—as in II.i.VII. 3, *et al.* 皇 考, is, of course, king Woo. 永 世＝终 身, 'all his life.' The young king proposes the filial conduct of his father as the great thing to be imitated by himself.

In ll.6—9 king Woo is still the subject of ll.6,7. 祖, 'grandfather,' refers to king Wăn, Ching's grandfather and Woo's father. 兹＝此 'this;' but we must substitute 'my' for it in the translation. L. 7 indicates how Woo kept the thought of his father before him, as if he were continually seeing him ascending and descending in the court (常 若 见 我 皇 祖 之 陟 降 于 庭). This is a much more likely construction than that proposed by Maou, who would take 庭, as he does elsewhere, as＝直, so that the line＝'who was upright above and below,' *i. e.*,

Heaven-wards and man-wards. The 止 in ll. 7, 9 are both the final particle.

Ll. 10, 11. The 皇 王 are to be taken of both Wăn and Woo. Maou defines 序 by 绪, 'the thread of a clue or cocoon,'＝the line of succession in the kingdom. 思 is emphatic,＝ 慕, 'to long for,' 'to strive.'

The rhymes are— 造 *, 疚 (prop. cat. 1), 考 *, 孝 *, cat.3, t.2; 庭, 敬, cat.11; 王 忘, cat. 10.

Ode 2. Narrative. SEEMS TO BE A SEQUEL TO THE FORMER ODE. THE YOUNG KING TELLS OF HIS DIFFICULTIES AND INCOMPETENCIES; ASKS FOR COUNSEL TO HELP TO COPY THE EXAMPLE OF HIS FATHER; STATES HOW HE MEANT TO DO SO; AND CONCLUDES WITH AN APPEAL OR PRAYER TO HIS FATHER. The Preface says that this piece relates to a council held by Ching with his ministers in the ancestral temple; but we can hardly affirm anything so definite about it.

L. 1. 访＝问, 'to ask,' or 谋, 'to take counsel.' 落 is defined by 始, 'the beginning,' *i.e.*, here, the commencement of Ch'ing's reign. The term is supposed to have this signification from the use of 落 to denote the feast or ceremony with which any great building was inaugurated (凡 宫 室 始 成，则 落 之，故 以 落 为 始). Ching's accession to the throne, or to the govt., would stand in that relation to his future reign. Ch'ing supposes that l.2 is the counsel which had been given by the ministers, but I prefer to take it as in the translation. 时＝是, 'this;' but we

陟降厥家。休矣皇考。以保明其身。

In his room, [I will look for him] to go up and come down in
    the court,
To ascend and descend in the house.
Admirable art thou, O great Father,
[Condescend] to preserve and enlighten me.

III. *King che*

敬之

敬之敬之。天维显思。命不易哉。无曰高高在上。陟

Let me be reverent, let me be reverent, [in attending to my
    duties];
[The way of] Heaven is evident,
And its appointment is not easily [preserved].
Let me not say that It is high aloft above me.

must render it by 'my.' 昭考,—as in [ii.]
VIII. Ll. 3, 4. 悠 = 远, 'far-reaching;' referring to the plans of king Woo. 艾 is here
defined by 尽, 'to carry on and out,' which is
not found in the dictionary. A reference is
made, in illustration of this meaning, to the use
of 艾 in II. iii. VIII. 2, *q.v.* L. 5. 将 is with
many of the critics taken as = 扶 推, (comp its
use in II. vi. 2), or = 助, 'to help;' so that
Ching is asking his ministers to support him
and help him to attain to the example of his
father. But we may understand it of his expressing his own purpose to try and advance
(就) in that direction; and then l. 6 says that
though he might do so, his course would be
diverging still, and like a dispersion of his father's achievements. 判 = 分; 涣 = 散.
L. 8. 堪 = 胜, 'to be equal to bear,' or 'to
cope with.' Ll. 9, 10 are puzzling, but I think
we have the key to them in l. 7 of last ode. As
Woo, there, is represented as keeping his father's
example always before him, as if he saw him
ascending and descending in his court, so does
Ching here say that he would keep Woo's example before him. 绍,—'to continue;' *i. e.*,
Ching was now in his father's room continuing
the line of Chow. Këang takes 绍 rather differently, but his general view of the lines is
what I have given:—念 我 皇 考 之 绍

我 皇 祖 也, 上 下 于 庭 陟 降 于
家, 时 时 见 之 无 一 事 不 相 契
合. In ll. 11, 12, the king addresses himself to
his father, and indicates his dependence on his
help.

The only rhyme which Twan-she makes out is
一涣, 难, cat. 14.

Ode 3. Narrative. KING CHING SHOWS HIS
SENSE OF WHAT WAS REQUIRED OF HIM TO PRE-
SERVE THE FAVOUR OF HEAVEN, A CONSTANT
JUDGE; INTIMATES HIS GOOD PURPOSES; AND ASKS
THE HELP OF HIS MINISTERS TO BE ENABLED TO
FULFIL THEM. The Preface says that in this
piece his ministers present cautionary warning to
the king; but that can be an account of the first
six lines only. The general view is that in those
lines we have the admonitions of the ministers,
and in the remaining six the reply of the king.
In ll. 7—12 the king speaks certainly in the
first person, and in the others I think the king
is also the speaker, recapitulating, it may be,
with his own view of it, the counsel which
had been given. The only claim which the
piece has to a place among the Temple odes is
that it may be a portion of the consultation
which, it is affirmed, took place between king
Ching and his ministers,—in the temple.

Ll. 1—6. The 之 after 敬 serves to bring
out its meaning as in the translation. In l. 2,
思 is the final particle. 显 = 明, 'evident;'
and this makes us take 天 as = 天 之 道,
' the way or course of Heaven.' L. 3—see III. i.

降厥士。日监在兹。○维予小子。不聪敬止。日就月

将。学有缉熙于光明。佛时仔肩。示我显德行。

It ascends and descends about our doings;
It daily inspects us wherever we are.

I am [but as] a little child,
Without intelligence to be reverently [attentive to my duties];
But by daily progress and monthly advance,
I will learn to hold fast the gleams [of knowledge], till I arrive
    at bright intelligence.
Assist me to bear the burden [of my position],
And show me how to display a virtuous conduct.

IV.   *Sëaou pe.*

小毖

予其惩。而毖后患。莫予荓蜂。自求辛螫。肇允彼桃

I condemn myself [for the past], and will be on my guard
    against future calamity.
I will have nothing to do with a wasp,
To seek for myself its painful sting.

l, 6,7.   L.4. It might be supposed that Heaven being so high above us, does not take account of our affairs. The reply to this is given in ll. 5,6. 士＝事, 'affairs;'—compare its use in I. xv. IV. 1. Ho K'ëae says, ' 士 is a designation of men of talent, as being equal to the management of affairs (其 人 足 任 事), and hence the term has the signification of "affairs" in the text.' The indefinite 厥 must be rendered by 'our.' 在 兹,—'here;' *i. e.*, in every place, wherever we are.

Ll. 7—12.   In l. 8 止 is the final particle. There may, possibly, be a reference in the line to the rumours about the disloyalty of the duke of Chow, which the young king had given credit to for a time. L.9='Daily going towards, monthly advancing (将 ＝ 进).' The words have given rise to a variety of expressions for continuous progress:—日 有 所 就，月 有 所 进；日 成 月 长；日 有 所 造．月

有 所 往, &c.   L. 10. 'Learning,' it is said, is opening the door of intelligence, the way by which one enters into reverent attention to duty. 缉 is the continuation of the daily and monthly progress. 熙 has reference to the light which, from day to day and month to month, is so obtained. We are to regard ll. 11, 12 as addressed by the king to his ministers. 佛 —*i. q.*, 弼, ＝ 辅, 'to assist.' 仔 ＝ 任, 'to sustain a burden.' 时 仔 肩, 'this burden on my shoulders;'—the duties incumbent on me. Choo seems to take 显, as an adjective (示 我 以 显 明 之 德 行). The construction is simpler if we take it as a verb.

The rhymes are— 之, 思, 哉, 兹, cat. 1, t. 1 ;? 子, 止, *ib.*, t. 2 ; 将, 明 *, 行 *, cat. 10.

Ode 4. Narrative.   KING CHING ACKNOW-LEDGES THAT HE HAD ERRED, AND STATES HIS

虫。拼飞维鸟。未堪家多难。予又集于蓼。

At first, indeed, the thing seemed but a wren,
But it took wing and became a [large] bird.
I am unequal to the many difficulties of the kingdom;
And I am placed in the midst of bitter experiences.

V. *Tsae shoo.*

载芟

载芟载柞。其耕泽泽。○千耦其耘。徂隰徂畛。○

They clear away the grass and the bushes;
And the ground is laid open by their ploughs.

In thousands of pairs they remove the roots,
Some in the low wet lands, some along the dykes.

PURPOSE TO BE CAREFUL IN THE FUTURE; HE WILL GUARD AGAINST THE SLIGHT BEGINNINGS OF EVIL, AND IS PENETRATED WITH A SENSE OF HIS OWN INCOMPETENCIES. This ode may be considered as the conclusion of the service in the ancestral temple with which it and the previous three are connected. The Preface says that in it king Ching asks for the assistance of his ministers. No such request, however, is directly expressed.

L.1. 惩,—'to reprimand,' 'to warn.' Ching had offended somehow in the past,—probably in indulging suspicions of the duke of Chow. 其 gives emphasis to the declaration. 毖 = 慎, 'to be careful against;'—compare its use in III. iii. III. 5. Ll. 2, 3. Maou and most of the critics take 莫 = 'do not;'—addressed to the ministers. Then 荓 is defined by 掣曳, as if the ministers had dragged him into contact with a wasp; but if this were a correct, ex-egesis, l.3 would not begin with 自求, 'seek-ing for myself.' Choo defines 荓 by 使, as in III. iii. III. 6, meaning 'to cause or employ,' or, more generally, 'to have to do with.' This gives a more satisfactory meaning, and the 莫 will be indicative, or='let me not.' By the 'wasp' is intended, I suppose, the king's uncles, who had joined in rebellion with the son of Chow of Shang, and whom the king had been inclined to trust in preference to the loyal duke. Ll. 4,5 are intended to set forth how evil at first looks small, but becomes large as it developes. 桃虫, 'the peach-tree insect' is the name of a small bird, called also 鹪鹩, 巧妇

('the clever wife,' from the artistic character of its nest), and by other names. Williams says it is 'a wren, turin, tody, or some such small bird.' 拼 = 飞貌, 'the appearance of fly-ing,' the bird on the wing. 鸟 = 大鸟, 'a large bird.' Choo refers to a fabulous be-lief that the wren grows into a hawk; but it took its origin probably from these lines, which do not necessarily imply it. What we have to see in them is what is small at the beginning (肇 = 始) developing to be something great. Ll. 6, 7 again express the sense which the king had of his insufficiency, and l.7, perhaps, of the trouble which it had brought him into in the past. 蓼 is the name of 'a plant with a red stalk, and of a bitter taste;'—perhaps the smart-weed. Ching's experience had brought him, as it were, into the midst of a patch of it.

The only rhyme which Twan-she gives is that of 鸟 *, 蓼 *, cat.3, t.2. To this we may add, 蜂, 虫, cat. 10.

Ode 5. Narrative. THE CULTIVATION OF THE GROUND, FROM THE FIRST BREAKING OF IT UP, TILL IT YIELDS ABUNDANT HARVESTS;—AVAIL-ABLE SPECIALLY FOR SACRIFICES AND ON FES-TIVE OCCASIONS. WHETHER INTENDED TO BE USED ON OCCASIONS OF THANKSGIVING, OR IN SPRING WHEN PRAYING FOR A GOOD YEAR, CAN-NOT BE DETERMINED. The Preface says the ode was sung in spring, when the king ploughed a furrow in the field set apart for that purpose, and prayed at the altars of the Spirits of the land and the grain for an abundant year. Choo says he does not know on what occasion it was intended to be used; but comparing it with

侯主侯伯。侯亚侯旅。侯强侯以。有嗿其馌。思媚其

妇。有依其士。有略其耜。俶载南亩。○播厥百谷。

There are the master and his eldest son;
His younger sons, and all their children;
Their strong helpers, and their hired servants.
How the noise of their eating the viands brought to them
    resounds!
[The husbands] think lovingly of their wives;
[The wives] keep close to their husbands.
[Then] with their sharp plough-shares,
They set to work on the south-lying acres.

[ii.] IV., he is inclined to rank it with that as an ode of thanksgiving. The imperial editors give a decision, more positive than is their wont, in favour of the earlier view. The student will see that there is absolutely nothing in the ode itself to determine him in favour of either view. It brings before us a series of pleasing pictures of the husbandry of those early times, and has more interest for the reader than most pieces in the She. The imperial editors also say that its place in the Sung makes it clear that it was an accompaniment of some royal sacrifice; but, without controverting this, the poet evidently singled out some large estate, and describes the labour upon it, from the first bringing it under cultivation to the state in which it was before his eye, and concludes by saying that the picture which he gives of it had long been applicable to the whole country.

Ll. 1, 2 seem to commence with the first breaking up of the ground, which has not been brought under cultivation before. The redoubled 载 is merely the initial particle. 芟＝除草, 'to remove or clear away grass;' 柞＝除木 'to remove bushes and trees.' When this was done, the plough could be set to work, and, as it turned up the ground, the earth became pulverized through the action of the elements which now found free admission to it. This seems to be the meaning of 泽泽, which is explained by 解散, 'to be opened and dispersed.'

Ll. 3, 4. If ll. 1, 2 be explained correctly of the first taking in of the ground, then the 耘 or 'weeding' here will be the clearing away of the roots of the grass and bushes;—so, Ch'ing (耘 为除根株). At one time Choo took the same view, but in his 'Collected Comments' he defines 耘 as 'the removal of the grass among the growing corn.' But he is incorrect, for it is not till l. 13 that mention is made even of the

sowing. 'A thousand pairs would be two thousand men. 隰 denotes the low wet grounds, specially intended for the fields; 畛, the raised banks, serving for paths, which were made alongside the ditches and channels by which the ground was divided. 徂＝往, 'to go to;' here indicating the places where the labour was applied.

Ll. 5—12. We are now, I conceive, to withdraw our thoughts from the labours thus far indicated, and to have before us a large, cleared estate, on which the proprietor and his dependants are at work in the spring of the year. The redoubled 侯 in ll. 5, 7 is evidently a particle like the 载 in l.1. 主＝家长, 'the Head of the family;' 伯＝长子, 'his eldest son;' 亚 ＝仲叔, 'the younger sons (Ying-tah says, 亚训次也, 次于伯, 故知仲叔 也;' 旅＝子弟, 'the younger members of the family' (Ying-tah says, 旅训众也, 幼者之众, 即季弟(?)及伯 仲叔之诸子也); 强＝有力者, 'the able-bodied men (By these, I apprehend, we are to understand the labourers of different clans, regularly attached, as helpers, to the family. Ying-tah supposes they were strong men who, after doing their own work, were able to go and give a hand where they were needed).' 以＝能左右之者, 'men who could be sent to the left or the right (Choo says that they were like the hired labourers of a later time,—若今时佣力之人, 随主 人所左右者也).' But they must have got some remuneration for their labour even in those early days.

实函斯活。○驿驿其达。有厌其杰。○厌厌其苗。绵

绵其麃。○载获济济。有实其积。万亿及秭。为酒为

醴。烝畀祖妣。以洽百礼。○有飶其香。邦家之光。

They sow their different kinds of grain,
Each seed containing in it a germ of life.

In unbroken lines rises the blade,
And well-nourished the stalks grow long.

Luxuriant looks the young grain,
And the weeders go among it in multitudes.

Then come the reapers in crowds,
And the grain is piled up in the fields,
Myriads, and hundreds of thousands, and millions [of stacks];
For spirits and for sweet spirits,
To offer to our ancestors, male and female,
And to provide for all ceremonies.

Maou defines 喷 by 众貌, 'the appearance of a multitude,' and then 饎 will indicate those bringing their food to the workers in the fields. He understands 士 in l. 10 of 子弟, all the younger people who have come with the wives bringing the viands. Much more pleasing, and I believe correct also, is Choo's view of ll.8—10. 喷 is the sound made by the workers as they partake of the viands brought to them (众饮食声). L. 9 belongs to the husbands lovingly regarding their wives, and l. 10 to the wives keeping close to their own husbands. 士＝夫, 'husband.' I do not think that Maou's explanation of the term by 子弟 is admissible. There is hardly a picture in the She equal to that which these three lines give us;—'a picture,' says Yen Ts'an, 'of a well-ordered, happy age (治世之气象).' 略＝利, 'sharp.' The meal is over, and the husbandmen go to work. 俶＝始, 'to begin.' 载＝事, 'to set to work on.'
Ll.13,14. We come to the work of sowing. 实＝种子; 'the seed.' 斯＝则, so that l. 14＝'what the seed contains is living.' The 'Flower and Essence of the She' seems to take 斯 as＝此 in a vague sense,—not more than our the; 其谷实之种子, 皆含此生活之气.
Ll. 15,16 tell of the first appearance and subsequent progress of the plants. 驿驿,—苗生貌, 'the appearance of the young grain growing;'—we must understand it of the blade. 达＝出土, 'developing from the earth.' 杰 is the same, 'growing long (先长者),' through the abundance of the moisture (有厌,—受气足也). Ll. 17,18. 苗 is the plant now risen to a considerable height, and looking fresh and well-nourished (厌厌). 麃＝耘, 'to weed,' 'weeders.' 绵绵 describes the weeders as many and close on one another (详密).
Ll. 19—24. We come to the reaping. 载,—the particle. 实 is here the fruit of the fields,—the corn cut down, and gathered into sheaves or bundles. 积,—as in III. ii. VI. 1. Ll 21—24,—comp. in [ii.]. IV., only l.20 here belongs to the number of stacks, and there to the measures of grain in the granaries.

有椒其馨。胡考之宁。○匪且有且。匪今斯今。振古

如兹。

Fragrant is their aroma,
Enhancing the glory of the State.
Like pepper is their smell,
To give comfort to the aged.

It is not here only that there is this [abundance];
It is not now only that there is such a time:—
From of old it has been thus.

VI. *Lëang sze.*

良耜

畟畟良耜。俶载南亩。○播厥百谷。实函斯活。○

Very sharp are the excellent shares,
With which they set to work on the south-lying acres.

They sow their different kinds of grain,
Each seed containing a germ of life.

Ll. 25—28. 馥＝芬香, 'fragrant.' Choo does not know of what things l. 25 is spoken. L. 27 is understood to be descriptive of the spirits, and Fan Ch'oo-e would refer l. 25 to the viands of a feast. The paragraph shows the further use which the results of the husbandry would serve, in addition to sacrifices direct;—for the feasts to visitors and guests at the royal court, which would be the glory of the State; and especially for the comfort of the old, whom we have seen, in III.ii.IV. 4, specially attended to at the conclusion of sacrificial services; or on other occasions. 胡＝寿, 'advanced in years,' or 遐, 'with nearly the same meaning,—in the connection.

Ll. 29—31 say that the country had for very long been blessed with abundant years. 且 ＝此, 'this.' The first 且＝此处, 'here;' the second＝此有年之事, 'this abundant harvest.' Similarly, the first 今 ＝'the present time;' the second ＝ 'the present prosperity.' Maou defines 振 by 自, 'from'; Choo,

by 极, so that 振古 = 'from very ancient times.'

The rhymes are—柞, 泽 *, cat. 5, t. 3; 耘, 畛 *, cat. 13; 以, 妇, 士, 耜, 亩 *, cat. 1, t. 2; 活, 达, 杰, cat. 15, t. 3; 苗, 麃, cat. 2; 济, 积 (prop. cat. 16), 秭, 醴, 妣, 礼, cat. 15, t. 2; 香, 光, cat. 10; 馨, 宁, cat. 11.

Ode 6. Narrative. MUCH AKIN TO THE PRECEDING:—PRESUMABLY, AN ODE OF THANKSGIVING IN THE AUTUMN TO THE SPIRITS OF THE LAND AND GRAIN. This is the account of the piece given in the Preface. Choo, indeed, says that as there is nothing in ode 5 to lead us to think of it as a prayer for a good harvest, so there is nothing here about thanksgiving. But in the concluding paragraph there is a description of the victim in a sacrifice; and the whole character of the ode suits well with a service of thanksgiving. Yen Ts'an says, 'This ode was made for the thanksgiving to the Spirits of the land and the grain in autumn, and it was proper therefore that it should set forth the beginning

或来瞻女。載筐及筥。其饟伊黍。○其笠伊纠。其镈
斯赵。以薅茶蓼。○荼蓼朽止。黍稷茂止。○获之挃
挃。积之栗栗。其崇如墉。其比如栉。以开百室。○

There are those who come to see them,
With their baskets round and square,
Containing the provision of millet.

With their light splint hats on their heads,
They ply their hoes on the ground,
Clearing away the smart-weed on the dry land and wet.

These weeds being decayed,
The millets grow luxuriantly.

They fall rustling before the reapers,
And [the sheaves] are set up solidly,

and the end of the labours of husbandry. Hence, though the sacrifice was in the autumn, it recapitulates the ploughing of the spring, and anticipates the harvest of the winter.' The imperial editors say that l.20 plainly indicates, in the use of a bull, a royal sacrifice, and l.23, as plainly, that it did not take place in the ancestral temple, so that the account given of it in the Preface should be received without hesitation; while, as this is thus an ode of thanksgiving, the connection between it and the preceding is sufficient evidence that that was one of supplication.

Ll. 1, 2, — comp. ll. 11, 12 in last ode. 畟
畟=严利, 'very sharp;' descriptive of the plough-shares. Some say that the phrase expresses the appearance of the shares going into the soil (耜入地之貌). The meaning is much the same.

Ll. 3, 4,—as ll. 13, 14 of last ode.

Ll. 5—7 are all to be referred to the wives and children of the workers, bringing their food to them in the fields. L.5 is difficult, and the sudden change of person in the use of 女, 'you,' is to me inexplicable; and I have adhered to the 3d person in the translation. 瞻, 'to see,' is also a strange term, and 或 also. Ll. 6, 7 show that we are to understand l. 5 of the wives and children bringing the food of the workers (妇子之来馌者). Fan Ch'oo-e gives, indeed, a different view of l.5, as to be taken of the

surveyor of the fields (I.xv.I.1) coming to inspect the ploughing; but I cannot entertain it. 载 is the particle. 筐,筥,—as in I. ii. IV. 2. 其 饟,—'the food brought' in the baskets. 伊 =维, having the force of the copula.

Ll. 8—10. The workers have partaken of their meal, and go to their weeding. 纠 is descriptive of their hats as light, and easily moved. Maou says nothing on the term, but Ch'ing says,—戴纠然之笠; and Choo says that 纠然 denotes the ease with which the hat was lifted (笠之轻举). In the 'Complete Digest' we read, 首动则笠动, 'when the head moved, the hat moved.' The line altogether is obscure to me. 镈,—as in [ii.] I. 赵=刺, 'to cut;'—descriptive of the action of the hoes upon the ground. 伊 and 斯 are synonymous, and cannot be attended to in the translation. 薅=去, 'to remove,' 'to clear away.' Choo observes that 荼 and 蓼 are here one plant, with different names; called 荼 in the dry soil, and 蓼 (smartweed) in the wet. Ying-tah also observes that the 荼 here is not the 苦菜.

百室盈止。妇子宁止。○杀时犉牡。有捄其角。以似

以续。续古之人。

High as a wall,
United together like the teeth of a comb;
And the hundred houses are opened [to receive the grain].

Those hundred houses being full,
The wives and children have a feeling of repose.

[Now] we kill this black-muzzled tawny bull,
With his crooked horns,
To imitate and hand down,
To hand down [the observances of] our ancestors.

VII.　*Sze e.*

丝衣

丝衣其纻。载弁俅俅。自堂徂基。自羊徂牛。鼐鼎及

In his silken robes, clean and bright,
With his cap on his head, looking so respectful,
From the hall he goes to the foot of the stairs,
And from the sheep to the oxen.

Ll. 11, 12. 朽＝烂, 'to rot.' The writer seems to say that the weeds, being destroyed and left to rot in the soil, help the growth of the millets. 止,—the final particle.

Ll. 13—17. 挃挃 is understood to give the sound of the reaping. 栗栗 describes the solidity with which the sheaves of the cut grain were set up (积 之 密). L. 15 seems to describe the height of the grain, and 16, the appearance of the ears, close together as the teeth of a fine comb. L. 17. The 'hundred houses,' or chambers in a hundred houses, are those of the hundred families cultivating the space which was bounded by a 洫　They formed, says Choo, a clan (一 族 之 人), whose members all helped one another in their field-work, so that their harvest might be said to be carried home to their stack-yards at the same time. Then would come the threshing, or treading, and winnowing, after which the grain would be brought into the houses. So, the 'Flower and Essence of the

She:'—所 获 所 积, 既 已 在 场, 蹂 践 治 之, 于 是 百 家 开 户 纳 之. I cannot conceive where Lacharme found the suggestion of his—'*Familia numerosior facta est, et in centum familias dividuntur.*'

Ll. 20—23. A bull, yellow and black-lipped, was called 犉. Chów, it has been more than once observed, used victims of a red colour in sacrifice; but that was in the ancestral temple. For the sacrifice to the Spirits of the land and grain, the animals were as here described. 捄 ＝ 曲 貌, 'crooked.' The concluding two lines must be taken, I think, together, as in the translation. As the 'Flower and Essence of the She' expands them, 夫 犉 牡 报 祭 之 礼, 我 先 祖 也 行 之 矣, 今 似 而 效 之, 续 而 举 之, 盖 继 续 古 人 之 旧 典, 庶 几 答 神 贶 于 万 一 耳.

鼐。兕觥其觩。旨酒思柔。不吴不敖。胡考之休。

[He inspects] the tripods, large and small.
The good spirits are mild;
There is no noise, no insolence:—
An auspice, [all this], of great longevity.

VIII. *Choh.*

酌

於铄王师。遵养时晦。时纯熙矣。是用大介。我龙受

Oh! powerful was the king's army;
But he nursed it in obedience to circumstances while the time
    was yet dark.
When the time was clearly bright,
He thereupon donned his grand armour.

The rhymes are— 耟, 亩 *, cat.1, t. 2; 女,
笞, 黍 , cat.5, t.2; 纠, 赵 (prop. cat. 2),
蓼 *, 朽, 茂 *, cat. 3, t.2; 挃, 栗, 楬,
室 , cat. 12, t.3; 盈, 宁, cat.11; 角, 续,
cat. 3, t. 3.

Ode 7. Narrative. AN ODE, APPROPRIATE TO
A SACRIFICE, AND THE FEAST AFTER IT. Few
pieces in the odes give more trouble to a translator than this one, short and apparently trivi-
al as it is. The Preface says that it belongs to
the entertainment of the personators of the dead
in connection with the supplementary sacrifice
on the day after one of the great sacrifices in
the ancestral temple (绎, 宾 尸 也);—see
III. ii. IV. Choo says that this view is not correct, and gives the argument of the ode as stated
above; but he does not say what sacrifice he
thought was intended. The imperial editors argue
at length in favour of the old view, to which I
am half inclined to give in my adhesion.
Ll. 1,2 bring before us an officer, or officers
(士, an officer of inferior rank) in the sacrificial dress in which they assisted at the services
of the ancestral temple (士 祭 于 王 之
服). 纻 describes the appearance of the
silken robes as pure and clean (洁 貌). 载
= 戴, 'to wear on the head.' 弁 is what
was called the 爵 弁, 'a cap of linen, dyed
purple.' 俅 俅 = 恭 顺 貌, 'reverent
and deferential-looking.' Ll.3—5 describe the

movements of this officer (or officers) preparatory to the sacrifice (if we are to find a sacrifice
in the ode), or to the feast (if it relate only to
a feast). 基 is defined by 门 塾 之 基,
'the foundation (*i. e.*, the foot of the stairs) of
the apartments at the gate;'—intending, I suppose, what we may call the vestibule at the
gate leading to the ancestral temple. Two
buildings there were outside the gate, fronting the
south, and two inside it fronting the north. We
are to suppose that the officer goes from the
hall to the foot of the stairs to inspect the
various dishes arranged for the sacrifice or the
feast, and then similarly goes to see the animals, and the tripods for the boiling of the flesh,
&c. Whether the 堂 be the great hall in the
temple, or merely the hall in the inner buildings
of the vestibule, we cannot say. I incline to the
latter view, as it was in that hall that the personators of the dead were feasted; and if the ode
speaks only of the entertainment to them, which
consisted of the provisions of the previous day
heated up again, the 羊 and the 牛 will simply be the meat remaining over. 鼐 is 'a
small tripod,' and 鼐, 'a large one.'
Ll. 6—9 are understood to describe the good
order which characterized the drinking at the
feast, or at the conclusion of the sacrifice. The
cup of rhinoceros horn was drunk as a punish-
ment; but we are to conceive of it here as standing idly, with no occasion to resort to it. 思
is the particle;—having the force of the copula.
Choo, after Maou and Ch'ing, defines 吴 by
哗, 'noisy.' The dict. gives it as = 娱, 'plea-

之。蹻蹻王之造。载用有嗣。实维尔公允师。

We have been favoured to receive
What the martial king accomplished.
To deal aright with what we have inherited,
We have to be sincere imitators of thy course, [O king].

IX. *Hwan.*

桓

绥万邦。屡丰年。天命匪解。桓桓武王。保有厥士。

There is peace throughout our myriad regions;
There has been a succession of plentiful years:—
Heaven does not weary in its favour.
The martial king Woo

sure,' adding the gloss of Ying-tah, that when people are enjoying themselves, they become noisy (人自娱乐，必喧哗). 敖＝ 傲 or 骜, 'to behave with impropriety,' 'to be insolent.' These lines must belong to the feasters, and not to the officer or officers in ll. 1—5; and of the feasters, therefore, we must understand l. 9. 胡考，＝as in ode 5. 休＝征, 'a proof;' here an admirable thing from which an auspice might be drawn.

The rhymes are— 纻*, 俅 (prop. cat. 3), 基, 牛*, 鼟, cat. 1, t. 1; 觩, 柔, 敖, (prop. cat. 2), 休, cat. 3, t. 1.

Ode 8. Narrative. AN ODE IN PRAISE OF KING WOO. The Preface says that this ode was made to announce in the temple of king Woo the completion, by the duke of Chow, of the *Woo* dance, intended to represent the achievements of the king in the overthrow of Shang and the establishment of the Chow dynasty. The 10th ode of last section was also sung, we saw, in connection with that dance. The same thing is affirmed of several of the odes that follow this. The whole may be portions of a larger composition which has not been preserved in its integrity. The name (酌) does not occur in the piece itself. Attempts are made to explain it from the term as meaning 'to deliberate,'—as if we were to find in the lines the proof of Woo's movements being regulated by a deliberate consideration of the times (酌时而行). The Preface says,— 言能酌先祖之 道以养天下也, 'It means that Woo

was guided by the ways of his ancestors, in nourishing the kingdom;' which is very far-fetched. The name should probably, be Choh (勺), which we find twice in the Le Ke (X. ii. 34), and in the E Le (燕礼), apparently as the name of a dance. L. 1. 铄＝盛, 'complete,' 'powerful.' The most likely meaning of l. 2 is that which I have given in the translation. As Ying-tah says, 'High Heaven's time to take off Chow was not yet come, and king Woo quietly waited its arrival, thus acting in accordance with the way of Heaven (上天诛纣之 期未至，武王靖以待之，是 遵天之道也).' Gow-yang Sëw says, 'He had his army, but he did not display its warlike terrors, but nursed it in obscurity (有师而 不耀其威武，养之以晦也).' L. 3 is in opposition to the 时晦 of l. 2. The darkness passed away; the bright light (熙＝ 光) clearly shone; and Woo acted accordingly. L. 4. 是用＝是以, 'thereon;' 介＝ 甲, 'mail.' 大介＝the 一戎衣 of the Shoo, V. iii. 8. L. 5. 我 is to be understood in the first place of king Ching. 龙＝宠,—as in II. iii. IX. 2.; meaning, I suppose,—'by the favour of Heaven.' L. 6 is in apposition with the 之. 蹻蹻＝武貌, 'martial-looking.' 造＝为, 'achievement.' For l. 7 the 'Complete Digest' gives 我将何所用以

于以四方。克定厥家。於昭于天。皇以间之。

Maintained [the confidence of] his officers,
And employed them all over the kingdom,
So securing the establishment of his Family.
Oh! glorious was he in the sight of Heaven,
Which kinged him in the room [of Shang].

X. *Lae.*

赉

文王既勤止。我应受之。敷时绎思。我徂维求定。时
周之命。於绎思。

King Wăn laboured earnestly;—
Right is it we should have received [the kingdom].
We will diffuse [his virtue], ever cherishing the thought of him;
Henceforth we will seek only the settlement [of the kingdom].
It was he through whom came the appointment of Chow;
Oh! let us ever cherish the thought of him.

嗣之哉, 'what shall we do to inherit it?' *i.e.*, to secure and carry out Woo's achievement. L. 8,—lit., 'Truly only your course (公＝事) sincerely imitate.'

Twan-she does not give any rhymes.

Ode 9. Narrative. CELEBRATING THE MERIT AND SUCCESS OF KING WOO. I have mentioned on the last ode, that this is considered (on the authority of the Tso-chuen), as having been a portion of the larger piece which was sung to the dance of *Woo.* Evidently its subject is king Woo. The Preface says that it was used in a declaration of war in sacrificing to God and the Father of war, which Ying-tah explains as if it had been made by king Woo when he finally took the field against Show. But this is evidently absurd, as it contains the honorary title given to the first king of Chow after his death,—'king Woo.' It may be that the piece came to be used on the occasion which the Preface mentions; but we must refer it in the first place to the reign of Ching.

Ll. 1,2 are descriptive of the happy condition of the kingdom under Ching. A revolution is generally followed by famine; but it was not so, when Woo had overthrown the dynasty of Shang. L. 3. 天命＝'the favour of Heaven;' —its favour towards the House of Chow. 解＝懈, 'to be remiss,' 'to be tired.' L. 4.

桓桓 ＝ 武貌, 'martial-looking.' L. 6. 有士,—'the officers which he had;'—meaning, probably, the great leaders whom king Wăn had gathered around him, and whom Woo retained equally attached to himself. L. 5. 于以四方＝用于四方 meaning that Woo employed those officers throughout the kingdom, subduing its difft. parts, and securing their allegiance. So, K'eang;—武王保文王所有之多士,保守正与播弃相反,谓爱惜之. 以＝用; 于以＝用于, 于 being transposed according to a usage which has already been pointed out. L. 6. 家 is the House, of Chow. L. 7 is understood of the virtue of Woo, as recognized by Heaven. 皇,—as in [i.] IX. Choo says he does not understand 间, but he accepts Maou's definition of it by 代, and 间之＝代商,—as in the translation.

It is hardly worth while making a rhyme out of 王, 方.

XI. *Pan* or *Pwan.*

般

於皇时周。陟其高山。嶞山乔岳。允犹翕河。敷天之
下。裒时之对。时周之命。

Oh! great now is Chow.
We ascend the high hills,
Both those that are long and narrow, and the lofty mount-
ains;
Yes, and [we travel] along the regulated Ho,
All under the sky,
Assembling those who now respond to me.
Thus it is that the appointment belongs to Chow.

Ode 10. Narrative. CELEBRATING THE PRAISE OF KING WAN. This is the only account of the piece that can be given from itself. The Tso-chuen says, however, that it was the third of of the pieces sung to the dance of Woo; and the Preface says it contains the words with which Woo accompanied his grant of fiefs and appanages to the chief of his followers in the ancestral temple (大封于庙). On this view the 我 is to be understood of king Woo, speaking of himself. Choo's exposition of the lines is more or less affected by this; but if the piece ought to be understood in this way, the author has very imperfectly expressed his meaning. The name Lae (赉＝予, 'to give') has contributed to this interpretation, as it has been connected with the use of the term in the Analects, XX.i.4, 周有大赉，善人是富, and in the Shoo, V.iii.9, 赉予四海，而万民悦服.

L. 1. 止 is the final particle. 勤＝劳, 'to labour diligently.' The 'Complete Digest' observes that 既 is here not 'since,' nor the sign of the past tense, but ＝ 尽 'entirely;'—Wăn left nothing undone. L. 2. 我, it seems to me, is not naturally referred to king Woo; but to all the descendants of Wăn; and to his virtue they attribute their possession of the kingdom. L. 4. Their right to the kingdom being such, they would occupy in it accordingly. 时 ＝ 是, 'this;' which we can only explain by referring it to the virtue of king Wăn. 绎 ＝ 寻绎, 'repeatedly,' 'ever.' L. 4. 徂 ＝ 往；自今以往, 'hence-

forth.' The line, literally,＝'we henceforth only seek settlement;' *i. e.*, tranquillity and order. L 5. 时, here again, is to be referred to king Wăn, so that the line ＝ 盖我文王当日之勤劳，是周之所以受命;—as in the translation. Choo makes it ＝ 凡此皆周之命，非复商之旧矣, 'all these fiefs are now the appointments of Chow, and not. as heretofore, of Shang.' L. 6. is a repetition of part of l. 3, an admonition of the descendants of Wăn to themselves. Following out his interpretation of l. 5, Choo understands it as addressed to the appointed feudal chiefs.

There are no rhymes.

Ode 11. Narrative. THE GREATNESS OF CHOW, AND ITS FIRM POSSESSION OF THE KINGDOM, AS SEEN IN THE PROGRESSES OF ITS REIGNING SOVE-REIGN. In [i.] VIII. we have an ode akin to this, relating a tentative progress of king Woo, to test the acceptance of his sovereignty. This is of a later date, and should be referred, probably, to the time of king Ching, when the dynasty was fully acknowledged. Many critics, however, maintain that this piece likewise was a portion of the ode so often referred to;—in which case we should have to translate in the 3d person, and not the first. The meaning of the title is very uncertain. Maou makes it *pwan* ＝ 乐; Soo Ch'eh, the same, ＝ 游. Këang makes it *pan*, ＝, according to the Shwoh-wăn, 旋.

L. 1. 时 is, probably,＝今时, 'now,' Ll. 2, 3. The hills were ascended in the course of a royal sacrifice, and sacrificed to. 嶞山 ＝

山 狹 而 長 者 ;—as in the translation. L. 4 is very obscure, Choo does not profess to understand 允 猶 , and we are obliged, as usual in such cases, to fall back on Ch'ing, who takes 允 in its usual signification of 信, 'tru-ly,' and 猶 = 由 , 'to travel along.' 翕 = 和 , 'harmonious,' referring, we may suppose, to the Ho, prone to inundation, but now keep-ing its channel. L.5. 敷 天 之 下 = 普 天 之 下 ,—as in the translation. L.6. 裒 = 聚, 'to collect,' 'to assemble;' 对 = 答, 'to respond to.' The line refers to the king's assembling the princes in the different quarters of the kingdom, during his progress, and giving audience to them. They all now responded loy-ally. L. 7,—nearly as l. 5 of last ode.

There are no rhymes.

BOOK II. PRAISE-ODES OF LOO.

I. *Këung.*

鲁颂四之二

驷

一章

驷驷牡马。在坰之野。薄言驷者。有骄有皇。有骊有
黄。以车彭彭。思无疆。思马斯臧。

1　Fat and large are the stallions,
　　On the plains of the far-distant borders.
　　Of those stallions, fat and large,
　　Some are black and white-brecched; some light yellow;
　　Some, pure black; some, bay;
　　[All], splendid carriage horses.
　　His thoughts are without limit;—
　　He thinks of his horses, and they are thus good.

TITLE OF THE BOOK.—鲁 颂, 四 之 二,
'Praise-odes of Loo; Book II. of Part IV.' It
is impossible to render here 鲁 颂, by 'Sacrificial odes of Loo,' because they are not such.
Choo says, 'King Ching, because of the great
services rendered to the kingdom by the duke
of Chow, granted to Pih-k'in [the duke's eldest
son, and the first marquis of Loo], the privilege
of using the royal ceremonies and music, in
consequence of which Loo had its *Sung*, which
were sung to the music in its ancestral temple.
Afterwards, they made in Loo other odes in
praise of their rulers, which they also called
Sung.' In this way it is endeavoured to account
for there being such pieces as the four of this
Book in this Part of the She. Confucius found
them in Loo, bearing the name of *Sung*; and it
was not for him to do otherwise than simply
edit them as he did, and he thereby did not
commit himself to anything like an approval
of their designation. This is the best explanation of the name which can be given; but it is
not complimentary to the discrimination or the
moral boldness of the Sage.

The statement of Choo that such a privilege
was ever granted to the first marquis of Loo is
very much controverted. If it were granted to

him, how is it that we do not have a single sacrificial ode of that State? It is then contended
that the royal ceremonies were not usurped in
Loo till the time of duke He (僖 公 ; B. C. 658
—626). Without entering into this question, it
will be seen that it does not affect the application to the odes here of the name of *Sung*. We
cannot suppose that such application was made
by Confucius; he used it, because he found it
in use; and he allowed it just as he published
the events of the Ch'un Ts'ëw, without any indication of his own opinion about them, whether
in the way of censure or approval. It has often
been asked why there are no *Fung* of Loo in the
1st Part. The question cannot be answered
further than by saying that the pieces of this
Book are really *Fung*; but as they were wan-
tonly called Sung, we have them here instead
of in their proper place.

Loo was one of the States of the east, having
its capital in K'ëuh-fow (曲 阜), which is
still the name of one of the districts of the department of Yen-chow, Shan-tung. Choo says
that king Ching appointed the duke of Chow's
eldest son directly to it. Sze-ma Ts'ëen's account is rather difft.:—that the duke of Chow
was himself appointed marquis of Loo, but that,

二章

骃骃牡马。在坰之野。薄言駉者。有雅有驳。有骍有

骐。以车伾伾。思无期。思马斯才。

2   Fat and large are the stallions,
    On the plains of the far-distant borders.
    Of those stallions, fat and large,
    Some are piebald, green and white; others, yellow and white;
    Some, yellowish red; some, dapple grey;
    [All], strong carriage horses.
    His thoughts are without end;—
    He thinks of his horses, and they arc thus strong.

being unable to go there in consequence of his duties at the court, he sent his eldest son instead; and that the territory was largely augmented after the termination of his regency, he still remaining in Chow.

Ode 1. Narrative. CELEBRATING SOME MARQUIS OF LOO FOR HIS CONSTANT AND ADMIRABLE THOUGHTFULNESS,—ESPECIALLY AS SEEN IN THE NUMBER AND QUALITY OF HIS HORSES. The Preface says that the marquis was Shin (申), known as duke He, who is mentioned in the preceding note. It refers indeed all the four pieces to duke He, who was the 19th marquis of the State, reckoning from the duke of Chow. But, as Choo observes, it is only the 4th ode of which it can be alleged with certainty that it belonged to the time of He.

Ll. 1,2, in all the stanzas. 骃 骃 is descriptive of the body of the horses—'the belly and ribs'—as fat and large (腹 干 肥 张 貌). L. 2 gives the breeding and pasture grounds of the studs. 'The region beyond the city is called 郊, or *suburb;* beyond the suburb it is called 牧, or *pasture;* beyond the pasture it is called 野, or *wilderness;* beyond the wilderness it is called 林, or *forest;* beyond the forest it is called 坰, or *waste.*' Morrison, after thus translating the classical passage on the subject, gives for the line—'In the wastes of the wilderness.'—But 野 in the text can only mean 'uncultivated plains;' and 坰 is better rendered as I have done.

Ll. 3—5, 薄 言 is the compound particle, which we have often met with. Many of the colours which are mentioned in ll. 4,5 may seem strange to connoiseurs of the animal; but I can only follow the definitions of the terms in critics and the dictionaries. 骄 is defined as 'a black horse, white in the stride (骊 马 白 跨);' 骊 is 'a pure black horse;' 皇 is 'a horse, yellow and white (黄 白 曰 皇);' 黄 is 'a horse, yellow and red (黄 骍 曰 黄);' 雅 is 'a horse with green and white intermixed (苍 白 杂 毛);' 驳, 'a horse with yellow and white intermixed (黄 白 杂 毛);' 骍, 'a red yellow (赤 黄; probably, a chestnut);' 骐, 'a greenish-black (青 黑);' 骓, 'a greenish-black scaly-like, the colour here deep, there light, marked like the scales of a fish (青 骊 骓, 色 有 深 浅, 斑 驳 如 鱼 鳞);' 骆, 'white and black-maned(白 马 黑 鬣);' 骝, 'a red horse, black-maned (赤 身 黑 鬣);' 雒, 'a black horse, white-maned (黑 身 白 鬣);' 骃 is probably a cream-coloured horse (阴 白 杂 毛, 今 泥 骢);' 騢, 'red and white, intermixed (彤 白 杂 毛);' 骒 is described as having white hairy legs (豪 在 骭 而 白), and also as 'black with a yellow spine (骊 马 黄 脊);' 鱼 is 'a horse, with its eyes white like those of a fish (二 目 白 曰 鱼, 似 鱼 目 也).'

三章
駉駉牡馬。在坰之野。薄言駉者。有驒有駱。有駵有

雒。以車繹繹。思無斁。思馬斯作。

四章
駉駉牡馬。在坰之野。薄言駉者。有駰有騢。有驔有

魚。以車祛祛。思無邪。思馬斯徂。

3　Fat and large are the stallions,
　　On the plains of the far-distant borders.
　　Of those stallions fat and large,
　　Some are flecked as with scales; some, white and black-maned;
　　Some, red and black-maned; some, black and white-maned;
　　[All], docile in the carriage,
　　His thoughts never weary;—
　　He thinks of his horses, and such they become.

4　Fat and large are the stallions,
　　On the plains of the far-distant borders.
　　Of those stallions, fat and large,
　　Some are cream-coloured; some, red and white;
　　Some, with white hairy legs; some, with fishes' eyes;
　　[All], stout carriage horses.
　　His thoughts are without depravity;—
　　He thinks of his horses, and thus serviceable are they.

L. 6 tells the quality of the horses. 以車 = 以此馬而駕車, 'use or yoke these horses in a carriage.' 彭彭 = 盛貌, 'looking everything that could be desired;' as Maou says, 'both strong and handsome (有力有容).' 伾伾,—'strong (有力).' 繹繹,—不絕貌, = keeping together, i. e., obedient to the driver. 祛祛 = 强健, ' very strong.'

Ll. 7,8 praise the thoughtfulness of the marquis to whom the ode refers, and the result of that as seen in his horses. 无疆 = 深廣无窮, 'deep, wide, and inexhaustible;' 无期 denotes the penetration of his thoughts,— unending; 无斁, that they were unwearied; 无邪, that they were without any element of depravity or perversity. One is startled to find here this last characteristic, which Confucius mentions (Ana. II. ii.) as covering the whole of the *She*, or indicating the result to which the study of it will lead. We should not expect to meet with it in such an ode. 斯 = 則, 'then;' with a vivid descriptive force. The 'Complete Digest' says that it indicates the marvellous quickness with which the thing was realized (斯字見神效之速). 臧 = 善, 'good;' 才 = 材力, 'of capable strength;' 作 = 奮起, 'to start up;' 徂 = 行, 'to go,' or 'proceed,' referring, probably, as Ho Këae says, to the speed of the horses.

II. *Yëw peih.*

有駜

一章

有駜有駜。駜彼乘黃。夙夜在公。在公明明。振振

鷺。鷺于下。鼓咽咽。醉言舞。于胥乐兮。

1   Fat and strong, fat and strong,
    Fat and strong, are the chestnut teams.
    Early and late are the [officers] in the court,
    In the court, discriminating and intelligent.
    [They are as] a flock of egrets on the wing,
    Of egrets anon lighting on the ground.
    The drums emit their deep sound;
    They drink to the full and then dance:—
    Thus rejoicing together.

The rhymes are—in all the stanzas, 马, 野*, 者*, cat. 5, t. 2; in 1, 皇, 黄, 彭*, 疆, 臧, cat. 10; in 2, 駓*, 骐, 伾*, 期, 才, cat. 1, t. 1; in 3, 骆, 雒, 绎*, 致*, 作, cat. 5, t. 3: in 4, 骃*, 鱼, 祛, 邪*, 徂, *ib.*, t. 1.

Ode 2. Allusive. The happy intercourse of some marquis of Loo with his ministers and officers;—how they deliberated on business, feasted together, and the ministers and officers expressed their good wishes. The Preface refers this piece, like the others, to duke He.

Ll. 1, 2 in all the stanzas. 駜 denotes 'the app. of a horse fat and strong (马肥强貌).' 'A green-black horse is called *keuen* (青骊日駽);'—equivalent, probably, to our iron-grey (今铁骢也). These lines may be descriptive of the horses with which the ministers of Loo drove to the court; but the writer sets forth their good condition that he may introduce their masters, as worthy of equal praise in their way.

Ll. 3,4 belong to the officers of Loo (卿大夫), though they are not expressly mentioned. On 夙夜 the 'Complete Digest' observes that the phrase is not be taken as 'from morning to night' but as indicating generally the length of time (时之久) that the marquis

and his officers spent together, such was the good understanding and fellowship between them. 在公 = 在公所, 'in the prince's,' or 'with the prince.' Këang, however, observes, correctly, that in st. 1 the 公 = 朝廷, 'the court of audience,' where the business of govt. was transacted, and in the other stanzas, it indicates some other place to which they adjourned to feast together. 明明 = 辨治, 'discriminating and well-ordered;'—with reference to the discussion and adjustment of affairs. Duty over, they proceeded to pleasure. 饮酒 and 燕 are evidently synonymous; and we cannot translate 载 in st. 3. It is the particle, filling up the line and connecting its parts.

Ll. 5,6, in stt. 1,2. 振振 = 群飞貌, like 振 alone in i. [ii.] III. 鷺,—also as in that ode; meaning the egrets themselves, and not their feathers merely, as Choo says. The prince's guests are compared to a flock of egrets, pure and beautiful in their plumage, and seemingly methodical in their motions, whether circling over the ground as they are going to alight, or rising aloft from it on the wing. The 于 is merely the expletive particle. As these birds frequent the water, Këang thinks the feasting took place in the 泮宫 of next ode, and that the writer wrote thus of the officers from what was to be seen about the semi-circular pool connected with that building.

二章
有驰有驰。驰彼乘牡。夙夜在公。在公饮酒。振振

鹭。鹭于飞。鼓咽咽。醉言归。于胥乐兮。

三章
有驰有驰。驰彼乘骃。夙夜在公。在公载燕。自今以

始。岁其有。君子有谷。诒孙子。于胥乐兮。

2　Fat and strong, fat and strong,
　　Fat and strong are the teams of stallions.
　　Early and late are the [officers] with the prince,
　　With the prince drinking.
　　[They are as] a flock of egrets on the wing,
　　Of egrets flying about.
　　The drums emit their deep sound;
　　They drink to the full, and then return home:—
　　Thus rejoicing together.

3　Fat and strong, fat and strong,
　　Fat and strong are the teams of iron-greys.
　　Early and late are the [officers] with the prince,
　　With the prince feasting.
　　'From this time forth,
　　May the years be abundant.
　　May our prince maintain his goodness,
　　And transmit it to his descendants!'—
　　Thus they rejoice together.

Ll. 7—8 in stt. 1,2. The drum is mentioned, but we are not to suppose that it was the only instrument of music employed on the occasion. Choo says that 咽 here is equivalent to 渊, so that its reduplication indicates the long roll of the drum;—as 渊, in iii. I. 2. Maou keeps to the sound of *yin*, in the character, meaning the rapid changes of sound with the drum near at hand. See the dict. on the character. 言 is the expletive particle. The 归 is understood to intimate that the festivity was conducted with decency and order.

L. 9, in all the stt., sums up the whole. 于 may be taken as = 于是, 'thus.' 胥＝相, 'mutually,' 'together.'

Ll. 5—8 in st. 3 contain the expression of their good wishes and prayers by the officers (颂 祷 之 辞). L. 5; 'From this time as a beginning' seems to intimate that there was then a good year. 其 gives the line the force of a prayer. 有＝有年, 'abundant years.' 谷＝善, 'goodness.'

The rhymes are—in st. 1, 黄, 明 *, cat. 10; 下 *, 舞, cat. 5, t. 2: in 2, 牡 *, 酒, cat. 5. t. 2; 飞, 归, cat. 15, t. 1: in 3, 骃 *, 燕 *, cat. 14; 始, 有 *, 子, cat. 1, t. 2. The 乐 in the three stanzas are understood to rhyme together, cat. 2.

III. *Pwan-shwuy.*

泮水

一章

思乐泮水。薄采其芹。鲁侯戾止。言观其旗。其旗茷

茷。鸾声哕哕。无小无大。从公于迈。

1   Pleasant is the semi-circular water,
     And we will gather the cress about it.
     The marquis of Loo is coming to it,
     And we see his dragon-figured banner.
     His banner waves in the wind,
     And the bells of his horses tinkle harmoniously.
     Small and great
     All follow the prince in his progress to it.

Ode 3. Allusive and narrative. IN PRAISE OF SOME MARQUIS OF LOO, CELEBRATING HIS INTEREST IN THE STATE COLLEGE, WHICH PERHAPS HE HAD BUILT OR REPAIRED, TESTIFYING HIS VIRTUES, AND AUSPICING FOR HIM A COMPLETE TRIUMPH OVER THE TRIBES OF THE HWAE, WHICH WOULD BE CELEBRATED IN THE COLLEGE. It is not unlikely that the marquis in this ode is Shin or duke He, for we know that he was engaged in operations against the tribes of the Hwae. His part, indeed, was but a secondary one in them, and he was only a follower of duke Hwan of Ts'e, who had the supremacy among the feudal States; but it was not for the poet to dwell on the inferior position to which his State and ruler were reduced. To Loo had in the first place been assigned the regulation of the east; and in this ode and the next the writer, or the writers, would fain auspice a return of its former glories. There was a muttering at the time of an expedition against the barbarous hordes, and the piece predicts, or at least auspices, its triumphant conclusion,—all due to the troops and civilizing influence of Loo. The immediate occasion of its composition must have been some opening or inauguration service in connection with the repair of the State college.

Ll. 1, 2 in stt. 1—3. 思 is the initial particle, and the whole line may be compared with l. 4 in III. i. VIII. 3. 思 corresponds to 于 there; and 泮水 to 辟宫. That was, under the Chow dyn., the name of the principal royal college, and this was the name of the corresponding building in the feudal states. That we have seen was surrounded by a circlet of water; this only by a semi-circle, the edifice connecting on the north with the adjacent ground. This semi-circle of water gave its name of 泮宫 to the college, 泮 being one of the characters of the third class, where the meaning of the whole

combines the signification of both the elements; here 水, 'water,' and 半, 'half,' which latter is also the phonetic portion of the compound. In the Le Ke, however, III.ii.20, *et al.*, the name appears as 頖宫. The situation is said to have been in the western suburb of the capital. It is not easy to describe all the purposes for which the college was used. In this ode the marquis of Loo appears as feasting in it, delivering instructions, taking counsel with his ministers in it, and receiving the spoils and prisoners of war. In the Le Ke, VIII. ii. 7, it is mentioned as connected in Loo with sacrifices to Howtseih; Wang Taou says, 'In the *Pwan Kung* the officers of a state, in autumn learned ceremonies; in winter, books; in spring and summer, the use of arms; and in autumn and winter, they practised dancing. It was the great college of the States, and there especially were trials of archery, and the feasting of the aged.' 芹,—as in II. vii. VIII. 2. 藻,—as in I.ii.IV. 1. 茆 is probably another name for one of the duckweeds (凫葵). Williams says, 'An aquatic vegetable like mallows. The leaves are smooth.' 薄 is the initial particle. These plants about the water of the college are all understood to be allusive of the men of talents about the marquis, whom he was careful to encourage (皆是言僖公能育人才也).

Ll. 4—8 in stt. 1, 2. The writer describes the marquis of Loo coming to the college on the day of its inauguration, and occupied there. 戾= 至, 'to come to.' 止 is the final particle. 言 is the initial particle. 茷茷=旆旆, in II. i. VIII.2. Ts'een Wǎn-tsz says, that the characters

二章.
思乐泮水。薄采其藻。鲁侯戾止。其马蹻蹻。其马蹻

蹻。其音昭昭。载色载笑。匪怒伊教。

三章.
思乐泮水。薄采其茆。鲁侯戾止。在泮饮酒。既饮旨

酒。永锡难老。顺彼长道。屈此群丑。

2 Pleasant is the semi-circular water,
And we will gather the pondweed in it.
The marquis of Loo has come to it,
With his horses looking so grand.
His horses are grand;
His fame is brilliant.
Blandly he looks and smiles;
Without any impatience he delivers his instructions.

3 Pleasant is the semi-circular water,
And we will gather the mallows about it.
The marquis of Loo has come to it,
And in the college he is drinking.
He is drinking the good spirits;
And may there be given him the old age that is seldom enjoyed!
May he accord with the grand ways,
So subduing to himself all the people!

denote the appearance of a cluster of leaves, and that so did the streamers of the banner hang down. L. 6, in st. 1,—as in II. iii. VIII. 2. The 'small and great' of l. 7 are probably to be understood of the old and young of the capital, all following the marquis towards the college on the great occasion. We cannot translate the particle 于 in l. 8. 迈=行, 'to go;'—as often.

In st. 2, ll. 4, 5, 蹻 蹻,—as in III. iii. V. 4. On l. 6 Choo says nothing; Ch'ing takes the 音 as =德 音, 'fame for virtue.' 载 in l. 7 is the particle. According to the usage of the reduplication in the She, the 色 and 笑 must be taken together, and show us the countenance of the marquis wreathed with smiles. 匪怒, —'without anger;' but anger is too strong a term in the case;—'without impatience.' 伊

is the particle, = 维. On what subjects he gave forth his instructions we do not know.

Ll. 3—8 in st. 3. The marquis is now feasting, and the writer expresses his wishes for him. All the other stanzas are the sequel of this, partly praise and partly prayer; yet the prayer is not direct, and we get the spirit better by translating in the future tense, the writer feeling sure that what he auspiced would be fulfilled. L. 6. 难老 may mean old age that is seldom reached, or the perpetual youth which refuses to put on the appearance of age. This last is the view of Ying-tah;—难 老 者, 言 其 神 力 康 强, 难 使 之 老. The critics understand 神 or 天, 'the Spirits,' or 'Heaven,' as the nominative to 锡. Our passive voice enables me to leave the line as indefinite in this respect as it is in the original. L. 7.

四章
穆穆鲁侯。敬明其德。敬慎威仪。维民之则。允文允武。昭假烈祖。靡有不孝。自求伊祜。

五章
明明鲁侯。克明其德。既作泮宫。淮夷攸服。矫矫虎臣。在泮献馘。淑问如皋。陶在泮献囚。

4　Very admirable is the marquis of Loo,
　　Reverently displaying his virtue,
　　And reverently watching over his deportment,
　　The pattern of the people.
　　With great qualities truly civil and martial,
　　Brilliantly he affects his meritorious ancestors.
　　In everything entirely filial,
　　He seeks the blessing for himself.

5　Very intelligent is the marquis of Loo,
　　Making his virtue illustrious.
　　He has made this college with its semicircle of water,
　　And the tribes of the Hwae will submit in consequence.
　　His martial-looking, tiger leaders
　　Will here present the left ears [of their foes].
　　His examiners, wise as Kaou-yaou,
　　Will here present their prisoners.

长道,—'ways of length,' or 'permanence.' Choo says the phrase is equivalent to 大道, 'grand ways.' L. 8. 屈 = 服, 'to subdue,' or 收服, 'to keep in subjection.' 群丑 = 群众, 'the multitudes of the people.' The phrase means, acc. to most critics, the people of Loo (鲁国之群众), though some find also a reference in it to the tribes of the Hwae (已含淮夷在其中; Foo Kwang).

St. 4 is altogether of praise; celebrating the good and gracious qualities of the marquis. 穆穆 is here simply 美, intensified = very admirable. L. 6. 昭假 = 昭格, 'brilliantly reaching to.' The idea is that the fine qualities of the marquis affected his great ancestors in their Spirit-state, and would draw forth their protecting favour. L. 8. 'What he seeks of himself—by the natural outgoing of his qualities—is blessing or prosperity.'

St. 5. L. 3. 作 need not mean that the marquis had built any college which did not exist before, but that he had executed important repairs. As the 'Flower and Essence of the She' says, 仍其故址而修治之. L. 4 seems to say that the making of the college would make the tribes of the Hwae submit. They would care very little or nothing about it, but it pleased the poet thus to write. The 'Flower and Essence' goes round about the text, saying that he who thus showed his interest in the welfare of the State would have the means to subdue the tribes (伐淮夷自有所以服之也). L. 5. 矫矫 = 武貌, 'martial-looking.' L. 6. 泮 stands

六章
济济多士。克广德心。桓桓于征。狄彼东南。烝烝皇
皇。不吴不扬。不告于讻。在泮献功。

七章
角弓其觩。束矢其搜。戎车孔博。徒御无斁。既克淮
夷。孔淑不逆。式固尔犹。淮夷卒获。

6 His numerous officers,
   Men who have enlarged their virtuous minds,
   With martial energy conducting their expedition,
   Will drive far away those tribes of the east and south,
   Vigorous and grand,
   Without noise or display,
   Without having appealed to the judges,
   They will here present [the proofs of] their merit.

7 How they draw their bows adorned with bone!
   How their arrows whizz forth!
   Their war chariots are very large!
   Their footmen and charioteers never weary!
   They have subdued the tribes of the Hwae,
   And brought them to an unrebellious submission!

alone for 泮宫. 馘,—as in III. i. VII. 8.
The left ears of the slain were cut off. Those
who surrendered or were taken prisoners (囚)
were questioned, and in l.7 it is said their ques-
tioners would be as skilful (淑 = 善) as the
famous Kaou-yaou, Shun's minister of Crime;
—see the Shoo, II. iii., et al.
   St. 6 is an auspice concerning the body of the
officers who would be engaged in the expedition
to the Hwae,—those inferior in rank to the 虎
臣 of last stanza. L. 4 狄,—i. q. 逷 (III. ii.
IX., et al.) or 逖, 'to keep back,' 'drive to a
distance.' 'The east and south,' means the
tribes of the Hwae. Ll. 5—7 set forth the or-
derliness and discipline of the officers, and also
their mutual complaisance, one not disputing
the claims of another to any particular merit.
Maou defines 烝烝 by 厚, 'generous,' 'magnanimous;' and 皇皇, by 美, 'admirable,'
Choo says the two phrases together give the
idea of 盛, 'all-complete.' The Urh-ya makes

烝烝 = 作, 'rising up,' 'vigorous.' 不
吴,—as in i. [iii.] VII.; 不扬 = 肅, 'grave.'
Yen Ts'an defines it by 不轻浮. 讻 is
here the judges who decided questions of dis-
pute in the army (治讼之官).
   In st. 7, the writer describes a battle with the
wild tribes as if it were going on before his eyes,
and celebrates the complete victory, concluding
with a word of admonition to the marquis. Ll. 1
—4. 角弓,—as in II. vii. IX. 1. 其觩,
represents the bows drawn with strength into a
curve (持弦急; Ch'ing). 其搜,—the
whizzing sound of the rapid arrows. 束矢,
—'the bundles of arrows;' consisting, some say
of 50, others of 100. We must drop the 束 in
translating. 博 = 广大, 'wide and large.'
无斁 = 无厌倦, as in the translation.
Ll. 5, 6 give the result of the victory, l. 6 describing the wild tribes as transformed and no more
rebellious (淮夷甚化于善，不逆

八章

翩彼飞鸮。集于泮林。食我桑黮。怀我好音。憬彼淮夷。来献其琛。元龟象齿。大赂南金。

> Only lay your plans securely,
> And all the tribes of the Hwae will be got!

8 They come flying on the wing, those owls,
And settle on the trees about the college;
They eat the fruit of our mulberry trees,
And salute us with fine notes.
So awakened shall be those tribes of the Hwae;
They will come presenting their precious things,
Their large tortoises and their elephants' teeth,
And great contributions of the southern metals.

IV. *Peih kung.*

閟宫

閟宫有侐。实实枚枚。赫赫姜嫄。其德不回。上帝是

1 How pure and still are the solemn temples,
In their strong solidity and minute completeness!
Highly distinguished was Këang Yuen,
Of virtue undeflected.

其命). I must take ll. 7, 8 as a counsel to the marquis suddenly interjected. In no other way can we deal fairly with the 尔, 'you.' 式 is the initial particle. 卒=尽, 'entirely.'

St. 8. As the result of the expedition, the writer sees the tribes of the Hwae coming to the college with their articles of tribute. Ll. 1—4. 翩 is defined in the Shwoh-wan as 'the rapid flight of a bird.' 林 = 'trees.' There might be a grove about the college, but there could not be a forest. 黮 is the fruit of the mulberry tree; *i. q.* 葚. 怀 presents a difficulty. Both Maou and Choo are silent about it; but Ch'ing brings it under the category of 归 or 归就, 'to come to.' An owl is a bird with a disagreeable scream, instead of a beautiful note; but the mulberries grown about the college of Loo would make it sing delightfully. And so would the influence of Loo, going forth from the college, transform the nature of the wild tribes about

the Hwae! Ll. 5—8. 憬=觉悟, 'to awaken to a proper consciousness.' Standing as the character does, it brings the *E* before us so quickened and transformed. 琛 is defined by 美宝, 'admirable, precious things.' 元 — 大, 'large.' 赂 = 遗, 'to give,' 'to contribute.' By the 'metals of the south' are understood metals from King-chow and Yang-chow. Of both those provinces it is mentioned in the Shoo that among their articles of tribute were 金三品, 'gold, silver, and copper;'—see the Shoo, III. i. Pt. i. 44, 52.

The rhymes are—in st. 1, 芹, 旗 *, cat. 13; 茷, 哕, 大, 迈, cat. 15, t. 3: in 2, 藻, 跷 *, 跷 *, 昭, 笑, 教, cat. 2: in 3, 茆 *, 酒, 酒, 老 *, 道 *, 丑, cat. 3, t. 2: in 4, 德, 则, cat. 1, t. 3; 武, 祖, 祜, cat. 5, t. 2: in 5, 德, 服 *, 馘 *, cat. 1, t. 3; 陶 *, 囚, cat.

依。无灾无害。弥月不迟。是生后稷。降之百福。黍

稷重穋。稙穉菽麦。奄有下国。俾民稼穑。有稷有黍。

God regarded her with favour;
And without injury or hurt,
Immediately, when her months were fulfilled,
She gave birth to How-tseih.
On him were conferred all blessings,—
[To know] how the millet ripened early, and the sacrificial
 millet late,
How first to sow pulse, and then wheat.
Anon he was invested with an inferior State,

3, t. 1: in 6, 心, 南 *, cat. 7, t. 1; 皇, 扬,
cat. 10; 讻, 功, cat. 9: in 7. 觥, 搜, cat. 3,
t. 1: 博, 敄 *, 逆 *, 获 *, cat. 5, t. 3: in 8,
林, 黮 *, 音, 琛, 金, cat. 7, t. 1.

Ode 4. Narrative. In praise of duke He,
and auspicing for him a magnificent career
of success, which would make Loo all that
it had ever been:—written, probably, on
an occasion when He had repaired on a
grand scale the temples of the State, of
which pious act his success would be the
reward. Ll. 5,6 of stt. 3 and 8 leave no doubt
that the marquis Shin or duke He is the hero
of this piece. It is a great offence to Këang,
who deplores the sanction which it gives to the
opinion, false according to his view, that the
princes of Loo were privileged to employ royal
ceremonies and sacrifices, and condemns the
exaggerated representations in it of the character and successes of duke He. But it was not
for the writer, a minister, probably, of Loo, to
call in question the legality of celebrations in
which he took part, and which he considered to
be the glory of the State, and he was evidently
in a poetic rapture as to what his ruler was and
would do. Këang thinks Confucius would have
cast the ode out of the She, but that there are
certain admonitions and cautions gently insinu-
ated in it (夸 诞 巳 极, 而 圣 人 弗
削, 则 以 犹 有 箴 规 责 难 之
微 意 焉)!
St. 1. Ll. 1,2, and the concluding stanza, give
us the occasion on which the ode was made,
—some great temple-repairs executed by order of the marquis. Maou thinks the temples
were those of Këang Yuen, mentioned here, and
of He's predecessor, duke Min, mentioned in st.
9; but Këang Yuen is introduced as being the
mother of How-tseih, and without any reference
to her being sacrificed to. The opinion of Choo,
that He had repaired all the temples of the

State (鲁 之 群 庙), commends itself even
to Këang. There were in Loo the Chow temple
(周 庙), specially dedicated to king Wăn; the
Grand temple (太 庙), dedicated to the duke of
Chow; the temple of Pih-k'in, the first marquis,
called 世 室; and the temple of duke Woo, called 武 世 室. In later times we find mention
of a 高 祖 庙, a 曾 祖 庙, a 祖 庙,
and the 祢 庙. 宫 = 庙, 'temple.' Maou
explains 閟 by 闭, 'shut,' meaning, acc. to
Ying-tah, that the temple had been shut up and
not used. Choo's account of it is 深 闭 'deeply
shut;' Këang's 深 邃, 'deep and far-reaching;'
and Ch'ing's, 神 'Spirit-tenanted.' I must believe that our 'solemn' gives the idea. 侐 =
清 静, 'pure and still.' 实 实 describe the
solidity of the temples (巩 固, Choo; Maou
says, not nearly so well, 广 大; Tsow Ts'euen,
well, 下 之 盘 基 固 也); 枚 枚, their
completeness, furnished with every thing which
temples ought to have (器 物 完 备, Këang;
Choo explains these characters of the fine and close
structure, especially in the roof, 砻 密 (so,
also, Tsow Ts'euen, 上 之 结 构 密 也).
Ll. 3—17 are intended to magnify Loo and its
rulers tracing their origin up to How-tseih. On
ll. 3—8, about Këang Yuen's birth of How-tseih,
see III. ii. I. 1, 2. The idea of being distinguished, rather than of being majestic or awe-inspir-
ing, seems to be conveyed here by 赫 赫.
依 = 眷 顾, 'to regard with favour.' L. 7—
'Her months being fulfilled, without delay,'—

有稻有秬。奄有下土。缵禹之绪。

二章
后稷之孙。实维大王。居岐之阳。实始翦商。至于文

武。缵大王之绪。致天之届。于牧之野。无贰无虞。

And taught the people how to sow and to reap
The millet and the sacrificial millet,
Rice and the black millet;
Ere long all over the whole country;—
[Thus] continuing the work of Yu.

2　　Among the descendants of How-tseih
There was king T'ae,
Dwelling on the south of [mount] K'e,
Where the clipping of Shang began.
In process of time Wǎn and Woo
Continued the work of king T'ae,
And [the purpose of] Heaven was carried out in its time,

Ll.9—17 pass to How-tseih, giving a summary of his doings and the distinction which he gained. Compare i. [i.] X., and III. ii. I. 天 is understood as the subject of 降 in l. 9, but our passive voice enables us to make the line as indefinite as the original. In l. 10, 种 belongs to 黍, and 穋 to 稷. 'What, though earlier sown, ripens later is called 种, and what, though later sown, ripens earlier, is called 穋.' L. 11. 稙 is applied to what is planted early, and 稚 to what is planted late. Ying-tah observes that 重,穋,稙, and 稚 are denominations applied to the growth and ripening of plants as early or late, and not names of kinds of grain (生 熟 早 晚 之 异 称,非 谷 名). L. 12 is most naturally understood of the investiture of How-tseih with the principality of T'ae, as mentioned in III. ii. 1. 5. The only difficulty is with l. 16. Ying-tah, indeed, gives to the two lines the same meaning, and considers ll. 13—16 to be no more than a repetition of ll. 9—12. But 下 土 may very well mean the whole kingdom, 'the land below,' in correlation with 上 天, 'the sky above,' but such a meaning of 下 土 is, I believe, unexampled. Nor am I sure that 下 土 denotes an *inferior* State. The phrase occurs in the next Book, as a designation of the feudal States generally. How-tseih was invested with T'ae, and made minister of agriculture subsequently by Shun, and gradually the benefits of his husbandry extended throughout the land. He did not become king like Yu, and immediately found a dynasty; but as Yu's labours had extended to all, so did his, and therefore he might be said to continue the line or work of Yu (绪 = 业).

St. 2 gives a very summary outline of the growth of the family of Chow, down to the overthrow of the Shang dyn. by king Woo, and the establishment of the State of Loo by king Ching. Ll. 1—4 relate to king T'ae;—comp. III. i. VII. 1, 2. Dukes Lëw and T'an-foo are passed over without notice. The 'clipping' in l. 4 is not to be understood of any active operations of king T'ae against Shang, nor even, says Choo, of any thought or purpose in his mind. But his management of his territory drew the thoughts of the people in other States to the lords of Chow. A new centre of attraction was established, and served to increase the dissaffection to the govt. of Shang. Ll. 5—8. Passing over king Ke, the poet sketches the career of Wǎn and Woo, and especially of Woo. Of him only are we to think in ll. 7, 8. 届 = 'to come

上帝临女。敦商之旅。克咸厥功。王曰叔父。建尔元

子。俾侯于鲁。大启尔宇。为周室辅。

三章

乃命鲁公。俾侯于东。锡之山川。土田附庸。周公之

孙。庄公之子。龙旗承祀。六辔耳耳。春秋匪解。享

In the plain of Muh.
'Have no doubts, no anxieties,' [it was said];
'God is with you.'
[Woo] disposed of the troops of Shang;
He and his men shared equally in the achievement.
[Then] king [Ching] said, 'My uncle,
I will set up your eldest son,
And make him marquis of Loo.
I will greatly enlarge your territory there,
To be a help and support to the House of Chow.'

3　Accordingly he appointed [our first] duke of Loo,
And made him marquis in the east,
Giving him the hills and rivers,
The lands and fields, and the attached States.
The [present] descendant of the duke of Chow,

to.' Heaven had now reached the limit of its forbearance with Shang, and its time to give the sovereignty to Chow was fully come. There is no necessity to give to 届 the meaning of 殛 = 诛, 'to cut off,' as Këang does. 致,— 'to carry out.' The subject of it is king Woo. Ll. 9—12 continue the sketch of the overthrow of Shang. Ll. 9, 10,—see III. i. II. 8, ll. 7, 8. The words spoken to Woo on the day of battle by his principal commander had laid deep hold on the minds of the people. 敦 (tuy) = 治 之, 'to deal with.' Compare the use of the term in i. [ii] IX. It is here equivalent to our slang expression,—'to polish off.' 咸 = 同, with reference to the enthusiasm and unanimity which possessed all the army of Woo. Ll. 13—17. The sketch now converges to the State of Loo. The 'king' is king Ching as appears from 叔 父 or 'uncle,' meaning the duke of

Chow. 元 子 is the duke's eldest son, Pih-k‘in. 启 = 开, 'to open;' here equivalent to 'to enlarge.' 宇 = 土 宇, 'territory,' Pih-k‘in was to be the first marquis, yet the State is still spoken of as belonging to the duke, his father.

The principal subject in st. 3 is duke He's offering the border sacrifice to God, in the spring-sacrifice for a good year, with How-tseih as His correlate, and his seasonal sacrifices in the ancestral temple. Ll. 1—4 are a sequel to ll. 13—17 of last stanza, stating the fact of the investiture of Pih-k‘in with the marquisate of Loo. 附 庸,—see on Ana. XVI. i. 1, where mention is made of one of the small States attached to Loo. Ll. 5—8 belong to duke He, and the state with which he proceeded to the sacrifices. The immediate successor of duke Chwang was a boy, called K‘e and K‘e-fang

祀不忒。皇皇后帝。皇祖后稷。享以骍牺。是饗是

宜。降福既多。周公皇祖。亦其福女。

四章
秋而载尝。夏而楅衡。白牡骍刚。牺尊将将。毛炰胾

The son of duke Chwang,
With dragon-emblazoned banner attends the sacrifices,
His six reins soft and pliant.
In spring and autumn he does not neglect [the sacrifices];
His offerings are all without error.
To the great and sovereign God,
And to his great ancestor How-tseih,
He offers the victims, red and pure.
They enjoy, they approve,
And bestow blessings in large number.
The duke of Chow, and [your other] great ancestors,
Also bless you.

4   In autumn comes the sacrifice of the season,
But in summer the bulls for it have had their horns capped.
They are the white bull and the red one;

(启; 启方), known as duke Min (闵公) who was murdered in the second year of his rule; and then, our duke He, an elder brother by a lady of the harem was raised to the State. 承祀,一奉祀, 'to offer the sacrifices,' or 视祭祀, 'to look after the sacrifices.' 耳耳 = 柔从,--as in the translation. Ll. 9—17. L. 9 refers to the seasonal sacrifice in the ancestral temple. Spring and autumn, two of the seasons, are mentioned by *synecdoche* for all the four. 匪解,—as in i. [iii.] IX. L.10= 所 献所祀,不有差忒. Kĕang insists on taking this of the offerings at the border sacrifice; but it connects more naturally with l. 9. Ll. 11—15. Lacharme gives for l. 11— '*Summus rerum dominus qui per se regnat.*' 皇 皇, = *maximus*, 'the most great;' 后,= 君, 'ruler,' 'sovereign;' 帝,—'God.' L. 13 = 所 献, 则用骍色之牺牛, 'For his offerings he employs perfect bulls of red colour.'

L.14= 上帝与后稷于是饗之, 于是宜之,—as in the translation. Ll. 16, 17, are in connection with ll. 9, 10. 皇祖 must be understood of Pih-k'in and the other dukes sacrificed to in the ancestral temple. 女,— 'you.' The writer turns suddenly, and addresses duke He directly.

St. 4 continues the subject of the seasonal sacrifices, and auspices, or prays for, the blessing which duke He might expect from his reverent discharge of them. Ll. 1, 2 refer to the autumnal sacrifice and the preparation in summer for it;—a specimen of the provision made for the sacrifices of the other seasons. 尝 is the name of the autumnal sacrifice, used as a verb, — to offer that sacrifice. 载 = 始, 'to begin,' showing that line 2 mentions what was a preparation for the service. 楅衡 was the name of a piece of wood fixed across both the horns of the victim-bulls to prevent their goring; but one does not see how this could contribute to improve their condition. Acc. to Ying-tah's definitions in the Chow Le (XII. or II. 5),

羹。笾豆大房。万舞洋洋。孝孙有庆。俾尔炽而昌。

俾尔寿而臧。保彼东方。鲁邦是常。不亏不崩。不震

不腾。三寿作朋。如冈如陵。

[There are] the bull-figured goblet in its dignity;
Roast pig, minced meat, and soups;
The dishes of bamboo and wood, and the large stand;
And the dancers all-complete.
The filial descendant will be blessed.
[Your ancestors] will make you gloriously prosperous!
They will make you long-lived and good,—
To preserve this eastern region,
Long possessing the State of Loo,
Unwaning, unfallen,
Unshaken, undisturbed!
They will make your friendship with your three aged [ministers],
Like the hills, like the mountains!

the 楅 was fixed on the horns, and the 衡 was another thing, fitted to the nose. L. 3 specifies the victims. 刚＝特, 'a bull fit for sacrificing.' Williams erroneously speaks of it as '*a bullock*.' K'ang-he's dictionary does not give this usage of the character; but under 牨, it mentions that 刚 is interchangeable with it. In sacrificing to the duke of Chow a white bull was used by way of distinction. His great services to the dyn. required that the victim offered to him should bear some mark of his peculiar dignity. A white bull therefore was employed, and he was thereby put on a level with the kings of the former dynasty of Shang. For Pih-k'in and the other dukes of Loo a red victim was employed,—according to the usual practice of the Chow dyn. L.4. is descriptive of a goblet or vase used to contain the spirits for libation and other purposes. It is called 'the victim vase (尊 ＝樽),' because there was the figure of a bull upon it (画牛于尊腹), or because it was made in the form of a bull, with a hollow chiselled out in the back to contain the spirits (尊作牛形,凿其背以受酒). 将将＝严正貌,—as in the translation.

L.5. 毛炰 is explained from the Chow Le, II.v. 4, where we have 毛炰之豚, 'a pig, from which the hair has been scalded off, and then roasted (焰去其毛而炰之).' 胾 ＝切肉, 'meat cut up fine.' Two kinds of soup are to be understood:—plain soup, the water in which meat has been boiled; and the same with salt and vegetables added to it. L.6. 大房 was a species of the 俎 (see II.vi. V. 3), and was also called 房俎. It was large enough to receive half the roasted body of one of the bulls (半体之俎), having from its size and the form of the supporting frame the app. of a small room or apartment. L. 7. 万舞,—see on I. iii. XIII. 1. 洋洋＝盛貌, 'complete-looking.'
Ll. 8—17. 'The filial descendant' is duke He. Sacrificing to his ancestors as he did, he might expect their blessing (有庆, 言祭 而获福). We may translate from l. 9 in the future tense (假尸祝之言以报 僖公；Fan Ch'oo-e), or as a prayer 祝愿

五章

公车千乘。朱英绿滕。二矛重弓。公徒三万。贝冑朱

绠。烝徒增增。戎狄是膺。荆舒是惩。则莫我敢承。

俾尔昌而炽。俾尔寿而富。黄发台背。寿胥与试。俾

5   Our prince's chariots are a thousand,
[And in each] are the vermilion tassels and the green bands
    of the two spears and two bows.
His footmen are thirty thousand,
With shells on vermilion-strings adorning their helmets.
So numerous are his ardent followers,
To deal with the tribes of the west and north,
And to punish [those of] King and Shoo,
So that none of them will dare to withstand us.
May [the Spirits] make you grandly prosperous!
May they make you long-lived and wealthy!
May the hoary hair and wrinkled back,

其 获 福 寿；Lëw Kin). I prefer the former construction. L.10. 炽而昌,—'blazing and prosperous.' L.13 = 鲁邦是可 常守而无失,'That you may always keep the region of Loo, and not lose it.' L. 14.—see on II. i. VI. 6, l. 4. L. 15. In II. iv. IX. 3, 滕 is used of a river rising and overflowing its banks. Ts'aou Suy, on ll. 14, 15, says finely:— 不亏,如日常盈；不崩,如山 常固；不震,如地常静；不腾, 如水常平。 Ll. 16, 17. The meaning of 三寿, 'three longevities,' is very obscure. Ch'ing thinks they refer to the three principal ministers of Loo (三 卿); and Yen Ts'an says, 愿有三寿考之三卿为朋 友,皆如冈陵之固,祝其君 臣同庆也,'The line contains a prayer for blessing to be shared by the ruler and his ministers together, he and his three aged ministers associating together in friendship, firm as the hills and mountains.' Nothing better can be made of the text.
St. 5 passes from the marquis's sacrifices to his resources for war, and ability to cope with his enemies, and concludes with a prayer or auspice for him, which is not so warlike as we

might have expected. Ll. 1—9. 'A thousand chariots' was the regular force which a great State could at the utmost bring into the field. Each chariot contained three mailed men;—the charioteer in the middle, with a spearman on his right, and an archer on his left. And there were attached to it 72 foot-soldiers and 25 other followers, 100 men in all; so that the whole force would amount to 100,000 men. But in actual service, the force of a great State was restricted to three armies, or 375 chariots, attended, inclusive of their mailed occupants, by 37,500 men, of whom 27,500 were what were called foot-soldiers, given in round numbers, in l. 4, as 30,000. 朱英, 二矛,—see on I. vii. V. 1. 绿滕, 重弓,—see on I. xi. III. 3. 贝, —see on II. v. VI. 1. These shells were connected together, and attached to the helmets by means of strings of vermilion colour (朱绠,所以 缀贝而饰冑也). 增增=众, indicating the number of the soldiers. 戎= 西戎, 'the hordes of the west.' 狄=北 狄, 'those of the north.' In the 10th year of duke He, Hwan of Ts'e had led an expedition against these, but Loo took no part in it. Perhaps He had been engaged in some operations against them of which we have no record, or, which is more likely, his encomiast is only speaking of what he could do. 荆 is another name for the great southern State of Ts'oo

尔昌而大。俾尔耆而艾。万有千岁。眉寿无有害。

六章

泰山岩岩。鲁邦所詹。奄有龟蒙。遂荒大东。至于海

邦。淮夷来同。莫不率从。鲁侯之功。

Marking the aged men, be always in your employment!
May they make you prosperous and great!
May they grant you old age, ever vigorous,
For myriads and thousands of years,
With the eyebrows of longevity, and ever unharmed!

6　The mountain of T'ae is lofty,
Looked up to by the State of Loo.
We grandly possess also Kwei and Mung;
And we shall extend to the limits of the east,
Even the States along the sea.
The tribes of the Hwae will seek our alliance;—
All will proffer their allegiance:—
Such shall be the the achievements of the marquis of Loo.

(楚); and 舒 was applied to several half-civilized States to the east of it, which it brought, in the Ch'un Ts'ëw period, one after another, under its jurisdiction. The marquis of Loo had taken part under Ts'e, in his 4th year, in a great expedition against Ts'oo, which came to an unsatisfactory conclusion with the treaty of Shaou-ling (召陵之盟). 膺=当, 'to withstand;' 惩=艾, 'to punish.' Chang Foo (章甫; Ming dyn.) distinguishes the two words thus;—彼入寇而我当之,为膺;我伐寇而彼畏之,为惩. 承=御, 'to withstand,' 'to resist.'

Ll. 10—17, like the latter half of last stanza, may be taken either as auspice or prayer. L. 12, —comp. l. 5 in III. ii. II. 4. 'The Flower and Essence of the She' connects this line with the next thus:—且愿黄色之发,鲐文之背,此寿考者,相与为公所试用, adding 盖不特三寿作朋而已,其所用皆老成之人也. 试=用, 'to employ.' 艾=养, 'to nourish;' here,=vigorous, well-nourished.

Stt. 6, 7 auspice great achievements for the marquis in forcing the acknowledgment of the superiority of Loo on all the territories lying to the south and east of it, which could be considered as included in the original grant and commission of king Ching. L. 6. Mount T'ae was the great hill of Loo, between it and Ts'e. Kwei and Mung were also two hills in Loo. The latter was probably the eastern hill of Mencius, VII. Pt. i. xxiv. 1, q. v. 奄有,—'We grandly have.' These were all in Loo proper; but the marquis would extend his sway beyond. 遂荒,—遂 is the conjunction,='and thereon;' but 荒 is not easily construed. Choo simply repeats Ch'ing's 荒=奄. The likeliest meaning here, given in the dict., is that of 蒙, 'to cover over.' 'That which covers the sides is called 帷, "a curtain;" that which covers above is called 荒.' I take the term, therefore, as here='to overspread.' 大东, 'the great east,'= 极东, 'the extreme east.' 同=同盟, 'to covenant together.' The tribes of the Hwae would come, and seek for treaties,—acknowledging the superiority of Loo,

七章
保有凫绎。遂荒徐宅。至于海邦。淮夷蛮貊。及彼南

夷。莫不率从。莫敢不诺。鲁侯是若。

八章
天锡公纯嘏。眉寿保鲁。居常与许。复周公之宇。鲁

侯燕喜。令妻寿母。宜大夫庶士。邦国是有。既多受

7 He shall maintain the possession of Hoo and Yih,
 And extend his sway to the regions of Seu,
 Even to the States along the sea.
 The tribes of the Hwae, the Man, and the Mih,
 And those tribes [still more] to the south,
 All will proffer their allegiance;—
 Not one will dare not to answer to his call,
 Thus showing their obedience to the marquis of Loo.

8 Heaven will give great blessing to our prince,
 So that with the eyebrows of longevity he shall maintain Loo.
 He shall possess Chang and Heu,
 And recover all the territory of the duke of Chow.
 Then shall the marquis of Loo feast and be glad,
 With his admirable wife and aged mother;

as l. 7 more fully declares,— 莫 不 相 率 以 从 于 鲁 国 , 'all will lead one another on to follow Loo.'

St. 7. Hoo and Yih were two hills of Loo,—in the pres. district of Tsow (邹县). 徐 宅,—'where Seu dwells,' *i. e.*, all the States in the region of Seu. In l. 4 the writer expresses himself wildly and extravagantly. 蛮貊 means properly the wild tribes of the south and of the north;—see Ana. XV. ii. 2, and the Shoo, V. iii. 6; but it is impossible to understand here by the expression any but the wild hordes south of the Hwae. Then in l. 5 he seems to go farther south still. 诺 ='yes,' *i. e.*, to respond obediently. 若 =顺, 'to accord with;'—in the connection,— 顺 服 , 'to submit to.'

St. 8 is akin to the two preceding, auspicing for the marquis,—through the help of Heaven, the recovery of all the territory which had at any time been taken from Loo, and then the enjoyment of purest domestic and social happiness to a great and hale old age. L. 1. 纯

may here be defined by 大 , 'great.' Ll. 3, 4. 常 (or 尝) was a city, with some adjacent territory,—in the pres. dis. of T'ǎng (滕), dep. Yen-chow, which had been taken from Loo by Ts'e. 许, called in the Ch'un Ts'ëw, 许 田 , 'the fields of Heu,' was on the west of Loo, and had been granted as a convenient place for the princes of Loo to stop at on their way to the royal court; but it had been sold or parted with to Ch'ing in the first year of duke Hwan. The writer of this ode desires that He might recover possession both of Chang and Heu, and so have got back all the territory, which the duke of Chow could have claimed. 宇 = 土 宇 , 'territory.' Ll. 5—7. The marquis would feast in the inner apartment appropriate to such a purpose (内 寝) with his wife (called Shing Keäng, 声 姜), and his mother (called Ching Fung, 成 风); and in the outer banqueting room (外 寝), with his worthy officers and ministers. 宜 = 鲁 侯 所 宜 有 , 'such

祉。黄发儿齿。

九章
徂来之松。新甫之柏。是断是度。是寻是尺。松桷有

舄。路寝孔硕。新庙奕奕。奚斯所作。孔曼且硕。万

民是若。

> With his excellent ministers and all his [other] officers.
> Our region and State shall he hold,
> Thus receiving many blessings,
> To hoary hair, with a child's teeth.
>
> 9   The pines of Tsoo-lae,
> And the cypresses of Sin-foo,
> Were cut down and measured,
> With the cubit line and the eight cubits line.
> The projecting beams of pine were large;
> The large inner apartments rose vast.
> Splendid look the new temples,
> The work of He-sze,
> Very wide and large,
> Answering to the expectations of all the people.

as he ought to have.' Ll. 8—10. 有 is emphatic, 一常有, 'ever have.' 儿齿, 'child's teeth,' is perplexing. The Urh-ya quotes the line with 鲵齿, and the Shwoh-wan explains that phrase by 老人齿, 'old men's teeth.' I think, however, the meaning must be this, that the marquis would ever be renewing his youth, and never be sans teeth. They might fall out, but they would be replaced by others, as in the case of a child.'

St. 9 returns to the subject with which the ode commenced,—the temples, duke He's repair of which gave occasion to the composition of the piece. The materials were got from Tsoo-lae and Sin-foo, two hills in the pres. dep. of T'ae-gan. When the trees were felled, and prepared for use, they were sawn up into the proper lengths, determined by the fathom and cubit measures. L. 5. 桷 = 榱, meaning, I think, the 榱题, of Mencius, VII. xxxi v. 2,

q. v. 舄 = 大貌, 'large-looking.' L. 6. 路寝 is the back apartment of the temples put for the whole; 路 being simply = 大, 'large.' Or we may take 路寝 of the state, retiring apartment of the marquis. It was on a grand scale, but the renewed temples were on a grander. 奕奕 = 美, 'beautiful,' 'admirable.' The work had been executed under the superintendence of He-sze, a brother of the marquis, known as 'Duke's-son Yu (公子鱼).' 曼 = 长 or 广, 'long,' or 'wide.' L. 8 = 顺万民之望;—as in the translation.

Maou arranges the whole piece in 8 stanzas; 1, 2, of 17 lines, each; 3, of 12; 4, of 38; 5, 6, of 8, each; and 7, 8, of 10, each. The present arrangement was fixed by Choo, after Soo Ch'eh. Subsequent scholars,—Woo Ch'ing, Kin Le-ts'ëang, Hwang Kwang-shing, Ho K'ëae, and others, have proposed various alterations;—but, as Këang says, to no purpose.

The rhymes are—in st. 1, 枚, 回, 依, 迟, cat. 15, t. 1; 稷, 福 *, 穆 (prop. cat. 3), 麦, 国, 穑, cat. 1, t. 3; 黍, 秬, 土, 绪, cat. 5, t. 2: in 2, 王, 阳, 商, cat. 10; 武, 绪, 野 *, 虞, 女, 旅, 父, 鲁, 宇, 辅, cat. 5. t. 2: in 3, 公, 东, 庸, cat. 9; 子, 耳, cat. 1, t. 2; 解, 帝 *, cat. 16, t. 3; 牺 *, 宜 *, 多, cat. 17; 祖, 女, cat. 5, t. 2: in 4, 尝, 衡 *, 刚, 将, 羹 *, 房, 洋, 庆 *, 昌, 臧, 方, 常, cat. 10; 崩, 腾, 朋, 陵, cat. 6: in 5, 乘, 滕, 弓 *, 縢 (prop. cat. 7), 增, 膺, 惩, 承, cat. 6; 炽, 富 *, 背 *, 试, cat. 1, t. 2; 大, 艾, 岁, 害, cat. 15, t. 3: in 6, 岩, 詹 *, cat. 8, t. 1; 蒙, 东, 邦, 同, 从, 功, cat. 9: in 7, 绎 *, 宅 *, 貊 *, 诺 *, 若 *, cat. 5, t. 3: in 8, 嘏 *, 鲁, 许, 宇, cat. 5, t. 2; 喜, 母 *, 士, 有 *, 祉, 齿, cat. 1, t. 2: in 9, 柏 *, 度, 尺 *, 舄 *, 硕 *, 奕 *, 作 *, 硕 *, 若 *, cat. 5, t. 3.

BOOK III. THE SACRIFICIAL ODES OF SHANG.

I. *Na.*

商颂四之三

那

猗与那与。置我鞉鼓。奏鼓简简。衎我烈祖。○汤孙
奏假。绥我思成。鞉鼓渊渊。嘒嘒管声。既和且平。
依我磬声。於赫汤孙。穆穆厥声。庸鼓有斁。万舞有

How admirable! how complete!
Here are set our hand-drums and drums.
The drums resound harmonious and loud,
To delight our meritorious ancestor.

The descendant of T'ang invites him with this music,
That he may soothe us with the realization of our thoughts.
Deep is the sound of the hand-drums and drums;
Shrilly sound the flutes;
All harmonious and blending together,
According to the notes of the sonorous gem.
Oh! majestic is the descendant of T'ang;
Very admirable is his music.

TITLE OF THE BOOK.—商 颂, 四 之 三,
'Sacrificial odes of Shang; Book III. of Part IV.'
Here we return, for several odes at least, to the
proper meaning of 颂 in this Part of the She, the
character having the same meaning as in the title
of Book I. Shang is the name of the second of the
three ancient feudal dynasties, and remains still
as the name of the small department of Shang
Chow in Shen-se. The ancestor of the dynasty
was Sëeh (契), who appears in the Shoo as
minister of Instruction to Shun. Whether he
received his investiture from Yaou or from
Shun is a disputed point. In the 14th generation
from Sëeh was a T'ëen-yih (天 乙), the celebrated T'ang, who overthrew the dynasty of
Hëa, and made himself master of the kingdom;
—in B. C. 1,765, (or B. C. 1,557, acc. to the
Bamboo Annals). His descendants ruled in
China, down to B. C. 1,120 (or 1,101), when
Chow or Show, the last sovereign, was put to
death by king Woo of the dynasty of Chow. Among
them there were three, more particularly distinguished:—T'ae-këah, T'ang's grandson
and successor, who received the title of 太 宗;
T'ae-mow (B. C. 1,636—1,560, or 1,474—1,398)
known as 中 宗; and Woo-ting (B. C. 1,323—
1,263, or 1,273—1,213 known as 高 宗). The
temples or shrines of these four sovereigns main-

tained their places in the ancestral temple of the dynasty, after their first establishment, and if all its sacrificial odes had been preserved, they would have been in praise of one or other of them. But it so happened that at least all the odes of which T'ae-tsung was the subject were lost. Of the others we have only a small portion,—five odes in all.

Of how it is that we have even these, we have the following account. The viscount of Wei was made duke of Sung, there to continue the sacrifices of the House of Shang; but the govt. of that State fell subsequently into great disorder, and the memorials of the dynasty seem to have been lost. In the time of duke Tae (戴 公 ; B. C. 798—765), one of his ministers, Ching-k'aou-foo, an ancestor of Confucius (Vol. I., proleg., p. 57) received from the Grand music-master at the court of Chow twelve of the sacrificial odes of Shang, with which he returned to Sung, and used them in sacrificing to the former kings of that dynasty. This story rests on a statement in the 'Narratives of the States (鲁 语 , 下 , art. 17)' by a contemporary of Confucius. As we have only five odes in the Classic, it is supposed that seven of those twelve had perished during the two centuries that elapsed between Ching-k'aou-foo and his descendant.

Choo adds that in the odes that remain there are many *lacunæ*, and passages of which the meaning is doubtful, so that he could not presume to be positive in the interpretation of them. To the same effect is a remark of Fan Ch'oo-e on the 1st ode, that the student must deal with these pieces as in reading the Pwan-kang and the Announcements in the Shoo, not insisting on the literal meaning of the text, but well satisfied if he can catch the writer's drift (学 者 要 当 如 读 盘 诰，不 必 以 文 义 相 属，识 其 大 旨 可 也).

Ode 1. Narrative. APPROPRIATE TO A SACRIFICE TO T'ANG THE SUCCESSFUL, THE FOUNDER OF THE SHANG DYNASTY, DWELLING ESPECIALLY ON THE MUSIC, AND ON THE REVERENCE WITH WHICH THE SERVICE WAS PERFORMED. By which of the sovereigns of Shang the sacrifice to which the ode refers was performed we cannot tell. He is simply spoken of as 'a descendant of T'ang.' Are we to take the piece as from him, whoever he was, or as narrative rather, composed by some one, probably a member of the royal House, who had taken part in the service? On the former view the several 我 in the piece, and especially the 予 in the last line but one, find an easy explanation, but on the other hand, I cannot conceive the principal in the sacrifice speaking of himself simply as 汤 孙 , or that he could say of himself 於 赫 汤 孙 , as in l. 11. I understand the whole therefore as narrative, and translate the personal pronouns in the plural.

Ll. 1—4. Sacrifices, during the Shang dynasty, were commenced with music; during the Chow dynasty with libations of fragrant spirits;—in both cases with the same object, to at-

tract the Spirit or Spirits sacrificed to, and secure their presence at the service. Ch'in Haou (陈 澔 ; Ming dyn.) says:—'The departed Spirits hover between heaven and earth, and sound goes forth filling all the region of the air. Hence, in sacrificing, the people of Yin commenced with a performance of music, wishing thereby to call the attention of the Spirits, who, hearing it, would perhaps come to be present at the service and to enjoy it.' I do not vouch for the correctness of this explanation; but the sacrifices of Yin or Shang did begin with music; and hence we have so much about it in this ode. L. 1. 猗 与 ,—as in i. [ii.] VI.; but I translate here—'How admirable,' as we must take the terms as an exclamation of admiration (美 而 叹 之 ; Ying-tah). 那 ,—as in II. vii. I. 3. The line must refer, I think, to the instruments of music. L. 2. 置 ＝ 陈 , 'to set forth.' 鞉 鼓 ,—as in i. [ii.] V. L. 3. 奏 denotes the striking up of all the drums. 简 简 is defined by 和 大 ,—as in the translation. Ll. 4. 衎 ,—as in II. vii. VI. 2. 'The meritorious ancestor' is T'ang.

Ll. 5—12. L. 5. 'The descendant of T'ang' is the sacrificing sovereign. Ch'ing, erroneously insisting on 孙 as meaning 'grandson,' says we are to understand T'ae-këah. Maou takes 假 ＝ 大 , so that the line ＝ 'The descendant of T'ang performs this grand music.' Much better is it to take 假 as ＝ 格 , 'to come to,' so that the meaning of 奏 假 is as I have given it. or, perhaps, stronger. L. 6 has perplexed the critics very much, though Ch'ing got hold of what seems to be the correct view of it. In the Le Ke, XXVI. Pt. i. 2, 3, we are told how the sacrificer, as preliminary to the service, had to fast for several days, and to think of the person of his ancestor,—where he had stood and sat, how he had smiled and spoken, what had been his cherished aims, pleasures, and delights; and on the 3d day he would have a complete image of him in his mind's eye. Then on the day of sacrifice, when he entered the temple, he would seem to see him in his shrine, and to hear him as he went about in the discharge of the service. The line seems to indicate the realization of all this. The 'Complete Digest' says on it 一 绥，安 也；思 成，言 未 祭 而 有 所 思，既 祭 而 若 有 形 声 可 接，则 所 思 者 于 是 乎 成 矣，谓 神 命 来 格 也 . Ll. 7, 8. 渊 渊 indicate the deep sound of the drums. and 嘒 嘒 the clear, shrill notes of the flutes. Ll. 9, 10. These sounds were in harmony and blended together (高 上 相 均 谓 之 平), being regulated by the music which came from the hall above the court. Of the music in the

奕。我有嘉客。亦不夷怿。○自古在昔。先民有作。

温恭朝夕。执事有恪。○顾予烝尝。汤孙之将。

The large bells and drums fill the ear;
The various dances are grandly performed.
We have admirable visitors,
Who are pleased and delighted.

From of old, before our time,
The former men set us the example;—
How to be mild and humble from morning to night,
And to be reverent in discharging the service.

May he regard our sacrifices in summer and autumn,
[Thus] offered by the descendant of T'ang!

hall only one instrument is mentioned,—the *k'ing*. This, we are told, was not the ordinary *k'ing*, or sounding stone (石磬), which was among the instruments in the court, but the 'gem *k'ing* (玉磬, or 玉球).' I cannot describe it more particularly. Ll. 11,12. I have said I cannot conceive of the sacrificer speaking, as in l. 11, of himself. Këang says the line is in praise of T'ang, and not the sacrificer's boasting of himself (颂汤, 非自夸也); but that is a mere evasion of the difficulty.

Ll. 13—16. The preceding paragraph is supposed to cover the offering of the sacrifice, and all the feasting of the departed T'ang through his representative. In this the service is drawing to a conclusion. L. 13. 庸 —the same character with 金 at the side, in III. i. VIII. 3. Both Maou and Choo say on 有敦, 敦敦然, 盛也, meaning the richness and compass of the notes of the bells and drums. There is nothing in the dict., under the character, to give us this meaning of it; but Wang Taou observes that 敦, 驛, and 绎 were anciently interchanged. Either of the latter forms will suggest the meaning adopted here. L. 14. 有奕 = 奕奕然, 有次序, denoting the orderly gracefulness with which the dances were performed.

Ll. 15,16. 客,—as in i. [ii.] III, *et al.;* only the term should here, perhaps, be taken in the singular, the visitor being the representative of the former dynasty of Hëa. There may have been another also, the representative of the Family of Shun. L. 16 must be construed interrogatively. 夷 and 怿 are synonymous,— 悦, 'to be pleased.'

Ll. 17—20 celebrate the mildness and reverence of the sacrificer in all the service, showing him to be the true representative of all the great men of former times. Choo Kung-ts'ëen refers the 'former men' to such as T'ang, noted for his 敬; Yu, for his 祇; Shun, for his 恭; and Yaou for his 钦. The force of the 作 — 行, 'to practise,' must be carried on to the next line. 恪 = 敬, 'to be reverent.'

Ll. 21, 22 are expressive of a prayer or wish (言汤其尚顾我烝尝哉). Two of the seasonal sacrifices are mentioned, by *synecdoche,* for all the four. 将 = 奉, 'to offer;'—the offering of the descendant of T'ang.

The rhymes are— 鼓, 祖, cat. 5, t. 2; 成, 声, 平 *, 声, 声, cat. 11; 敦 *, 奕 *, 客 *, 怿 *, 昔 *, 作 *, 夕 *, 恪, cat. 5, t. 3; and 尝, 将, cat. 10.

II. *Lëeh tsoo.*

烈祖

嗟嗟烈祖。有秩斯祜。申锡无疆。及尔斯所。○既载

Ah! ah! our meritorious ancestor!
Permanent are the blessings coming from him,
Repeatedly conferred without end:—
They have come to you in this place.

The clear spirits are in our vessels,
And there is granted to us the realization of our thoughts.
There are also the well-tempered soups,

Ode 2. Narrative. PROBABLY LIKE LAST ODE, APPROPRIATE TO A SACRIFICE TO T'ANG, DWELLING ON THE SPIRITS, THE SOUP, AND THE GRAVITY OF THE SERVICE, AND THE ASSISTING PRINCES. It is the view of Choo that the object of the sacrifice here was also T'ang the Successful. The Preface says that it was T'ae-mow, the second of the three Honoured ones (中宗) among the sovereigns of Shang. The imperial editors go at length into a discussion of the question, and say all that can be said in favour of the earlier view. But I am persuaded that Choo is correct. There is no getting over the 烈祖 of l. 1, and the 汤孙 of l. 22. It would be very strange to have a sacrifice to T'ae-mow, and not a word in the piece in praise of him, which can be interpreted in any way of him, unless it be l. 4.

There is the same difficulty with the personal pronouns as in the former ode, and I can see no other method to dispose of it but that which I there adopted. The student can try if he can get any satisfaction from the following remarks of Lëw Kin, who has on this ode endeavoured to cope with it:—'The Sung odes all celebrate the complete virtue and set forth the accomplished merit of their subjects; but this is done by the singer (or writer), giving expression to the sentiments of the principal at the sacrifice. When from the stand-point of his own person he refers to that principal, he calls him "you." From the stand-point of the ancestor (sacrificed to), he calls him "the grandson of T'ang." When he introduces him in his own person, he uses the first personal pronoun. It is one and the same person who is indicated by these different forms of expression. The case is the same in the previous ode. So in the Chow *Sung*, [ii.] VII., the writer, from the stand-point of his own person mentions the sacrificer as "the Son of Heaven;" then, as "the filial son," also as here we have "the grandson of T'ang;" and again we have the sacrificer speaking in the first person just as here（颂诗所以美盛德, 告成功, 而皆

之主身, 自我, 人也, 若称予, 称我, 亦若此诗称予我也）.'

L1. 1—4. 嗟嗟,—as in i. [ii.] I. 'The meritorious ancestor'is, with all critics, T'ang,—as in last ode. The 'Flower and Essence of the She' expands l. 2 into 烈祖眷顾后人有常者此福, 'This happiness with which our meritorious ancestor blesses his posterity is his permanent possession.' Being permanent, he could confer it on one descendant after another. The 尔 in l. 4 must be referred to the principal in the sacrifice with reference to which the ode was first made. On which of the kings of Shang he was, not even a conjecture can be hazarded. 斯所, 'this place;'=in this place. His sacrificing to T'ang in the ancestral temple was the greatest possible proof of his inheriting from him the royal dignity.—Of course those who hold by the Preface refer the 'you' to T'ae-mow;—against all natural interpretation.

L1. 5—12. 酤 = 酒, 'spirits.' These are mentioned here as for the purpose of libation, at the commencement of the sacrifice. 载 indi-

清酤。赉我思成。亦有和羹。既戒既平。鬷假无言。

时靡有争。绥我眉寿。黄耇无疆。○约軝错衡。八鸾

鸧鸧。以假以享。我受命溥将。自天降康。丰年穰

穰。来假来飨。降福无疆。○顾予烝尝。汤孙之将。

Prepared beforehand, the ingredients rightly proportioned.
By these offerings we invite his presence, without a word,
Nor is there now any contention [in any part of the service].
He will bless us with the eyebrows of longevity,
With the grey hair and wrinkled face, in unlimited degree.

With the naves of their wheels bound with leather, and their
　　　ornamented yokes,
With the eight bells at their horses' bits all tinkling,
[The princes] come and assist at the offerings.
We have received the appointment in all its greatness,
And from Heaven is our prosperity sent down,
Fruitful years of great abundance.
[Our ancestor] will come and enjoy [our offerings],
And confer [on us] happiness without limit.

May he regard our sacrifices in summer and winter,
[Thus] offered by the descendant of T'ang!

cates their being 'contained' in their proper vessel. L. 6,—like l. 6 in last ode. The soup is, I suppose, spoken of in ll. 7, 8,—a part of the articles used in the sacrifice for the whole. 和 denotes the harmonious mixture or tempering of all the flavours in it. The same idea is repeated in the 平, and so the 戒 also must refer to the soup as carefully prepared beforehand. Ll. 9, 10 are quoted in the 'Doctrine of the Mean,' XXXIII. 4, with 奏 instead of 鬷, and Choo adopts the former as the true reading, so that 鬷假＝奏假 in l. 5 of last ode. The rest of the lines describe the stillness and gravity with which all the service was gone about. Ll. 11, 12 express the blessing which T'ang, so worshipped, would confer. Comp. l. 4 in II. iii. VII. 5.

Ll. 13—20. Ll. 13—15 relate to the feudal princes who were present and assisted in the service. Ll. 13, 14. See on II. iii. IV. 2, 鸧鸧 here being evidently equivalent to 玱玱 in l. 9 there. L. 15. The 以 indicates the object of the princes in coming to the court of Shang. 享, 'to offer,'＝to take part in offering. In ll. 16—20 the ode returns again to the principal in the sacrifice, as the descendant of T'ang, rejoicing in the favour of Heaven, and the blessing which he would receive from his ancestor. 溥＝广, 'wide;' 将＝大, 'great.' L. 18,—comp. in i. [i.] IX. The subject of ll. 19, 20 is T'ang. 来 ＝ 是, blending its meaning with the verbs that follow.
Ll. 21, 22,—as in last ode.

III. *Heuen nëaou.*

玄鸟

天命玄鸟。降而生商。宅殷土芒芒。古帝命武汤。正
域彼四方。○方命厥后。奄有九有。商之先后。受命

Heaven commissioned the swallow,
To descend and give birth to [the father of our] Shang.
[His descendants] dwelt in the land of Yin, and became great.
[Then] long ago God appointed the martial T'ang
To regulate the boundaries throughout the four quarters.

[In those] quarters he appointed the princes,
And grandly possessed the nine regions [of the kingdom].

The rhymes are 祖, 祜, 所, cat. 5, t. 2;
成, 平∗, 争, cat. 11; 疆, 衡∗, 鸧, 享∗,
将, 康, 穰, 飨, 疆, 尝, 将, cat. 10.

Ode 3. Narrative. APPROPRIATE TO A SACRI-
FICE IN THE ANCESTRAL TEMPLE OF SHANG;—
INTENDED SPECIALLY TO DO HONOUR TO THE
KING WOO-TING. The Preface says that the
sacrifice to which the piece refers was entirely
to Woo-ting (祀 高 宗). Choo on the contrary says nothing about Woo-ting, but simply
that it belonged to the sacrifices in the ancestral
temple, tracing back the family of Shang to its
origin and its attaining the sovereignty of
the kingdom. If we accept the view of the Preface, we are obliged to adopt what seems to me
an unnatural interpretation of ll. 10, 11; but if it
were not intended in some way to do honour to
Woo-ting, we cannot account for the repeated
mention of him in it. Ch'ing would change the
祀 of the Preface into 祫, maintaining that the
sacrifice was in the third year after the death
of Woo-ting, and paid to him in the temple of
Sëeh, the ancestor of the Shang dynasty. Woo-
ting is mentioned in the Shoo, V. viii., and ix.

Ll. 1—5. Ll. 1, 2. 玄 鸟, 'the dark bird,'
is a name for the swallow (玄 鸟, 鳦
也, 燕 也), derived from this passage and
the traditions connected with it. The mother
of Sëch, it is said, was a daughter of the House
of Sung (有 娀 氏 女), belonging to the
harem of the ancient emperor K'uh, and named
Këen-teih (简 狄). Acc. to Maou, she accompanied the emperor at the time of the vernal
equinox, when the swallow made its appearance, to sacrifice and pray to the first Match-

maker, and the result was the birth of Sëeh;—
see a very similar legend as to the birth of
How-tseih, on III. ii. I. Sze-ma Ts'ëen, and also
Ch'ing, after him, make the birth of Sëeh still
more marvellous. Këen-teih was bathing in
some open place, when a swallow suddenly
made its appearance and dropt an egg, which
she took and swallowed; and from this came
the birth of Sëeh. We need not believe the
legends, say the imperial editors;—the important point is to believe that the birth of Sëeh
was specially ordered by Heaven. 生 商,—
'gave birth to Shang;' *i.e.*, to Sëeh who became
lord of Shang :—see the note on the title of the
Book.

L. 3. 宅 = 居, 'to dwell in.' We must understand 子 孙, 'Sëeh's descendants' as the
subject of 宅. As it was not till the reign of
Pwan-kang, that the name of Shang came to be
interchanged with Yin, we must suppose that
the land of *Yin* is here improperly spoken of. 殷
was a name for the district about 亳, where
Pwan-kang fixed his capital. The poet, writing
after him, gives the denomination to the early
seat of the family. 芒 芒 = 大 貌, 'great-
looking;'—to be understood of Sëeh's descendants and their territory. As the 'Flower and
Essence of the She' expands the line,— 其 子
孙 宅 居 殷 土, 国 遂 芒 芒 然
大. Ll. 4, 5, 古 = 昔, 'anciently.' The 帝
is 上 帝, 'God.' I translate l. 5 acc. to Gow-
yang Sëw's exposition of it, which is the simplest I have met with :— 谓 汤 始 受 命
以 正 四 方 之 疆 域.

不殆。在武丁孙子。○武丁孙子。武王靡不胜。龙旗
十乘。大糦是承。○邦畿千里。维民所止。肇域彼四
海。○四海来假。来假祈祈。景员维河。殷受命咸

The first sovereign of Shang
Received the appointment without any element of instability in it,
And it is [now] held by the descendant of Woo-ting.

The descendant of Woo-ting
Is a martial king, equal to every emergency.
Ten princes, [who came] with their dragon-emblazoned banners,
Bear the large dishes of millet.

The royal domain of a thousand *le*
Is where the people rest;
But there commence the boundaries that reach to the four seas.

Ll. 6—10. 方＝四方,—throughout the four quarters, or in each of the four quarters. 厥后,＝诸侯,' the feudal princes.' 九有 is explained by 九州, both by Maou and Chow, with reference to the division of the country by Yu into nine provinces;—see the Shoo, III. i. The dictionary repeats the same definition without attempting to account for this signification of 有; nor will I set myself to do so. Ll. 8—10 seem plain enough, but the meaning of them is very much disputed. To begin with l. 10—武丁孙子＝武丁之孙子, ' the descendant of Woo-ting.' So say Gow-yang Sëw, and Fan Ch'oo-e, the latter adding that the expression denotes the sacrificing sovereign (指主祭之君). On this view, 在＝the appointment is now *in the person of* the descendant of Woo-ting. If we adopt this view of l. 10, the other lines present no difficulty, and I understand 先后 of T'ang, rather than, in the plural, of the former kings of Shang anterior to Woo-ting. Many of the critics, however, Wang Suh the first among them so far as I have been able to ascertain, take 武丁孙子 as＝武丁之为人孙子,＝武丁善为人之孙子, and 在＝'lay in,' 'depended on,' so that the meaning of the three lines is that the permanence of the appointment to the sovereignty of the kingdom, which T'ang received,

was owing to Woo-ting's approving himself a worthy descendant of him. Ying-tah claims Maou as in favour of this view; but it is merely by way of inference. I do not think it would ever have been heard of but for the statement of the Preface that the sacrifice celebrated in the ode was one to Woo-ting. It is not a fair construction of the text.

Ll. 11—14. The difft. views of l. 10 of course affect the interpretation of ll. 11, 12; but I need not enter on them again. Choo says that 武王 is properly a denomination of T'ang, but that his descendants also so designated themselves. This hardly seems to be necessary, if we translate—'a martial king.' 胜＝任 'to bear,' 'to sustain.' 靡不胜＝无所不胜,—as in the translation. Ll. 13, 14 relate to the feudal princes who came to assist the king in sacrificing. I do not think we are to lay stress on the specification of *ten* chariots. Yen Ts'an says we are to take the ten as referring to the more illustrious among the princes;—if they came, all the others would be sure to do so. Ch'ing and Ying-tah have other ways of accounting for the number. 大糦 is explained as a denomination of ' millet and sacrificial millet.' The dict. quotes, under the character, this line, and also l. 1 of II. i. VI. 4, where we read 饎. The two characters are interchanged, but Ying-tah observes that the radical 米 determines the meaning here to be what I have just stated. 承 must be under-

宜。百禄是何。

From the four seas they come [to our sacrifices];
They come in multitudes;—
King has the Ho for its outer border.
That Yin should have received the appointment [of Heaven]
    was entirely right;—
[Its sovereign] sustains all its dignities.

IV.   *Ch'ang fah.*

长发

一章
濬哲维商。长发其祥。洪水芒芒。禹敷下土方。外大

1   Profoundly wise were [the lords of] Shang,
    And long had there appeared the omens [of their dignity].
    When the waters of the deluge spread vast abroad,
    Yu arranged and divided the regions of the land,

stood of the presenting the dishes of millet at the sacrifice, and not of contributions by the princes to the Government.

Ll. 15—17. Ll. 15—16,—see in the 'Great Learning,' Commen. III.1. 肇 = 始, 'to begin.' There may, possibly, be a reference in the lines to the vigour of Woo-ting and his martial descendant, as re-establishing the ancient sway of T'ang over all the kingdom. On 'the four seas,' see Ana. XII. iv. 祈祈 = 众多貌, 'the app. of multitudes.' L. 17 is very obscure, and Choo acknowledges that he does not understand it. The most likely construction is to take 景 as the name of a hill, near which was the capital, to which it served as a shelter and defence. 员, —like 阪 in the next ode, l. 6; but it is there explained by 周, 'all round.' As we must take 河 of *the* Ho, the Yellow river, I do not see how it could be represented as going all round the capital. The translation gives what I conceive the line may have been intended to say. La-charme has—'*Regio King (ubi urbs regia) tota fluviis cingitur.*' L. 22. 何 = 任 'to sustain.' Ch'ing says that the line = 担负天之多福, 'He sustains (or enjoys) the many sources of happiness conferred by Heaven.'

The rhymes are— 商, 芒, 汤, 方, cat. 10; 有 *, 殆 *, 子, cat. 1, t. 2; 胜, 乘, 承 cat. 6; 里, 止, 海 *, cat. 1, t. 3; 河, 宜 *, 何, cat. 17.

Ode 4. Narrative. CELEBRATING SEEH, THE ANCESTOR OF THE HOUSE OF SHANG; SEANG-T'OO, HIS GRANDSON; T'ANG, THE FOUNDER OF THE DYNASTY; AND E YIN, T'ANG'S CHIEF ADVISER.—ON OCCASION OF WHAT SACRIFICE THE PIECE WAS MADE DOES NOT APPEAR. The Preface, indeed, says it was made on occasion of the great *Te* sacrifice (大 禘), when the principal object of honour would be the emperor K'uh, with Sëeh as his correlate, and all the previous kings of the dynasty and the lords of Shang, and their famous ministers and advisers, would be associated in the service. Choo is of opinion that the occasion was the *Heah* sacrifice (祫 祭). Other views have been advanced; but it is not necessary to enter into a discussion of them. There are many difficulties in construing and explaining the paragraph and lines, and the remark of Fan Ch'oo-e quoted in the note on the title of the Book is often brought to mind;—if we think we have got the drift of the writer's meaning, we must be satisfied.

St. 1. Ll. 1, 2. 濬哲 = 深知, 'deep and wise,' or 'profoundly wise.' The lines must be referred, I think, to the ancestors of the Shang dynasty, when they occupied the territory of Shang. 长 = 久, 'long,' 'for long.' 祥,— as in II. iv. V. 7;—'happy omens.' As those omens issued in the sovereignty of T'ang, I think that l. 1 must be restricted as I have done. Similarly Lëw Kin:— 泛言濬哲之君, 盖自汤以上, 契以下, 皆是也. Ll. 3—6. The work of Yu is referred to, not, apparently, with any purpose to sing the praises of

国是疆。幅陨既长。有娀方将。帝立子生商。

二章
玄王桓拨。受小国是达。受大国是达。率履不越。遂

And assigned to the exterior great States their boundaries,
With their borders extending all over [the kingdom].
Then the State of Sung began to be great,
And God raised up the son [of its daughter], and founded [the
　　Family of] Shang.

2　The dark king exercised an effective sway.
　Charged with a small State, he commanded success;
　Charged with a large State, he commanded success.
　He followed his rules of conduct without error;
　Wherever he inspected [the people], they responded [to his in-
　　structions].

that monarch, but to give the point of time when Sëeh came into notice, and to connect his labours with those of Yu as of universal benefit, just as we have Yu's work and How-tseih's brought together in ii. III. 1. 洪水,—as in the Shoo I. 11, *et al.* 芒芒,—as in last ode, =the 浩浩 of Shoo, I.11. 禹敷下土方＝禹随下土之方而敷治之. The line = 敷土 in the Shoo, III. i. 1. It is difficult to determine exactly the meaning of 下土. The connection might seem to justify the meaning of 'the low-lying land;' but the phrase may be only a designation of the kingdom, as in many other places. Choo explains 方 by 四方, the 'four quarters,' meaning all the different regions. 外大国 means the feudal States, as lying outside the domain or State of the sovereign. If the great States had their boundaries assigned them, the same was done for the small ones. 幅＝边幅, 'an end or border;' 陨＝周, or 员 in last ode, l. 20. Wang Ying-lin says, 'The boundaries, spoken of as straight, are called 幅; spoken of with reference to the extent they embraced, 陨(自其直言之,曰幅,自其周围言之,曰陨). Ll.7, 8. It has been mentioned, in the introductory note, that the mother of Sëeh was a daughter of the State of 有娀. 方将＝始大,—as in the translation. 帝＝上帝, 'God.'

So, all the critics, except Ch'ing, who says that the 帝 was the 黑帝, one of his five elemental Gods, whom he called 叶光纪 (see the *proleg.* to the Shoo, pp. 97, 98).
St. 2. Ll. 1—5 are occupied with Sëeh, who is styled 'king' in l. 9; not that he ever was a king himself, but the title of his descendants is carried back to him. It is vain to inquire why he is styled the *dark* king. 拨 is defined by 治, 'to rule;'—with reference to the meaning of the term as 'to scatter,' 'to remove:'—Sëeh took away the confusion and ignorance that prevailed. 桓 is explained, by Choo, by 武, 'martial,' and by Wang Taou, by 大, 'great.' It does not seem proper to speak of Sëeh's rule as warlike, his work being to instruct the people in the social duties;—see the Shoo, II. i. 19. Ll. 2, 3. 'A small State,' 'a great State,' may refer to Shang, small at first, but increased by subsequent grants; but I prefer to understand the expressions of the States small and large, as they were subjected to the influence of Sëeh's lessons. 达＝通, 'to have free course,'＝to be successful. Ll. 4, 5 tell us how Sëeh exemplified his lessons, and how rapidly he accomplished his object. 履 is taken as＝礼, 'the rules of conduct to be trodden by men.' 不越＝不过, 'without transgression.' L. 5＝遂视其民,则发以应之, 'thereon he looked at the people, and they had stirred themselves to respond to him.' As Wang Che-Ch'ang (王志长; Ming dyn.) says, 契能

視既发。相土烈烈。海外有截。

三章
帝命不违。至于汤齐。汤降不迟。圣敬日跻。昭假迟

迟。上帝是祗。帝命式于九围。

[Then came] Sëang-t'oo, all-ardent,
And all [within] the seas, beyond [the middle region], acknow-
    ledged his restraints.

3   The favour of God did not leave [Shang],
And in T'ang was found the subject for its display.
T'ang was not born too late,
And his wisdom and virtue daily advanced.
Brilliant was the influence of his character [on Heaven] for
    long,
And God appointed him to be a model to the nine regions.

以 身 教, 故 在 宽 而 奏 效 捷). Ll. 6, 7 introduce Sëang-t'oo, who appears in the genealogical lists, as the grandson of Sëeh. 烈 烈,—'all-ardent,' or 'very meritorious.' L. 7 is very obscure. 海 外 is literally, 'outside the seas;' but we cannot think of the influence of Sëang-t'oo as extending beyond the China of his day. The phrase=四 海 之 外, 'the outside of the four seas,' the 'four seas' being a denomination of the kingdom in all its extent, and the 'outside' leading us to conceive of all the feudal States in distinction from the royal domain. Choo defines 截 by 整 齐, 'to be adjusted and made regular;' but that is merely a portion of Ch'ing's account of the line, and a result of the 有 截. He says, 四 海 之 外 率 服 截 然 整 齐. 截 means 'to cut off,' 'to intercept; 有 截 sets the States before us as submissive to the restraints put upon them by the lord of Shang, whatever they were. Ch'ing says that Sëang-t'oo was employ-ed by the then king of Hëa as a sort of director or president of all the other princes; but that is merely an inference drawn from this line.

St. 3. The writer passes over all the other lords of Shang, and brings us, with a bound, to T'ang, the founder of the dynasty. Ll. 5,2. 违 =去, 'to go away,' 'to leave.' The favour of Heaven, to be seen in due time, in its appoint-ment of the House of Shang to the sovereignty of the kingdom, had never left it, but it was not till T'ang that the proper man to receive it appeared. This seems to be the meaning of 汤 齐, which Choo says he does not under-stand. Soo Ch'eh, Fan Choo-e, and others, explain 齐 by 会, 'to meet with,' as if in T'ang the man and the decree of Heaven met together (Maou says, 至 汤 与 天 心 会; Soo, 与 天 命 会; Fan, 至 于 汤, 则 德 与 命 会). Ll. 3, 4. 降 = 生, 'to be born.' 不 迟, 'not late,'= at the proper time. 圣 敬,—'his sagely reverence,' 跻 = 升, 'to ascend,' = to increase. Ll. 5—7. 昭 假 expresses how the virtue of T'ang brilliant-ly affected Heaven (其 德 昭 明 感 格 于 天), and this it did by a continuous and gradual process (迟 迟; comp. the phrase in I. xv. 2, et al.). 祗=敬, 'to reverence.' 式 =法, 'to be, or to give, the law.' 九 围 = 九 有 in last ode. Ying-tah says, 'All under heaven being divided into nine parts, there they were, distinct as if each part had been marked out by a compass (九 分 天 下, 各 为 九 处, 若 规 围 然).

四章 受小球大球。为下国缀旒。何天之休。不竞不绒。不

刚不柔。敷政优优。百禄是遒。

五章 受小共大共。为下国骏厖。何天之龙。敷奏其勇。不

4 He received the rank-tokens [of the States], small and large,
Which depended on him, like the pendants of a banner;—
So did he receive the blessing of Heaven.
He was neither violent nor remiss,
Neither hard nor soft.
Gently he spread his instructions abroad,
And all dignities and riches were concentrated in him.

5 He received the tribute [of the States], large and small,
And he supported them as a strong steed [does its burden];—
So did he receive the favour of Heaven.
He displayed everywhere his valour,
Unshaken, unmoved,

St. 4. T'ang appears now as sovereign of the kingdom. Ll. 1, 2. Choo does not understand l. 1. 球 is explained as 美玉, 'an admirable kind of jade.' We must give it the same meaning as 瑞, in the Shoo, II. i. 7, the jade-tokens of rank;—the 圭 of the Chow dynasty, varying in shape and size, according to the rank of the princes. They received them from the king in the first place, and they brought them to the court, when they appeared there, as the tokens of their dignity. 小球, 大球 will be the tokens belonging to small and to great States respectively. The princes now rendered them to T'ang, acknowledging his sovereignty. L. 2 expresses his sovereignty in another way. 旒 denotes the tassels or pendants attached to a banner. 缀,—'to be connected.' To T'ang all the States were now attached as the pendants to a banner (言为天子而为诸侯所系属,如旗之缀·为旒所缀著也). L. 3. 何=荷, 'to bear,' 'to sustain.' Ll. 4—7, describe the manner of T'ang in his government. 绒=缓, 'to be slow or remiss.' 优优 is expressive of gentleness and magnanimity. L. 29. 遒=聚, 'to be

collected.' 百禄,—'all the dignities and their emoluments.'

St. 5. Ll. 1, 2 are both in themselves unintelligible to Choo. Taking 共 as = 供 in the sense of contributions, and keeping in mind the analogy of l. in last st. 1, we get the meaning of l.1 which I have here given. Other explanations have been tried, but I need not dwell upon them. L. 2 is more perplexing. 骏, indeed, has commonly the meaning of 大, 'great;' but 厖 seems to baffle critical ingenuity. Maou explains it by 厚, and Ying-tah gives the meaning as— 为下国大厚,谓成其志性,使大纯厚也;—which is very unsatisfactory. Evidently this stanza and the last are of similar structure, and as the 2d line there contained a comparison, so ought the line before us to do. Now, the Ts'e copy of the She read here 骏 骃, a character which K'ang-he's dictionary does not acknowledge, but which is found in the Urh-ya, the Yuh-p'een, and the Shih-wǎn, meaning a horse, with characteristics variously defined (See in the 皇清经解, ch. 1,408.) I must adopt this reading, and then the line may be translated as I have done (是喻汤 有力量,能负重致远之意·

震不动。不憼不竦。百禄是总。

六章

武王载斾。有虔秉钺。如火烈烈。则莫我敢曷。苞有

三蘖。莫遂莫达。九有有截。韦顾既伐。昆吾夏桀。

七章

昔在中叶。有震且业。允也天子。降予卿士。实维阿

Unterrified, unscared:—
All dignities were united in him.

6 The martial king displayed his banner,
And with reverence grasped his axe.
It was like [the case of] a blazing fire,
Which no one can repress.
The root, with its three shoots,
Could make no progress, no growth.
The nine regions were effectually secured by him.
Having smitten [the princes of] Wei and Koo
He dealt with [the prince of] Keun-woo, and with Këeh of Hëa.

7 Formerly in the middle of the period [before T'ang],
There was a time of shaking and peril,

下国皆于我乎负载也)。L. 3.
何,—as in last stanza. 龙＝宠, as often.
L. 6 大进其武功, 'grandly exhibited
his warlike merit.' L. 8. 憼 and 竦 are of
kindred meaning＝恐 or 惧, 'to be afraid.'
L. 9. 总, 'to be together;'＝道 in last stanza.

St. 6 details the military achievements by
which T'ang made himself master of the kingdom. Ll. 1,2. 斾 is a streamer attached to a
flag; but it is here used for the flag itself, and
with a verbal force,—'he raised his banner.'
载 is the particle. 有虔＝'reverently.'
T'ang had no wish to dethrone Këeh, but it was
a duty which he owed to Heaven to take the
course he did. Ll. 3,4. 曷,—here, i. q. 遏, to
repress,' 'to check.' 我 had better be translated in the 3d person. L. 5 is a metaphorical

way of describing Këeh the last king of Hëa,
and his three principal adherents. He was the
root (苞＝本); they were the shoots springing from it. L. 6. 莫遂, 莫达 are to
be explained with reference to the figure in
l. 5. As Ho K'ëae says, 皆从蘖字生
出. L. 7 九有 as in last ode. 有截,—
as in the translation. Ll. 8,9. The three great
helpers of Këeh were the princes of Wei (or Ch'e-
wei, 豕韦), Koo, and Keun-woo; but the exact
site of those principalities I have not been able to
make out. Their chiefs are represented as descended from Chuh-yung, a son of the ancient
Chuen-hëuh. We must repeat the 伐 at the
commencement of l. 9.

St. 7 叶＝世, 'age;' 中叶,—'the mid-
dle age;' i. e., some time between Seang-too and
T'ang. As Ho K'ëae says, 此诗前言相
土后言成汤所谓中叶者

衡。实左右商王。

But truly did Heaven [then] deal with him as its son,
And sent him down a minister,
Namely A-hǎng,
Who gave his assistance to the king of Shang.

V.　*Yin woo.*

殷武

一章

挞彼殷武。奋伐荆楚。罙入其阻。裒荆之旅。有截其

1　Rapid was the warlike energy of [our king of] Yin,
　And vigorously did he attack King-ts'oo.
　Boldly he entered its dangerous passes,
　And brought the multitudes of King together,

其 世 数 居 于 相 士 成 汤 之
中 者 也。 L. 2 describes the state of Shang
during that period of decadence. 业＝危,
'to be in a perilous condition.' L. 3. Choo takes
this line as meaning—'But truly did he—T'ang
—prove himself the Son of Heaven.' I much
prefer the view of Ch'ing, which is followed in
the 'Flower and Essence,' taking 子 as in i. [i.]
VIII. 天 子 ＝ 天 爱 汤 而 子 之,
'Heaven loved T'ang, and made him its son.'
Ll. 4—6. Heaven showed its favour for T'ang,
by raising up (降) and giving him the famous
E Yin, who became his principal minister and
director. See on him the note in the Shoo on
the title of IV. iv; and on 阿 衡, his name, or
the name of his office, under IV. v. 1.

Choo and the critics generally resume in regard to this ode the arrangement of the lines in
stanzas, which seems to me to show that it is
not a Sung piece.

The rhymes are—in st. 1, 商, 祥, 芒, 方,
疆, 长, 将, 商, cat. 10: in 2, 拨, 达,
达, 越, 发, 烈, 截, cat. 15, t. 3: in 3, 违,
齐, 迟, 跻, 迟, 祗, 围, ib., t. 1: in 4, 球,
旒, 休, 绿, 柔, 优, 遒, cat. 3, t. 1: in 5,
共, 厖, 龙, 勇, 动, 竦, 总, cat. 9: in 6,
斾, 钺, 烈, 曷, 蘖, 达, 截, 伐. 桀,
cat. 15, t. 3: in 7, 叶 *, 业, cat. 8, t. 3: 子,
士, cat. 1, t. 2; 衡 *, 王, cat. 10.

Ode 5. Narrative. CELEBRATING THE WAR
OF WOO-TING AGAINST KING-TS'OO, ITS SUCCESS,
AND THE GENERAL HAPPINESS AND VIRTUE OF
HIS REIGN;—MADE, PROBABLY, WHEN A SPECIAL
AND PERMANENT TEMPLE WAS BUILT FOR HIM
AS THE 'HIGH AND HONOURED' KING OF SHANG.
The Preface merely says that this was made on
occasion of a sacrifice to Woo-ting. The concluding stanza indicates further that it was
made on the occasion which I have indicated in
the argument. After his death his Spirit-tablet
would be shrined in the ancestral temple of
Shang, and he would have his share in the
seasonal sacrifices; but several reigns would
elapse before there was any necessity for making
any other arrangement, so that his tablet should
not be removed and his share in the sacrifices not
be discontinued. Hence Këang refers the composition of the piece to the reign of Te-yih
(帝 乙), the last but one of the sovereigns of
Shang.

St. 1. L. 1. 挞＝疾 貌, 'rapid-looking.'
殷 武＝殷 王 之 武, —as in the translation. L. 2. In 荆 楚 we have two names of
the same State combined together, just as we have
so often the combination Yin-shang as the name
of the Shang or Yin dynasty in II. iii. 1. But
the combination here is more strange and perplexing. Both the names of Yin and Shang
were in common use in the time of king Wǎn,
who uses them combined in III. iii. 1.; but we
should say, but for this ode, that the name of
Ts'oo was not in use at all till long after the
Shang dynasty. The name King appears in the
Ch'un Ts'ëw several times in the annals of duke
Chwang, and then it gives place to the name
T'soo in the 1st year of duke He, and subsequently disappears itself altogether. The common

所。汤孙之绪。

二章

维女荆楚。居国南乡。昔有成汤。自彼氐羌。莫敢不

来享。莫敢不来王。曰商是常。

Till the country was reduced under complete restraint:—
Such was the fitting achievement of the descendant of T'ang.

2 'Ye people,' [he said], 'of King-ts'oo
Dwell in the southern part of my kingdom.
Formerly, in the time of T'ang the Successful,
Even from the Këang of Te,
They dared not but come with their offerings;
[Their chiefs] dared not but come to seek acknowledgment:—
Such is the regular rule of Shang.'

opinion is that the name of Ts'oo first came into use about the beginning of duke He's rule of Loo, *i. e.*, about B.C. 658,—between four and five centuries after the overthrow of Shang. If the ode before us be genuine, that opinion of course is incorrect. Han Ying, however, referred this piece to the time of duke Sëang of Sung;—and I must say that the balance of the argument rather inclines in favour of that view. I introduce here a long note from Këang on this point, and King-ts'oo, or King and Ts'oo, generally:—楚雄南服,立国在江汉之间,其强最久,周以前世系无所考,武王封熊绎为楚子,春秋庄公之世,楚皆书荆,至僖元年,乃书楚人伐郑,严氏疑商时未有荆楚之说,殊不思禹贡荆州既旅岐,别有荆楚哉,李夷曰,荆楚在商周之时,世乱则先叛,世治则后服,当汤之时,不敢抗衡,商中微,为中国患,此高宗所以讨之也,按郝氏敬援二南

为证,谓天下有道,则荆楚首善,非也,夫文王之化,及于江汉之间,乃德化之成,非雍豫后而江汉转先也,盖楚最难服,天下视为向背,责一不享之楚,而天下莫敢不享,责一不王之楚,而天下莫敢不王,平荆楚者,平天下之大机也.

L.3. Maou defines 来 by 深, 'deeply;' Choo, after Ch'ing by 冒, 'daringly.' Either meaning suits the connection. 阻 = 险阻,—as in the translation. L.4. 袠 = 聚, 'to collect;' 旅 = 众, 'multitudes.' Perhaps the 'Essence and Flower of the She' is correct in understanding the line of the king's making all the people of King-ts'oo prisoners (荆州之众,负固不服者,袠聚而俘虏之). L.5. 其所, 'their places;'—meaning the whole territory. 有截,—as in last ode. L.6. 绪 = 功, 'meritorious achievement;' but it also indicates that the merit was a sequence of that of T'ang and other sovereigns.

St. 2 contains an address which we are to suppose Woo-ting to have spoken to the people or chiefs of King-ts'oo. L.2. Maou explains 乡 by 所, 'place,' so that 南乡 simply = 'the south,' or 'the southern parts.' Woo-ting's capital being in the north of the present Ho-nan, he might very well speak thus of King-ts'oo,

三章
天命多辟。设都于禹之绩。岁事来辟。勿予祸适。稼

穑匪解。

四章
天命降监。下民有严。不僭不滥。不敢怠遑。命于下

国。封建厥福。

3 Heaven has given their appointments [to the princes],
But where their capitals had been assigned within the sphere
　　of the labours of Yu,
For the business of every year, they appeared before our king,
[Saying], 'Do not punish nor reprove us;
We have not been remiss in our husbandry.'

4 When Heaven by its will is inspecting [the kingdom],
The lower people are to be feared.
[Our king] showed no partiality [in rewarding], no excess [in
　　punishing];
He dared not to allow himself in indolence:—
So was his appointment [established] over the States,
And he made his happiness grandly secure.

which was in Hoo-pih. Ll. 3—6. The Te-këang still existed in the time of the Han dynasty, occupying portions of the present Kan-suh. 享＝献, 'to offer,' *i. e.*, to present as a tribute the productions of their country. 王 is used in a technical sense,＝世一见, 'once in the life-time to appear at the king's court.' This was the rule laid down anciently for the chiefs of the wild tribes, which lay beyond the nine provinces of the kingdom. Every chief once in his time was required to present himself at court. The rule, in normal periods, was observed by a chief, immediately after he succeeded to the headship of his tribe. L. 7 is an explanatory remark of the king, and 曰 is merely ＝盖, 'for.' 商是常＝此商之常礼—as in the translation. If the tribes of the Te-këang had thus acknowledged the sovereignty of T'ang so long ago, much more might those of King-ts'oo be expected now to acknowledge that of Woo-ting.

St. 3 relates how all the feudal princes loyally presented themselves at the court of Woo-ting; —the more so, we are to suppose, because of the way in which he had subdued the tribes of King-ts'oo. Two ideas seem to underlie ll. 1, 2 — that though the princes had their appointments from the king, these might also be ascribed to Heaven. The same ideas occur in the Shoo, IV. viii. Pt.ii.2, in the words of Yueh, the chief adviser

of Woo-ting. 多辟＝诸侯; like 辟公, in i. [i.] IV., *et al.* 于禹之绩, 'in the merit of Yu,'＝于禹功所及之处;— as in the translation. In l. 3, 辟 is here the king, and 来辟 is analogous to 来王 in last stanza, meaning that the princes appeared at the royal court (来朝觐于我殷王). The 'yearly affairs' which brought them there, were that they might take their part in the seasonal sacrifices, and to report on the condition of their States. We are to take ll. 4, 5 as spoken by the princes, praying the king to deal gently with them, and promising to attend to the husbandry of their States,—their most important duty.

St. 4 seems to refer to the general govt. of Woo-ting as strictly just, and regulated by a regard to the sentiments of the people, and to the firm establishment of his throne in consequence. The sentiment in ll. 1, 2 is understood to be the same as that in the Shoo. V.i. Pt. ii. 7, 天视自我民视，天听自我民听, 'Heaven sees as my people see; Heaven hears as my people hear.' 严＝威可畏, 'an awfulness which is to be feared.' The 命 in l. 1 is perplexing, as the whole is equivalent to saying that 'Heaven descends and inspects,'

五章

商邑翼翼。四方之极。赫赫厥声。濯濯厥灵。寿考且

宁。以保我后生。

六章

陟彼景山。松柏丸丸。是断是迁。方斫是虔。松桷有

梴。旅楹有闲。寝成孔安。

5   The capital of Shang was full of order,
     The model for all parts of the kingdom,
     Glorious was his fame;
     Brilliant, his energy.
     Long lived he and enjoyed tranquillity,
     And so he preserves us, his descendants.

6   We ascended the hill of King,
     Where the pines and cypresses grew symmetrical.
     We cut them down, and conveyed them here;
     We reverently hewed them square.
     Long are the projecting beams of pine;
     Large are the many pillars.
     The temple was completed,—the tranquil abode [of his tablet].

or that 'Heaven exercises an inspection here below.' The 命 is to be taken adverbially, or as expressive of the law or method of procedure which Heaven prescribes to itself. Woo-ting recognized this, and showed that he did so, as is described in ll. 3, 4. 僭 is understood of 'error in rewarding or bestowing favours (賞 之差),' and 滥 of 'excess in punishing (刑 之过).' 遑 = 暇, 'to have — or to allow one's-self—leisure.' L. 5,—' Being appointed (*i.e.* by Heaven) over all the feudal States.' L. 6. 封 = 大, 'grandly,' 'on a great scale.' 'His happiness' will mean his firm possession of the throne, and the prosperity of the country.

St. 5 may be considered as an expansion of l. 6 in last stanza. L. 1. 邑 = 都, 'capital,' as in III. i. X. 2, so that 商邑 = 王都, 'the royal capital.' 翼翼 = 整救貌, 'the appearance of the city as well-built and ordered.' L. 2. 极 = 表, 'a model,' the type of what a city and government should be. L. 4. 灵 has

the meaning of 'energy,' 'majesty.' On ll. 3,4 Yen Ts'an says, 声誉赫赫乎显盛, 威灵濯濯乎光明. L. 5. Woo-ting's reign is said to have lasted 59 years. L. 6. 后生 = 后嗣子孙, 'his heirs and descendants.'

St. 6. relates to the temple which had been built for Woo-ting, and which was to last as long as the Shang dynasty should last;—for ever, as the writer of the ode imagined. Choo remarks on the similarity of structure between this stanza and the last stanza of ii. IV., and says he does not know how to account for it. It is certainly suspicious, and must be added to the peculiarity in the use of the name King-ts'oo in st. 1, as suggestive of the later origin of the piece. L. 1. 景, 山,—see on III., l. 20. L. 2. Choo explains 丸丸 by 直, 'to be straight;' Maou by 易直, 'easy and straight.' The meaning of 丸, 'anything round,' suggests the symmetrical appearance of the trees as the real meaning of the phrase. **L. 4.** 方＝正, 'square,' 'exact (以 绳 墨 取 方 正).' I take 虔 in its most frequent sense of 敬, 'to do reverently.' The dict., with reference to this passage, defines it by 棋, of which it is difficult to see the meaning in the connection. Equally obscure is the 亦 截 of Choo. **L. 5.** 梴＝长 貌, 'long-looking.' **L. 6.** 闲＝大, 'large.' **L. 7.** 寝 is 'the inner apartment of the temple,' put for the whole. 安 ＝ 所 以 安 高 宗 之 神, 'wherewith to give repose to the spirit of Kaou-tsung.'

The rhymes are—in st. 1, 武, 楚, 阻, 旅, 所, 绪, cat. 5, t. 1: in 2, 乡, 汤, 羌, 享., 王, 常, cat. 10: in 3, 辟, 绩, 辟, 适, 解. cat. 16, t. 3: in 4, 监, 严, 滥, 遑 (prop. cat. 10), cat. 8, t. 3; 国, 福 ., cat. 1, t. 3: in 5, 翼, 极, *ib.*; 声, 灵, 宁, 生, cat. 11: in 6, 山, 丸, 迁, 虔, 梴, 闲 安, cat. 14.